LITERARY SWORDSMEN AND SORCERERS: THE MAKERS OF HEROIC FANTASY

OTHER BOOKS BY L. SPRAGUE DE CAMP

S. H. Sime

L. Sprague de Camp

LITERARY SWORDSMEN AND SORCERERS

THE MAKERS OF HEROIC FANTASY

For Charles N. Brown —

L. Sprague de Camp

8/30/80

ARKHAM HOUSE
Sauk City · Wisconsin

International Standard Book Number 0-87054-076-9
Library of Congress Catalog Card Number 76-17991

This book is based upon a number of magazine articles, rewritten and expanded, as follows:

Chapter II is based upon "Jack of All Arts," in *Fantastic Stories* for September 1974, copyright © 1974 by Ultimate Publishing Company, Inc.

Chapter III is based upon "Two Men in One," in *Fantastic Stories* for February 1972, copyright © 1971 by Ultimate Publishing Company, Inc.

Chapter IV is based upon "Eldritch Yankee Gentleman," in *Fantastic Stories* for August and October 1971, copyright © 1971 by Ultimate Publishing Company, Inc.

Chapter V is based upon "Superman in a Derby," in *Fantastic Stories* for November 1974, copyright © 1974 by Ultimate Publishing Company, Inc.

Chapter VI is based upon "Memories of R.E.H.," in *Amra*, II, no. 38, copyright © 1966 by L. Sprague de Camp, and "Skald in the Post Oaks," in *Fantastic Stories* for June 1971, copyright © 1971 by Ultimate Publishing Company, Inc.

Chapter VII is based upon "Pratt's Parallel Worlds," in *Amra*, II, no. 35, copyright © 1968 by L. Sprague de Camp, and "Pratt and His Parallel Worlds," in *Fantastic Stories* for December 1972, copyright © 1972 by Ultimate Publishing Company, Inc.

Chapter VIII is based upon "Sierran Shaman," in *Fantastic Stories* for October 1972, copyright © 1972 by Ultimate Publishing Company, Inc.

Chapter IX is based upon "White Wizard in Tweeds," in *Fantastic Stories* for November 1976, copyright © 1976 by Ultimate Publishing Company, Inc.

Chapter X is based upon "The Architect of Camelot," in *Fantastic Stories* for December 1975, copyright © 1975 by Ultimate Publishing Company, Inc.

Chapter XI is based upon "Conan's Imitators," in *Amra*, II, no. 20, copyright © 1961 by L. Sprague de Camp, and "Knights and Knaves in Neustria," in *Amra*, II, no. 41, copyright © 1971 by L. Sprague de Camp.

To Nan and Gerry Crook

CONTENTS

LITERARY SWORDSMEN & SORCERERS:
  The Makers of Heroic Fantasy

by L. Sprague de Camp

11/24/76 $ 10.00

We take pleasure in sending you this
    book for review and we shall
    appreciate receiving two
    copies of any notice you
        may give it.

ARKHAM HOUSE
Sauk City, Wisconsin

INTRODUCTION: NEOMYTHOLOGY

"SWORD AND SORCERY" is the term by which *aficionados* affectionately refer to that school of fantastic fiction wherein the heroes are pretty much heroic, the villains thoroughly villainous, and action of the derring-do variety takes the place of sober social commentary or serious psychological introspection.

In a word, then, Sword & Sorcery is written primarily to *entertain:* a motive generally suspect and largely obsolete in modern letters.

This heroic school of fantasy dates, of course, from remote antiquity and boasts an illustrious lineage. The prototypes of swordly-and-sorcerous swashbuckling can be clearly traced back to the voyagings of Odysseus, the adventures of Jason, the labors of Hercules, the wanderings of Aeneas, the explorations of Sindbad, the exploits of Beowulf, Siegfried, and St. George, and the chivalric questings of Amadis and Orlando, of Lancelot and Galahad.

Most national literatures spring from bodies of heroic and fabulous legendry—except in countries like America, too recently founded to have enjoyed a myth-making period. Persia has her Rustum, Germany her Nibelungs, Norway her Volsungs, India her Rama, Arabia her Antar, France her Carolingian peers, Russia her Ilya Murometz, Spain her Cid, and even smaller nations like Ireland and Finland their Cúchulainn and their Lemminkainen. But America—whose age, measured in centuries, can still be counted on the fingers of one hand—has to make do with such feeble follow-ups to the doughty dragon-slayers of yore as the likes of Hiawatha, Davy Crockett, and Dan'l Boone.

This may explain why, although the modern revival of heroic fantasy began in the mid-nineteenth century, when William Morris penned his inimitable medieval romances, it remained for some half a century a predominantly British field of literary endeavor. Having once been transported across the Atlantic to these shores, fantasy took root. It proliferated so abundantly that today the primary living practitioners of this ancient craft of legend-spinning are all Americans, with the lone exception of England's Michael Moorcock.

In a nation too young to have a mythology of its own, heroic fantasy has created a unique neomythology, in which so recent a creation as Superman has the status of an antediluvian epic figure, and Conan and Jirel, Fafhrd and the Gray Mouser, Vakar of Lorsk and Thongor of Lemuria form a new Round Table.

It is difficult to praise *Literary Swordsmen and Sorcerers* enough, and even harder to give it its fair and just proportion of criticism. This is, after all, only the second book ever published to attempt anything like a history of modern fantasy— the first being my own *Imaginary Worlds,* published by Ballantine Books in 1973.

Instead of attempting a comprehensive approach to fantasy as a whole, going back to MacDonald and *Vathek* as I did in my own book, L. Sprague de Camp has, I think wisely, chosen to examine the evolution of Sword & Sorcery through the works of key writers whose *œuvres* were central to the growth of the genre. He begins quite properly with Morris, therefore, the "man who invented fantasy," upon whose monuments later generations upreared their own. He follows with Lord Dunsany, the first writer to introduce an element of the Oriental fable into Morris's predominantly medieval and Malorian invention, who was also the first to adapt the genre to the short-story

form. He then looks at E. R. Eddison, the British romancer of
the 1920s who revolutionized fantasy by bringing in docu-
mentation. Whereas Morris had set his scenes in a dim world-
scape remote from history or geography, and Dunsany had
established his little kingdoms at the World's Edge or in the
Third Hemisphere, it was Eddison who buttressed his romances
with firm chronological tables and detailed, seemingly-realistic
maps—imaginary historical dates, to be sure, and invented
geographies, of course: but they *looked real.*

De Camp then goes on to consider major writers in the development of Sword & Sorcery such as Robert E. Howard, T. H.
White, J. R. R. Tolkien, and Clark Ashton Smith.

If I felt minded to quarrel, or even quibble, with de Camp,
it would be not so much with the writers he includes in his
study, as with those writers he leaves out. I don't see how you
can discuss major British literary figures like Morris and Dunsany and Tolkien, without discussing so major an American
literary figure as James Branch Cabell, who is barely mentioned. And I would have given more space to the gigantic
A. Merritt.

Obviously, de Camp reasoned that he lacked sufficient room
to treat each of the dozen or so primary fantasy authors in the
depth and detail he wished, and narrowed his choice of authors
to be so discussed to the few seminal figures about whom he
had something interesting and insightful to say. I really cannot
fault him for his choice of writers—a critic has to deal with the
book as it exists, not with the book as it *might* have been written—but it is precisely in this area, the writers who were left
out, that my main gripe originates.

For, when it comes to the major living fantasy writers,
Sprague has limited himself to those who wrote before the
1940s. This arbitrary choice of a cut-off date forces him to ig-
nore any writer in the field later than the redoubtable Fritz
Leiber.

I'm delighted that he was able to include the creator of

Fafhrd and the Gray Mouser in this book, which is only Fritz's due: Fritz is, after all, unquestionably the finest living Sword & Sorcery writer, and to have left him out of this book would have been an unforgivable omission.

But Sprague has chosen to leave out other living masters of heroic fantasy as well, and this is most unfortunate. I would enjoy reading a judicious and clear-eyed appraisal of such as the Dying Earth stories of Jack Vance, or Andre Norton's Witch World books, or Lloyd Alexander's Prydain pentalogy, or the Brak the Barbarian yarns of John Jakes, or Michael Moorcock's saga of Elric of Melniboné and his several avatars and incarnations, or Jane Gaskell's Atlantis trilogy. For that matter, I'd be interested to see what Sprague *really* thinks of my own Lemurian books, my Green Star cycle, or the three volumes so far published of my Gondwane epic.

But the most indispensable author L. Sprague de Camp has omitted from *Literary Swordsmen and Sorcerers* is, of course, L. Sprague de Camp. I don't for a minute believe he couldn't have stretched his self-imposed cut-off date by another year or two, to include his fantasy novels *The Undesired Princess* and *Solomon's Stone* (written in 1941 and published in *Unknown Worlds* the next year), or his Harold Shea novels in collaboration with Fletcher Pratt, which began to appear in print in 1940. Nosirree; it was sheer modesty on de Camp's part. To paraphrase Madame Roland, O Modesty, what crimes are committed in thy name! Modesty in authors is an overrated, even a superfluous, almost an unexpected, virtue. Thank Cthulhu, Noshabkeming, and Crom I possess little of it, myself. . . .

In this particular case, an attack of the modesties has incontrovertibly robbed this book of whatever pretensions it could have had to authoritative completeness. The omission of the one living writer who runs Fritz Leiber a hair-thin second is lamentable. And, since Sprague, rather carelessly, gave me *carte blanche* in the composition of my introduction, and promised beforehand not to tamper with my judgments, I will take

him at his word and squeeze herein one more essay in the
Literary Swordsmen and Sorcerers series, to wit:

QUIXOTE WITH A PEN

In 1950 a small publishing firm called Gnome Press, which
operated out of Hicksville, New York, began publishing hard-
cover books made up of Robert E. Howard's deservedly popular Conan stories, which had run in the magazine *Weird Tales*
in the 1930s. The man behind the Gnome Press imprint, an
old-time fan and collector named Martin W. Greenberg,
launched the series with an edition of "The Hour of the
Dragon," the only full-length novel about Conan which Howard ever wrote.

Greenberg retitled the novel *Conan the Conqueror* in order
to capitalize on the magic of that character's name. In due
course, a reviewer's copy was dispatched to Fletcher Pratt. Pratt,
a diminutive man with a wispy, straggling beard, owlishly-
thick eyeglasses, and a taste for plaid shirts of the most excruci-
ating loudness, gave the book short shrift. Although fond of
the Icelandic sagas and the romances of William Morris, and
enthralled by the word-witchery of Dunsany and the ringing
Tudor gusto of Eddison, Pratt had little patience with the
muscle-bound hero who could only batter his way out of sticky
predicaments, relying on beef and brawn rather than brains.
Pratt handed the book to his friend, colleague, and collaborator,
L. Sprague de Camp, with some casual remark to the effect
that here, perhaps, was something he might find amusing.

De Camp was then, as he is now, a tall, lean, distinguished-
looking man with piercing black eyes, a stiff, military manner,
and short, neatly-trimmed dark hair (his short, neatly-trimmed
Van Dyke beard he added to the ensemble later). He was
forty-two years old and had been writing fantasy or science-
fiction stories for the pulp magazines for thirteen years, and was
the author of some ten books. His first published story was

"The Isolinguals" in John W. Campbell's *Astounding Stories* for September 1937; his first book was a nonfiction item called *Inventions and Their Management,* done in collaboration with Alf K. Berle and published by the International Textbook Company in Scranton, Pennsylvania, in 1937.

Pratt was a war-gamer before the term had even been coined, and conducted elaborate naval war-games complete with carefully detailed, whittled-out models of warships. These games, which sometimes drew as many as fifty participants, were played out on the floor of Pratt's apartment in Manhattan. In 1939 de Camp's old friend John D. Clark, Ph.D. (they had been college roommates at the California Institute of Technology in Pasadena, California, from which de Camp took a Bachelor of Science degree in aeronautical engineering in 1930) introduced de Camp into Pratt's war-gaming circle, and, of course, to Pratt himself.

They hit it off, despite many differences between them of age (Pratt was de Camp's senior by ten years), background (Pratt was the son of an upstate New York farmer, born on an Indian reservation near Buffalo; de Camp came from an old family of certain social pretensions, and had a more-or-less upper-class upbringing), experience (Pratt had been a prize-fighter, flyweight class, reporter on two newspapers, and held down a desk in one of those semi-legit "writers' institutes" which, for a fee, guarantee to turn every would-be wordsmith into another Wordsworth; de Camp held several educational and editorial jobs before settling down to free-lancing full time), education (Pratt never got past his freshman year at Hobart College at Lake Seneca, New York; besides de Camp's B.S. in Aeronautical Engineering, he also took a Masters in Engineering and Economics from Stevens Institute of Technology, and studied at M.I.T.), temperament (Pratt was ebullient, impulsive, and sometimes quick-tempered; de Camp is always the suave, courtly gentleman whom I have never seen even slightly ruffled), and height (Pratt stood five feet three inches;

de Camp tops six feet and looks even taller, with his habitual ramrod-stiff military bearing).

De Camp, a hearty naval buff, joined in the war-games; and before very long, he and Pratt joined in a close literary partnership which made their dual by-line one of the delights of fantasy buffs from the 1940s on. The year they first met, 1939, John Campbell launched a new magazine called *Unknown,* which was to specialize in fantasy, but not just the fairly routine swashbucklement which had made Howard famous in the pages of *Weird Tales:* fantasy that was written with intelligence, not merely with verve; wit, not just the occasional pratfall; modern literary style, not the old, adjectival guff.

Responding to Campbell's challenge for new, thought-provoking, original ideas in fantasy, Pratt cooked up the notion for a sequence of novelettes about a snooty, self-important young psychologist whose experiments with symbolic logic catapult him and his friends into a variety of alternate world-lines "where magic works, and the gods are real." In particular, these worlds would be imaginary worlds, drawn either from legend, i.e., the world of Norse mythology, or from literature, i.e., Ariosto, Spenser, Coleridge & Co.

The first fruit of their efforts, "The Roaring Trumpet," took their itinerant psychologist, Harold Shea, into the above-mentioned world of the sagas and the Eddas. It appeared in the May 1940 issue of *Unknown,* and the readers loved it. They loved even more "The Mathematics of Magic" in the August 1940 issue, when Harold and his pals ventured into the universe of *The Faerie Queene.* The following year, in a short novel called *The Castle of Iron,* my personal favorite of this series, Shea wandered into the chivalric cosmos of Ariosto's Italian verse romance, *Orlando Furioso.* The acclaim for this series was truly remarkable. Even more remarkable, before the ink was dry on that issue, the staid, very legitimate (and literary) publishing house of Henry Holt issued the first two Harold Shea stories in book form under the title of *The Incomplete Enchanter.*

Nowadays it is not at all unusual for a science-fiction novel or magazine serial to appear in the dignity of hard covers after its initial baptism of printer's ink on pulp pages. But in 1941 this was unheard of: I cannot think of a single fantasy or science-fiction novel or collection of stories which traversed the enormous gulf then separating the science-fiction pulp magazine world from the prestigious world of hard-bound book publishing before *The Incomplete Enchanter,* save for de Camp's previous time-travel novel *Lest Darkness Fall* (1939–41). The scientific romances of Wells, Verne, Burroughs, Merritt, and Cummings had been translated into book form earlier, of course, but with the single exception of *The Master Mind of Mars* by Edgar Rice Burroughs, which had been reprinted from *Amazing Stories Annual* of 1927, those others who had bridged the gap were taken from the loftier adventure pulps, *Argosy* and *Blue Book* and the like, not from the lowly and despised SF magazines, with their gaudy cover art and flamboyant titles in which a blatant adjective—Weird, Astounding, Thrilling, Startling, Amazing, Fantastic—played so prominent a rôle in the largest possible lettering style. Only Burroughs did it earlier than they: and his novel appeared in *Amazing* only because it had already been rejected by everyone else!

Several things had happened to make the Harold Shea stories such a success with the readership of *Unknown.* In the first place, the stories were well-written in a neat, trim, modern prose that neither dripped with prose poetry, *à la* Merritt, nor with spooky adjectives, as with Lovecraft, nor weltered in reeking gore as was the case with Howard and his earlier imitators. The prose—as *prose*—was good, tight, decent modern journalistic prose. It was not hokey. It did not rant and rave, clamoring to pile marvel upon marvel, massacre on top of massacre.

Then again, there was the novelty of the background and of the situation: once precipitated into the world of Ariosto or Spenser, Shea had to learn the laws of magic in order to cope with more occultly-gifted adversaries, whereas a hero of Conan's

breed would simply bash and bludgeon his way out of tight
spots by brute force. Then again, there was the matter of characterization: Harold Shea was really a character, not just something cut from cardboard. Sure, he was a hero, but heroes in
most fantastic romances before *The Incomplete Enchanter* were
either indomitable physical supermen like Conan and Tarzan,
or just natural-born master swordsmen, like John Carter of
Mars, who could hold twenty rampaging Tharks at swordpoint
simultaneously.

Shea was no Hercules or D'Artagnan, but an ordinary bloke:
a flashy dresser, a bit of a fop, brash, conceited, known on occasion to affect a phony British accent, a remarkably unsuccessful man with the ladies, and not even particularly good-looking.
In all, a most decidedly *un*heroic hero!

The success of these early stories, and of the other Shea
stories, "The Green Magician" and "The Wall of Serpents,"
and of the further novels and stories Pratt and de Camp collaborated upon, such as *Land of Unreason* (*Unknown,* October
1941—the issue in which the magazine's title became *Unknown Worlds*), and *The Carnelian Cube* (Gnome Press,
1948), were a tremendous impetus to de Camp's career. He had
only had seventeen stories published by the time he and Pratt
pooled their talents on the first Harold Shea yarn, whereas
Pratt was an old hand at the game and had been selling science fiction since 1929.

Sprague learned quite a bit from Fletcher during their period of collaboration: the early or pre-Prattesque stories of de
Camp's had been clever enough, but unmemorable: cute, but
not trophy-winners. Only in one story, the celebrated *Lest
Darkness Fall* (*Unknown,* December 1939), which de Camp
was working up during his first year's acquaintance with Pratt
but in the making of which Pratt played no part whatever, is
it possible to discern something of de Camp's future excellence.
Indeed, that novel, in which a modern American ordinary man
is accidentally precipitated back into history, to Rome during

the twilight age of the Gothic occupation, displays one of de Camp's primary interests: the minor nooks and crannies of history.

De Camp himself credits Fletcher Pratt with having exerted a powerful shaping influence on the development of his style—as emphatic an influence, he acknowledges, as that of John Campbell himself, the most exacting, as he was the most excellent, of editors. But de Camp's fiction, on the whole, demonstrates another faculty gained neither from Pratt nor Campbell, and that is *humor,* which both of de Camp's literary gurus doubtless possessed in their private social lives, but for which their literary productions are not particularly noted. De Camp's keen appreciation of the ridiculous element in human affairs is probably innate and unlearned; his employment of it in his fiction, however, perhaps derives from his fondness for the fictional hilarities of P. G. Wodehouse and Thorne Smith. From the first writer he may have learned how to bring out the humorous frailties and failings of his characters purely through their dialogue, while the second writer probably served as a model for farcical action of the pratfall and funny-predicament sort.

Like every other writer worth his salt, de Camp was sharp enough to learn from his betters, and honest enough to admit to the fact.

When Pratt tossed that historic copy of *Conan the Conqueror* into his colleague's lap, he started something that, even now, is not finished. De Camp read, and yielded helplessly to Howard's gusto and driving narrative energies. He had never before read any of Howard's fantasies that he can recall, although he was certainly around while they were being published in *Weird Tales.* The reason for this, simply, is that he had never read an issue of *Weird Tales.*

How any red-blooded reader of omnivorous taste and strong inclinations towards fantastica could possibly have avoided snatching up the monthly *Weird Tales* during the decade of the

1930s seemed to me, when Sprague first confessed his failure to have ever done so, thoroughly inexplicable. He offers the explanation, I would say the remarkably feeble explanation, that he had for some reason gotten the notion that *Weird Tales* was a magazine devoted wholly to ghost stories, and as he had always been immune to the theoretical fascination exerted by the macabre, he passed it by, notwithstanding those luscious Margaret Brundage covers which adorned the prince of pulps during its most legendary decade.

It also baffled me that de Camp's friends, like John D. Clark, and colleagues, like P. Schuyler Miller—both of whom collaborated on an "informal biography" of Conan and were among the first and most devoted of Howard's fans—never tipped Sprague off to the good stuff he was missing every month in *WT*. I asked Doc Clark about this, and he points out that when he and de Camp were college roommates, Howard had only begun to be published, and that later on, when his Kull and Conan and Kane stories were the rage of *Weird's* readership, de Camp was off in Scranton or somewhere, and Clark buried away in upstate New York, and they were just not that closely in touch.

At any rate, once introduced to the magic of Howard, de Camp made up for lost time by reading everything by Howard he could obtain, and when Donald A. Wollheim published a previously unknown Howard story in his *Avon Fantasy Reader* not long thereafter, de Camp tracked down its source—a trove of forgotten manuscripts left in the hands of Otis Adelbert Kline, Howard's agent, at Howard's death. Among these papers were some previously unknown Conan stories and others that could be rewritten as Conan stories. The rest is history.

A year later, de Camp tried his hand at some Howardian heroica, in a novella called *The Tritonian Ring*. It appeared in the Winter 1951 issue of Larry Shaw's magazine, *Two Complete Science-Adventure Books*. Although hampered by one of the ghastliest titles any magazine ever labored under, *TCSAB* coaxed some remarkably good novels out of some remarkably good writers like de Camp, James Blish, and Arthur C. Clarke. For his *Tritonian Ring,* Sprague concocted an elaborately-invented world *à la* Howard's Hyborian Age: but, where Howard's imaginative integrity, or forethought, or something, lapsed, leading him into gross errors of taste in the devisal of pseudo-geography, de Camp took patient care and had the expertise to do the thing right. *The Tritonian Ring* is laid in a post-Atlantean era, "the Pusadian Age," like Conan's world in general, but far more cleverly and thoroughly done.

The novel was followed by a number of Pusadian Age short stories, such as "The Eye of Tandyla" (1951), "The Stronger Spell" (1953), "Ka the Appalling" (1958), and so on. Twayne published a hard-cover edition of the novel and the first three Pusadian stories in 1953. The cycle is not yet finished: I coaxed a new Pusadian yarn from de Camp as recently as 1971 ("The Rug and the Bull" in *Flashing Swords!* #2).

But even in *The Tritonian Ring,* where his literary model, clearly and obviously, was Howard, de Camp's sense of the ridiculous in human doings insists on rising into view despite his determined efforts to squelch it. The characters are all faintly comical: the hero, Vakar of Lorsk, albeit bound on a world-saving quest, has sufficient leisure to debate philosophy and fool around with women. Queen Porfia, like Catherine the Great, views healthy specimens of masculinity who visit her realm primarily as potential bedmates. Even magicians, both of the benign sort and of more proper villainy, tend to be amusingly grumpy or forgetful, or both. In subsequent fantasy novels, like *The Goblin Tower* (Pyramid, 1968), *The Clocks of Iraz* (Pyramid, 1971), and especially in *The Fallible Fiend* (Signet, 1973), his knack for humor, or his inability to resist the humor in a situation or a character, comes more fully to the fore. In *Fiend,* for example, the fact that the narrative is told from the viewpoint of a genuine demon trapped on the human plane and forced to observe human behavior at close range, gives de Camp a perfect position from which to score the foibles and inanities of his fellow men.

De Camp is too sane and civilized really to *believe* in heroes *per se*. He knows enough about history to realize that too often the heroes of this world, from Richard Francis Burton to Lawrence of Arabia, act in what seems to observers as a heroic manner because of inner weaknesses, compulsions, or desperate needs to overcompensate for what they dread is cowardice or less than complete masculinity. Knowing this, he finds it difficult to create fictional heroes who do not suffer from *something* which serves to goad them into acting like heroes—incurable gas pains, post-nasal drip, deviated septums, or a galloping mother fixation, let us say.

He is also, I suspect, too sane and civilized to be able to swallow whole such pretty notions as patriotism, saintliness, nobility, without their leaving a bad taste in his mouth. Puritanism can be a mask for perversion; saintliness has been known to stem from the most masochistic motives; and patriotism, like politics, is more than occasionally a comfy and remunerative refuge for scoundrels.

De Camp is gifted with that clarity of vision that is more often a curse than a blessing, and which enables one to see in unpleasantly keen detail the realities, often sordid, frequently venal, behind patriotic flag-waving, political sloganeering, and the call to crusading zeal which often masks cynicism, corruption, greed, and the lust for power. He sees as clearly as ever did Voltaire or, for that matter, Socrates, that men often act from base or ignoble motives—while loudly proclaiming their nobility of purpose and purity of character.

But he is no crusader against pomposities and inanities, however obvious they are to him. Don Quixote imagined the windmills were hostile and monstrous giants, therefore the born enemies of man; he so firmly accepted his own delusion that he charged those same windmills, armed only with a spear, ready to give his life in battle to support his own delusions.

De Camp has no delusions; or, if he has them at all, he has only those few which men need in order to permit their existence to continue in the face of the ultimate futility of all existence. He sees the men around him as inexplicable beings, often acting from sordid and selfish motives, all too blatantly venal and silly, convincing themselves that they believe in the most transparent hoaxes and hocus-pocus. However swinish, they seem to him irresistibly comic. The ignorance, superstition, and vapid biases to which they cling tickle his funnybone, whereas in another these qualities might arouse fury or loathing.

Voltaire laughed at humanity; Cabell saw endeavors as pricelessly ironic: de Camp belongs with that company, and is one with them and with Rabelais, Aristophanes, Lucian, and Apuleius, who saw humanity as raw material for comedy. At the other end of this spectrum is a writer such as Swift, who saw humanity as bestial but who was too incensed at men's folly and blindness and ignorance to see anything remotely funny about it.

Swift wrote with savagery. He would have killed the object of his rage, if he could, like Quixote with the lance. But such as Voltaire and Cabell and de Camp prefer a subtler instrument: the pen. As keen as any lancehead, the penpoint, and able to sting as sharply. But somehow or other, it is a more civilized weapon.

Although he has yet to win a Hugo or a Nebula—to say nothing of a Pulitzer—de Camp enjoys his work, and works at it assiduously. At 68, he is hale and hearty, in excellent health after a recent operation or two.

A former Lieutenant Commander in the U.S. Naval Reserve, who fought World War II from a desk in a research facility along with Isaac Asimov and Robert Heinlein, de Camp still rises at six A.M., still holds himself with the erect bearing of an officer treading the quarterdeck, or a corridor in the Pentagon.

He enjoys a convivial martini before dinner, and smokes an occasional pipe or two of evenings, but these remain his only known fleshly weaknesses except for the pleasures of connubial life (de Camp and his petite blond wife, Catherine, have two tall sons, Lyman and Gerard).

He is what most Sword & Sorcery writers ought to be, but only Dunsany and he actually were: he rides horseback, goes yachting, speaks several languages fluently (including a little Swahili), knows a genuine maharaja. An inveterate globe-trotter, de Camp has seen the ruins of Carthage and jungle-lost Tikal by moonlight, and was most recently a visitor to the Galápagos Islands. He even fenced in his college days.

His fund of colorful anecdotes about the far lands he has seen, the interesting people he has known, is delightful. De Camp is what most storytellers are not—a charming raconteur. Indeed, he does so many things so very well that he is, I suspect, the envy and despair of many of his fellow-writers less disciplined, less traveled, and less common-sensical about things in general. I, who tend to pry myself grudgingly from bed about noon—by which time Sprague has easily put in a full day's work at the typewriter—regard him at times with incredulity. The way he takes care of himself, Sprague will still be going strong at ninety, by which point I, twenty-two years his junior, will probably have been a good ten years in a cigarette-smoker's grave.

His affable and generous nature is known to few of the many who know his wit. When I was a raw beginner, toiling over my first Sword & Sorcery novel, *The Wizard of Lemuria,* he inquired, without my even hinting, if he might read it. He returned the manuscript with a five-page, single-spaced criticism, flawlessly pinpointing every mistake of grammar, spelling, internal logic, and consistency. Having taken my poor manuscript apart, he admitted having read it "with gusto."

Years later, after I had completed a bookful of Howard's fragmentary King Kull stories, Sprague thrilled, delighted, and completely astonished me by diffidently asking if I would mind collaborating with him on some new Conan tales. I said "yes" very quickly, before he could change his mind. To date we have written close to a quarter of a million words together. The process has been exasperating, enjoyable, exhilarating, and exhausting; but on that topic I will unburden myself in more detail at another time, when once he has entered that Fiddler's Green reserved for storytellers and yarn-spinners, and is trading tall tales with Gulliver and Sindbad over a tankard of ale and a fragrant pipe.

As to de Camp's genuine and lasting importance as a fantasy writer, it is hard to appraise his work, for he is, happily, still with us and still writing. But some observations, however premature, can be made even at this interim point in time. He was the first great popularizer of heroic fantasy and its most tireless and eloquent champion. He edited the very first anthology of Sword & Sorcery ever published—a book titled, with great aptness, *Swords and Sorcery* (Pyramid, 1963). He continued in this vein with *The Spell of Seven* (1965), *The Fantastic Swordsmen* (1967), and *Warlocks and Warriors* (1970), the first anthology of heroic fantasy in hard cover. With four books to his credit thus far, he has edited more anthologies of literary swordsmanship and sorcery than anyone else.

Singlehandedly he has laid the foundations for all future scholarly studies of heroic fantasy in a voluminous series of articles, essays, memoirs, and reviews so immense by now that the articles which comprise *Literary Swordsmen and Sorcerers* are only a small portion of this body of work. In *Amra* and other magazines, both fan and pro, he has written knowledgeably and with wit, insight, and appreciation concerning Howard, Smith, Pratt, Eddison, Lovecraft, Morris, Dunsany, Tolkien, Ball, Moore, Kuttner, Derleth, White, Mundy, Rohmer, Lamb, Moorcock, Barringer, and just about anybody else who has had anything to do with the Sacred Genre, however peripherally. The present book is only one of several volumes which include these articles.

His work on reviving interest in Robert E. Howard, in getting Howard's work back into print again and before the public, in completing the unfinished manuscripts, in collaborating with me or Björn Nyberg on new Howardian pastiches, is singularly important. He has performed for Howard the same splendid service that Derleth did for Lovecraft: writing him up, anthologizing him, keeping his work alive and his name before the readers. De Camp not only edited some of the Conan stories for Gnome Press but was also instrumental in getting the entire series into paperback editions by Lancer Books.

For this alone, de Camp has earned the gratitude and esteem of all fantasy buffs the world over. Derleth, at least, *knew* Lovecraft, corresponded with him, regarded him quite rightly and with good reason as his literary mentor. But de Camp never met Howard and never so much as exchanged a postcard with the man whose life work he was to spend a quarter of a century getting into print. A more sincere and unselfish devotion to another man's work by a later writer I cannot call to mind.

But then there is the question of de Camp's own fiction. Just how good *is* it, and just how lasting? This is a difficult question to answer right now, although easy enough from the perspective of time. Give me another twenty years post de Camp, and I guarantee an accurate estimate. (Hindsight is so easy in questions of literature, you know.)

I am persuaded that a goodly number of his novels and stories will survive the test of time, at least for a while. Few—*very* few—writers are lucky enough, or gifted enough, to have their writings survive them by more than half a century. Looking at those fantasy writers who died twenty or thirty or forty years ago, you see that such as Burroughs, Merritt, Lovecraft, Haggard, and Howard are still very much "alive." But writers of comparable worth, or nearly so, are flirting narrowly with oblivion. By how slim a margin—and for how long—did the

Ballantine Adult Fantasy Series postpone extinction for Morris, Dunsany, Ernest Bramah, and Hannes Bok? George Allan England and John Taine, to say nothing of Clifford Ball or Nictzin Dyalhis, are forgotten, except by a few buffs; neither Ball nor Dyalhis has received book publication.

When it comes to de Camp, any guess as to the viability of his work must essentially be based on personal preference. But some informed estimates may be put forth. I should hazard the opinion that his nonfiction study of the Atlantis theme, *Lost Continents,* has a strong claim to permanence, not only because it is written with zest and wit, but because the scholarship is exhaustive and impeccable. For those reasons, and because no comparably comprehensive study of this field has ever been written, it should become a standard reference work, and should remain deservedly popular. I have much the same opinion concerning *The Ancient Engineers.* De Camp has a rare gift for making scholarly writing entertaining to read and enjoyable.

Of his work with Pratt, surely *The Castle of Iron,* at very least, will last during our time. It is the strongest and the most thoroughly exemplary of their collaborations, while the other works are more or less flawed in one way or another and reveal their pulpish origins all too plainly.

While even the best of de Camp's science fiction—even *Divide and Rule*—now seems dated, the most purely entertaining of the Krishna stories have the timeless appeal of good, vivid storytelling. *The Tower of Zanid* (1958) should continue to find its way into the hands of new generations without difficulty. *Lest Darkness Fall,* his first novel and still perhaps his best, is so completely original, refreshing, and entertaining that I cannot imagine its being easily forgotten. Of the Pusadian stories, "Ka the Appalling" and "The Eye of Tandyla" can be endlessly anthologized as long as a sufficient readership exists to encourage the publication of fantasy. *The Goblin Tower* seems to be the most perfect of his Sword & Sorcery novels. But these are merely personal preferences: time, as always, will have the last word in these matters.

As a writer of heroic fantasy, L. Sprague de Camp brought a unique personal talent for injecting humor into even the most serious plots of quest and war and adventure, and a delightful whimsical irreverence to the creation of heroes, heroines, and villains. The best of his prose is so cleanly written, so well constructed, that for it ever to seem quaint or outmoded is difficult to imagine. To the craft of world-inventing he brought several ingenious and insightful new techniques: no writer I can think of before him quite so thoroughly realized that preliterate people, such as generally inhabit fantasy worlds, will quote from apothegms, tales, and legends in lieu of the written word. For superior use of this device, see in particular the *Zanid*. And no writer before him who dealt with imaginary prehistoric ages had so thoughtfully, carefully, and intelligently constructed his invented milieux—certainly not Howard or any of the Atlantis novelists.

Among fantasy writers, he stands out virtually alone as being devoid of annoying eccentricities of taste or invention. It is possible to enthuse over Morris, Eddison, Lovecraft, Howard, Merritt, or Smith, while admitting serious flaws in their command of the narrative art. I do not think it is possible to do that with de Camp. He wrote purely to entertain, not to convert or crusade or complain. Behind his choice of the literary craft lies no neurotic compulsion, lurks no guilty fears as to his lack of masculine machismo, whimpers no inferiority complex's hunger for attention. Quite early on he saw where his best abilities lay, and pursued perfection in his craft from that moment.

Somewhere in the qualities listed in the paragraph above may be found the secret of his greatness in our field. Perhaps in all of them.

LIN CARTER

Hollis, Long Island, New York

LITERARY SWORDSMEN AND SORCERERS: THE MAKERS OF HEROIC FANTASY

I

THE SWORDS OF FAËRIE

O hark, O hear! how thin and clear,
And thinner, clearer, farther going!
O sweet and far from cliff and scar
The horns of Elfland faintly blowing![1]

TENNYSON

In 1965–66, a publishing phenomenon took place. Two American paperback publishers issued rival editions of an immensely long fantasy novel by an elderly Oxford don. The story had appeared a decade before in three big clothbound volumes. It had received reviews—more in its native United Kingdom than in the United States—from the wildly enthusiastic to the sternly damnatory and had become the ikon of a small cult of enthusiasts. Its sales had not been spectacular.

Now it became a paperback best-seller, with sales of more than a million a year for a number of years. It sold especially well to—of all people—college undergraduates. Some of these wore buttons reading FRODO LIVES, Frodo being one of the story's heroes. A fierce quarrel arose among the two publishers, the author, and his admirers as to which publisher was doing right by the author.

The author was J. R. R. Tolkien; the book, his *Lord of the Rings* trilogy or three-volume novel. However excellent of their kind, books of this type had not up to then aroused much general public enthusiasm. The story was a fantasy-adventure in an

3

imaginary setting—a kind of adult fairy tale. It was not a story of skullduggery in Washington, or of fornication in Hollywood, or of the woes of an anti-hero, a wretched twerp with neither brains nor brawn nor character, who can do nothing right and whose only function is to suffer. At that time, all these themes were popular in mainstream fiction. This story was about as far from the real world of the here-and-now as one could imagine.

Theretofore, adult fantasy had seldom shown much profit. True, there had been several adult fantasy magazines. One, *Weird Tales,* had run for thirty-one years before perishing in 1954; most others had proved ephemeral. It looked, in fact, as if fantasy could never be successfully revived.

Close on the heels of *The Lord of the Rings* came another success in the same genre: Lancer Books' paperbacked series of Robert E. Howard's stories of Conan the barbarian, hero of gore-spattered adventures in an imaginary, magic-fraught prehistoric world. The Conan paperbacks did not sell so well as *The Lord of the Rings* but went well over the million mark. Then other authors persuaded publishers to purchase similar tales of swordplay and sorcery in imaginary settings, where magic works and modern science and technology do not exist. Such fiction is now a well-developed sub-genre in the general class of imaginative fiction—that is, science fiction and fantasy.

This sub-genre is sometimes called "heroic fantasy" and sometimes "sword-and-sorcery fiction." The names are about equally descriptive, although neither exactly fits all the stories in the field. I prefer "heroic fantasy" as more concise but have no objection if others prefer the other term. It will, I hope, be interesting to trace the development of the genre from its revival in the 1880s down to the Second World War, through the lives and works of its leading authors of that period. These writers include some very singular personalities indeed—individuals whom some consider even more interesting than their stories.

With the revival of heroic fantasy in the last quarter-century, the Hero rides again. For a time, it looked as if he had been buried for good. During and after the Second World War, writers of science fiction and fantasy gave us many stories of anti-heroes; sentimental, psychological, introverted stories; stories using the "slice-of-life" technique instead of that of the "well-wrought tale" previously favored; stories with experimental narrative techniques, like those pioneered by James Joyce half a century before. The results were often more confusing than stimulating.

Then the Hero reappeared in heroic fantasy. He strides through landscapes in which all men are mighty, all women beautiful, all problems simple, and all life adventurous. In such a world, gleaming cities raise their shining spires against the stars; sorcerers cast sinister spells from subterranean lairs; baleful spirits stalk crumbling ruins; primeval monsters crash through jungle thickets; and the fate of kingdoms is balanced on the bloody blades of broadswords brandished by heroes of preternatural might and valor.

Such stories, written in recent decades and still coming off the press, are not all of equal value. They come good, bad, and indifferent like the other works of man. But they have action, color, vigor, and recognizable heroes. This gives them an advantage, as pure escape reading, over fiction of some other kinds. And heroic fantasy is the purest escape fiction there is; the reader escapes clean out of the real world.

Much ink has been spilled in trying to define "science fiction" and "fantasy." Practically speaking, we can divide all fiction into two kinds: realistic and imaginative. Realistic fiction, let us agree, consists of stories laid in the known world, either in the present or in the historical past. It tells of people like real human beings, doing the ordinary things that real people do and governed by the same natural laws. Realistic fiction does not tell what *actually* happened (save when, as in a historical novel, the storyteller brings in some real event or person) or it would not be fiction. But, as far as the reader knows, the events *could* have happened.

Then let us use "imaginative fiction" for stories that could not have happened. They may be laid in the future, which has not yet come to pass, or in the prehistoric past, about which no detailed information survives, or on another world. Or they contain elements like ghosts, magic, and miracles, in which most readers—at least the more sophisticated ones—do not really believe.

There is no sharp line between these two classes. For instance, many stories, otherwise realistic, have been laid in an imaginary place, like the Balkan kingdom of Ruritania in Anthony Hope's *The Prisoner of Zenda* (1894).

Anyone can open an atlas to prove that no such place exists. That, however, is to be like the literal-minded German publisher who, offered Tolkien's fairy tale *The Hobbit,* turned it down on the ground that his people had searched dictionaries and encyclopedias, and they reported that there was positively no such thing as a Hobbit. Any fiction involves some make-believe, and a reader incapable of flights of fancy had better stick to nonfiction.

A story may be realistic to one reader and imaginative to another. To a firm believer in ghosts, a ghost story is "realistic." The difference between realistic and imaginative fiction is one of degree rather than of kind.

Likewise, no sharp line divides science fiction from fantasy. We use "fantasy" for stories based on supernatural ideas or assumptions, such as demons, ghosts, witches, and workable magical spells. "Science fiction," on the other hand, is used for stories based upon scientific or pseudo-scientific ideas, such as revolutionary new inventions, life in the future, or life on other worlds. Some stories, like several of H. P. Lovecraft's, fall on the border.

Whether the things in the story are possible does not necessarily classify the tale. There is more evidence for werewolves than for the possibility of time travel. Yet a werewolf story is classed as a fantasy, while a time-travel tale is deemed science fiction. Neither is much more unlikely than the assumptions of many detective stories, such as the little old lady who always comes upon freshly-cooled corpses and solves the mystery after the bungling police have failed.

We find a curious thing in the history of fiction. Nearly all the stories told around primitive campfires, in ancient royal palaces, or in medieval castles and huts were what we now call imaginative fiction. Before 1700, realistic fiction—stories of ordinary people doing ordinary things—hardly existed. Save for a few scattered early examples, it is only in the last three centuries that realistic fiction has come into being, become widely popular, and grown into the main kind of fictional entertainment. Hence its name of "mainstream fiction." To this day, however, imaginative fiction continues to thrive beside its younger competitor.

Imaginative fiction took shape in the myths and legends of ancient times and of primitive peoples. These tales of gods and heroes were passed along by word of mouth before people learned to write.

In their most primitive form, myths and legends are often childishly irrational and exuberantly inconsistent and contradictory. As barbarism evolves into civilization, bards piece this amorphous mass together and iron out the most obvious inconsistencies. The resulting narratives take the form of long narrative poems or epics, like the *Iliad*, the *Mahâbhârata*, and the *Völsungá Saga*.

Early epics are full of details that modern readers recognize as elements of science fiction or fantasy. In Homer's *Odyssey*, composed about 800 B.C., the witch Circe turns the companions of Odysseus into pigs, and Odysseus has to threaten her with his sword to make her turn them back. Robots had a fictional fore-bear in Talos, a bronzen giant who ran around the island of Crete, throwing boulders at unwanted visitors.

As literacy developed, a class of literary men appeared. Some, tired of copying and recopying ancient epics, decided to compose their own. These tales, imitating the traditional form, are called pseudo-epics or romances. About 20 B.C., the Roman poet Virgil (Publius Vergilius Maro) wrote his *Aeneid* in imitation of the *Odyssey*. A little over a thousand years later, a Welsh monk, Geoffrey of Monmouth, wrote a *History of the Kings of Britain* in imitation of Virgil.

Many science-fictional ideas took shape among the Classical Greeks. Aristophanes invented the mad scientist and the artificial earth satellite; Plato proposed tunnels in the earth, islands in the sky, an ideal commonwealth where everybody was healthy, wealthy, and wise, and the sunken continent of Atlantis. Loukianos of Samosata sent his characters to the heavens and involved them in an interplanetary war.

After the West Roman Empire fell to the barbarians in the fifth century of the Christian Era, literacy in Europe all but vanished. For several centuries, most fiction took the form of hagiographies. In these imaginary lives of saints, some martyrs, after being beheaded, went about carrying their heads in their hands.

During the Dark Ages, civilization continued much as before in the Near and Middle East, India, and China; but, because of poor communications, the writings of these lands had but little effect on barbarous Europe. At this time, however, writers set down many traditional tales told among the barbarians on the fringes of the former Roman Empire. Thus the Scandinavian sagas, the German *Nibelungenlied,* the Welsh *Red Book of Hergest,* and the Irish epics of the Red Branch were saved from oblivion. Some of the old stories were given a thin Christian veneer to save them from the hostility of the Church.

With the revival of European learning after the eleventh

century, some of the earlier Classical literature was copied and circulated. Inspired by Virgil and others, European storytellers began composing their own romances, of which more than a hundred appeared in the next few centuries. Anyone who likes to read of parfit gentle knights rescuing maydenes faire from vile enchauntours will find here material to occupy his time for years.

Among these romances were tales of the more or less legendary King Arthur and his knights of the Table Round. Others told of Arthur's adviser Merlin, the prototype of the good magician, the wise, white-bearded old wizard, who so often appears in modern fantasy. Another cycle dealt with Charlemagne and his twelve paladins. Outstanding in this group is the *Orlando Furioso* ("Mad Roland") of the early 1500s, by Lodovico Ariosto, later imitated by Edmund Spenser in his *Faerie Queene*. The *Orlando Furioso* revived the theme of a voyage to the moon; one of Ariosto's heroes flies thither on the back of a hippogriff.

The medieval romance came to an ignominious end about 1600. A Spaniard, Miguel de Cervantes, had fought against the Turks in the great naval battle of Lepanto and had been wounded there. Later, he was captured and enslaved by the Moors. Having led a rough, adventurous life, Cervantes knew that real adventures were seldom so picturesque, sanitary, and enjoyable as those of the romances. So he wrote a long novel, *Don Quixote de la Mancha,* about a woolly-minded would-be knight. This work so hilariously burlesqued the medieval romance that nobody thereafter dared to write one.

Freed of the conventions of the traditional romance, writers continued to play with imaginative ideas. Thomas More, Francis Bacon, and Tommaso Campanella revived Plato's concept of the ideal commonwealth. Stories of marvelous journeys, like those of Jonathan Swift's Captain Lemuel Gulliver, continued popular. Stories were written about flying, about journeys to the moon, and about trips through those hollows inside the earth of which Plato had written. Cyrano de Bergerac sent his hero to the moon in a rocket ship; Voltaire brought to earth visitors from other planets.

Aside from some ghost stories, tales of witchcraft, and religious tracts, few supernatural fantasies were written in the seventeenth and early eighteenth centuries. Cervantes had slain the medieval romance. Moreover, after 1650 came a general decline in belief in the supernatural. The eighteenth century saw the growth of a skeptical, rationalistic, materialistic outlook. It also saw the rise of the realistic novel, of which Daniel Defoe's *Robinson Crusoe* (1719) was one of the first. Books for children, pioneered by John Bunyan in the seventeenth century, also began to be written, although for a long time they consisted of grimly moralistic tales with a maximum of uplift and a minimum of entertainment.

In the eighteenth and early nineteenth centuries, however, fantasy reëntered the stream of European fiction. It sprang from three sources. One was the oriental extravaganza. In 1704 a French scholar, Antoine Galland, found an Arabic manuscript containing tales of Sindbad the Sailor. After he had translated them into French, Galland learned that these stories were only part of a much larger collection called *The Arabian Nights* or, more accurately, *The Book of the Thousand Nights and a Night*. These stories, mostly composed in Egypt between the years 900 and 1400, have since been translated into many European tongues.

Another source of modern fantasy was the Gothic novel, invented in Germany and introduced to England by Horace Walpole's *The Castle of Otranto* (1764). This lively and still surprisingly readable novel of medieval murder and spookery contains all the elements that became standard props of the Gothic horror story: an Italian locale, a lecherous tyrant, an imperiled virgin, an impoverished young hero of noble blood, a monk, a castle with trapdoors and secret passages, eldritch legends, a ruined monastery, and *two* ghosts. Who could ask for more?

Otranto was followed by a flood of Gothic novels in England and Germany: for example, by William Beckford's *Vathek* (1786) about a caliph who, avid for power and knowledge, sells himself to the Evil One; by *The Mysteries of Udolpho* and others by Mrs. Ann Radcliffe in the 1790s; by Charles Maturin's endless *Melmoth the Wanderer* (1820). The best-remembered is *Frankenstein* (1818) by Mary Wollstonecraft Godwin, mistress and later wife of the poet Shelley. Mrs. Shelley's melancholy, murderous monster is the ancestor of all the robots and androids that shamble through modern science fiction.

The third source of modern fantasy was the fairy tale. In medieval and Baroque times, the European peasantry continued to hand down traditional tales as they had before the rise of Western civilization. In the nineteenth century, people like the Grimm brothers in Germany began to collect and publish such tales. Then others like Lewis Carroll and George MacDonald began composing original stories in the genre.

During the nineteenth century, many eminent writers like Hawthorne, Melville, and Bulwer-Lytton tried their hands at an occasional imaginative story. Dickens introduced the theme of time travel in *A Christmas Carol* (1843). Fitz-James O'Brien had an invisible monster attack his protagonist in "What Was It? A Mystery" (1859). Edward Everett Hale described an artificial earth-satellite vehicle in "The Brick Moon" (1869). Stanley Waterloo gave a naïve picture of caveman life in "Christmas 200,000 B.C." (1887).

Edgar Allan Poe (1809–49) made major contributions to the imaginative genre, writing of hypnotism, alchemy, a flight to the moon, and a future transatlantic balloon flight. After Poe died, poor and neglected, his work came to the notice of the French writer Charles Baudelaire, a leader of the self-styled Decadents. Fascinated, Baudelaire translated Poe's works into French in the 1850s and 60s.

This translation much impressed an unsuccessful young

French lawyer, stockbroker, and playwright named Jules Verne (1828–1905). As a result, Verne became the world's first successful full-time science-fiction writer, with nearly a hundred novels to his credit. Most of his stories take the form of a marvelous journey, on which the author sends along one or two learned characters to explain the wonders of science to the other characters and the reader. After Verne, Rudyard Kipling, H. Rider Haggard, and A. Conan Doyle made distinguished contributions to imaginative fiction, while Herbert George Wells (1866–1946) outshone them all.

Fantasy evolved along parallel lines. Bulwer-Lytton, Dickens, Hawthorne, O. Henry, Henry James, and many others tried their hands at ghost stories. In O'Brien's "The Diamond Lens," the hero makes contact with the spirit of Leeuwenhoek, the inventor of the microscope, through a Spiritualist medium. Alexander Dumas *père* brought the werewolf theme into current fiction with *The Wolf Leader,* while Joseph Sheridan Le Fanu revived the vampire motif in *Carmilla,* later and more effectively exploited in Bram Stoker's *Dracula.*

While the Gothic novel bloomed, Sir Walter Scott launched the modern historical novel with his *Waverly* (1814) and its many successors. Many earlier writers had composed stories laid in a time well before their own. Homer's *Iliad* and Xenophon's *Youth* (or *Education*) *of Cyrus* belong in this class. Such writers, however, made no special point of the differences between their own times and those whereof they wrote. Often they were not even aware of these differences.

Scott discovered not only that the past was different in significant ways from the present but also that these differences could be turned to account. The costumes and customs of a bygone age had entertainment value in themselves. To an ordinary man in any civilization, harassed by the petty everyday needs of a drab existence, life in an earlier century seems more colorful and dramatic than that of his own world. Hence Scott looked back to the Middle Ages, just as medieval men looked back to Rome, the Romans to Greece, and the Greeks to the days of Minoan Crete and Mycenae.

Needless to say, those who fancy that they would relish life in a bygone era assume that they would arrive in the earlier milieu with all the health, wealth, and social status needed to enjoy their visit. Nobody would wish to find himself an Irish peasant during the Famine of the 1840s, or a medieval serf, or a slave in the Athenian silver mines at Laureion. Actually, if one were translated to the body of such a dweller in former times, chosen at random, one would be hundreds of times more likely to find oneself a downtrodden proletarian than a baron or an Athenian eupatrid, because the affluent in those days were such a tiny fraction of the whole. For that matter, such a translation would drastically cut one's life expectancy, because there were so many illnesses and injuries that in those days were fatal.

Scott's novels touched off a wave of romantic medievalism in the British Isles. Rich men built synthetic medieval ruins on their estates, where they could sit and brood like Shelley's Alastor.

In 1817, a man named Ashford accused another, Thornton, of murdering Ashford's sister. Thornton then challenged Ashford to appear in the lists in full armor for trial by battle. When Ashford failed to appear, armored or otherwise, Thornton claimed to have won his case. The lawyers found to their amazement that indeed he had, for Parliament had never gotten around to abolishing trial by battle. Then in 1839 a sporting young peer, Lord Eglinton, and his friends, at enormous expense, staged the last authentic medieval tournament on Eglinton's Scottish estates. Alas for romance; it poured!

This wave of medievalist enthusiasm affected a generation of British architects, who speckled Britain with Gothic churches and public buildings; of British artists, who painted Arthurian characters in anachronistic plate armor and soulful attitudes; and of British writers, who wrote medieval romances in prose and verse.

In the 1880s William Morris revived heroic fantasy, moribund since the death of the medieval romance. In effect, Morris combined the antiquarian romanticism of Scott and his imitators with the supernaturalism of Walpole and *his* imitators, in a series of novels laid in imaginary pseudo-medieval worlds, where magic works. Practically speaking, this began the modern sub-genre of heroic fantasy or swordplay-and-sorcery fiction: stories laid on another world—in a parallel universe, or on another planet, or on this world in the remote past or future—where gunpowder and machinery are unknown and where spirits and workable magic are part of the nature of things.

In the medieval romances on which Morris's novels were modeled, the storytellers sited their tales on this world, usually in some time a few centuries earlier. Spirits and magic gave no trouble, because they (or at least most of their audience) believed in such things. The advances of science and history since then, however, have made it harder for a modern reader to become emotionally involved in a story of this kind, if laid in a real, well-documented earthly scene. So most modern heroic fantasists place their narratives in completely exotic milieux.

A strong element in modern heroic fantasy is that of romantic primitivism. This is the concept of the primitive, the lusty barbarian, as the hero, the superman, superior to the decadent weaklings of urban civilization.

Romantic primitivism goes back to the "noble savage" proclaimed by Jean Jacques Rousseau (1712–78). In 1672, John Dryden published a verse drama, *The Conquest of Granada*. At the beginning, one of Dryden's characters declaims:

> I am as free as Nature first made man,
> 'Ere the base laws of servitude began,
> When wild in woods the noble savage ran.

The phrase "noble savage," epitomizing the idea of the primitive as the superhuman hero, was taken over by Rousseau's critics when that weepy Swiss philosopher praised primitive life. The notion that primitive men were better than those of today goes back to the Greek myth of the Golden Age and the Judaeo-Christian myth of Eden, but it got an enormous boost from the writings of Rousseau. So far as I know, Rousseau did not himself use the term "noble savage"; neither did he ever know any savages, noble or otherwise.

In 1755, Rousseau published a *Discourse on the Origin and the Foundations of Inequality Among Men.* He headed the second chapter: "That Nature has made man happy and good, but that Society depraves him and makes him wretched." "Man," he declared, "is naturally good," but civilization, especially the institution of private property, renders him evil. Seven years later, Rousseau developed the same argument on more conservative lines in *The Social Contract.*

When Rousseau wrote, scientific anthropology hardly existed. Philosophers speculated about the "state of nature," preceding civilization, by analogies with Genesis and with existing primitives. European navigators were then discovering the South Sea Islands and sending home idyllic but fanciful, unrealistic accounts of Polynesian life. These descriptions were taken as portraying "noble savages" in actual fact. Fiction writers made supermen out of American Indians and other barbarians. This attitude is sometimes called "soft primitivism" in contrast to the more realistic "hard primitivism," which took a less idealized view of primitive life. Generally, the further that writers were from first-hand observation, the softer was their primitivism.

In 1791, one of these writers, François René de Chateaubriand, came as a youth to America to see the noble savage in his native haunts. In the Mohawk Valley in upstate New York, he was enchanted by the forest primeval until he heard music coming from a shed. Inside, he found a score of Iroquois men and women solemnly dancing a fashionable French dance to the tune of a violin in the hands of a small, powder-wigged

Frenchman. This Monsieur Violet had come to America with Rochambeau's army in the Revolution, stayed on after his discharge, and set himself up as a dancing teacher among the Amerinds. He was full of praise for the dancing talents of *Messieurs les Sauvages et Mesdames les Sauvagesses*. Chateaubriand's disillusionment did not prevent him from later writing an Amerind novel, *Atala,* which became a classic of romantic primitivism.

Rousseau was not the utter fool that selected quotations from his writings can make him appear, even though his reasoning powers, while not negligible, were usually overborne by his intense emotionalism, and his principal emotion was a passionate love of Jean Jacques Rousseau. But consistency was never one of his virtues. He condemned intolerance but proposed an official "civil religion," compulsory to all on pain of exile. He praised chastity and wrote a revolutionary treatise on education but sent his own several illegitimate children to orphanages as soon as they were born. He sang the praises of liberty but idealized Sparta, whose serfs suffered under the world's most grinding class tyranny, enforced by terrorism.

Rousseau's arguments were often ingenious and subtle. Sometimes he even made sense, or as much sense as one should expect of a political philosopher before modern anthropology, sociology, and psychology. He preached effectively for republican government.

On the other hand, he argued mainly by definition—an elementary fallacy. He juggled abstractions like "mankind," "society," "natural law," "the sovereign," and "the general will," having little connection or none with the real world; Jeremy Bentham called such terms "nonsense on stilts." Rousseau explained that his "state of nature . . . perhaps never existed, and probably never will." It was an ideal to shoot for. He did not, he said, mean the hypothetical "original state of man," when the "war of all against all" prevailed and, as Hobbes had said, "the life of man [was] solitary, poore, nasty, brutish, and shorte."

Rousseau had in mind a "patriarchal" culture, when people lived in families and clans and had perhaps begun to enjoy the fruits of husbandry, but before private property was invented. Indications are that there was no such time. Families and small, coöperative bands probably go back to our australopithecine ancestors. Even the most primitive of living men have ideas of property, if only in the form of hunting and fishing rights. But Rousseau lacked our advantage of living after Darwin, Mendel, Freud, Lewis H. Morgan, and their successors.

The search for the fictitious "state of nature," when all men were peaceful, happy, and good, continued through the Romantic Era, fathered by Rousseau and dominant roughly 1790–1840. The movement continued afterwards, for example in the utopian colonies formed in the nineteenth-century United States. The romantic illusion of a primitive Golden Age has, in fact, flourished right down to the present, as witness the commune movements of the so-called counterculture of the 1960s. (The only such cults that have shown any real staying power are those like the Amish and the Hutterites, which, recruited from the stolid German peasantry, combine intense religious convictions, puritanical austerity, and a passion for hard work. Would-be founders of communes may take note.)

During the nineteenth century, the windy German philosopher, Friedrich Nietzsche, played a similar tune with his talk of the Superman, the "great blond beast," who would some day reappear, smash the Judaeo-Christian "slave morality," and impose proper discipline upon the masses of Europe. Nietzsche was vague as to how this hero was to be created, save for the interesting suggestion that the mating of German army officers with Jewish women might engender him.

The romantic illusion was further fostered by several very popular writers of the late nineteenth and early twentieth centuries. Jack London, who incongruously combined Marxism, racism, and romanticism, was full of it. Rudyard Kipling's *Jungle Books* (1894–95) presented one of the purest examples before Tarzan. Kipling's Mowgli, reared from babyhood by wolves in India:

> . . . must have been nearly seventeen years old. He looked older, for hard exercise, the best of good eating, and baths whenever he felt in the least hot or dusty had given him strength of growth far beyond his age. He could swing by one hand from a top branch for half an hour at a time, when he had occasion to look along the tree-roads. He could stop a young buck in mid-gallop and throw him sideways by the head. . . . The Jungle-People, who used to fear him for his wits, now feared him for his mere strength, and when he moved quietly on his own affairs the whisper of his coming cleared the wood-path.[2]

Kipling's animal characters make snide remarks about "civilized" men: "Men are only men, Little Brother, and their talk is like the talk of frogs in a pond." "Men must always be making traps for men, or they are not content." "Men are blood-brothers to the *Bandar-log* [monkeys]." "Who is Man that we should fear him—the naked brown digger, the hairless and toothless, the eater of earth?" (By "Man," Kipling meant the Indians, whom he never much liked. He was more respectful of his imperial fellow-Britons.)

In 1912 appeared in *All-Story Magazine* the first successful novel by one of the most voluminous writers in the genre of imaginative fiction. The story was "Under the Moons of Mars," by "Norman Bean." The author was a Westerner in his thirties, who had unsuccessfully tried several occupations, including bookkeeper, cowboy, prep-school teacher, railroad detective, salesman, and soldier. Once, when he read a magazine story that struck him as especially bad, he swore that even he could do better. Thus did Edgar Rice Burroughs (1875–1950) write his first story. In 1917, the tale was republished as a book, *A Princess of Mars,* under the writer's true name.

John Carter, an adventurer and professional soldier who cannot remember his childhood, is mustered out of the defeated Confederate army and goes west to try prospecting. Trapped in a cave by Apaches, he hears a rustling noise behind him and finds himself paralyzed. Presently he leaves his material body lying unconscious. He sees the Indians approach the cave, look in, and flee in terror. Watching them go, Carter sees the planet Mars on the horizon. He focuses his will upon it—and finds himself (or perhaps his astral body) standing naked on the moss-covered dead sea bottoms of Mars. The mysterious rustle is never explained.

Carter is captured by four-armed green men fifteen feet tall, with eyes at the sides of their heads. Mars harbors other humanoid races, and Carter falls in love with a fellow captive, a princess of the red race, altogether human save that they lay eggs.

Life on Burroughs's Mars, with its four-armed giants and its boat-shaped aircraft supported by the Eighth Barsoomian Ray, is suspiciously like life in Atlantis as described by the Theosophists, Helena Petrovna Blavatsky and William Scott-Elliot. Several interplanetary novels of earlier decades have been named as possible precursors of *A Princess of Mars,* but the connection is uncertain. What is certain is that Burroughs used the speculations of the astronomer Percival Lowell, a few years earlier, that the straight lines astronomers thought they saw on Mars were canals built by intelligent Martians to carry water from the poles to the arid equatorial regions of their planet.

This was the first of ten Martian novels (and two novelettes): *The Gods of Mars, The Warlord of Mars,* and so on. In 1932, Burroughs started a companion series: *Pirates of Venus* and its successors. These, however, never had quite the grip of his Martian stories.

After "Under the Moons of Mars," Burroughs wrote a historical novel, *The Outlaw of Torn,* but this did not see publication for years. He followed this medieval tale with the most popular story he ever wrote: *Tarzan of the Apes,* which appeared in *All-Story* for October 1912. When this tale came out as a book in 1914, it made Burroughs's fortune. Tarzan became the hero not only of more than a score of books but also of a long series of movies and comic strips.

The story is too well known to need a summary. Burroughs told contradictory stories of where he got the basic idea for Tarzan, sometimes admitting and again denying that he had read Kipling's Mowgli stories. Burroughs gave the credit to the legend of Romulus and Remus. But then, Burroughs never admitted that he got his ideas for Barsoom[3] from Madame Blavatsky's Theosophical Atlantis, either, although the resemblances seem too close for coincidence.

The Tarzan stories show the romantic illusion of primitive simplicity and virtue in its purest form. Tarzan is forever contrasting the vices of civilization with the supposed virtues of the wild: "In reality he had always held the outward evidences of so-called culture in deep contempt. Civilization meant to Tarzan of the Apes a curtailment of freedom in all its aspects. . . . Clothes were the emblems of that hypocrisy for which civilization stood. . . . In civilization Tarzan had found greed and selfishness and cruelty far beyond that which he had known in his familiar, savage jungle. . . . in the bottom of his savage heart he held in contempt both civilization and its representatives. . . . Always he was comparing their weaknesses, their vices, their hypocrisies, and their little vanities with the open primitive ways of his ferocious jungle mates. . . ."[4]

Romantic primitivists like to think of barbaric or savage life as *simpler* than that of civilization. According to some who have tried it, it is anything but simple. The preliterate peasant must carry in his head a vast amount of knowledge of when and how to plant what crop, how to foster its growth, and how to gather and process it. The same applies to his flocks and herds.

The true savage—that is, the primitive hunter and food-gatherer, who has not yet learned husbandry—must likewise be, in his own way, a highly educated man to survive. Moreover, if the primitive makes one bad mistake, he dies. Nor is his way eased by the fact that much of what he thinks he knows is untrue.

The yawning gap between the romantic primitivists' fictitious "state of nature" and the real thing has often been exposed. Thor Heyerdahl's recent *Fatu-Hiva* tells of the attempt of young Heyerdahl and his bride to go native in the Marquesas Islands. After a year, they were heartily glad to get back to civilization before primitive life killed them, as it nearly did.

Civilized men, however, still cling to the illusions of romantic primitivism. The Tarzan stories appealed to a huge and largely male audience, to whose deepest emotions tales of "righteous violence in primitive settings" appealed.

Burroughs also wrote other imaginative novels, laid on the moon, inside a hollow earth, or on an unknown island in the Pacific. Many of these stories, especially the Tarzan novels, are based on the lost-race theme. Tarzan blunders into some lost city, inhabited by Atlanteans, or ancient Romans, or ape-men left over from the Pleistocene. He is captured and imprisoned, escapes, is recaptured and forced to fight in the arena, escapes again, and so on.

Burroughs's stories, with interplanetary adventures and super-scientific gadgetry, are science fiction rather than fantasy. Still, Burroughs furnished themes and concepts often used in later heroic fantasy. Although Burroughs's own outlook was anti-supernatural, he did use a few touches of fantasy, such as the phantom bowmen of Lothar in *Thuvia, Maid of Mars.*

Besides his imaginative fictions, Burroughs harbored, at least for a while, a yearning to be deemed a serious artist. So he tried to write some realistic novels. They brought little money and no fame, and Burroughs suspected that publishers brought them out solely on the strength of his name. To test the theory, he submitted some of these manuscripts under pseudonyms. All bounced, confirming his suspicion.

Burroughs tired of Tarzan, as Conan Doyle got bored with Holmes. Burroughs said: "It is difficult and even impossible for me to take these Tarzan stories seriously, and I hope that no one else will ever take them seriously." But, as in Doyle's case, the public would not let him abandon his hero.

In later years, soured by the failure of his "serious" writings and by his discovery that wealth did not necessarily bring happiness, Burroughs offered a cynical formula for success as a popular writer: "1. Be a disappointed man. 2. Achieve no success at anything you touch. 3. Lead an unbearably drab and uninteresting life. 4. Hate civilization. 5. Learn no grammar. 6. Read little. 7. Write nothing. 8. Have an ordinary mind and commonplace tastes approximating those of the great reading public. 9. Avoid subjects that you know anything about."[5]

Burroughs did himself an injustice; but his faults, which he here exaggerated, are well-known. He admitted that he owed the sale of over 35,000,000 copies of his books (and that before the days of cheap paperbacks) to his care never to subject his readers' minds to the slightest strain. He cared little for scientific plausibility or even internal consistency. His Martians, although they have radium rifles that shoot a hundred miles, prefer to fight with the more glamorous swords and spears. His Martian animals have eight or ten legs, which in that feeble gravity they would not need.

In the magazine version of *Tarzan of the Apes* appeared a character called "Sabor the Tiger." H. P. Lovecraft wrote to the magazine, pointing out that there are no tigers in Africa—at least, outside of zoos. In the book version, Sabor became a lioness; but Burroughs still adorned the African fauna with nonexistent deer.

Like most popular-fiction writers of his generation, Burroughs had no qualms about using ethnic stereotypes: the arrogant German, the avaricious Jew, the childish Negro, the treacherous Mexican, and so on. While Tarzan is supported by his native band of "faithful Waziri" warriors, his attitude towards the other natives of Black Africa is that of a ruthless colonial overlord. In his youth, he amuses himself by "black baiting"—terrifying the Africans by cruel practical jokes, up to murder. (Some of the passages about Negroes have been toned down in later paperback editions.)

On the other hand, Burroughs sometimes brings in a sympathetic or admirable Negro or other ethnic, as if to show that he was not irredeemably prejudiced. When the Nazis came to power in Germany, they burned the Tarzan books as not racist enough.

Still, there are sound reasons for Burroughs's popularity. His books are good juveniles. He gets his action going right at the start and never slows down. The style of his early books is cluttered with some of the useless verbiage then deemed "fine writing," but he learned in time to write in good, brisk, straightforward English. His narrative drive keeps the uncritical reader from noticing the sameness of his plots and the blankness of his characters. He had imagination, ingenuity, and humor, and there is something charming about his unabashed romanticism, wherein princesses are always beautiful *ex officio.*

Despite his faults, there is much solid entertainment in Burroughs's works. His Mars, like Lewis Carroll's Looking-Glass Land and Howard's Hyborian Age, has the vividness that a potent imagination imparts to a fictional setting, so that its glamor lingers long after one has forgotten the author's shortcomings. We can thus understand the strong influence that Burroughs had on some successors, notably Robert E. Howard.

Robert E. Howard caught the romantic illusion from London, Kipling, and Burroughs and idealized primitive life accordingly. Like some other writers of heroic fantasy, he made sweeping statements about barbarians and based stories upon these assumptions. Thus he said of Conan:

> Now the barbaric suggestion about the king was more pronounced, as if in his extremity the outward aspects of civilization were

stripped away, to reveal the primordial core. Conan was reverting
to his pristine type. He did not act as a civilized man would act
under the same conditions, nor did his thoughts run in the same
channels. He was unpredictable.[6]

Others, too, have stressed the barbarian's supposed unpredict-
ability, unconventionality, and freedom from civilized tabus and
inhibitions. From all I can learn, however, it seems that barbarians are on the whole more conventional, predictable, and
inhibited than civilized men. They may not observe civilized
tabus and inhibitions, but they have plenty of their own. The
few barbarians whom I have known personally were all individuals of diverse characters, with the usual spread of virtues
and faults. None bore the slightest resemblance to Conan.

Among barbarians, the force of custom must be greater than
among civilized folk, to enable them to survive in the absence
of our elaborate framework of laws, police, and courts to keep
the unruly in order. Hence real barbarian societies have been
more conventional and tabu-ridden than civilizations.

Barbarian cultures (those that have advanced beyond primitive hunting and food-gathering to farming and stock-raising
but have not yet achieved writing and cities) varied widely.
Some were sexually permissive and promiscuous; others like
the Zulus punished adultery by the death of both culprits. Some
were peaceful; others like the Comanches were so devoted to
war that they thought it the only decent, manly occupation. A
reason for the ferocity of Howard's barbarians is that the barbarians he knew the most about, the Comanche Indians of
Texas, were one of the most warlike peoples on earth. Having
just been promoted from food-gathering savagery by acquiring
horses, they were not about to sit down and master the techniques of dry farming when murder and robbery were so much
more fun.

In general, however, each barbarian society was extremely
rigid, conformist, and resistant to change. Such barbarians are
not at all like the adaptable, uninhibited adventurers of fiction.

The only exception occurs when the barbarians live near a civilization and are conquering or being conquered by it.

When barbarians have lived near a civilization weakened by civil war or other disorder, population pressure or bad weather may impel the barbarians to seek their fortunes elsewhere. If their military techniques, say as a result of contact with the civilization, have come to equal those of the civilization, the barbarians may overrun the civilization and set themselves up as a new ruling class. (This can no longer happen, because of the vast destructive powers that the advances of science have given civilizations.)

Then, if ever, the barbarian conqueror sheds his inhibitions. He has left the toilsome, dreary, humdrum round of normal barbarian life. He has escaped his usual milieu, with its tabus and etiquette, but he has not accepted the mores of the con- quered, whom he despises because he has beaten them. Hence he feels that he can get away with anything. He sees no reason not to obey every whim and lust. He acts like a bumptious adolescent, liberated from his parents' control but not yet fitted into the mold of civilized life.

The result is a catastrophic decline in the culture and living standards of the conquering adventurer's civilized subjects, since he is more interested in confiscating property, prosecuting feuds, and indulging his appetites than in maintaining roads, harbors, and aqueducts. He is happy to squander the capital that others have saved up over the centuries and let the future take care of itself. The ensuing squalid chaos can perhaps be enjoyed by one with a gangster mentality but not by many others.

Hence the resemblance of many heroes of ancient epics and modern sword-and-sorcery fiction to overgrown juvenile delin- quents. Such uninhibited behavior, in the real world, does not make one a good life-insurance risk. There are always other *conquistadores,* watching for a chance to sink something into the conqueror's back. So life expectancy, like that of today's juvenile gangsters, is short.

An Odovakar might, like Howard's Conan, rise to become general of an empire. He might even, like Conan, kill his employer (the regent Orestes, father of the boy-emperor Romulus Augustulus) and seize the throne. But Theodoric the Ostrogoth besieged Odovakar, got him to surrender on a promise of immunity, and coolly murdered him.

There have been many such downfalls, as when the Aryans overran Iran and India about 1500 B.C., or the Turks seized the Caliphate in the eleventh century. Often, a civilization has beaten off the barbarians, as the Byzantine Empire did the Avars and the Slavs.

The case we most think of is the overthrow of the West Roman Empire in the fifth century by Teutons from Germany and Sweden, Alani from Russia, and Huns from Mongolia. Western Europe suffered so sharp a decline in culture that the time is called the Dark Ages. We know the fall of the West Roman Empire best because it is the best documented. It gave rise to a large legendary literature, as in the tales of Arthur, Sigurð, and Charlemagne.

The heroes of these epics differ from real barbarian leaders, having been romanticized out of recognition. They strike nobly self-sacrificing attitudes, go on long solitary quests, and converse with supernatural beings, none of which their real-life prototypes did. But, like the real barbarians, they usually come to a bad end. Bellerophon is bucked off Pegasus in flight; Siegfried is stabbed in the back; and Arthur's skull is split by his bastard son.

Nonetheless, from these tales, modern heroic fantasy descends directly through the medieval romances and Morris's imitations of them.

Morris was followed by Lord Dunsany, who early in this century adapted heroic fantasy to the short-story form. Blackwood, Cabell, and Machen contributed to the growing stream of adult fantasy. Eric R. Eddison carried on the tradition of the long adventure-fantasy novel.

Several stories in this genre were contributed by Abraham Merritt (1884–1943). A journalist, Merritt edited Hearst's *American Weekly* from 1912 to his death. His hobbies included archaeology, witchcraft, and raising exotic plants containing rare drugs and poisons. Merritt's nine imaginative novels show strong imagination, vivid description, complex plots, and glacial slowness of pace. He often used the lost-race theme.

In *The Ship of Ishtar* (1926), often deemed Merritt's best, the scholar Kenton gets a model of an ancient galley. As he scrutinizes the model, he suddenly finds himself aboard the real ship, sailing in some extra-dimensional world of strange natural laws. The story belongs in the tradition of heroic fantasy. In the December 1942 issue of *Unknown Worlds,* the fantasy illustrator Hannes Bok had a novel called *The Sorcerer's Ship,* a so-so imitation of *The Ship of Ishtar.*

Another novel by Merritt, *Dwellers in the Mirage* (1932), is on the borders of heroic fantasy. In this story, however, Merritt threw in so many fantastic ingredients—a "lost valley" in Alaska, a "Shadowed-land," the spirit of an ancient Asian emperor, a race of Vikinglike women warriors, a race of yellow dwarfs, two beautiful sorceresses, and an evil trans-dimensional octopus—that the story bogs down under the sheer weight of so many concepts.

From 1890 on, the habit of reading magazines grew rapidly in the English-speaking world. Their number and circulation rose accordingly. By 1900, several general-circulation magazines published occasional imaginative fiction, such as the stories of H. G. Wells. In the early 1900s, the Munsey Company's magazines, such as *Munsey's Magazine, The Argosy,* and *All-Story Weekly,* ran many such "different" stories, as they called them, like the novels of Edgar Rice Burroughs.

This was an era of increasing specialization in magazines. It was, therefore, only a matter of time before someone put out a periodical devoted to imaginative fiction. The first such effort was *The Thrill Book,* launched in 1919 by Street & Smith

Publications. It ran for sixteen issues, until editorial inexperience and a printer's strike put it out of business.

The idea next came to Jacob Clark Henneberger, publisher of the successful *College Humor*. Henneberger was inspired to start *Weird Tales* by Poe's lines:

> From a wild weird clime that lieth, sublime,
> Out of SPACE—out of TIME.

Henneberger hired Edwin F. Baird, a mystery writer, to edit *Weird Tales* and its companion *Detective Tales*. The first issue of *Weird Tales,* with a cover picture of a man and woman in combat with an octopoidal monster, appeared with the date of March 1923. While the magazine ran both science fiction and fantasy, it published more of the latter.

In 1924, the magazine met financial difficulties. In a complicated deal, Baird and another employee took over the publication of *Detective Tales,* while the management of *Weird Tales* was assumed by still another employee and a new editor, Farnsworth Wright. A San Franciscan, then writing in Chicago, Wright was a gaunt Shakespearean scholar with Parkinson's disease, which made his fingers twitch uncontrollably.

Despite this handicap and a low budget, which forced him to print much inferior copy, Wright achieved signal results with *Weird Tales.* He bought stories of permanent interest, still reprinted. His contributors included Robert E. Howard, Frank Belknap Long, H. P. Lovecraft, C. L. Moore, and Clark Ashton Smith, all of whom made distinguished contributions to fantasy.

In the late 1930s, several leading contributors to *Weird Tales* died, while others departed for better-paying markets. In 1938, the magazine's owners sold it. Two years later, Wright's health worsened, his new employers fired him, and he soon died.

As the new editor, they assigned Dorothy McIlwraith, a middle-aged Scotswoman. Although an experienced editor, Miss

McIlwraith lacked Wright's touch with the fantastic. The magazine struggled along, suffered from the competition of other fantasy magazines, and ceased publication in 1954.

Meanwhile other imaginative-fiction magazines, most of them limited to straight science fiction, had arisen. In 1926, *Amazing Stories* was launched by Hugo Gernsback, an inventor and publisher who for eighteen years had been publishing popular-science magazines like *Science and Invention. Wonder Stories* (later *Thrilling Wonder Stories*) and *Astounding Stories* (later *Astounding Science Fiction,* now *Analog*) soon followed. All underwent changes of ownership.

During 1939–41, science fiction grew rapidly in popularity. The number of magazines swelled to over twenty. The Second World War ended this boom, when shortages of editors, writers, and paper caused the death of many magazines.

With the end of the war, many discontinued science-fiction magazines were revived and new ones were started, until by 1950 their number reached about twenty-five. The demand, however, was not large enough to support so many periodicals. The number again shrank and for the last decade has varied between five and ten.

In 1937, a young engineering graduate of Duke University, John W. Campbell (1910–71), became editor of *Astounding Stories.* In the thirty-four years of his editorship, Campbell, who had been writing stories as a free lance, earned the repute of the greatest science-fiction magazine editor of all time. Campbell was largely responsible for the marked rise in literary quality that took place in science fiction during the early years of his editorship. He had a sound knowledge of literary techniques and actively coached his writers.

From 1939 to 1943, under Campbell's editorship, Street & Smith Publications issued a fantasy companion to *Astounding,* called *Unknown* (later *Unknown Worlds*). In its short life, *Unknown* printed many stories of the kind later known as heroic fantasy. These included stories by Fritz Leiber, Fletcher Pratt in collaboration with the present writer, and others. Much of this material was later reprinted in book form.

The paper shortage slew this magazine along with many others. When, after the war, the publishers thought of reviving it, they decided that its percentage of returns had been too high to make it profitable. While it had not lost them money, it had not made so much as they thought they could get by using their capital otherwise.

Other fantasy magazines appeared after the Second World War. Most of them lasted a few issues only, save for *The Magazine of Fantasy and Science Fiction* and *Fantastic Stories*. These, started in 1949 and 1952 respectively, still thrive.

The limitations of magazines as markets for heroic fantasy have been more than made up for by the growth of the paperbacked book business. These, in the form of "dime novels," had been known in the United States before the First World War but had gone out of use, although they continued in use in Europe. Between the two World Wars, paperbacks were almost unknown in America. The Second World War revived them, because they used less paper and shipping space than similar clothbound books.

For a decade after 1945, all fantasy fared badly. With the end in 1954 of *Weird Tales* and the failure of its would-be successors, it seemed as if fantasy had become a casualty of the Machine Age. Then came a surprising revival, beginning with the publication of Tolkien's *The Lord of the Rings*.

Now let us consider, one by one, the founding fathers of the genre of heroic fantasy.

II

JACK OF ALL ARTS:
WILLIAM MORRIS

A nameless city in a distant sea,
White as the changing walls of faërie,
Thronged with much people clad in ancient guise
I now am fain to set before your eyes....[1]

MORRIS

Of all the people influenced by the current of romantic medievalism that flowed through Victorian England, one of the
most eminent was John Ruskin (1819–1900), critic, lecturer,
teacher, writer, and reformer. The son of a rich Scottish liquor
dealer, Ruskin gave away his inherited fortune piece by piece,
having in late years become convinced that it was wicked to
live on interest. Having annulled their marriage on grounds of
Ruskin's impotence, Ruskin's wife then married his friend, the
painter John Everett Millais. This seems to have been a more
satisfactory arrangement all around.

Ruskin wrote voluminously on art, architecture, economics,
education, morals, politics, and religion. Appalled by the lot of
the Victorian workingman, he thought that the common man
had been better off in the Middle Ages. One of his utopian
proposals was for a commune based on the laws of fourteenth-
century Florence.

In fact, the picture of the Middle Ages entertained by romantic medievalists like Ruskin was about as accurate as the
"noble savage" concept of Jean Jacques Rousseau. Medieval

31

European feudalism was, outside of India, one of the most closed, caste-bound, and rigidly stratified societies that the world has seen.

Dante Gabriel Rossetti (1828–82), painter, poet, son of an Italian refugee and nephew of Byron's physician, was a friend of Millais and a protégé of Ruskin. Rossetti, Millais, and several others founded the Pre-Raphaelite Brotherhood, which pursued the ideal of painting with minute, literal accuracy. They were trying to do what we now do with color photography.

Under the influence of these idealists and esthetes came William Morris (1834–96), one of the most versatile, vigorous, and accomplished creators of them all. Like Ruskin, Morris inherited money; unlike Ruskin, he developed a hard business head and made a good living. Architect, decorator, designer, novelist, painter, poet, and printer, Morris tried his hand at most of the arts and did outstanding work in most of those that he tried. That he took a key position in the history of heroic fantasy was an incidental afterthought. In his last years, Morris wrote the novels in which he pioneered this genre, for relaxation rather than with a commercial motive.

Morris was a short young man who became a stout middle-aged man. Strong and athletic, he was a furious fencer. His mop of dark, curly hair earned him the nickname of "Topsy." His manner was boisterous, energetic, abrupt, and brusque, with a loud, explosive way of speaking. Excitable and hot-tempered, he had a congenital nervous instability, which appeared in more acute form in his epileptic daughter. His explosions of temper soon blew over and were usually followed by humble apologies. In character he was upright, generous, kind, and idealistic.

At Oxford, Morris studied at first for the Church, then switched to architecture. On graduation, he worked for nine months in an architect's office but then quit to devote his full time to painting.

At Oxford he also formed several lifelong friendships. When

he had become an able painter, he and Rossetti, together with Edward Burne-Jones and several other friends, launched a scheme to paint and decorate the new Union Society building at Oxford. The young men had a glorious time, although their inexperience caused their murals to fade away and vanish during the following decades.

For use in his drawings, Morris designed a set of early fourteenth-century arms and armor and had it made by a local blacksmith. When Morris tried on the helmet, the visor stuck. His colleagues were convulsed to see Morris dancing about, tugging at the refractory basinet and roaring with rage inside it.

At this time, in the late 1850s, Rossetti and Morris employed two beautiful working-class young women as models. One was Elizabeth Siddal, to whom Rossetti became engaged. The other was Jane Burden, with whom Morris fell in love. Shy and awkward with women, he wooed her by reading aloud to her and writing yearning poems to her eyes:

> So beautiful and kind they are,
> But most times looking out afar,
> Waiting for something, not for me.
> *Beata mea domina!*

Although an irresponsible wastrel, Rossetti had a Victorian sense of propriety. Therefore he felt honor bound to marry Elizabeth Siddal, even though he had cooled towards her and begun to cast amorous eyes on Jane Burden. To keep Jane within the group as a model and either (one may guess) to give his friend happiness or to keep her within pouncing distance, Rossetti persuaded Jane to marry Morris.

Morris wedded Jane in 1859; Rossetti married Elizabeth the following year. Morris begat two daughters, of whom the elder became an epileptic. The younger shed her husband after a brief marriage (involving a triangle with the young George Bernard Shaw) and devoted the rest of her life to enshrining her father's memory.

Elizabeth died of tuberculosis after two years of marriage—
or to be strictly accurate, of an overdose of laudanum taken to
relieve her terminal sufferings. Rossetti buried a manuscript of
his poems in her coffin; but, when he needed money, he dug her
up and retrieved the manuscript.

For a few years, Morris was happy with Jane but then was
made aware that he did not seem to be good for her. Jane—tall,
black-haired, long-necked, and aquiline-nosed—was a stable-
man's daughter who easily made the transition into the gentry.
But her health declined, with possibly psychosomatic back-
aches and fainting fits.

In the late 1860s, by all indications, Jane had begun an
active if discreet love affair with Rossetti. This continued for
the next decade, until Rossetti's health broke down from alcoholism and narcotics.

Poor Morris made the best of a sticky situation, since the
modern facilities for easy divorce and remarriage were not available. In that time and place, divorced persons were automati-
cally barred from "society" along with tradesmen, workingmen,
Jews, illegitimates, and persons caught cheating at cards or
welshing on gambling debts.

In the other departments of life, however, Morris enjoyed
spectacular success. In 1861, Morris and several friends formed
Morris, Marshall, Faulkner & Company to engage in house
decoration and the manufacture of the materials therefor:
textiles, tapestries, hangings, furniture, wall paper, carpets, and
stained glass. Morris, who was very handy, insisted on learning
the technique of each step of his manufacturing operations himself. When an associate suggested an armchair with an adjust-
able back, Morris adopted and marketed it as the Morris chair.

An implacable perfectionist, Morris turned out exquisite
work, charged high prices, and deferred to no customers no
matter how exalted. They found a burly, full-bearded man in a
workman's smock and one of those little round hats that were
the Victorian substitute for the topper. Spattered with paint or

smeared with grease, he gruffly quoted his steep prices to the gentry on a take-it-or-leave-it basis. If he sometimes blew up and roared at his workmen, they took it in good part, since he treated them on a basis of man-to-man equality.

Morris moved both his home and his plant several times, to places in London and its suburbs. Each time, he decorated his new house himself.

The company had ups and downs but in the long run proved successful; a series of good accountants saved it from some of Morris's more eccentric decisions. In 1874, Morris forced a reorganization, which put him in sole charge. This move left some hard feelings among the other shareholders. Morris's friendship with Rossetti, which had survived their *ménage à trois,* broke up at last.

This, however, was but one activity of this many-sided man. In the 1860s, Morris wrote book-length poems, still well-regarded, such as *The Life and Death of Jason* and *The Earthly Paradise.* The latter retells Greek and Norse myths, alternating. One of his most effective poems is "The Haystack in the Floods," a grim, 160-line account in blank verse about a medieval French girl, rescued from some unnamed accusation by an English knight. Then they are captured by a robber baron and the knight is murdered.

Morris also became interested in the Viking Age and studied Icelandic. With the help of an Icelander, Eirikr Magnússon, he translated several sagas, including the great *Völsungá Saga,* which tells the story of Sigurð.

In 1871 and 1873, Morris visited Iceland with his friend Faulkner. Looking like Santa Claus in the kind of broad sombrero then called a "wide-awake," Morris trotted on a shaggy Icelandic pony over fields of lava through fog and rain. He harangued the Icelanders in what he fondly thought was their native tongue, but of which they could scarcely understand a word. At one stop, his hostess made the visitors take off their pants before sitting down to dinner.

Meanwhile, as secretary of the Society for the Protection of Ancient Buildings, Morris tirelessly campaigned to save England's medieval relics from being either demolished by developers or "restored" out of all recognition. He was active in the National Liberal League, which campaigned against the government's pro-Turkish foreign policies, and similar organizations.

In 1883, disillusioned with these groups, Morris joined the Democratic Federation (later the Social Democratic Federation), founded two years before by a disciple of Karl Marx. Morris had long wanted a better deal for the British working class. In his translation of the *Völsungá Saga* (published as *The Story of Sigurd the Volsung and the Fall of the Nibelungs*), he had made the dragon-slaying Sigurð an unlikely crusader for social justice.

Thus Morris became a Socialist, as that term was then understood. The concept of Socialism was much vaguer, more variable and amorphous and inconsistent, than it is now. The democratic, legalistic Socialists had not yet split with the revolutionary, authoritarian Communists.

Morris fretted a little about being a Socialist and a capitalist at the same time. He once considered giving up his business to resolve this contradiction, but common sense prevailed. As it was, he spent much of his money financing the League and even sold his library to give the proceeds to the cause of Socialism. He took part in demonstrations and was twice arrested. He was furious when the judge let him, as a "gentleman," off with a scolding or a small fine but sent his working-class comrades to jail.

Morris's Socialism was, however, of a very individual kind. For all his Socialistic professions, he clung to his medievalism. His medievalistic "Socialism," with its guilds and handicrafts, led Friedrich Engels to dismiss him as a "sentimental" and "utopian" Socialist.

Morris tried to read Marx but confessed that he could not

make head or tail of Marx's theory of surplus value. (This is not to Morris's discredit, since the theory contains a major logical fallacy.) When Morris read Edward Bellamy's *Looking Backward* (1888), which portrayed a highly regimented Socialist utopia, he said that he "wouldn't care to live in such a Cockney paradise." If they brigaded him into such a regiment of workers, he would "just lie on his back and kick."[2]

As an antiquarian and devout medievalist, Morris had long opposed the less esthetic aspects of the Industrial Revolution. In his early twenties, when touring French cathedrals, he had denounced railroads as "abominations."[3] Later, he insisted that he was not against all labor-saving machinery. Some, he thought, was needed to perform the more repulsive kinds of necessary drudgery. In general, though, he cherished the illusion of the well-fed, healthy, contented medieval workman, happily whacking out gargoyles with hammer and chisel for the next cathedral.

It is amusing to compare Morris with another great literary archaist and anti-industrialist, H. P. Lovecraft. But, where Morris idealized the Middle Ages, Lovecraft idealized the eighteenth century, and each wholeheartedly despised the other's favorite period.

To support the population of Great Britain in the 1880s with medieval technology, it would have been necessary to get rid of all but a small fraction of the people. Morris, however, was oblivious to such considerations.

In 1886, Morris wrote a novella or imaginative tract, *A Dream of John Ball,* in which he imagined himself back in the England of 1381, at the time of the peasant rebellion. Morris credited the rebels with Socialistic or Communistic aims of which they never dreamed. He did, however, realize the dangers of such mass uprisings to littérateurs like himself. The rebels of 1381, viewing literacy as an enemy, made a bonfire of the books and manuscripts of Cambridge University, crying: "Let this learning of the clerks die!" and cut off the heads of persons caught carrying pen and ink.[4]

Morris wrote one more Socialistic-utopian tract, *News from Nowhere,* and then abandoned propaganda for pure romance. He had become a little disillusioned. Although still for Socialism in theory, he had been ousted from his editorship of *The Commonweal,* the SDF's organ, by an anarchist faction. Moreover, failing health compelled him to give up active speaking, demonstrating, and organizing. Despite his energy and robustness, he did not age well. He had long suffered from gout and in his fifties was increasingly assailed by exhaustion.

Morris's novels of heroic fantasy were all written in the last nine years of his life, from 1888 to 1896. They were *jeux d'esprit,* done for fun and relaxation, rather than attempts to write great literature or to garner money and fame—although Morris saw to it that they were published. At this time, besides his decorator business, Morris was running a small press. The Kelmscott Press turned out books by Morris and others in beautifully printed and bound collectors' editions.

The novels were written off and on during this time, sometimes overlapping and not published in the order in which they were written. In the story of Morris and his colleagues, these tales play but a minor part, but in the story of heroic fantasy they bulk large.

Two of Morris's earlier works of this group were *The House of the Wolfings* (1888) and *The Roots of the Mountains* (1889). These are non-fantastic historical novels, somewhat in the tradition of Scott. Both are full of the Nordicism that Morris had absorbed from the sagas and from his Icelandic journeys. As in his later works, they are written in a heavily archaistic style (sometimes called "pastiche Jacobean") with vast prolixity and glacial slowness.

The first, *The House of the Wolfings,* tells of the defeat by a German tribe of the invading Romans. The German barbarians (in history a singularly dirty, treacherous, and bloody lot) are cleaned up, prettified, and imbued with noble motives almost to the point of burlesque.

Next, *The Roots of the Mountains* tells of a similar conflict between the men of Burgdale and a swarm of bloodthirsty invaders called the Dusky Men. The Burgdalers are led by Face-of-god, a proper Nordic hero. The Dalesmen vaguely resemble Goths and the Dusky Men the Huns. Thence it is sometimes assumed that Morris had the historical conflict between these peoples in mind. Neither Goths nor Huns are named, however; and the terrain does not resemble the Russian prairie, where in the fourth century the Huns overthrew Hermanarich's short-lived Gothic steppe empire.

The Dusky Men are driven out, and Face-of-god is united with his Sun-beam. Such is Morris's prolixity, however, that to read this huge novel through were a task to daunt the stoutest. His insistence on telling everything that befalls his characters day by day, whether it affects the outcome or not, reminds one of the old story about "Then another locust came and carried away another grain of corn."

In one episode, Face-of-god's father, Stone-face, warns his son of supernatural dangers:

> "Even such an one have I seen time agone, when the snow was deep and the wind was rough; and it was in the likeness of a woman clad in such raiment as the Bride bore last night, and she trod the snow light-foot in thin raiment where it would scarce bear the skids of a deft snow-runner. Even so she stood before me; the icy wind blew her raiment around her, and drifted the hair from her garlanded head toward me, and she was fair and fresh as in the midsummer days. Up the fell she fared, sweetest of all things to look on, and beckoned on me to follow. . . ."[5]

Compare this with Conan's encounter with Atali, in "The Frost Giant's Daughter" (*Conan of Cimmeria*, 1969, pp. 54ff) and it is hard not to suspect that Robert E. Howard had read this passage. I know of no direct evidence that Howard had read Morris; but it is likely that a voracious reader of Howard's tastes and interests would have come across *The Roots of the Mountains.*

In this novel, the supernatural element is trivial, since Stoneface's female wood-wight never appears on stage. In Morris's next, *The Glittering Plain,* however, the author definitely sets sail upon the seas of Faërie. He combined (whether consciously or, more probably, not) Scott's antiquarian romanticism with Walpole's supernaturalism, in language beautifully poetic and artfully archaic. Thus heroic fantasy was born.

In (to give its full title) *The Story of the Glittering Plain, Which Has Been Also Called the Land of Living Men or the Acre of the Undying,* the Nordic hero Hallblithe finds that his betrothed, the Hostage, has been kidnapped by pirates from the Isle of Ransom. Going in search of her, at this isle he falls in with a local, called Puny Fox because the others there are real giants and he stands a mere seven feet.

The wily Puny Fox kids Hallblithe along until the latter leaves and goes to the Land of the Glittering Plain. This is a fairyland where nobody ages and old men are rejuvenated. Hallblithe declines the king's offer of his daughter's hand, escapes from the land, and returns to the Isle of Ransom. There he recovers his beloved. The trickster Puny Fox becomes his friend, and all go back to Hallblithe's home and live happily ever after.

At 65,000 words, this novel is shorter than most of Morris's fantasies, which is all to the good. It starts off well but tends to peter out. For one thing, Morris was not strong on plot. His adventures and encounters "just happen." Morris could no doubt have defended himself by saying that he was writing, not a "modern" novel, but a medieval romance of the type of those of Chrestien de Troyes, Gottfried von Strassburg, Lodovico Ariosto, and Sir Thomas Malory. They never worried about intricate, logical, self-consistent plots either.

Morris was trying to revive the kind of medieval prose narrative that had perished with the publication of *Don Quixote.*

Hence, when for instance Hallblithe returns to the Isle of Ransom and plays a minor trick on the pirates to regain his betrothed, they amiably let him go with her instead of more plausibly killing him in some lingering, humorous, and anatomically ingenious manner. There is no explanation—not even why they kidnapped the maid in the first place.

Another weakness of Morris the storyteller also appears. His stories suffer, not from Victorian prudery—his characters enjoy a good roll in the hay as well as the next—but Victorian optimism. His imaginary worlds are just too mild and safe; there is too much sweetness and light and not enough conflict. His heroes have a relatively easy time. When they do get into trouble, there is usually a magical weapon or a good witch to get them out of it. His villains are not very villainous and are often cajoled into reforming their evil ways.

In this respect, Morris stands at the other extreme from Robert E. Howard. Howard's heroes are grim, somber, hard-bitten fellows who suspect, usually rightly, that everyone they meet is out to cheat, rob, or murder them. Howard suffered from some profound internal maladjustment or unhappiness, which finally slew him but which gave him a tragic sense of life. Morris, on the other hand, aside from his marital complications, seems to have been a basically happy, jolly man, convinced of the fundamental goodness of his fellow men.

One more weakness of *The Glittering Plain,* to my way of thinking, is the very concept of the Acre of the Undying. To one who enjoys life, the idea of a land of eternal youth would have so strong an appeal that it would take the strongest possible motive—comparable to that which makes a man sacrifice his life in other contexts—to induce him to forgo it. The mere presence of such a concept in a story, therefore, makes the attainment of such a land the central plot element. To treat it casually is to introduce a jarring inconsistency, like bringing the atomic doom into one of P. G. Wodehouse's social comedies. The same difficulty appears in Tolkien's Grey Havens,

Lloyd Alexander's Summer Country, and even in Baum's later Oz.

Still, the story has lasting historical interest as the first heroic fantasy, in my sense of the term, to be written. It combines an imaginary, invented, pre-industrial world with the supernatural beings and forces that our own pre-scientific forebears believed in, as in a child's fairy tale but on an adult level.

The next of the series was *The Wood Beyond the World* (1894). Golden Walter is a typically tall, fair-haired, gray-eyed youth, whose wife betrays him with another man. Not wishing to start a feud with her family, he considers a trading voyage:

> So this went on a while till the chambers of his father's house, yea the very streets of the city, became loathsome to him; and yet he called to mind that the world was wide and he but a young man. So on a day as he sat with his father alone, he spake to him and said: Father, I was on the quays even now, and I looked on the ships that were nigh boun, and thy sign I saw on a tall ship that seemed to me nighest boun. Will it be long ere she sail? Nay, said his father, that ship, which hight the Katherine, will they warp out of the haven in two days' time. But why askest thou of her? The shortest word is best, father, said Walter, and this it is, that I would depart in the said ship and see other lands. Yea and whither, son? said the merchant. Whither she goeth, said Walter, for I am ill at ease at home, as thou wottest, father.[6]

The lack of quotation marks has good biblical precedent; but in his later books, Morris put them back in. This prose is one at which the reader must work a little harder than in briskly contemporary English; but one can get used to it and find a certain musical charm in it. One is well-advised, however, to keep a dictionary handy for obsolete words like "boun" (ready). But it does no harm to enlarge one's vocabulary.

Walter sets out. En route, the family scrivener catches up with him to say that his father has been slain in a brawl with Walter's wife's family.

Here appears Morris's weakness as a plotter. We are prepared for the story of Walter's return and revenge. But then the tale goes off on an entirely different tack. Walter never does get home, so that these complications prove irrelevant. Did Morris find the theme of the adulterous wife too painful to pursue?

Instead, Walter is blown to a far land. He has adventures in a castle run by an enchantress, who is served by a captive maiden and a wicked, apelike dwarf. Walter and the maiden flee the castle and have more adventures in the land of a race of giant stone-age hunters.

At last they come to a city. Here they are hailed as king and queen. It transpires that the king of that city has just died without issue, and their custom is to enthrone the next passing stranger. Presumably, nobody is likely to serve Walter with a bigamy warrant there.

This plot has three glaring defects. First is the change in direction of the story, already mentioned. Second is that the most exciting part, the escape from the enchanted castle, is in the middle of the book instead of just before the end as in a well-wrought tale. Finally, the coronation of Walter and his maiden is perhaps the longest reach of the arm of coincidence on record. It baldly exposes Morris's tendency to "legislate himself out of trouble."

Still, the novel has many pleasant parts and considerable suspense in the castle episode.

At about the same time as the previous novel, Morris wrote *The Water of the Wondrous Isles,* beginning:

> Whilom, as tells the tale, was a walled cheaping-town hight Utterhay, which was builded in a bight of land a little off the great highway which went from over the mountains to the sea.[7]

The heroine is Birdalone, stolen as an infant from her native town by a witch, who rears her in the wood of Evilshaw to be her maid-of-all-work. Coming to maturity, Birdalone steals the witch's magical boat and is taken by it to a series of marvelous islands, the Isle of the Young and the Old and others.

On one island, Birdalone falls in with three more maidens, who are captives of another witch. The three maids mourn their lovers, three paladins who dwell in the Castle of the Quest.

Birdalone reaches the Castle of the Quest and sets the three heroes on the track of their loves. After complications, kidnappings, fights, and enchantments, one paladin is slain. The maidens are rescued. One gets her original paladin; the one whose paladin is dead gets another man; and the third loses her man to Birdalone and is left lamenting.

One captive maiden is named Aurea. This name also appears, probably not by coincidence, as that of the heroine's sister in Fletcher Pratt's *The Well of the Unicorn.* Birdalone also has a fairy godmother, Habundia, who appears to help her through crises.

Although the story is more logically plotted than its predecessors, I have, I regret to say, enjoyed it the least of any. I found it dreadfully prolix, long-winded, and icky-sweet.

Next came the magnum opus of the series: *The Well at the World's End* (1896). Morris seems to have found glamor in the letter *w*. This story is, with the possible exception of *The Roots of the Mountains,* much the longest of these novels. With nearly a quarter of a million words, it belongs in the class with Tolkien's *The Lord of the Rings.* It is also, probably, the best of the lot, even though the reader may weary of Morris's technique of "another locust took away another grain."

The tale tells of the King of Upmeads, whose four sons set out to seek their fortunes. The story follows the youngest, Ralph, who undergoes many adventures. He is involved in the war between the Champions of the Dry Tree and the Burg of the Four Friths, and with the Lady of Abundance, with whom he has a hot love affair until one of her other suitors jealously slays her.

Hearing of the miraculous Well at the World's End, Ralph sets out for it. He becomes involved with the tyrant of Utterbol and his queen, who wants Ralph for her fancy man. Ralph

escapes with a young woman whom he has already met elsewhere. They get to the Well, drink of its waters, and are trans-
formed into super-persons. On the way back, whenever they
meet a gang of villains, Ralph has only to wave his sword and
scowl. The scoundrels, recognizing his power, flee in terror or
grovel in submission.

Tolkienians will be interested to learn that the tyrant of
Utterbol is named "Gandolf," and that Ralph's horse is called
"Silverfax."[8] Tolkien was influenced by Morris along with
many others. Among widely-read literary men, it is hard to be
sure by whom they have *not* been influenced.

The last story of the group, save for some fragments, is *The
Sundering Flood,* published after Morris's death in 1896. Morris finished a rough draft less than a month before his end, following a rapid decline of several months. The final pages were
dictated to a friend when Morris could no longer write. May
Morris edited the manuscript, tidying up inconsistencies and
adding a few passages to bridge the gaps. In the present paperback edition, these interpolations are put in brackets.

The story tells of Osberne Wulfgrimsson, who lives in an
isolated stead at Wethermel, east of an uncrossable river. He
loves the maiden Elfhild, who lives across the river. He is also
befriended by a supernatural being, who takes divers forms and
gives him the invincible sword Boardcleaver.

A foreign horde, the Red Skinners, invade the land, and Elfhild vanishes. Sorrowing, Osberne becomes a soldier for Sir
Godrick of Longshaw. Osberne learns of the city at the mouth
of the Sundering Flood. As an officer for Sir Godrick, he helps
to overthrow the king of this city and the clique of rich mer-
chants who oppress the virtuous workers of the guilds. (Here
Morris's Socialism surfaces.)

At last Osberne finds Elfhild, living with an old kinswoman
of magical powers in a house in the Wood Masterless. Thither
they had fled after adventures and perils. All return to Wethermel and live happily.

The story is better plotted than most of Morris's. In entertainment quality, it is perhaps second to *The Well at the World's End*. On the other hand, *The Sundering Flood* has serious flaws. The tale starts with glacial sloth, since Osberne does not even leave Wethermel until more than halfway through.

Elfhild's adventures, which had the potential of strong suspense, are not presented directly but are narrated by Elfhild after her reunion with her lover. Morris would have done better to condense his leisurely first half down to a fraction of its present length and to have used the space in direct narration of Elfhild's adventures—perhaps alternating with Osberne's, as Burroughs did with John Carter and Dejah Thoris.

The hero's supernatural friend and magical weapon are clichés of Morris's novels. In providing the hero with too easy a way out of his plights, they detract from rather than add to the strength of the story. (Tolkien also was given to "legislating his way out of trouble"; so was Howard, in giving his heroes invincible thews.)

Morris would doubtless have explained, had we asked him, that thus things were done in medieval romances; and he was writing, not a modern novel, but a synthetic medieval romance. That is all very well, but it still remains that fictional techniques have advanced since medieval times. While in one sense it is true that "there is no such thing as progress in the arts," from the technical point of view there have been advances. A modern artist may be no more gifted than the Crô-Magnards who painted spirited horses, bison, and mammoths on the walls of Font-de-Gaume in southwestern France; but the modern painter has far better paints, brushes, and painting surfaces than his paleolithic predecessor.

Likewise, in storytelling techniques, we now know how to do things better than they did in the days of Layamon and Hartmann von Aue. To scorn this knowledge were like a modern painter who insists on grinding his own pigments and applying them with fingers and sticks to the bumpy walls of the nearest cave.

Still, we must excuse many shortcomings in a pioneer, and Morris pioneered in heroic fantasy. His successors stand on his shoulders. He has been widely read among other literary swordsmen and sorcerers. The battle on the causeway in *The Sundering Flood,* for instance, reads suspiciously like the similar battle in Pratt's *The Well of the Unicorn.* Not that the latter was a conscious plagiarism; but characters and incidents that a writer has read of in his youth are apt to turn up in his fiction later, even though he may have consciously forgotten them.

Lastly, the works do contain much beauty, music, and color. Any fan of heroic fantasy should have tried at least one of these novels. Who knows? He may find that something in them strikes a chord in his own soul, so that he cannot rest until he has tracked down and read the remainder.

III

TWO MEN IN ONE: LORD DUNSANY

It does not become adventurers
to care who eats their bones.[1]

DUNSANY

A medieval Irish historian once wrote: "There be two great robber barons on the road to Drogheda, Dunsany and Fingall; and if you save yourself from the hands of Fingall, you will assuredly fall into the hands of Dunsany." Dunsany (rhymes with "one rainy") is a village twenty-odd miles northwest of Dublin, in County Meath, near An Uaimh (pronounced a-NOO-if). For most of the twentieth century, nearby Dunsany Castle was occupied by Edward John Moreton Drax Plunkett, eighteenth Baron Dunsany (1878–1957). Dunsany was an amazing man: soldier, sportsman, hunter, politician, world traveler, writer, novelist, poet, dramatist, artist, lecturer, and one of the main influences on modern fantasy.

About 1155, finding the Irish clergy too independent for his taste, Pope Adrian IV (the only English pope) gave Ireland to the brilliant, energetic, and terrible-tempered Henry II of England (as if it had been his to give) on condition that Henry reduce these fractious Hibernians to obedience. Henry was then too busy elsewhere to take possession. But an exiled Irish kinglet, Dermot MacMurrough, got Henry's permission to recruit Norman adventurers to put him back on his throne.

There is a question of the authenticity of the pope's gift, but all parties concerned acted as if it were real. When the Normans saw Ireland, they thought it would be much more fun to take over the country themselves than to fight for King Dermot. They despised, as bare-arsed barbarians, the unarmored, kilted Irish, who were slaughtered by the mailed Norman knights. The new ruling class so afflicted the Irish that in 1171 the latter submitted to the English king (who was actually more of a Frenchman) in the hope that he would protect them from the Normans. The hope was cruelly disappointed, and the Irish have never had a moment's peace since.

One Norman freebooter was John Plunkett, who seized land in County Meath near the sacred hill of Tara, where the High Kings had long been crowned. In the 1440s, John Plunkett's descendant Christopher Plunkett was made Baron Dunsany. The barons of Fingall were another branch of the family.

During the religious conflicts of the seventeenth century, the Dunsanys adhered to the Catholic Church for some years after the battle of the Boyne (1690) and were exiled. They nonetheless managed by fast footwork to hold on to their property through all the persecutions and confiscations, until in 1713 the then Baron Dunsany was converted to Protestantism. The subject of this chapter, however, was a skeptic or atheist—although, after his hairbreadth escape from Greece in 1941, he did not mind going to the cathedral in Cairo to give thanks.

One member of the family was the Blessed Oliver Plunkett, an Irish Catholic archbishop. Archbishop Plunkett became the last victim of the Popish Plot hoax engineered in the 1670s by Titus Oates. This Plunkett was hanged, drawn, and quartered on flimsy charges of plotting to land a French army in Ireland. He has lately been made a saint.

In the nineteenth century, the Dunsanys shrewdly invested in coal mines, which for many decades supported the family in properly baronial style.

Dunsany Castle dates from 1190. About 200 years ago, however, it was drastically rebuilt. The Dowager Lady Dunsany

(widow of the writer) once told me: "If you're going to mod-
ernize a castle, the eighteenth century is the very best time to
do it." The present structure is in the Neo-Gothic style of the
Romantic Revival, with medieval battlements but tall windows
instead of arrow slits. In a final spasm of romanticism, a nineteenth-century Dunsany built a "folly"—a synthetic ruin in the
form of a Norman guard tower, with arrow slits—by the front
gate. Three television antennae sprout among the battlements
of the castle.

Inside, suits of armor stand in corners and paintings by Van
Dyck and other masters behang the walls. A sword rack holds
a dozen or so dress swords worn by the last two lords during
their military careers. There are still a priest hole and a secret
stair, from the days of persecution of Catholics. The castle has
seen visits of a multitude of eminent literary names: O. St. J.
Gogarty, George Moore, G. W. Russell, G. B. Shaw, H. G.
Wells, T. H. White, W. B. Yeats, and so on.

The eighteenth Dunsany, the writer, was six feet three or
four inches tall, and lean, with large hands and feet. He was
sometimes called "the worst-dressed man in Ireland." He could
dress up when an occasion, such as a fox hunt or a coronation,
demanded; but in the country he wore clothes in the last stages
of decrepitude, saying: "Why spoil good ones?" In youth he
wore a short mustache, to which in eld he added a straggly
goatee or imperial.

A garrulous, fun-loving, sociable man of lively, enthusiastic
spirit and extraordinary versatility, he was esteemed by those
who liked him as genial, delightful, and fascinating. "A grand
man," a working-class Englishman who had known him said to
me; "the most representative man I know," said his longtime
friend Gogarty.[2] My colleague Lin Carter, who heard him lecture in New York, wrote:

> . . . the old baron, then in his seventy-sixth year, was tall, lean,
> erect, with twinkling frosty eyes, apple cheeks and a white little

spike of a goatee. He wore a completely shapeless gray tweed suit whose baggy pockets were stuffed with scraps of paper, and he had a soft white silk shirt on, with a loose, floppy *foulard*. He spoke in a rich, resonant voice wherein just the slightest trace of Irish lilt sang.[3]

A man of strong personality is never liked by everybody. Those who did not like Dunsany found him arrogant, opinionated, self-centered, and sometimes testy and inconsiderate. When I asked one who had known him well whether he had been an easy man to live with, the reply was an emphatic "No! He was the artist . . . completely absorbed. . . ."

Dunsany had strong opinions on many subjects. He esteemed Walter de la Mare as the greatest living Anglophone poet but denounced the turgid free verse, which most poets have written from mid-century on, as "bells of lead." T. S. Eliot's work he dismissed as "*frightful* nonsense." He had positive ideas of how prose should be written and said: "I can't think of any great prose writers who have come up to the standards I have set for prose."[4] He deemed Irish English superior to the standard upper-class Southern British accent on which he had been reared. In late years he became something of a food faddist, insisting on rock salt in place of ordinary refined table salt.

Born in London, Dunsany spent much of his childhood at his mother's home. This was a Regency house in Kent called Dunstall Priory, doubtless because a monastery had once stood there. He was not allowed to read newspapers—lest they spoil his English, he said; because they contained divorce-court news, said others.

Educated at Cheam School, Eton, and Sandhurst (the British West Point), young Plunkett lost his father the year he graduated from Sandhurst and succeeded to the title. He had admired his father, but from a distance. The seventeenth baron and his wife lived apart, in Dunsany Castle and Dunstall Priory respectively, and Edward had shuttled between them.

The new Lord Dunsany was commissioned in the Coldstream Guards and sent to duty at Gibraltar. There he took long rides about the Spanish countryside, gathering impressions that he later used in his Spanish fantasies, *Don Rodriguez* and *The Charwoman's Shadow*. (These impressions do not seem to have included much knowledge of Spanish, judging from the way he mangled the tongue in his stories.)

In the Boer War, Dunsany fought in the battles of Graspan and Modder River. His younger brother, with whom he did not get on well, went into the Navy and in time became Admiral Sir Reginald Drax-Plunkett. In August 1939, Neville Chamberlain sent Admiral Drax as head of the ill-fated British mission to Moscow in the forlorn hope of forming an alliance with Stalin against Hitler.[5]

Back home, Dunsany retired from the army and married the slender and beautiful Lady Beatrice Villiers, daughter of the Earl of Jersey. Dunsany's biographer says of this marriage: "She knew nothing of sex, he scarcely more; it was never important to them." Nevertheless they lived quite happily—if not ever after, at least to a ripe age.

Dunsany and his mother-in-law were much given to mutual ribbing. Dunsany's mother had been a cousin of Captain Sir Richard Francis Burton, the great, swashbuckling Victorian soldier, explorer, scholar, writer, linguist, diplomat, swordsman, and general man of the Renaissance. When Dunsany asked the Countess of Jersey: "I believe you knew a relation of mine, Richard Burton?" she snapped: "Yes. He drank."[6] That ended the subject.

Dunsany and Beatrice had one son, Randal Arthur Henry Plunkett, who (as nineteenth baron) is now a retired lieutenant-colonel of the Guides Cavalry of the Indian Army. Tall, tweedy, mustached, monocled, and snuff-sniffing, the present baron commanded an armored-car unit at the battle of El Alamein. ("The four-wheeled drive," he said, "has abolished the impassable desert. We proved that.") He married a Brazilian

lady, and they had one son. After the war, the wife returned to
Brazil, where she had spent the war years, and they were divorced. Randal Plunkett then married the widow of a brother
officer who had been killed in the war. The Dunsanys are active
in Dublin's literary and artistic circles, own a marina, and are
restoring a ruined Welsh castle as a tourist attraction. The son,
the Hon. Edward John Carlos Plunkett, is an artist.

Dunsany (our Dunsany, that is) was abstemious in his
tastes. He smoked and drank but little, had no interest in gambling, and even disliked ribald jokes. Nevertheless, he took
enthusiastically to the fox-hunting, shooting, partying, games-
playing life of the country gentry. But about 1903 the scenario,
which had typed him as a typical Anglo-Irish country squire,
began to go awry. He began to write dreamy little stories about
gods and godlets and heroes in imaginary worlds. The first
began:

> Before there stood gods upon Olympus, or ever Allah was Allah,
> had wrought and rested MĀNA-YOOD-SUSHĀĪ.
>
> There are in Pegāna—Mung and Sish and Kib, and the maker
> of all small gods, who is MĀNA-YOOD-SUSHĀĪ. Moreover, we have
> a faith in Roon and Slid.
>
> And it has been said of old that all things that have been were
> wrought by the small gods, excepting only MĀNA-YOOD-SUSHĀĪ,
> who made the gods, and hath thereafter rested.
>
> And none may pray to MĀNA-YOOD-SUSHĀĪ but only to the gods
> whom he hath made. . . .

Dunsany either wrote with a quill pen or dictated to his
wife. In 1905 he found a publisher willing, if subsidized, to
bring out a volume of these exotic vignettes. The book, *The
Gods of Pegāna,* made Dunsany some literary reputation, and
he never resorted to vanity publishing on subsequent books.
He continued to write all his long life and turned out over
sixty volumes, including short stories, novels, plays, poems,
and memoirs.

He said that, actually, he had spent ninety-odd per cent of

his adult life in sport and soldiering, giving only odd moments to writing; but this may have been a gentlemanly pose. He did write fast, and he said: "I never rewrite and I never correct." If this be true, his brilliantly polished prose must have been the product of a mind with the enviable power of organizing and editing everything he wrote before putting it on paper.

So Dunsany pursued a Jekyll-Hyde existence, as a rich, fashionable, sporting aristocrat and as a serious littérateur. Since he did not talk about his writings to his horsy, unintellectual titled friends and kinsmen, many were unaware of these writings after Dunsany had been publishing for years. He was like two men in one, each having its own activities, interests, and circle of friends with hardly any overlap.

In the literary world, on the other hand, so far from his title's being an advantage, "I have found it of the greatest disadvantage; and all critics who have concentrated on the cover of a book, where the writing is large and clear and is quickly read, have been inclined to take the line that here was an aristocratic idler designing to take the bread out of the mouths of honest men."[7] This inverted snobbery infuriated him but also, perhaps, stimulated him. Having once made a reputation as "Lord Dunsany," it would have been quixotic to change his by-line to "Edward Plunkett."

In literature, he did not show the exuberant self-confidence that he displayed in social and sporting matters. He was easily discouraged by adverse criticism. He did not aspire to be thought a deep thinker, but he liked to hear that his poetical fantasies had touched a sympathetic emotional chord in his readers.

Looking for an illustrator for his stories, Dunsany had been impressed by the drawings of Sidney H. Sime. He was lucky to find Sime alive, active, and willing. Dunsany's stories and Sime's pictures (the originals of which hang today on the walls of Dunsany Castle) perfectly complemented each other. Sometimes Dunsany asked Sime to draw a fantastic picture and then wrote a story around it. "Distressing Tale of Thangobrind the Jeweller" was thus begotten.

In 1905, while the 27-year-old Dunsany was staying in Wiltshire, Conservative friends asked him to stand for Parliament. Since his father had been an active and eloquent M.P., Dunsany was willing. He found he enjoyed making speeches but lost anyway. After continuing active for a few years in that district, he decided that he was away too much to do the party justice and quit politics.

Dunsany alternated between Dunstall Priory and Dunsany Castle. He played chess and cricket and continued to write. In 1908–09 he made a trip to Egypt.

In Dublin, Dunsany became involved with the Abbey Theatre, the Irish Renaissance, and William Butler Yeats. Although he and Yeats were close friends for a while and had many interests in common, in the long run they did not get on well. Dunsany suspected Yeats of sharing the common prejudice against titled dilettantes. He also thought, with some reason, that Yeats and Lady Augusta Gregory, who between them ran the Abbey, had gone out of their way to make sure that Dunsany's plays should not outshine their own. One they canceled when it was doing well, and another was put on with a slipshod performance.

Years later, in 1932, Yeats founded an Irish Academy of Letters, ostentatiously omitting Dunsany on the ground that Dunsany wrote, not about Ireland, but about imaginary places. Dunsany was stimulated by the rebuff to write a good fantasy novel, *The Curse of the Wise Woman,* with an Irish locale. He also got even with Yeats by suggesting a society to honor medieval Italian writers—which would, however, omit Dante. He said: "Dante did not write about Italy, but of a very different place. Most unsuitable."[8]

A mutual friend of Dunsany and Yeats was Oliver St. John Gogarty, the amiable literary surgeon, friend of all the Irish Renaissance figures, and the original of Joyce's "plump, stately Buck Mulligan." Gogarty surmised that Yeats was simply jealous of Dunsany's title. According to Gogarty, Yeats thought that if anybody had a title, it should be William Butler Yeats. There was, however, no active feud between the two. When they met in later years, they treated each other pleasantly enough.

At this time, Dunsany wrote the stories comprising one of his best collections of fantasy, *The Book of Wonder* (1912) and several plays including two of his most successful: *The Gods of the Mountain* and *King Argimēnēs and the Unknown Warrior*. Several of these plays were produced in London and in Dublin with gratifying success and were paid the compliment of being pirated in Tsarist Russia. The real success of these plays, however, came later and in the United States.

In 1911, the Dunsanys went to London for the coronation of King George V. At the last minute, they discovered that Dunsany had left his coronet, a necessary part of the regalia, behind at Dunsany Castle. There was a fine uproar; Dunsany at first refused to attend at all. Then it was recalled that a fellow peer was in Scotland and so would not need his coronet. En route to Westminster Abbey, ermine-robed but coronetless, Dunsany stopped at this lord's house, borrowed the coronet from the unflappable butler, and made the Abbey just in time to be let in and take his proper place.

In 1912, Dunsany was hunting wild goats in the Sahara. His guide insisted on what a healthy place the desert was. "The Arabs in the desert are never ill," quoth Smail ben-Ibrahim. "If an Arab is ill he dies."[9] Next year, Dunsany hunted big game in East Africa. In later years, he sometimes wondered how one who loved wild nature as he did should also enjoy killing game.

Then came August, 1914. Dunsany volunteered for the Inniskilling Fusiliers in Ireland. Captain Dunsany was still training his company when the Easter Rising of 1916 broke out. Dunsany and a fellow officer drove back from the Castle to Dublin but ran into a street barricade manned by a company of the Irish Republican Army. These rose up and began shooting, making up in volume what they lacked in marksmanship. Dunsany's car was riddled. While running for cover, Dunsany was hit in the face by a ricochet, which lodged in his nasal sinuses. A rebel took Dunsany prisoner and, seeing the blood flow, said: "I am sorry." His comrades cried: "Where's a doctor? Here's a man bleeding to death!"[10]

Dunsany was put in a hospital and tenderly cared for until the rebellion was crushed. By the end of the year, Dunsany was on duty in France in the most dismal of all wars. In reference to his own stature, he later remarked: "Our trenches were only six feet deep; I shall never fear publicity again."[11]

He survived the war without further damage and in 1919 made the first of a number of lecture tours to America, where he found that readers appreciated him more than did his own countrymen. Sometimes he had to flee back across the Atlantic to escape American hospitality, fearing lest he should never get any more writing done. His plays, too, took hold in the New World; at one time he had five running at once on Broadway. During the 1920s and 30s, declining finances compelled him to learn to economize and to pay closer attention to the earnings from his writing and lectures.

During the Troubles, Dunsany, despite his loudly voiced pro-British, Tory, Unionist sentiments (to him Lloyd George was a "damned ruffian") was often in trouble with the authorities. He insisted on keeping up his shooting when being caught with gun in hand was a capital offense in Ireland.

During this time, Dunsany's gardener came to Dunsany and said he had gotten on the wrong side of the IRA and that he was due to be murdered if Dunsany could not lend him ten pounds to help him get to Canada. Dunsany paid and thought no more of it. Many years later, when Dunsany was lecturing in Chicago, a ruddy, prosperous-looking, middle-aged man came up and said: "Here's the ten pounds I owe you." Dunsany was delighted.

Dunsany hunted in Algeria and the Sudan, where he got the setting for some of his Jorkens stories. Running out of needles for his portable phonograph, he played Beethoven with mimosa thorns. He and his wife went to India to visit son Randal. Naturally, they moved in the most exalted circles. Lady Beatrice once wrote me about India:

> It has evidently changed since I last saw it over thirty years ago, but even so I can hardly believe the letter from an Indian friend who said that their great difficulty was getting good domestic staff, when I remember servants in swarms all over the place, sleeping on marble palace stairs and appearing as by magic when one's hosts clapped their hands.[12]

In 1924, Dunsany won the chess championship of Ireland. He once played the invincible Capablanca to a draw. He became a friend of Kipling, Elgar, and other eminences and went with H. G. Wells on a literary junket to Czechoslovakia.

He took up drawing, painting, and sculpture. His weird drawings may be compared to Clark Ashton Smith's—talented primitives, but often effective. His painting of a formal flower garden was touched up by the ultra-bohemian Augustus John. His sculpture consisted of a series of terra cotta figurines, mostly of men in fantastic uniforms, comparable to Smith's soapstone carvings. Dunsany learned by trial and error how to bake his statuettes so that they should not fall to pieces.

As war again approached, Dunsany drew obloquy on himself by predicting it and urging preparedness. In some of his earliest stories, he had not been above taking a few sly cracks at the Jews. Witness the vulgar parvenu, Lord Castlenorman, who appears in "How Nuth Would Have Practised his Art Upon the Gnoles" and "The Bird of the Difficult Eye," and at whose residence "Saturday was observed as Sabbath." This attitude was very common among Gentile writers of Dunsany's generation, such as Buchan, Hyne, and Shiel. Later, especially after the rise of Hitler, Dunsany swung round (somewhat as

Lovecraft did) and became a sympathizer with and defender of the Jews, as well as a strong opponent of dictatorship.

When the Hitlerian War broke out, Dunsany moved from Ireland back to Kent and joined the Home Guard. He commemorated the Battle of Britain, much of which took place right over his head, with a verse:

> One thing I know which Milton never knew:
> When Satan fell, hurled headlong to the shade
> Of Hell eternal out of Heaven's blue,
> I know the screaming wail his pinions made.

In 1940, the government persuaded him, as a goodwill gesture, to give a course on English literature at the University of Athens. He got there via South Africa and began lecturing. Then the Germans overran Greece. The Dunsanys escaped on a refugee-crammed ship just ahead of the conquerors, Dunsany wearing two hats because he saw no reason to abandon either to the foe.

When the Dunsanys got home, they moved back to Ireland and "gradually settled down to grow old there."[13] Dunsany made a few more American trips and died quietly at 79, in a nursing home in Dublin.

Lovecraft once called Dunsany's work, "Unexcelled in the sorcery of crystalline singing prose, and supreme in the creation of a gorgeous and languorous world of iridescently exotic vision. . . ."[14] which is a pretty iridescent piece of crystalline prose in itself. Some of Dunsany's tales are laid in Ireland, some in an Africa odder than anything thought up by Edgar Rice Burroughs, and some in never-never lands of his own creation. He constantly threw off quotably epigrammatic sentences: "The Gibbelins eat, as is well known, nothing less good than man"; or: "To be a god and to fail to achieve a miracle is a despairing sensation; it is as though among men one should determine upon a hearty sneeze and as though no sneeze should come."[15]

He wrote over a period of half a century and in some ways

got better as he did so. Although his stories were always told in richly poetic language (based, he said, upon extensive reading of the Bible) some early ones failed to support the peerless prose with any particular point or plot. Later, he pruned away pointless anecdotes and rhetorical extravagances. His stories are also notable for their lack of connection with the real world and lack of interest in human character. Few of his characters other than Jorkens are developed to any significant degree.

At least a dozen of Dunsany's books contain stories in the genre of heroic fantasy or something close to it. First came nine volumes of collections of plays and short stories, all published before 1920 and practically all written before or during the Kaiserian War: *The Book of Wonder, A Dreamer's Tales, Five Plays, The Gods of Pegāna, Plays of Gods and Men, The Sword of Welleran, Tales of Three Hemispheres, Tales of Wonder,* and *Time and the Gods.* Lovers of fantasy often prefer these early tales to Dunsany's later stories, holding that the latter, while more skillfully wrought, have less of the magic of Faërie. But, while Dunsany changed his literary approach with time, the whole range of his writings is endlessly entertaining.

After the First World War, Dunsany undertook novels, which he had never done. He went at each new branch of the arts, as he got around to it, as if he were putting his horse at a high fence on a hunt. In 1922 he published *Don Rodriguez: Chronicles of Shadow Valley* (also called *The Chronicles of Rodriguez*). This is a novel of Spain in that indefinite period called the Golden Age, with a gallant if naïve hidalgo, his Sancho-like servant, and a professor of magic.

Two years later came *The King of Elfland's Daughter,* the most swordly and sorcerous of Dunsany's works. It tells of Alveric, the son of the lord of Erl, who weds the king of Elfland's daughter and gets a son but then is separated from her. He spends years searching (rather ineptly, it must be admitted) for his lost love.

Like many Britons of his time, Dunsany thought hunting the

world's most fascinating occupation and gives it more space than non-hunters and wild-life lovers are likely to find pleasurable. *The King of Elfland's Daughter* is a splendid fantasy novel in a class with Pratt's *The Well of the Unicorn;* but it still gets bogged down in lengthy accounts of the hunting of deer and unicorns. This reflects the internal conflict between Dunsany's literary bent and the environment of unbookish, hunting-shooting Anglo-Irish gentry in which he was brought up.

In 1926, he produced a semi-sequel to *Don Rodriguez.* This was *The Charwoman's Shadow,* laid in the same imaginary setting, wherein a minor character is a descendant of Don Rodriguez. It is one of his best stories despite a rather unpromising title.

Dunsany went on to write many more books, including collections of verse (much of it rather pedestrian, albeit with occasional flashes of true poetic fulgor),[16] novels of Irish life, and many non-heroic fantasies, such as *The Man Who Ate the Phoenix* and the five volumes of Jorkens stories. (All Dunsany's short heroic fantasies belong to his earlier period.) Some of his later, humorous tales are very funny indeed. Many are laid in modern England or Ireland. One of his last works of fiction was a science-fiction novel, *The Last Revolution* (1951). The plot is a simple, conventional revolt of the robots, but the story is developed with masterly skill and suspense.

Dunsany wrote novels of modern Irish life and three volumes of autobiography: *Patches of Sunlight, While the Sirens Slept,* and *The Sirens Wake.* (He meant air-raid sirens, not the kind that beguiled Odysseus.) These are leisurely, charming reminiscences, full of delightful anecdotes, like the tale of the man who, during Prohibition, landed in New York from a liner with a hamper among his baggage.

> To the Customs officer he said: "Please don't open that, as I have a very valuable cat inside, and it might escape."
>
> "We know all about that cat," said the officer. "Open it."

So the traveller opened the hamper. Out leaped a cat and rushed away down the platform. The traveller ran after it with the empty hamper, and a long while after returned.

"I asked you not to open it," he said.

"I know that," said the officer; "but we have to deal with all sorts of people. Got your cat all right?"

"Yes, I got her at last," said the traveller. And no more was said. The cat was the ship's cat. And when it got out it ran straight to the ship, and the man with the hamper after it. But when he got to the ship he didn't put the cat into the hamper: he filled that hamper with bottles of whiskey.[17]

On the other hand, these autobiographies tell little about Dunsany's private or interior life. He brushed this over lightly, whether because of lack of interest or because of aristocratic reserve.

Although he had predecessors, such as the many exploiters of Arthurian legend and the lost-Atlantis theme, Dunsany was the second writer (Morris being the first) fully to exploit the possibilities of heroic fantasy—adventurous fantasy laid in imaginary lands with pre-industrial settings, with gods, witches, spirits, and magic, like children's fairy tales but on a sophisticated, adult level. He was a master of the trick or surprise ending. Sometimes the dauntless hero meets an ironic or gruesome fate: "And, without saying a word, *or even smiling,* they neatly hanged him on the outer wall—and the tale is one of those that have not a happy ending."[18]

Dunsany was a writer's writer. Although well known in his lifetime and having much influence on his younger colleagues, he never became an actual best seller, even though some of his plays had considerable success.

As an example of his influence, the eloquent contemporary scientific writer Loren Eiseley, author of *The Firmament of Time, Darwin's Century,* and so on, acknowledges Dunsany's influence. Dunsany's play *King Argimēnēs and the Unknown Warrior* served as a springboard for Fletcher Pratt's *The Well of the Unicorn.* The Jorkens stories, about a cadging old club-man who tells tall tales for his drinks, started a cycle of stories of fantastic barroom reminiscence, such as Arthur C. Clarke's White Hart stories, Pratt's and my Gavagan's Bar tales, and Sterling Lanier's stories of Brigadier Ffellowes. Dunsany's influence was fully acknowledged by H. P. Lovecraft.

Dunsany's influence is not a matter of accident but partly the result of thoughtful study of the craft of writing. He delivered lectures and wrote articles on writing techniques. He fulminated against such sloppy usages as "weather conditions" (a tautology, since weather *is* a condition) or "our Rome correspondent" (for "our Roman correspondent").

His lack of the widest popular success may be traced to several causes. One is his fondness for exotic made-up names, as when in "The Sword of Welleran" he tells of "the souls of Welleran, Soorenard, Mommolek, Rollory, Akanax, and young Iraine." Some, who learned to read by sight-reading methods, are exasperated by such unfamiliar word-shapes. Another cause is the fact that in some of his earlier stories, poetic eloquence hides a lack of solid substance. Then, Dunsany shared in the decline of fantasy that took place in the 1940s and 50s. In his later years, he sometimes sadly felt that he had outlived his time. But this trend was reversed by Tolkien's trilogy and Conan. Dunsany, too, has been reprinted in paperback.

Dunsany's tales are a necessary possession for any lover of fantasy. Like first-rate poetry, they are endlessly rereadable. Those who have not read them have something to look forward to.

IV

ELDRITCH YANKEE GENTLEMAN: H. P. LOVECRAFT

The oldest and strongest emotion of mankind is fear, and the strongest kind of fear is fear of the unknown.[1]

LOVECRAFT

Howard Phillips Lovecraft (1890–1937) merits attention in any study of heroic fantasy. In addition to his own substantial contributions to the genre, he had great influence on other fantasy writers, occupying a key position in the whole development of imaginative literature. Moreover, his was a most singular personality; he was the greatest bundle of contradictions that one can imagine. For examples:

He condemned poses and affectations but was himself the prince of poseurs, affecting the language, the attitudes, and even the spelling ("publick," "shoar," "ask'd") of an eighteenth-century English Tory, or at least of a Colonial Loyalist. Once he visited the monument in Lexington, Massachusetts, to the first Colonials to fall in the Revolution. When asked if he had gotten an emotional reaction, he replied:

"I certainly did! I drew myself up and cried in a loud voice: 'Thus perish all enemies and traitors to His lawful Majesty, King George the Third!' "[2]

He detested tobacco and liquor, although his experience with them was trivial. But the life he led in Providence must have been harder on his health than moderate smoking and drinking.

He went out usually at night and ate so spare and unbalanced a diet, even when he could afford better, that, although over 5 feet 10 inches tall, he kept his weight around 140 pounds. When he married Sonia Greene and moved to Brooklyn, she fed him up to a normal weight and got him to exercise. When he fled back to Providence, however, he soon restored his self-image as a gaunt, pallid recluse.

He abhorred sexual irregularities and deviations, yet his own approach to sex was so prissy and inhibited as to make some wonder whether he, too, had a touch of lavender. While he undoubtedly loved Sonia, the one really great love affair of his life was with Providence. It was, moreover, with the material city, not with the people, for whom he cared little and few of whom knew he existed.

A thorough materialist, he had a good knowledge of the sciences and a profound respect for the scientific method. Yet he was full of pseudo-scientific racial theories, notably Aryanism or Nordicism. He rhapsodized on "the lusty battle-cry of a blue-eyed, blond-bearded warrior," although he himself was as unlike a stalwart Viking marauder as can well be imagined.

He despised "the herd" or "the masses," denounced democracy, apologized for Mussolini and Hitler, and wrote: "We are proud to be definitely *reactionary*," albeit (as he realized) he would have been given short shrift by a fascist regime. But, later, he became a mild Socialist and an admirer of Franklin D. Roosevelt.

He wrote: ". . . my hatred of the human animal mounts by leaps and bounds the more I see of the damned vermin,"[3] yet all his friends described him as one of the kindest and most generous and unselfish persons they had ever known.

He long advocated a bloodthirsty nationalistic militarism, although he himself was too squeamish to take a dead mouse from a trap. He threw away trap and all rather than touch the tiny cadaver.

Until his last few years, he was ethnocentric to the point of mania. In the abstract, he hated all ethnics, especially Jews, Latins, and Slavs: "yellow, soulless enemies," "twisted ratlike vermin from the ghetto," "rat-faced, beady-eyed oriental mongrels." The "simian *Portuguese,* unspeakable *Southern Italians,* and jabbering *French-Canadians,*" together with Negroes, Mexicans, Chinese, and Japanese, also take their lumps. When he was rooming alone in Brooklyn and learned that his next-door neighbor was a Syrian, his reaction was like that of a man who finds a rattlesnake in his bathtub.

Yet, when he came to know members of these hated ethnoi in person—for example Sam Loveman, his wife Sonia, or the Italian owner of a quarry whence he got a minute income (a "good old Roman")[4]—he proved just as kind, friendly, generous, and affectionate toward them as he did towards "Aryans."

He gave good advice on literary matters but often failed to take it himself. He would not send stories to science-fiction magazines other than *Weird Tales,* although they paid better, because he deemed them too "commercial."

H. P. L. (as he often signed himself) was born in 1890 and lived his first thirty-four years on Angell Street, Providence, Rhode Island. Much of Lovecraft's youth was spent in the house of his grandfather, Whipple Van Buren Phillips, at 454 Angell Street.

Although Lovecraft recalled his childhood as happy, he had a bad start. His father, Winfield Scott Lovecraft, was a traveling salesman of English parentage. When young Lovecraft was three, Winfield Lovecraft went insane. He was committed to the care of a guardian, then to a mental home, and died of paresis in 1898.[5]

Lovecraft's mother, Sarah Susan Phillips Lovecraft, moved with her son to the house of her father W. V. Phillips, a cultivated and fairly successful businessman. Here young Lovecraft had the run of a big library and heard ghost stories from his grandfather. Lovecraft showed great precocity, learning his letters at two and reading at four.

Lovecraft's mother was a neurotic who smothered her son with protection. When he rode his tricycle, she walked alongside holding him lest he fall.

Lovecraft attended school for a year or two but then was removed on grounds of health. For several years, he was intermittently tutored, while educating himself by wide reading and dabbling in astronomy and chemistry. His memory was phenomenal. If asked about a gathering he had attended years before, he could tell just when and where it had taken place, who was there, and what was said.

He had little human contact outside his family. He said: "Amongst my few playmates I was very unpopular, since I would insist upon playing out events in history, or acting according to consistent plots. . . . The children I knew disliked me, and I disliked them."

Never wholly convinced by Christian doctrines, Lovecraft flirted with medieval Islâm. Then he became a devotee of Graeco-Roman lore, half believed its mythology, and "would actually look for fauns and dryads in certain oaken groves at twilight. . . ."[6] Soon, however, he became a scientific materialist and atheist and so remained throughout life.

In 1904, Lovecraft's grandfather died, leaving his three daughters a modest legacy, which would see them through life only by careful economy. Lovecraft and his mother rented one floor of a smaller house. Since tutors were no longer afforded, Lovecraft attended high school, 1904–08.

Upon graduation he would normally have gone to nearby Brown University. In 1908, however, he suffered a nervous and physical collapse, as a result of which he never even finished high school. The cause of his collapse is not definitely known, but Lovecraft's accounts of his symptoms suggest rheumatic fever, hypothyroidism, hypoglycemia, or some combination of these.

Like several of the writers discussed in this book, Lovecraft displayed, from childhood on, a schizoid personality. This is not to be confused with the form of insanity called schizophrenia. The schizoid is not necessarily abnormal or even neurotic, although some writers of this group were so. A "schizoid" is merely one of a number of common personality types.

In the schizoid, the connection between external stimuli and internal mental processes is weak. The schizoid is likely to be detached from and indifferent to worldly matters, to have difficulty in realistically adapting himself to his environment, to be shy, seclusive, and over-sensitive, to avoid close or competitive human relationships, and to be individualistic, often to the point of eccentricity. An individual may, of course, show these characteristics in varying degrees, or display some but not others.

Many psychologists and psychiatrists believe that the schizoid personality is likely to go with a creative, original mind—or conversely, that strongly creative persons, such as scientists, writers, artists, and other intellectuals, are more likely than most to have schizoid personalities.

It is easy to see why there should be such a connection. Where the non-schizoid's attention is fixed on the things and people around him, vigilantly watching them to protect himself and promote his own advantage, the mind of the schizoid is likely to wander off into daydreams, fancies, speculations, and theories. Thus the schizoid is more likely than most to make scientific discoveries or artistic creations. On the other hand, he is more likely to be absent-minded and impractical in everyday affairs.

For the next decade, Lovecraft lived at home, read voraciously, and did no gainful work. His reading included the early novels of Edgar Rice Burroughs, about which he was enthusiastic at the time. Later he held them in low esteem as commercial hackwork.

During this time, Lovecraft made little effort to equip himself to face the world. For several years, he vegetated as an almost complete recluse, seeing few people besides his doting mother. His scholastic failure and physical breakdown, coming on top of his family's financial decline, seem to have destroyed whatever worldly ambitions he had once harbored. He turned his back on the world, content to idle and dream his time away and let the future fend for itself. He became a self-made "outsider," the theme of which occurs in many of his stories. He later made sporadic efforts to rejoin the mainstream of human affairs, but these efforts were fatally handicapped by his failure to get either practical training or gainful employment during adolescence and young manhood.

Lovecraft was rescued from complete passivity by his discovery of amateur journalism. Beginning in late 1914, he took an increasingly active part in this hobby, writing, publishing, and engaging in lengthy correspondence with the circle of friends that he thus collected.

He also took long walks in the country, until in his thirties he could cover more than ten miles a day with little fatigue. He was rarely seen in Providence in daytime but often prowled its streets at night.

Oppressed by a feeling of uselessness, he made one effort to escape his mother's coddling. In May 1917, during the Kaiserian War, he applied for enlistment in the National Guard. He passed the cursory physical examination and was accepted as a private in the Coast Artillery. When his mother heard, she "was almost prostrated with the news." There were scenes, and in the end she and the family physician persuaded the Army to annul the enlistment. When conscription loomed, Lovecraft wrote: "My mother has threatened to go to any lengths, legal or otherwise, if I do not reveal all the ills which unfit me for the army." None knows how many of these ills were genuine and how many were invented by his mother and foisted upon the youth.

How an actual enlistment would have worked is also unknown. As Lovecraft wrote: "It would either have killed me or cured me." He suffered real psychosomatic ills, but some good soldiers have been made of equally unlikely material. As it

was, poor Lovecraft was left feeling more "useless" and "desolate
and lonely"[7] than ever.

In his twenties, Lovecraft looked much as he did through life.
He was a fraction of an inch under five feet eleven, with broad
but stooped shoulders, and lean to gauntness. He had dark eyes
and hair (which later turned a mousey gray) and a long, clean-
shaven face with an aquiline nose. His salient feature was a
very long chin—a "lantern jaw"—below a small, pursed-up
mouth, which gave him a prim look.

Although he said that his mother had called him ugly, he
was actually rather personable in his bony way. His skin was
pale from nocturnal habits. An acquaintance reported: ". . . he
never liked to tan, and a trace of color in his cheeks seemed
somehow to be a source of annoyance. He was the only person
I ever met to be ashamed of a coat of tan."[8] He got over this
quirk later, when he found how much good the sun of Florida
did him.

In dress he was clean and neat but preferred old clothes to
new. In youth he presented a deliberately old-fashioned appearance, affecting high-buttoned shoes, stiff-bosomed shirts,
starched wing collars, and black ties, with, he said, "austere
and reticent manners to match."

In time he gave up these sartorial quirks but remained ultra-
conservative in dress. When he looked at his reflection in the
new suit and overcoat that his wife bought him in 1924, he
said: "But, my dear, this is entirely too stylish for Grandpa
Theobald; it doesn't look like me. I look like some fashionable
fop!"[9] He usually wore a suit or an overcoat until it went into
holes. Then he darned the holes and continued to wear it until
it was in the last stages of decrepitude.

His voice was high and rather harsh; he called it a "raucous
squawk."[10] When excited, he stuttered. When affecting his
eighteenth-century pose, he used archaic pronunciations like
"me" for "my" and "sarvent" for "servant."

During his twenties, he conformed to his self-image "as a cadaverous, mysterious figure of the night—a pallid, scholarly necrologist—and cultivated a resemblance until he was almost the real thing."

A shy man, he practiced a gentlemanly reserve and imperturbability. He thought of himself as a kind of disembodied intellect, unswayed by human passions: "I shall never be very merry or very sad, for I am more prone to analyse than to feel. What merriment I have is always derived from the satirical principle, and what sadness I have, is not so much personal, as a vast and terrible melancholy at the pain and futility of all existence. . ."[11] Later, he showed that inside the old Lovecraft quite a different one had been struggling to get out: gregarious, garrulous, charming, warm-hearted, and physically active. This Lovecraft succeeded in emerging only partway.

Lovecraft's physical state is a puzzle. He thought himself a frail, nervous creature; yet the doctors could find nothing wrong, and he looked normal. He wrote:

> If you received G. J. Houtain's *Zenith* you will see how I impress a stranger—as a husky, pampered hypochondriac, tied down to indolence by indulgent relatives, and by false notions of heredity. If Houtain knew how constant are my struggles against the devastating headaches, dizzy spells, and spells of poor concentrating power which hedge me on all sides, and how feverishly I try to utilise every available moment for work, he would be less confident in classifying my ills as imaginary.[12]

The term "psychosomatic illness" had not yet come into wide use, but Lovecraft grasped the concept. Later he wrote:

> The more we know of psychology, the less distinction we are able to make betwixt the functional disorders known as "mental" and those known as "physical." Nothing is more unfortunate than a neurotic temperament, and I am just enough inclined that way myself to sympathise deeply with anyone else who suffers from shadowy depressions. Many times in my youth I was so exhausted by the sheer burden of consciousness and mental and physical

activity that I had to drop out of school for a greater or lesser period and take a complete rest free of all responsibilities; and when I was eighteen I suffered such a breakdown that I had to forego college. In those days I could hardly bear to see or speak to anyone, and liked to shut out the world by pulling down dark shades and using artificial light . . . my hypersensitive nerves reacted on my bodily functions to such a degree as to give the appearance of many different physical illnesses.[13]

His outstanding frailty was hypersensitivity to cold. He suffered from an inability, called "poikilothermia" (or "poikilothermism"), to keep his body temperature constant. At 90° he felt fine; in winter in Providence, he kept the house heated into the eighties. Below 80° he became increasingly unhappy; at 70° he was stiff, sniffling, and gasping. On a few occasions, when he was caught out of doors in winter by a sudden freeze, he collapsed on the sidewalk and had to be rescued by passers-by.

Lovecraft's sensitivity to cold may have been aggravated by his diet. His tastes were highly idiosyncratic. He abhorred milk, fat, and sea food but had a passion for cheese, chocolate candy, coffee saturated with sugar, highly spiced curry, and ice cream. In 1927, he and his friends Morton and Wandrei stopped at a place that advertised thirty-two flavors of ice cream.

"Are they all available?" asked Lovecraft.

"No," said the waiter; "only twenty-eight today, sir."

"Ah, the decay of modern commercial institutions!" sighed Lovecraft. Each of the three ordered a double portion in a different flavor and traded parts of his serving with the others, so that each got three flavors with each serving. Wandrei soon dropped out, but Morton and Lovecraft continued through the whole twenty-eight flavors, consuming more than two quarts apiece.[14]

Towards food in general, Lovecraft was indifferent, despising gourmanderie and priding himself on the cheapest and sparsest diet that would sustain life. He thought his brain worked better when slightly starved. Late in life he wrote: "Fortunately I have reduced the matter of frugal living to a science, so that I can get by on as little as $1.75 a week by purchasing beans or spaghetti in cans and cookies or crackers in boxes."[15]

He experienced vivid dreams and nightmares. Some he described in his letters or exploited in his tales.

He disliked dogs but loved cats. When he visited a friend and a kitten climbed into his lap and went to sleep, he sat up all night rather than disturb the creature.

He doted on eighteenth-century England and, next in order, on Classical Rome. He wrote: "I would actually feel more at home in a silver button'd coat, velvet small-cloaths, wig, Steenkirk cravat, and all that goes with such an outfit from sword to snuffbox, than in the plain modern garb that good sense bids me to wear in this prosaick aera."[16]

Along with his passion for the Baroque Age went his love of the oldest parts of Providence, where traces of this "aera" lingered. He was so opposed to change that he wrote a letter and a poem to the *Providence Journal* denouncing a proposal to tear down some old brick warehouses. He illustrates in extreme form Bertrand Russell's dictum: "Few men's unconscious feels at home except in conditions very similar to those which prevailed when they were children."[17] Lovecraft suffered from "future shock" long before Alvin Toffler made up the term.

Another source of Lovecraft's xenophobia was the pseudo-scientific Nordicism current in the United States during the first quarter of the twentieth century. This cult started with a French diplomat, the Comte de Gobineau, who in the 1850s wrote a book to prove that the tall, blond, blue-eyed type of northern Europe—the "Nordic" sub-race or type—was superior to all the lesser breeds of man. Gobineau deemed himself to belong to these folk, who as the Germanic Franks had conquered Gaul around A.D. 500 and made themselves the French aristocracy. He averred that France had ruined herself by destroying or exiling these "best people" in the Revolution.

Gobineau attracted many followers, all believing themselves Nordics, since nobody has ever written a book to prove his own ethnos inferior. Among these was Houston Stewart Chamberlain (1855–1927), a member of the Gobineau Society. The son of a British admiral, Chamberlain was educated in Switzerland and Germany. A frail little neurotic with hallucinations of being pursued by demons, he became a German citizen, a friend of Kaiser Wilhelm II, and a son-in-law of Richard Wagner. In his old age he hailed Hitler, then an obscure rabble-rouser, as the savior of Germany.

In 1899, Chamberlain published a book, *Die Grundlagen des 19en Jahrhunderts,* which a dozen years later appeared in English as *Foundations of the Nineteenth Century.* This is a windy, rambling, tendentious, verbalistic, and wholly worthless book (despite its huge sales in Germany), on a par with Churchward's Mu books or Madame Blavatsky's *Secret Doctrine.* The author undertakes to prove the superiority of the "Teutonic Aryan" by a perfectly circular argument: Any historical character he likes, such as Julius Caesar or Jesus, is proved a Teutonic Aryan by his virtues, and the virtues of all these Teutons prove Aryan superiority.

These ideas were popularized in the United States by Madison Grant (*The Passing of the Great Race,* 1916) and Lothrop Stoddard (*The Rising Tide of Color Against White World Supremacy,* 1920). These amateur ethnologists eloquently but quite unscientifically argued that the purity of the Nordic race must be guarded against dilution, lest civilization, whereof the Nordic was the author and prime mover, perish from the earth. Some Nordicists identified the Nordics with the supposed Aryan race, which in the second millennium B.C. spread the Indo-European languages from Portugal to India. Although completely unscientific in the light of present knowledge, these arguments influenced the immigration law of 1924.

From close resemblances of wording, I am sure that Lovecraft read Chamberlain's *Foundations* and was influenced by it. He did read Grant and probably Stoddard. In 1915, after

Foundations but before Grant's book, he brought out the first issue of his amateur magazine, *The Conservative.* This featured a long editorial, "The Crime of the Century," proclaiming:

> The Teuton is the summit of evolution. . . . Tracing the career of the Teuton through mediaeval and modern history, we can find no possible excuse for denying his actual biological supremacy. In widely separated localities and under widely diverse conditions, his innate racial qualities have raised him to preeminence. There is no branch of modern civilization that is not of his making. . . . The Teutonic mind is masterful, temperate, and just. No other race has shown an equal capability for self-government.[18]

His letters were likewise filled with statements like: "Science shows us the infinite superiority of the Teutonic Aryan over all others."[19] At the same time, he began venomously disparaging non-Nordics, fulminating against Jews and "niggers," and glorifying the "noble but much maligned" Ku Klux Klan. In one letter, he reversed the usual arguments for tolerance:

> Nothing is more foolish than the smug platitude of the idealistic social worker who tells us that we ought to excuse the Jew's repulsive psychology because we, by persecuting him, are in a measure responsible for it. This is damned piffle. . . . We despise the Jew not only because of the stigmata which our persecution has produced, but because of the deficient stamina . . . on his part which permitted us to persecute him at all! Does anybody fancy for a moment that a Nordic race could be knocked about for two millennia by its neighbours? God! They'd either die fighting to the last man, or rise up and wipe out their would-be persecutors off the face of the earth! ! It's *because* the Jews have allowed themselves to fill a football's role that we instinctively hate them. Note how much greater is our respect for their fellow-Semites, the Arabs, who *have* the high heart—shewn in courage. . . —which we emotionally understand and approve.[20]

Had Lovecraft lived to witness the Arab-Israeli wars of 1948–67, he might have found the experience educational. Today, such opinions would place a man in the right-wing lunatic fringe—although the New Left has made similar noises about

"Zionist imperialists." But, when Lovecraft began voicing such opinions in the 1910s, they were widespread and respectable, especially among Old Americans of Lovecraft's and earlier generations—that is, born before 1900. All the time, Lovecraft was warmly praising the intelligence, sensitivity, honor, and other virtues of his friend Samuel Loveman, "Jew or not."[21]

Most writers are, in my observation, less ethnocentric than the masses, because their reading has exposed them to many points of view. This is true *a fortiori* of science-fiction writers. After one has coped with the problem of the spider-men from Sirius, no human being seems alien. Lovecraft, however, continued to write in this xenophobic vein for nearly twenty years, long after most American intellectuals had abandoned this viewpoint.

Otherwise, Lovecraft was a thorough puritan. He once castigated his friend W. Paul Cook for publishing a harmless story about an artist's model who posed in the nude: "a horrifying example of decadence in thought and morals." As Lovecraft aged, however, while he maintained the same austere standards for himself, he became more tolerant of others' deviation from them. He became "convinced that the erotic instinct is in the majority of mankind far stronger than I could ever imagine . . ." and that laws and customs would have to be adjusted accordingly.

Likewise, once in favor of Prohibition, he turned against it, not because he had taken to drink himself but because he saw that it was unworkable. The only time he is known to have drunk anything alcoholic was at a New Year's Eve party in New York in 1933–34, where his host spiked his ginger ale. Lovecraft became "the very life of the party"[22] talking a streak, laughing, joking, and singing. He never learned what had befallen him.

He strove for a detached, objective view of human affairs and cynically believed "that the average person is governed by no moral law save appearances and self-interest"; that all governments, whether called Fascistic, democratic, or Communistic, were oligarchies wherein the able and aggressive few exploited the ignorant many; that war was inevitable because of "ineradicable human instincts"; and that pacifism, disarmament, and the "comic-opera League of Nations" were futile, even though, regrettably, "the next war will probably end civilisation."[23]

As a boy, Lovecraft composed detective and supernatural stories. Then his interests shifted to science, and for several years he issued a hectographed *Rhode Island Journal of Astronomy*. In 1908 he wrote a fantasy, "The Alchemist," published eight years later in an amateur journal, *The United Amateur*.

During the next six years, Lovecraft discovered amateur journalism. Begun in the nineteenth century, this hobby had greatly expanded after 1900 with the development of the Mimeograph and Hectograph machines. Like science-fiction fans later, amateur journalists printed little magazines and circulated them through their organizations, as they still do. By 1914, the movement was sundered into the United Amateur Press Association and the National Amateur Press Association. The UAPA, also, was split into factions.

Lovecraft joined one faction of the UAPA and also the NAPA, served terms as president of both, and plunged into the politics of amateur journalism. He took this avocation seriously because it gave him a chance to exercise his literary bent in a genteel, noncommercial manner. From 1915 to 1923 he published his own amateur paper, *The Conservative.* Thereafter, wearied of Byzantine politics and teapot tempests, he gave the movement less time, although he retained connections with it down to his death.

Amateur journalism afforded Lovecraft new literary outlets; if not paid, at least he was printed. From 1915 to 1925, he had over a hundred articles and essays published in amateur periodicals. He also wrote much youthful poetry. Since, however, his models were Pope, Addison, and their Baroque colleagues, his verse took the form of endless chains of rhyming couplets in iambic pentameter, which soon become unreadably dull.

In 1917, Lovecraft began his serious work in the field that was to bring him fame: weird fantasies. His short story "The Tomb," printed in the amateur journal *The Vagrant* in 1922, was a competent but uninspired story of the kind that *Weird Tales* published throughout its existence. The narrator tells how as a solitary, dreamy boy he was fascinated by the discovery of the burial vault of an extinct New England family near his home. Finding a key, he takes to spending nights in the vault. The spirits of the vanished Yankee gentlefolk invade his mind, until he speaks their kind of archaic English.

The echoes of Lovecraft's own past are plain. All his life he was obsessed by "every treasured memory of childhood," or of "other and better days." He meant his life as a spoiled little rich boy, after which life seemed to have gone steadily downhill. Therefore he steadfastly resisted or ignored the pressures upon him to grow up, like Barrie's Peter Pan insisting: "I want always to be a little boy and have fun!" So haunted by the past was he that in 1935 he played a bizarre nostalgic game with his surviving aunt, pretending that they were living around 1900 and talking as people would actually have spoken at that time.

"The Tomb" was followed by "Dagon," published before the other in 1919 in *The Vagrant*. More original than its predecessor, this story sets the pattern for most of Lovecraft's later tales. In a leisurely first-person narrative, the narrator, a reclusive, ineffectual, scholarly bachelor like Lovecraft, comes upon some anomaly, some apparent violation of natural law. A long, slow, moody build-up follows, with little or no dialogue. At last the narrator, who has passively watched his approaching doom, makes the shattering discovery that the anomaly is real after all. The discovery leaves him either facing death or broken in health and spirit.

"Dagon" tells of the narrator's capture by a German sea raider in the Kaiserian War, his escape in a lifeboat, and his grounding on a stretch of sea bottom suddenly raised above the surface. Floundering through mud and slime, he finds carvings of gigantic fish-men, one of whom emerges alive from the water. The narrator escapes and returns to civilization but remains obsessed by horror. The story ends: "The end is near. I hear a noise at the door, as of some immense slippery body lumbering against it. It shall not find me. God, *that hand!* The window! The window!"[24]

As an eight-year-old boy, Lovecraft discovered Edgar Allan Poe and became a lifelong devotee of Poe's work. He became a recognized Poe scholar and solved problems in the interpretation of Poe's story "The Fall of the House of Usher" and his poem "Ulalume."[25] In many of his stories, he copied Poe's style so closely that at least one of these stories might have been passed off as a newly discovered work of Poe. This imitation included one of Poe's worst stylistic vices: trying to give added emphasis to his narrative by the lavish use of capital letters, italics, and exclamation points.

The second strongest influence, which brings Lovecraft within our circle of heroic fantasists, was Lord Dunsany. Lovecraft began reading stories by Dunsany in 1919. In the fall of that year, he heard a lecture in Boston by Dunsany himself. Immensely taken with Dunsany, who was just the sort of man Lovecraft would like to have been, Lovecraft hastened to read all of Dunsany's works that he could.

Everything about Dunsany contributed to his massive impact on Lovecraft. Dunsany was British; Lovecraft was an extreme Anglophile. Dunsany was an aristocrat; Lovecraft spent his life mourning his family's loss of upper-class status. Dunsany was an unabashed dreamer, calling one of his volumes *A Dreamer's Tales;* Lovecraft had retreated from the real world into dreamland for a number of years following his breakdown of 1908 and was dragged back to earth again only with reluctance. Dunsany's fantasies were notable for their lack of connection with the real world and their indifference to human character; this, as far as Lovecraft was concerned, was all to the good.

Now Lovecraft began writing fiction regularly, although for several years his stories appeared only in the amateur press. During 1917–21 he turned out at least seventeen stories, albeit some were not published until years later. Of Lovecraft's stories of this time, many showed Dunsanian influence. A third influence on Lovecraft was the work of the Welsh fantasist Arthur Machen (1863–1947).

Lovecraft's stories fall into several classes. There are his Dunsanian fantasies, his dream-narratives, his stories of New England horror, the stories of what was later called the Cthulhu Mythos, and several tales that are *sui generis.* Several stories use the theme of the ghoul-changeling; several others, that of psychic possession. Still another theme is that of a man's efforts magically to recover his lost and idealized youth.

These classes are not mutually exclusive. "The Dream-Quest of Unknown Kadath" is at once a dream-narrative, a Dunsanian fantasy, and a Cthulhu Mythos story. The themes of the ghoul-changeling and of lost youth both appear in it.

In the story "Polaris," written in 1918 and published in the amateur press in 1920, Lovecraft began to assemble a definite dreamworld of his own. The story begins:

> Into the north window of my chamber glows the Pole Star with uncanny light. All through the long hellish hours of blackness it shines there. . . .
>
> And it was under a horned waning moon that I saw the city for the first time. Still and somnolent did it lie, on a strange plateau

between strange peaks. Of ghastly marble were its walls and towers. . . .

Ancestral memory tells the narrator how he was once a citizen of "Olathoe, which lies on the plateau of Sarkia," in the land of Lomar. The city is threatened by the barbaric Inutos. The narrator is posted to a watch tower to give warning of the Inutos' approach but falls asleep at his post. Although this story seems to be laid in the real world in some prehistoric time, in later stories Lovecraft moved Lomar to his dreamworld, which more or less coexists with the waking one.

The story is a modest success despite Lovecraft's indulgence in another of Poe's vices. This is the lavish use of adjectives and adverbs to convey a mood of horror and terror: "uncanny light," "hellish hours," "ghastly marble," and so on. A star winks "hideously." These modifiers denote, not physical facts, but the narrator's supposed emotional reaction to facts. Such rhetorical extravagance soon wearies the sophisticated reader.

During this period, Lovecraft collaborated on several short fantasies with fellow amateur journalists. He also experimented with "prose poems." These are sketches or vignettes of a few hundred words, which make up for lack of plot by lush, poetical language. Prose poems were popular with the nineteenth-century French Decadents, who liked to hint at sins too frightful to be put into words. Lovecraft had read Huysmans and perhaps other Decadents.

Most of Lovecraft's Dunsanian fantasies were written around this time, when Lovecraft was turning thirty. The purest otherworldly tales are "The Cats of Ulthar," "The Other Gods," "The Quest of Iranon," "The Doom that Came to Sarnath," and "Celephais." Other fantasies—"The Strange High House in the Mist" and "The White Ship"—are anchored in the here-and-now but soar off into Lovecraft's dreamworld of Ulthar beyond the river Skai.

The most successful of these tales are, perhaps, "The Cats

of Ulthar" and "The Doom that Came to Sarnath." The former of these is a charming little fable, wherein Lovecraft combines his Dunsanian style with his love of cats:

> It is said that in Ulthar, which lies beyond the river Skai, no man may kill a cat; and this I can verily believe as I gaze upon him who sitteth purring before the fire. For the cat is cryptic, and close to strange things which men cannot see. He is the soul of antique Aegyptus, and bearer of tales from forgotten cities in Meroë and Ophir.

In that village dwell an old couple who trap and kill their neighbors' cats. A caravan of dark, Gypsylike strangers passes through. Among them is an orphan boy, Menes, whose only companion is a small black kitten. The kitten vanishes. Menes prays to his gods, and the caravan departs. That night, all the cats of Ulthar disappear. Next day they are back, placid and well-fed. Of the old couple, all that remains is a pair of skeletons.

"The Doom that Came to Sarnath," written about the same time, is an excellent little Dunsanian fantasy:

> There is in the land of Mnar a vast still lake that is fed by no stream, and out of which no stream flows. Ten thousand years ago there stood by its shore the mighty city of Sarnath, but Sarnath stands there no more.

Before the days of Sarnath had stood the gray stone city of Ib, "peopled with beings not pleasing to behold." Hating the froglike Ibites, the Sarnathians destroyed them. On the thousandth anniversary of the destruction of Ib, King Zokkar of Sarnath gives a feast, to which he bids other princes. At midnight. . . .

Other stories of this period include "Arthur Jermyn," a purely science-fiction horror story, and "The Statement of Randolph Carter." The latter, based on a nightmare involving Lovecraft's friend Loveman, brings in, as narrator, Lovecraft's *alter ego* Randolph Carter, who appears in a number of later stories.

Carter is much like Lovecraft, except that he has two things for which Lovecraft vainly yearned. One is enough money to live on like a gentleman; the other is a military record, gained by service in the French Foreign Legion.

Lovecraft's stories of 1920 include "From Beyond," "The Temple," and "The Terrible Old Man." The first is a conventional horror-fantasy or science-fiction horror story, about a mad scientist who develops a machine that enables him to see into another dimension. "The Temple" is in the form of a memoir by a German submarine commander, placed in a bottle, and released from the submarine, which lies crippled on the bottom amid the ruins of Atlantis. "The Terrible Old Man" is a competent but conventional fantasy of how three thieves go to rob an old sea captain of peculiar powers.

The year 1921 saw the writing of "The Music of Erich Zann," often deemed one of Lovecraft's best. The narrator tells how, living in France, he took a cheap room in a decrepid old house. His neighbor overhead is a mute old German musician, who plays weird tunes. When the narrator strikes up an acquaintance, the mute lets him listen to his playing but prevents him from looking out his shuttered and curtained window, which should (but does not) command a view of the city.

In 1921, Lovecraft wrote the first of a series of loosely connected stories, comprising what later became known as the tales of the Cthulhu Mythos. The first of these was "The Nameless City." The narrator tells how he found these ruins in Arabia:

> There is no legend so old as to give it name, or to recall that it was ever alive. . . . It was of this place that Abdul Alhazred the mad poet dreamed on the night before he sang this unexplainable couplet:
>
>> That is not dead which can eternal lie,
>> And with strange aeons even death may die.

The narrator explores the ruins and finds carvings and mummies of a race of small, civilized dinosaurs. When he starts out from a tunnel, he is forced back by a shrieking wind, in which he thinks he hears the voices of the spirits of the former dwellers. As he struggles to the surface, he sees a "a nightmare horde of rushing devils; hate-distorted, grotesquely panoplied, half transparent devils of a race no man might mistake—the crawling reptiles of the nameless city."

Although not bought until Lovecraft's death, the story is good of its kind. Like many of Lovecraft's works, it was based upon a dream. "Abdul Alhazred," which is pseudo-Arabic, was a make-believe name he had taken as a child.

Two years later, Lovecraft wrote "The Festival," which he sold to *Weird Tales.* As in "The Nameless City," there is no dialogue, but a slow buildup to a climax of horror. The narrator comes to Kingsport in response to a tradition that he shall celebrate Yuletide with his kin. He joins a throng of silent, hooded folk streaming into a nighted church and follows them down into a crypt, where strange rites are taking place. A horde of bat-winged, webfooted things appear, and the people ride off on them. When they try to get the narrator to do likewise, he leaps into an underground river and escapes. Lovecraft mentions not only Abdul Alhazred but also Abdul's *chef d'oeuvre,* the *Necronomicon,* in the library of Miskatonic University at Arkham.

Other stories of Lovecraft in 1921 were "The Outsider" and "The Moon-Bog." The former is often considered one of Lovecraft's best stories, although I personally do not care for it. It is the most Poe-esque in theme and style. The narrator tells how he grew up in a deserted castle, got out at last, and discovered, by looking at himself in a mirror, that he was a ghoul.

"The Moon-Bog" is a minor story of supernatural horror, laid in Ireland. Lovecraft wrote it to present at a St. Patrick's Day meeting of amateur journalists in Boston.

Through his amateur journalism, Lovecraft met many would-be writers and poets who would pay him to revise their work.

When given a story to edit, Lovecraft sometimes rewrote the whole thing, using only a fraction of the original author's ideas. In other words, he became a ghost writer.

Lovecraft's charges slowly rose from an eighth to three-quarters of a cent a word, but these were mere asking prices; in practice he accepted much less. In 1933 he was still rewriting an 80,000-word novel for a mere $100.[26] Since he was a conscientious worker, this was a starvation wage for the time spent. He could have made more had he haggled with his clients and dunned them when they failed to pay him, but he would not behave in such an "ungentlemanly" way. During his last years, I estimate that he averaged around $1,000 a year from his "revision," plus perhaps around $200 to $300 a year from his original fiction.

Still, ghost writing gave Lovecraft his first earned income. He later said he could get along on $15.00 a week and only wished he could always be sure of making that much. Actually, he earned more than that in later years but saved the surplus for travel and for his huge consumption of postage. He was never in danger of starvation, since his aunts, with whom he lived after his mother's death, could always tide him over a lean spell.

Lovecraft's mother—a weepy, ineffectual, despairing woman —went into a nervous decline in 1919 and entered Butler Hospital, where she lingered for two years. Lovecraft regularly visited her on the grounds but for some reason would not enter the hospital, even when his mother was dying. His widowed aunt, Mrs. Franklin Chase Clark, moved in with him. For the rest of his life, save for his New York period, he lived with one aunt or the other.

When his mother died, Lovecraft came into legacies totaling, by my estimates, between $12,000 and $13,000. Although this money then had several times its present value, the interest was still not enough to live on, even when added to Lovecraft's meager earnings from revision and writing. Hence he kept dipping into his capital, so that by the time he died it was nearly all gone. His estate then consisted of three mortgage notes on a quarry, valued at $500.

In 1920, Lovecraft spent his first night since childhood away from home, at a gathering of amateur journalists in Boston. He was beginning to come a little out of his shell.

His substitute for a normal social life was letter writing. His epistolatory output was stupendous; he is thought to have written something like 100,000 letters. Clark Ashton Smith said his letters from Lovecraft averaged 40,000 words a year, and Lovecraft kept fifty to a hundred correspondences going at once. He spent about half his working hours on correspondence. This tremendous drain on his time explains in part his inability to earn enough to meet his frugal expenses.

After Lovecraft died, his admirer and correspondent August W. Derleth borrowed stacks of letters from many of Lovecraft's correspondents. When these were transcribed, the transcript came to 5,000 pages of single-spaced typing, of which several volumes have been published. These letters are learned, fascinating, and—especially for one who prided himself on aristocratic reticence—very self-revealing. Nearly all are in longhand; Lovecraft hated typing. His handwriting, fairly elegant in his youth, became more and more scribbly and illegible as he got older, until one correspondent took the word "hermit" for "haircut."

In 1921 came Lovecraft's first commercial sales of fiction. His fellow amateur journalist, George J. Houtain, issued a magazine called *Home Brew,* for which he ordered some horror stories from Lovecraft. The latter wrote six melodramatic, rather amateurish tales under the blanket title of "Herbert West —Reanimator," the protagonist of which is always getting into trouble by reviving corpses. Houtain printed the series as "Grewsome Tales," and Lovecraft followed this series with four more connected tales under the title of "The Lurking Fear." When Jacob Clark Henneberger launched *Weird Tales,*

Lovecraft's friend James F. Morton urged Lovecraft to send that magazine some stories. Others had been pushing Lovecraft to seek commercial outlets. At first he resisted, feeling that it would be ungentlemanly to ask money for the products of his art. At length he sent at least two stories to *Black Cat* and *Black Mask,* which rejected them.

Then, Lovecraft sent "Arthur Jermyn," "The Cats of Ulthar," "Dagon," "The Hound" (a minor story tenuously connected with the Cthulhu Mythos), and "The Statement of Randolph Carter" to *Weird Tales.* Although three of these stories had already been published in amateur magazines, Edwin Baird, the editor, bought them all and asked for more.

During the three years that began with the appearance of "Dagon," in the issue of *Weird Tales* for October 1923, Lovecraft appeared in about half the issues of the magazine. Hence some have said that 1924–26 was Lovecraft's most productive period. Actually, his production was always slow, and most of the stories published at that time were reprints from amateur periodicals. From 1927 to 1933, after the backlog of these had been used up, Lovecraft's stories appeared in this magazine in only about two issues a year.

When Farnsworth Wright took over *Weird Tales* in 1924, he continued to buy from Lovecraft but treated his submissions erratically. Some stories that he rejected were later deemed among Lovecraft's best. Sometimes he turned down a story and then, months or years later, asked to see it again and sometimes bought it.

Lovecraft's production remained low, not only because he was a painstaking writer who revised extensively and had little sense of time, but also because he deemed his main work to be ghost writing and composed his own fiction in his spare time, so to speak. Being a perfectionist, he was never satisfied, when he had finished a story, that he had achieved the effect he sought. He became discouraged and despondent, writing his friends that his work was "a failure" and that he was "finished for good."[27]

In 1921, at a convention in Boston, another amateur journalist, Rheinhart Kleiner, introduced Lovecraft to a divorcée of Russian-Jewish origin, seven years older than he and having an adolescent daughter. This was Sonia Haft Greene (1883–1972): a tall, well-built, handsome woman with a good job in a department store in New York. Although she had lived in the United States from the age of nine, Mrs. Greene showed all the extraversion, volatility, impulsiveness, and compulsive generosity attributed to pre-Revolutionary Russians. She was vigorous, enterprising, strong-willed, and "cannot keep still for two consecutive seconds." A greater contrast to the primly inhibited Lovecraft would be hard to find.

During the following year, Lovecraft corresponded with Mrs. Greene and sometimes saw her in Boston. In the spring of 1922, learning that Lovecraft's friend Loveman was coming to New York, she invited both men to use her apartment in Brooklyn while she moved in with a neighbor.

This was the farthest from home that Lovecraft, thirty-one, had been. Sonia took him to an Italian restaurant, where he ate Italian food for the first time and acquired a taste for spaghetti. He had many "evenings with the boys": Loveman, Morton, and others. Next August, Lovecraft went to Cleveland to visit Loveman, who showed him art work from Clark Ashton Smith in California and started correspondence between Lovecraft and Smith. Lovecraft also met the poet Hart Crane, destined to a career of poetical fame, homosexuality, alcoholism, and eventual suicide.

Otherwise, Lovecraft stayed in Providence for the next year and a half. On business trips to Boston, Sonia stopped off at Providence to entertain Lovecraft and his aunts and to go on long antiquarian walks with him. Once she submitted the outline of a weird story. When he waxed enthusiastic, she suddenly kissed him. "He was so flustered that he blushed and then he turned pale. When I chaffed him about it he said that he had not been kissed since he was a very small child."[28]

Lovecraft had been writing Sonia several letters a week.

Thenceforward the letters developed into a courtship, in which Sonia took the lead. Lovecraft wrote that he wanted to move to New York; Baird's buying of several stories had encouraged him.

But changes impended at *Weird Tales*. It had lost Henneberger many thousands of dollars, and Henneberger was looking for a new editor. He also made contact with Harry Houdini, the escape artist. Henneberger proposed that Houdini write a regular column for his magazine. Since Houdini knew little about writing, it was suggested that Lovecraft collaborate.

Only one instalment of the column was ever printed, but Lovecraft composed a tale, "Imprisoned with the Pharaohs," on the basis of suggestions from Houdini. The story, ostensibly written by Houdini in the first person, tells of his being seized at night near the Sphinx of Giza by a gang of Arabs and lowered down a burial shaft. At the bottom, he finds a horde of indescribable monstrosities performing unspeakable obscenities.

Lovecraft wrote a rough draft of "Imprisoned with the Pharaohs" in longhand and typed the final version. In March 1924, he took the train for New York—absent-mindedly leaving the typescript in the station at Providence. Luckily, he still had the rough draft.

Next day was his wedding day. He insisted upon St. Paul's Chapel in the Wall Street district, not because he had been converted to Episcopal theology but because Admiral Lord Howe and other Baroque notables had worshiped there. Sonia spent her wedding night reading the rough draft of Houdini's tale aloud while Lovecraft typed it with two fingers. Then they left on a one-day honeymoon in Philadelphia, which they spent alternately sightseeing and typing.

Writers have described Lovecraft as "sexless," which does not seem to have been really the case. He prepared himself for marriage by reading books on sex, and during the early months of his marriage he seems to have performed his husbandly duties adequately if without any great zest. It is probably true that Lovecraft had a low sexual drive. His idea of declaring his love for Sonia was to say: "My dear, you don't know how I appreciate you."

The charge of "latent homosexuality," which has been leveled at many notables, including Lovecraft, whose love life was the least unusual, seems unsupported. Late in life, with a certain wonderment at his own earlier innocence, Lovecraft wrote that he had reached his thirties before he learned that homosexuality actually existed in the modern world and not just in ancient Greece. His friend and fan Robert H. Barlow was a homosexual who, after dabbling in various arts and sciences, became a distinguished professor of archaeology in Mexico until his suicide in 1951. Lovecraft apparently never realized his friend's peculiarity.

Back in New York, the Lovecrafts settled into Sonia's apartment in Brooklyn. Lovecraft had his furnishings sent from Providence, because "I could not live anywhere without my own household objects around me—the furniture my childhood knew, the books my ancestors read, the pictures my mother and grandmother and aunt painted." His letters were full of high spirits and a determination to make his mark.

He soon had a chance. Henneberger wrote from Chicago, offering Lovecraft an editorship—perhaps of *Weird Tales,* perhaps of a projected new magazine, tentatively called *Ghost Stories.* Lovecraft was appalled by the idea of moving to Chicago. "[Sonia] wouldn't mind living in Chicago at all—but it is Colonial atmosphere which supplies my very breath of life. I would not consider such a move . . ." unless he had first exhausted every effort to persuade Henneberger to let him work in New York.[29] So, although his friend Long urged him at least to take a look at Chicago, he put Henneberger off with noncommittal replies and stayed in New York.

On a visit to New York, Henneberger told Lovecraft that he was definitely hired as the editor of the proposed new magazine. But Henneberger had by now lost active control of *Weird Tales.* It was to be managed by an employee named William

Sprenger and a new editor, Farnsworth Wright, who had sold several stories to the magazine. Henneberger failed to get financial backing for his proposed new magazine and finally gave up, leaving Lovecraft as jobless as ever.

Before coming to New York, Lovecraft had written a couple of tales of straight, non-fantastic horror. One was "The Picture in the House," a story of cannibalism in New England (1920). The second (1924) was a collaboration between Lovecraft and one of his few friends in Providence, Clifford M. Eddy: "The Loved Dead." It is a tale of necrophilia, whose narrator gets his fun out of snuggling up to corpses. It begins with a thinly veiled account of Lovecraft's own boyhood:

> My early childhood was one long, prosaic and monotonous apathy. Strictly ascetic, wan, pallid, undersized, and subject to protracted spells of morbid moroseness, I was ostracised by the healthy, normal youngsters of my own age. They dubbed me a spoil-sport, and "old woman," because I had no interest in the rough, childish games they played, or any stamina to participate in them, had I so desired.

Since the narrator's love of death is not fulfilled by his work as an undertaker, he becomes a mass murderer to satisfy his craving. The story so horrified some readers that in some towns legal action was brought to bar *Weird Tales* from the newsstands. Unnerved, the editor and the publisher were wary thereafter with more than a slight seasoning of grue.

Meanwhile hard blows rained on the Lovecrafts. Sonia quit her department-store job to open a millinery shop, which quickly failed. Lovecraft went job-hunting, with an almost complete lack of success. He got a job as traveling salesman for a debt-collection agency; but, after one day, the manager kindly explained that "a gentleman born and bred has very little success in such lines of canvassing salesmanship . . . where one must either be miraculously magnetic and captivating, or else so boorish and callous that he can transcend every rule of tasteful conduct and push conversation on bored, hostile, or unwilling victims."[30]

Other prospective employers asked Lovecraft what work he had done in their lines. When he said, none, they replied, sorry, nothing here. He ran an advertisement as a "writer and reviser" in the *New York Times.* He wrote and circulated a strange letter of self-recommendation:

> Dear Sir:—
>
> If an unprovoked application for employment seems somewhat unusual in these days of system, agencies, & advertising, I trust that the circumstances surrounding this one may help to mitigate what would otherwise be obtrusive forwardness. The case is one wherein certain definitely marketable aptitudes must be put forward in an unconventional manner if they are to override the current fetish which demands commercial experience & causes prospective employers to dismiss unheard the application of any situation-seeker unable to boast of specific professional service in a given line. . . .[31]

And so on for pages. Not surprisingly, this letter produced no jobs. Neither did the scores of personal calls he made in response to help-wanted ads.

He tried all the openings he could find for editorial work. Had he been taken on, he might, with a little seasoning, have proved an excellent editor. But all he got were a few little editorial tasks from Henneberger, whose *Weird Tales* was doing better under Wright.

By September, the Lovecrafts had to sell their piano. Sonia collapsed and entered a hospital. When she was released in a few weeks, they went to a farmhouse in New Jersey for her convalescence. In December, Sonia received a promising job offer from a department store in Cincinnati.

Lovecraft balked at moving, saying he dreaded living in the Midwest and would rather stay in New York "where at least he had some friends. I [Sonia] suggested he have one of them come to live with him in our apartment, but his aunts thought it wiser for me to store and sell my furniture and find a studio large enough for Howard to have the old . . . pieces he had brought from Providence." Now in his middle thirties, Lovecraft had not yet outgrown dependence upon his elder female relatives.

So he moved to 169 Clinton Street, Brooklyn, where he found to his horror that he had Orientals as housemates. No sooner was he settled than thieves made off with all the new clothes that Sonia had bought him.

Sonia's health failed again in Cincinnati, and she had to return to New York to rest. Then she got another department-store job in Cleveland and departed, leaving Lovecraft alone save for weekends.

Lovecraft continued his writing, ghostly and otherwise, and got a temporary job addressing envelopes. His main recreation was the weekly meetings of the Kalem Club, so called because the names of all the early members began with K, L, or M: Kirk, Kleiner, Leeds, Long, Lovecraft, Loveman, McNeil, and Morton. They met at the apartments of several members but most often at that of Frank Belknap Long, a young journalistic student who became a prolific writer of imaginative fiction. All the members had a strong interest in such fiction, thus foreshadowing the science-fiction fan clubs of the next decade.

Lovecraft had come to hate New York. The skyline, the Colonial relics, and the friends failed to balance his aversion for the masses, especially the immigrant poor. His letters were filled with rant against "a verminous corpse—a dead city of squinting alienage," "the organic things—Italo-Semitico-Mongoloid—inhabiting that awful cesspool," and "the foul claws of the mongrel and misshapen colossus that gibbers and howls vulgarly and dreamlessly." In one letter he proposed solving the "Jewish problem" by extermination or expulsion of all American Jews except those that showed "Aryan" traits.

When Lovecraft gave vent to anti-Jewish tirade, Sonia would gently remind him that, after all, she was of Jewish origin:

> Later H. P. assured me that he was quite "cured." But unfortunately . . . whenever we found ourselves in the racially-mixed

crowds which characterize New York, Howard would become livid with rage. He seemed almost to lose his mind. And if the truth must be known, it was this attitude toward minorities and his desire to escape them that eventually prompted him back to Providence.

Soon after our marriage he told me that whenever we had company he would appreciate it if "Aryans" were in the majority. As a matter of fact, I think he hated humanity in the abstract.[32]

It is strange that a man, emotionally low-keyed, kind and generous to friends and acquaintances, interested in the ancient and exotic, and priding himself on an objective, dispassionate outlook, should develop such venomous hatred for people who had never harmed him, merely because he disliked their appearance, accents, and other superficialities. In most scientific matters, moreover, Lovecraft was a hard-headed, skeptical materialist, giving short shrift to Charles Fort, Atlantis, Elliot Smith's heliocentric theory, and Montague Summers's medieval notions about witchcraft. Yet he fell for the pseudo-scientific Aryanist cult and continued to spout Aryanist nonsense for years after he, as a science buff, should have known that science had demolished the Aryan myth.

After Hitler came to power in 1933, although Lovecraft castigated Hitler's ideas as "asinine" and "ridiculous" and his methods as "grotesque" and "barbarous," he still condoned Hitler as "sincere and patriotic"—"an honest clown whose *basic* objects are all essentially sound." These "objects" were the protection of Germany's "Aryan culture stream" from "the stigma of Latin mongrelisation" and from being "debased and effeminated and contaminated" by the "profoundly alien and emotionally repulsive" Jewish culture.[33]

Posthumous psychoanalysis is at best highly conjectural. Still, there is some evidence for the unconscious drives that made Lovecraft, during most of his life, as xenophobic as the most violent Southern nigger-hater. As a child he was rejected by his peers; as an adult he had many failures. Now, xenophobia is a common defense against knowledge of one's own failures and shortcomings. The xenophobe consoles himself with the thought that he is at least better than *those* bastards.

Besides Lovecraft's own peculiarities, a cultural factor reinforced his prejudices. Old Americans of Lovecraft's time, place, and class often thought they had inherited a vested right to superior wealth, power, and status in the American scene, by virtue of their ancestors' long residence. When such a person saw ethnics getting ahead while he was not, and saw them elbowing their way into the upper ranks, he was filled with resentful rancor. It seemed to him that the recent immigrants must, by some underhanded means, have robbed him of his birthright.

Despite the vehemence of his anti-ethnic outbursts, Lovecraft maintained a friendly, kindly course towards individuals of these groups whom he knew. It was a case of the "some-of-my-best-friends" syndrome, then common among American gentiles. Rhetorically, one could express the greatest scorn and dislike for some other ethnos, an abstraction like "the Jews," and at the same time act in a reasonably friendly, fair-minded way towards individuals. Similar ambivalent attitudes towards outgroupers could doubtless be found everywhere and in all ages of human history.

In addition, like many intellectual introverts, Lovecraft was an outsider in his own world. That he felt this is shown by one of his comments on ethnics:

> One has to get down to Richmond to find a town which really *feels like home*—where the average person one meets looks like one, has the same type of feelings and recollections, & reacts approximately to the same stimuli. The loss of collective life—of a sharing of common traditions & memories & experience—is the curse of the heterogeneous northeast today.[34]

In supposing that he would find Richmond more congenial than other cities, Lovecraft was probably kidding himself; the South has not been notably more tolerant of iconoclastic eccentrics than the rest of the nation.

Furthermore, although a very erudite man, Lovecraft was

also wont to pontificate on subjects of which he had the merest
smattering, derived from books without the corrective of personal experience. And he never learned to distinguish objective
fact from subjective reaction. If I say that X is "good, right,
beautiful" or on the contrary "bad, wicked, horrible," I am not
saying anything significant about X. I am merely exposing my
own attitudes towards X. Likewise, when Lovecraft called Jewish culture (about which he knew nothing) "repulsive," he
was not making a factual statement about Jews. He was only
expressing his emotions towards what, in his ignorance, he
imagined Jewish culture to be.

Lovecraft wrote several stories during his New York period.
"The Shunned House" (1924), over 10,000 words in length,
showed Lovecraft's growing tendency to write longer tales. It
was composed around a real house, the Stephen Harris mansion
in Providence, which at one time, when it had stood vacant for
years, had become dilapidated and acquired some legends. The
story (a good yarn, although too slow and wordy at the start)
tells of a malign entity lurking beneath the house; it also brings
in much real Providence history from Colonial times down.

"The Horror at Red Hook," written the next year, showed
Lovecraft's increasing hatred of New York. He described that
section of Brooklyn as "a maze of hybrid squalor. . . . a babel of
sound and filth. . . ." It is otherwise a lively tale, with action
and color, but illogical and poorly thought out.

After Sonia left New York, Lovecraft became increasingly
unhappy and neurotic. In the story "He," he put his feelings
into an autobiographical passage, at the beginning, where a
young New Englander, who has come to New York full of
illusions, learns otherwise:

> Garish daylight showed only squalor and alienage and the noxious
> elephantiasis of climbing, spreading stone where the moon had
> hinted of loveliness and elder magic; and the throngs of people
> that seethed through the flumelike streets were squat, swarthy

strangers with hardened faces and narrow eyes, shrewd strangers without dreams and without kinship to a blue-eyed man of the old folk, with the love of fair green lanes and white New England village steeples in his heart.

Lovecraft's last story written in New York was "In the Vault," a short ghost story laid in New England, with a tight, well-integrated plot. It is thus an advance on the formless, haphazard plots of Lovecraft's earlier stories.

He did not write any more during his sojourn there because he got sidetracked. He let his friend W. Paul Cook persuade him to do an article on the history of fantasy for Cook's amateur magazine. This grew to a treatise of 30,000 words, "Supernatural Horror in Literature," which has drawn praise even from so severe a critic of Lovecraft as Edmund Wilson. But it took eight months of Lovecraft's time, was not finished until he returned from New York to Providence, and never earned Lovecraft a cent. He could hardly have carried his anticommercial, amateur attitude further.

When Sonia visited him, Lovecraft lamented: "If I could live in Providence, the blessed city where I was born and reared! I am sure, there, I could be happy."[35] He became so unhappy and neurotic that, according to his friend Loveman, he carried a bottle of poison to kill himself. His letters to his aunts show him as fast nearing a major breakdown.

One of the aunts wrote him, suggesting that he and she take a place that was available for rent in Providence. Lovecraft jumped at the chance. In April 1926, Sonia packed him and his belongings and sent them to Providence, promising to follow.

Lovecraft and his aunt settled into half of a big wooden twin-duplex house at 10 Barnes Street. Lovecraft wrote letters full of happiness at being home again. Then Sonia came.

Eventually we held a conference with the aunts. I [Sonia] suggested that I take a large house in Providence, hire a maid, pay the expenses, and we all live together; our family to use one side of the house, I to use the other for a business venture of my own. The aunts gently but firmly informed me that neither they nor Howard could afford to have Howard's wife work for a living in Providence.[36]

The aunts did not mind Lovecraft's living off his wife's earnings in New York. But in Providence, where they were known and had a social position to keep up, it would never do. Lovecraft had said that he would never abandon Sonia after all she had done for him; but he supinely let his aunts tell her that she was not wanted in Providence.

Sonia then worked in New York and Chicago, with visits to Providence. In the spring of 1928, she invited Lovecraft to visit her in New York. He came but declined to resume marital relations.

Lovecraft still wrote her reams of letters; but Sonia, dissatisfied with a marriage by correspondence, began urging divorce. "He tried every method he could devise to persuade me how much he appreciated me: a divorce would cause him great unhappiness; a gentleman does not divorce his wife without cause, and he had none."[37] She persisted, and in 1929 he got a divorce on grounds of desertion.

Sonia moved to California and married a retired professor, Nathaniel Abraham Davis. She lived happily with him for ten years, unaware that Lovecraft, for reasons unknown, had neglected to execute the papers making the divorce final. At the end of 1972, aged eighty-nine, she died in a nursing home.

In "The Nameless City," "The Hound," and "The Festival," Lovecraft mentioned elements of what became the Cthulhu Mythos: Abdul Alhazred, the mad Arabian poet, and Miskatonic University with its book of spells, the accursed *Necronomicon.* "The Call of Cthulhu," written after Lovecraft's return to Providence and published in *Weird Tales* in 1928, first gathered these concepts into a coherent whole. It was the first of a series of long novelettes, which Lovecraft wrote during his last decade and which are generally accounted his best work. These stories display Lovecraft's "cosmicism"—a supra-human, impersonal viewpoint, freely handling aeons, light-years of distance, and forbidden dimensions.

In "The Call of Cthulhu," the narrator inherits a clay tablet bearing the image of a squid-headed monster. A police inspector from New Orleans, reporting on a sinister cult in the bayous, produces a stone statuette of a similar monster and tells of the chant of the cultists: *"Ph'nglui mglw'nafh Cthulhu R'lyeh wgah'nagl fhtagn."* This is said to mean: "In his house at R'lyeh dead Cthulhu waits dreaming." The *Necronomicon* is cited.

The last link in the chain of evidence is the account of a sailor whose ship stopped at an unknown island. This is the submarine land of R'lyeh, raised (as in "Dagon") by a seismic convulsion above the sea. When the crew land, they come upon the giant, tentacled Cthulhu himself, and only the sailor escapes to tell the tale.

With "The Call of Cthulhu," Lovecraft's new fictional cosmogony, the Cthulhu Mythos, took shape. Lovecraft assumed that a hostile race of supernatural powers, the Great Old Ones or Ancient Ones, once ruled the earth but were later banished or restrained, either by other powers or by cosmic forces. The Great Old Ones, however, strive to resume their dominion over the earth. Now and then, foolhardy mortals tamper with the restraints laid upon the Ancient Ones, who thereupon begin terrifyingly to manifest themselves.

The Ancient Ones include Cthulhu,[38] who sleeps in R'lyeh at the bottom of the sea; Shub-Niggurath, "the Goat with a Thousand Young" (a kind of fertility goddess); Yog-Sothoth, coeval with space and time; and the demon sultan Azathoth,

> . . . who gnaws hungrily in inconceivable, unlighted chambers beyond time amidst the muffled, maddening beating of vile drums and the thin, monotonous whine of accursed flutes; to which de-

testable pounding and piping dance slowly, awkwardly, and absurdly the gigantic Ultimate Gods, the blind, voiceless, tenebrous, mindless Other Gods whose soul and messenger is the crawling chaos Nyarlathotep.[39]

This passage has always reminded me of one of the noisier night clubs. Lovecraft got the idea of making up his own pantheon from Dunsany. Other elements came from Poe's *Narrative of A. Gordon Pym,* from Robert W. Chambers's *The King in Yellow* (1895), and from Ambrose Bierce's "An Inhabitant of Carcosa" and "Haïta the Shepherd." Most of the Cthulhu tales are laid in New England, "Arkham" being a thinly-disguised Salem and "Kingsport," a Marblehead.

Lovecraft never used the term "Cthulhu Mythos," which his admirers invented after his death. About a dozen of Lovecraft's stories may be referred to the Mythos. The exact number depends on which marginal stories one includes. In some tales, the Cthulhuvian elements are central to the plot, while in others they are only casually alluded to.

The earlier stories of the series are pure fantasy. The later ones become more and more science-fictional, until the last few are straight science fiction. The stories of the Mythos are not mutually consistent, because Lovecraft never worked out a detailed, all-embracing scheme for his Cthulhuvian cosmos, as Robert E. Howard did with his Hyborian Age. The stories should therefore be read as independent entities. In stories of Lovecraft's type, which depend heavily on mood and atmosphere, mutual consistency does not greatly matter.

Lovecraft further created a set of pseudobiblia—imaginary books that, by familiarity, come to have a pseudo-life in the minds of readers. Lovecraft's fictive library includes the prehuman *Pnakotic Manuscripts,* the *Seven Cryptical Books of Hsan,* the "puzzling Eltdown Shards," and, most portentous of all, the accursed *Necronomicon.* We are told that this fearful work was written about A.D. 730 by Abdul Alhazred, a mad Yamanite poet, and later translated into Greek, Latin, and modern tongues. Abdul came to a bad end, being devoured in broad daylight by an invisible entity.

Lovecraft's scholarly quotations and references made the book seem so real that librarians and booksellers were plagued by people asking for it. It has been the subject of hoaxes, such as smuggling an index card for it into the files of the Yale University Library. Waggish dealers in rare books have listed it in catalogues. In the thirties, another *Weird Tales* writer, Manly Wade Wellman, entered a basement bookshop in New York, where shelves sagged and dust lay thick. A little old lady, who looked as if she had just parked her broomstick, asked him what he wanted.

Quoth Wellman in jest: "Have you by any chance a copy of the *Necronomicon?*"

"Why, yes, heh heh," cackled the crone. "Right—about—here!"

It proved a false alarm, but it gave Wellman quite a turn.

"The Call of Cthulhu" and its successors proved so popular that other writers joined the game, writing pieces in the same setting and adding gods to its pantheon and books to its reference shelf. Thus August Derleth furnished the entity Lloigor and the book *Cultes des Goules,* by "the Comte d'Erlette"; Clark Ashton Smith, Tsathoggua and the *Liber Ivonis* or *Book of Eibon.* Lovecraft welcomed these additions and adopted some for his own stories. He wrote: "I like to have other authors in the gang allude to it [the *Necronomicon*], for it helps work up a background of evil verisimilitude."[40]

Besides his completed Cthulhu Mythos stories, which straddle the border between fantasy and science fiction, Lovecraft left fragments of and notes for several more. Derleth later turned these into complete stories and wrote several additional Mythos tales of his own. Derleth added new elements to the Mythos, such as a race of benign deities, the Elder Gods, which sometimes help out mankind in its struggle with the Ancient Ones. Other writers, too, have tried their hands at this game. The total number of Mythos stories, counting the imitations, runs into hundreds.

For all his talk of "gods" in the Cthulhu Mythos stories, Lovecraft's attitude is wholly materialistic. These entities are merely beings of superior powers, which enable them to traverse interstellar space or slip through forbidden dimensions. But they still are bound by natural law. They are no more concerned with human problems and morals than are men with the problems of mice; they have no more compunction about eliminating men who get in their way than men have about mice. As Fritz Leiber once wrote:

> Perhaps Lovecraft's most important single contribution was the adoption of science-fictional material to the purpose of supernatural terror. The decline of at least naive belief in Christian theology, resulting in an immense loss of prestige for Satan and his hosts, left the emotion of supernatural fear swinging around loose, without any well-recognized object. Lovecraft took up this loose end and tied it to the unknown but possible denizens of other planets and regions beyond the space-time continuum.

In 1926, Lovecraft composed a novella (38,000 words) titled "The Dream-Quest of Unknown Kadath." In tone and atmosphere, this is like Lovecraft's early Dunsanian fantasies, albeit it also brings in the Cthulhuvian Ancient Ones.

The story follows Lovecraft's protagonist Randolph Carter on a journey through the world of dreams, looking for a wonderful city he has glimpsed. He adventures among the zoogs, ghasts, ghouls, night-gaunts, and other sinister dwellers in dreamland. Night-gaunts are lean, rubbery, faceless flying creatures, which had haunted Lovecraft's childhood nightmares. At last Carter confronts one of the most fell of the Ancient Ones, Nyarlathotep. He falls back into the waking world and finds that his marvelous city is his own Boston.

Some do not like this eerie dream-narrative, which was not published until after Lovecraft's death. He himself spoke of it as "pallid, second-hand Dunsanianism"[41] and meant to rewrite it. Despite its lack of plot and characterization, however, I find that I am still carried along by the author's sheer power of invention. It is a remarkable feat of sustained imagination and Lovecraft's strongest claim as a writer of heroic fantasy. Strangely, Lovecraft so dreaded the ordeal of typing the story that he never did type it. It remained in longhand in his files and was finally published in 1943.

Resettled in Providence, the middle-aging Lovecraft took up his ghost writing, his weird tales, and his voluminous letters again—but with differences. While alone in Brooklyn, he had enjoyed a sightseeing trip to Washington. During his last decade, he became an avid tourist and traveled more or less yearly. His goals were the remains of colonial architecture, of which he became a connoisseur, and historical sites. He also visited friends and correspondents.

He usually set out by bus in spring. When he headed south, he stopped in New York to see "the gang." While he never really liked New York, he no longer much minded the place if he did not have to remain there. In fact, he had a nostalgic memory of the good times he had enjoyed there while married.

From 1929 to 1935, he made three long trips through Virginia and the Carolinas to Florida. On the first journey, he visited another fantasy writer, the Rev. Henry S. Whitehead; on the second and third, his young admirer Robert H. Barlow. In 1932, he went through Tennessee and Mississippi to New Orleans. There he foregathered with Edgar Hoffmann Price, who wrote oriental weird tales; they talked around the clock.

In 1930, he joined a ten-dollar rail excursion to Quebec, the first of three trips he took to that city. He returned delighted with what he had seen, despite the hard things he had said about the French Canadians, whom he considered one of the "foreign hordes" polluting the soil of New England. After Quebec, he admitted that "the French are not bad," and the decline of his xenophobia may be dated from this visit.

At this time, when he was more active than ever, he felt more isolated. In 1931 he wrote:

> I did, surely enough, break away from belated juvenility enough to travel around independently so far as waning finances allowed; & to meet different people in person where previously I had conversed only through correspondence—but this long-deferred semi-introduction to the world did not "take" as thoroughly as it might have done had I been chronologically younger. The era of expansion & late-dawn was a relatively brief one, & it was followed by a sort of slow drift back to the hermit pattern of my early days. Vistas faded & contracted, & the glitter of adventurous expectancy receded farther & farther—till at length I saw the wider horizons fall off one by one. Before I knew it, I was virtually back in my shell.[42]

In fact, he never did "drift back into his shell." But his expectations widened, so that a life that was more gregarious than ever seemed irksomely restricted. In his late years, he was no more a recluse than are most writers who live neither in New York City nor in arty places like Taos and Carmel.

According to some of his friends of that time and some of his letters, he had given up brooding over his "uselessness." As middle-aged men often do, he had come to terms with himself. Knowing what he could and could not do, he settled down to make the best of his talents and limitations:

> It being settled that I'm a little man instead of a big man, I'd a damn sight prefer to let it go frankly at that—& try to be a good little man in my narrow, limited, miniature fashion—than to cover up and pretend to be a bigger man than I am.

Other letters of the time, however, show deepening depression and discouragement. He lamented his inability to achieve long-cherished desires like a trip to Europe or even to make a decent living. He mourned his lack of accomplishment and called himself a failure and a has-been. He repeatedly predicted his own suicide when his money gave out:

> . . . there are few total losses & never-was's which discourage &
> exasperate me more than the venerable Éch-Pi-El. I know of few
> persons whose attainments fall more consistently short of their
> aspirations, or who in general have less to live for. Every aptitude
> which I wish I had, I lack. Everything which I wish I could
> formulate & express, I have failed to formulate & express. Every-
> thing which I value, I have either lost or am likely to lose. Within
> a decade, unless I can find some job paying at least $10.00 per
> week, I shall have to take the cyanide route through inability to
> keep around me the books, pictures, furniture, & other familiar
> objects which constitute my sole remaining reason for keeping
> alive.

It does not follow that Lovecraft felt so despondent all the
time. He doubtless had his ups and downs like others. Still, the
general impression of these late letters is of steadily waxing
dejection and melancholy.

Some of his remarks imply that he realized, too late, that his
plight was largely of his own making. Ever since adolescence,
he had posed as a gentleman amateur who could not be bothered with vulgar commercial matters. Professionalism he
viewed as "tradesmanlike," to him a term of contempt. True
art, he averred, could only be produced by one who thought
nothing of monetary returns. When some of his friends became established as pulp-fiction writers, he deplored their
modest commercial success. He accused them of "charlatanry"
and of becoming "cheap magazine hacks." "And to think they
were once lit'ry guys!" he mourned.[43]

Evidently, Lovecraft shared a common illusion with one of
his severest critics, Edmund Wilson. This is that a critic can
pick, from the works that contemporary men create or perform
for the entertainment of their fellows, those that deserve to be
called "true art" or "great art." Actually, if such a work is done
with minimal competence, to pronounce it "great art" merely
expresses the critic's subjective emotional reaction. It means no
more than saying: "I like it," or "It gives me a thrill." People

have hailed as "true art" such unlikely subjects as subway graffiti, free verse by third graders, and the finger paintings of a captive orang-utan.

As far as we can fix an objective meaning to the term "great art," it means a work enjoyed not only when it was made but long after the death of its maker. Hence we speak of the works of Homer and Shakespeare, Praxiteles and Velazquez, Shelley and Brahms, as "great art," simply because they have outlasted, in public favor, the works of these artists' contemporaries. But we cannot realistically predict the fate of a contemporary work a hundred or a thousand years from now. Even the most durable artists have ups and downs. Shakespeare underwent an eclipse in the late seventeenth century, and a survey at that time would have excluded him from the ranks of great artists.

So picking the "true art" out of contemporary works of entertainment is an exercise in futility. The artist may as well do the best he can for those who like his work well enough to pay for it and leave to posterity the question of whether he has created true art.

Lovecraft had a perfect right to pursue this quixotic course; but one who tries to play Don Quixote in real life is liable to be knocked arsy-varsy by a windmill. Lovecraft's tragedy—and it *was* a tragedy to any but the most insensitive—was that he was unwilling (or, to put it more charitably, was unable) to face the facts of life until it was too late to do much good.

By the early 1930s, Lovecraft's xenophobia had been blunted by his friendship with gifted Jews like Robert Bloch and Henry Kuttner. During his last two or three years, it disappeared almost completely. While he never quite escaped from the Aryan myth, his former animosity toward non-Anglo-Saxons virtually vanished. Those who knew him only during that period have found it hard to believe that his earlier feelings towards outgroupers could have been so virulent as his letters and his wife's recollections imply. Conversely, some who have read these letters and reminiscences have found it hard to believe that he ever so completely changed his former attitudes. Such, however, seems to have been the case.

Lovecraft was influenced by *The Science of Life,* by H. G. Wells, Julian Huxley, and G. P. Wells, which briefly but firmly debunked the Nordic-Aryan cult. Lovecraft read the book in 1935 and found it "the most important book I have read in years."[44]

Likewise, his ultra-conservative political views shifted leftward as a result of the Great Depression and of reading such works as the iconoclastic Emanuel Haldeman-Julius and Sinclair Lewis's anti-Fascist novel *It Can't Happen Here.* He had become disillusioned with the upper class by knowing his surviving aunt's business-class friends, whom he found dull, stuffy, and unintellectual. His former approval of Fascism vanished in the face of "the crazy scientific fallacies such as one sees in Nazi Germany and Soviet Russia." He ended by approving Roosevelt's New Deal and preaching a gradualist, non-Marxist Socialism.

Another factor in Lovecraft's late change of front was a firsthand account of life in Hitler's Germany. The ground floor of his last residence was occupied by a high-school teacher of German, Alice Rachel Sheppard. Knowing and loving Germany from many sojourns there, Miss Sheppard intended, when she retired, to go to Germany to live for several years. She duly moved to Munich but was soon back in Providence, where the kindly Lovecraft was appalled by her eyewitness accounts of Nazi persecution of the Jews and horrified to learn how the racist ideals he had so long harbored worked out in practice.[45]

He also shed most of his eighteenth-century literary affectations. Hence his late poetry, notably the sonnet cycle *Fungi from Yuggoth,* is at least readable if not up to the best work of Clark Ashton Smith and Robert E. Howard.

In 1932 Lovecraft's senior aunt, Mrs. Clark, died. He and Mrs. Gamwell moved into a smaller house of Colonial design at 66 College Street, behind the John Hay Library of Brown University. They rented a five-room upstairs apartment in this house, built in 1825 by Samuel B. Mumford. Lovecraft was overjoyed to be able, at long last, to dwell in a house of genuinely Colonial type. To make room for collegiate expansion, this building has since been moved to 65 Prospect Street, a little over two blocks away.

During Lovecraft's last decade, a Lovecraft-*Weird Tales* circle took form. Lovecraft was the central figure by virtue of his tireless letter-writing and of the respect in which the others— most of whom never met him—held him. Around him orbited Robert E. Howard, Clark Ashton Smith, Frank Belknap Long, and E. Hoffmann Price. Younger members included Catherine L. Moore, Henry Kuttner, August Derleth, Robert Bloch, and (in Lovecraft's last year) Fritz Leiber.

Lovecraft had nicknames for all, as he did for most correspondents. Sometimes he Latinized their names, so that Long was "Belknapius." Clark Ashton Smith became "Klarkash-Ton," converting his solidly Anglo-Saxon name into something from forbidden dimensions; in "The Whisperer in Darkness," Lovecraft mentions "the Atlantean high-priest Klarkash-Ton." Howard was "Two-Gun Bob"; Price, "Malik Taus" or "the Peacock Sultan"; Derleth, "Comte d'Erlette."

Lovecraft headed his letters with phrases like "Caverns of Yuggoth, Night of the Black Moon" and "Sealed Tower of Pnoth—Hour of the Brazen Gong." He often signed them with an archaic "Yr. most obt. Servt., HPLovecraft"; or again as "Grandpa Theobald." He liked to affect a vast age and began letters to his aunts with "My darling daughter" or "granddaughter."

Among Lovecraft's late stories, the longest was "The Case of Charles Dexter Ward" (1927). At 48,000 words, this was at the minimum length for book publication. Laid in Providence, this fantasy is saturated with local color and history. It tells of the magical revival of persons long dead and the sorcerous evocation of beings from Outside. If successful, these activities may have dire, worldwide effects. It is an effective tale, although more loosely and less logically plotted than some of Lovecraft's.

As with "The Dream-Quest of Unknown Kadath," however, Lovecraft found himself daunted by the task of typing. Hence the story slumbered in his files until after his death. During his last years, he submitted collections of his shorter stories to several book publishers. These replied that they would not publish such a collection, since such a book by a comparatively obscure author is very likely to lose money. They would, however, like to see a novel from Lovecraft. He had "The Case of Charles Dexter Ward" in his files all the time but did nothing whatever about it.

Lovecraft had no high opinion of the Cthulhu Mythos stories, despite their posthumous popularity. In 1931 he wrote of his work:

> It is excessively extravagant and melodramatic, and lacks depth and subtlety. My style is bad, too—full of obvious rhetorical devices and hackneyed word and rhythm patterns. It comes a long way from the stark, objective simplicity which is my goal.

He sometimes burlesqued his own style. In 1934, he wrote that he could not write realistic fiction because he did not know enough about real people, and

> . . . the spark of creation and instinctive dramatic arrangement simply isn't there . . . the only "heroes" I can write about are *phenomena.* The cosmos is such a closely-locked round of fatality —with everything prearranged—that nothing impresses me as *really dramatic* except some sudden & abnormal *violation of that relentless inevitability* . . . something which cannot exist, but which can be imagined as existing. . . . Naturally one would rather be a broad artist with power to evoke beauty from every phase of experience—but when one unmistakably *isn't* such an artist, there's no sense in bluffing & faking & pretending that one *is.*[46]

In 1931, Lovecraft composed a 37,000-word novella: "At the Mountains of Madness." An Antarctic expedition from

Miskatonic University comes upon the colossal city of a race of the Ancient Ones, who resembled giant winged sea cucumbers standing on end. After many of the expedition perish, the narrator and one other survivor discover reliefs that give a history of the creatures. Coming from a distant star in the Mesozoic, they built the city with the help of gigantic ameboid servants called "shoggoths" in the *Necronomicon*. They died; but not all the shoggoths perished. . . .

Wright rejected it; he wanted short stories, while Lovecraft more and more found greater lengths more congenial. Three years later, Lovecraft wrote "The Shadow Out of Time" (27,000 words), but he was too discouraged even to try it on Wright.

Lovecraft would not bother with the other science-fiction magazines, deeming them suitable only for mass-production hacks, whereas he wished to be considered a serious artist. Nevertheless, at the end of 1935, Julius Schwartz persuaded Lovecraft to let him try to sell "At the Mountains of Madness" as Lovecraft's literary agent. Soon Schwartz sold the tale to *Astounding Stories*. At about the same time, Donald Wandrei obtained the manuscript of "The Shadow Out of Time," which Barlow had typed. Wandrei sold this story, too, to *Astounding*. Lovecraft got $595 for the two sales. This was the most he had ever received for his writings in so short a time.

In his late years, Lovecraft began to achieve recognition among connoisseurs of weird fiction outside the readers of *Weird Tales*. Several of his stories were reprinted in anthologies and mentioned in lists of "best short stories of the year," and he carried on inconclusive correspondence with several book publishers. Clifton Fadiman, then an editor for Simon & Schuster, asked him for a book-length novel; Lovecraft declined but offered a collection of shorter stories, which the publisher did not want.

The early 1930s saw the first appearance of organized science-fiction fandom. The early clubs and their publications were ephemeral; but, as fast as one died, another sprang up.

Lovecraft had a key rôle in this movement because several fanzine publishers belonged to his circle. Several were also fellow amateur journalists or were recruited into amateur journalism by Lovecraft. Their amateur journals specialized in stories of and articles about imaginative fiction and were thus pioneer science-fiction fan magazines. Publications by members of the Lovecraft circle included Barlow's *Dragon-Fly* and *Leaves,* Charles D. Hornig's *The Fantasy Fan,* and Donald A. Wollheim's *The Phantagraph.*

Lovecraft died just too soon to witness the growth of science-fiction fandom, to which he had acted as a kind of midwife, into a major socio-literary movement. The first World Science Fiction Convention was held in New York in July 1939, a little over two years after his demise.

Lovecraft took little care for his health, rarely seeing the physician or the dentist and expressing scorn for those who fussed about such things. In 1936, his health rapidly declined, and it transpired—much too late to do anything about it—that he was suffering from intestinal cancer. In March 1937, he entered a hospital. There, on March 15th, he died, aged forty-six.

Lovecraft's surviving aunt, Mrs. Edward F. Gamwell (with whom Lovecraft had lived from 1933) survived her nephew by four years. August Derleth, living in Sauk City, Wisconsin, obtained publishing rights to the greater part of Lovecraft's work. A prolific and versatile regional writer, Derleth devoted much of his subsequent life (1909–1971) to the promotion and publication of Lovecraft's work. With Donald Wandrei, he formed the company of Arkham House for this purpose.

The first collection of Lovecraft's stories, *The Outsider and Others,* appeared in 1939 at $5.00, with a pre-publication price of $3.50, for a book containing over 300,000 words. Four years later a second huge volume, *Beyond the Wall of Sleep,* came out. The two books sold slowly and at last went out of print. Then interest in Lovecraft arose, and so did the rare-book prices of these volumes. The last I heard, they were fetching $200.00 apiece.

Derleth continued publishing Lovecraftiana as well as collections of stories by other weirdists. Many paperbacked reprints of Lovecraft's stories have appeared, and in the 1960s and 70s he became one of the best-selling fantasy authors. Several of his stories have been made into motion pictures and television shows. As with many artists, notably Poe, Lovecraft achieved success, but posthumously.

Posthumous success is always sad. Dying in poverty and obscurity, Lovecraft became a best-seller thirty-odd years later. He used to console himself for his apparent failure by saying that the "vulgar herd" or "ignorant rabble" could not appreciate "real art" anyway. It turned out that enough of the rabble did like his writing, when properly presented, to have supported him in comfort. It is all very well to talk of "art for art's sake" and "making one's life a work of art," but almost anyone would prefer that such worldly success as he achieves take place while he is alive to enjoy it.

From the professional writer's point of view, Lovecraft's story is a horrible example of how not to do it. All that a writer could do to ruin his own prospects, Lovecraft did. He went about his literary affairs in a deliberately amateurish, unworldly way. He affected an aristocratic anti-commercialism, spent extravagant amounts of time on letters and amateur journalism, and ignored such things as word rates, subsidiary rights, and alternative outlets for his writings.

But then, Lovecraft did not consider himself a professional writer. He thought of himself as a ghost writer and "reviser," who wrote stories in his off time, for his own gentlemanly satisfaction. While he reconciled himself to accepting badly-needed money for his stories, he remained unwilling to let editors tamper with them or actively to push their sale.

It were meaningless to argue about what Lovecraft "ought" to have done. He did what he chose to do, and the results were what they were. Others may draw such lessons as they wish from his tale.

Lovecraft wrote sixty-two professionally published stories, totaling somewhat over half a million words. Considering that he worked hard all the while at his ghost writing, this is a modest but respectable output for a part-time writer. His Dunsanian tales, especially "The Dream-Quest of Unknown Kadath," are a lasting addition to the genre of fantasy. His writings were a mainstay of *Weird Tales* in its great days of the late twenties and early thirties, and the magazine furnished an outlet for writers of heroic fantasy when no other steady American market existed.

As he himself admitted and even exaggerated, Lovecraft suffered from literary faults. Too many of his tales read at once tire the reader by repetition of atmospheric tricks and the sameness of many plots. The stories are overloaded with adjectival rhetoric; one does not shudder because one has been repeatedly told that something is "horrible" or "blasphemous." Critics have had particular fun with his favorite adjective "eldritch."

On the other hand, Lovecraft had a powerful imagination, turned out much good, solid entertainment, and exercised wide influence. In the small puddle of weird fantasy, he was a big frog indeed. If some idolaters have over-praised him, some detractors have unjustly derogated him.

Whether Lovecraft was a "genius" is a matter of definition. Whatever his model Poe had, Lovecraft had a goodly share of the same stuff. If his best was not up to Poe's best, he never wrote anything for publication so awful as some of Poe's labored, dismal attempts at humor or his windy, meaningless "Eureka." Lovecraft was certainly neurotic, but he was never crazy—as Poe finally became—and he kept learning all his life. And to what better use can a man put his mind?

V

SUPERMAN IN A BOWLER:
E. R. EDDISON

Blood rains
From the cloudy web
On the broad loom
Of slaughter.
The web of man,
Grey as armour,
Is now being woven;
The Valkyries
Will cross it
With a crimson weft.[1]

NJAL'S SAGA

In 1922, a great heroic fantasy, *The Worm Ouroboros,* was published in a small collector's edition by R. & R. Clark of Edinburgh. When it made no splash, a cheaper edition was issued in 1924 by Jonathan Cape, Ltd., of London. This likewise had little impact, but two years later it begat an American edition by E. P. Dutton & Co., with an introduction by James Stephens, author of the immortal *Crock of Gold.*

For the next quarter-century, *The Worm Ouroboros* remained the private enthusiasm of a small circle of connoisseurs, including James Branch Cabell. When I was a fledgling writer, Fletcher Pratt introduced me to *The Worm.* This extraordinary novel failed, on first publication, to make a bigger impression because it belonged to a genre that never became popular until the 1960s, when Tolkien and Howard became best-sellers in paperback. The first printing of *The Worm* was forty-odd years ahead of its time.

The Worm Ouroboros begins with an "Induction":

> There was a man named Lessingham dwelt in an old low house in Wastdale, set in a gray old garden where yew-trees flourished that had seen Vikings in Copeland in their seedling time. Lily and rose and larkspur bloomed in the borders, and begonias with blossoms big as saucers, red and white and pink and lemon-colour, in the beds before the porch. . . .[2]

We meet Lessingham smoking his after-dinner cigar. He speaks to his wife, goes to bed, and dreams—or is it a dream? —that he flies in a chariot drawn by a hippogriff to the planet Mercury.

This Mercury is nothing like the astronomers'. Instead, it is a version of our own earth, with oceans, continents, moon, and tides. It is occupied by humanoid nations called Demons, Goblins, Witches, Imps, and Ghouls. But (save that the Demons have small horns growing from their skulls) these folk have nothing to do with the supernatural beings denoted by those names in earthly folklore. They are more like barbarian tribes of the post-Roman folk-wandering.

Lessingham alights in Demonland and becomes a passive spectator. He sees the four premier lords of Demonland: the brothers Juss, Spitfire, and Goldry Bluszco and their cousin Brandoch Daha. The author soon drops Lessingham, and we see him no more.

The rest of the book recounts a tremendous war between the Demons and the Witches, the latter under their redoubtable sorcerer-king Gorice XII. The atmosphere is like that of Europe in the Viking Age, with touches of the Renaissance. But everything is more splendid than in any earthly milieu. Characters talk Elizabethan English; they quote Shakespeare, Webster, and other writers of the sixteenth and seventeenth centuries as well as from the ancient Greek.

King Gorice, whose predecessor has been slain in a wrestling match by Goldry Bluszco, captures Goldry. He then ravages Demonland while the other three Demon lords are trying to rescue their comrade. To do this, they must climb the dizzy height of Koshtra Pivrarcha, which they do in a passage to make any acrophobe's viscera turn over. Then they must find and hatch a hippogriff's egg. Juss must fly on the hippogriff to the top of the mountain Zora Rach, where Goldry lies insensible.

After great adventures, battles, and encounters with foes both natural and supernatural, the Demons finally corner Gorice in his castle. Gorice perishes in a last attempt to use his sorcery. His henchmen likewise die, treacherously poisoned by one of their own number.

There is good reason to class this story—nearly 200,000 words long—as the greatest single novel of heroic fantasy. It is told in a marvelous, rolling, blazingly colorful, archaized English, reminiscent of William Morris but more skillfully done.

As more than one critic has said, however, the work is a "flawed masterpiece." If the beginning, with its clumsy device of Lessingham and his hippogriff-chariot, is unsatisfactory, the ending is equally so. When the Witches have been beaten, Juss and his fellows find peace an intolerable bore. So, in answer to Juss's prayer, the gods allow him to turn back time to the beginning and fight the same war over and over again *ad infinitum*. The thought of many readers at this point is: What a fate!

Evidently, the Demon lords—the Good Guys of this novel—fight more for the fun of whacking off arms, legs, and heads than for any humanly rational objective. As for the countless casualties of this ever-recurrent war, nobody gives them a thought.

To Eddison, apparently, war was a romantic adventure. This view was widespread in Western culture in Eddison's generation. People born before 1900 still visualized war as fought with bands and banners, and cavalry charging with sword and lance. Not until realistic accounts of the grim butchery of the Kaiserian War became current in the 1920s was there a reaction against this attitude.

The four Demon lords are not much developed as characters, save that Brandoch Daha has (if I may mix my allusions) a touch of Celtic *chutzpah*. On the other hand, the lords of Witchland are a fine, well-drawn set of mighty, indomitable, fearless scoundrels. So is Lord Gro of Goblinland, the intellectual *manqué,* whose weakness for lost causes makes him a perennial traitor to whichever side he espouses when that side begins to win.

The author of this work was one of the unlikeliest swashbucklers ever. In 1922, Eric Rücker Eddison (1882–1945) was a 39-year-old British civil servant, born in Yorkshire, who had served in the Board of Trade since 1906. A slender man standing five feet ten, he had light-brown hair, blue-gray eyes, and a fresh complection.

Eddison seems to have been the perfect bureaucrat. So distinguished was his work that in 1924 he was made a Knight Commander of the Order of St. Michael and St. George, and in 1929 a Companion of the Order of the Bath. He never became officially "Sir Eric," because he retired before the head of his department did. During his last years of public service, 1930–37, Eddison was Deputy Comptroller-General of Overseas Trade. If he had waited until the Comptroller-General retired, and he had succeeded to the post, he would have had the title; but he wanted to get on with his writing more than he wanted the honor.

Like every right-thinking British civil servant and businessman, Eddison went to work every day with bowler hat and furled umbrella. Daily he walked across Kensington Gardens and Hyde Park and lunched at his club, the Athenaeum.

Outside of his vocation, however, Eddison had long shown literary leanings. He began writing stories at the age of ten. In one of these appears a character named Horius Parry, destined to greatness in his later novels. Like William Morris an enthusiast for the Northern Thing, Eddison began while still a schoolboy to study Icelandic in order to read the sagas in the original. At Oxford he became devoted to Homer and Sappho. Besides Icelandic, he was at home in Greek, Latin, and French.

In 1909 he married Winifred Grace Henderson, with whom he lived happily until death them did part. They had one daughter, Jean.

An animal-lover and wild-life enthusiast, for years he took his daughter to the London Zoo every Sunday. He was a mountaineer, taking his family on walking tours every summer in the Lake District of England, in Scotland, Switzerland, Norway, Austria, Italy, France, and Germany. In 1926, he took them in a cargo ship to Iceland, then much more isolated than now. In Iceland he grew a Vikingesque full beard. When he returned to England, he removed the beard but kept the mustache thenceforth.

A genial man, occasionally ruffled by short-lived bursts of temper, he possessed a sharp but quiet sense of humor and a fondness for spirited but good-natured argument. His many friends included the noted British fantasist C. S. Lewis. He also knew Lewis's close friend Charles Williams.

A man of wide interests, Eddison loved music, ballet, and the theater. Like his super-hero Lessingham, he was a connoisseur of art as far as he could afford it; his collection included paintings by Matisse and Augustus John. He loved buying jewelry for his wife and daughter and collected cameo signet rings.

He also harbored prejudices of no small magnitude. One of the strongest was against short hair for women. He called such women "hermaphrodites" and forbade his wife to cut hers. He also despised the internal-combustion engine and, like Morris, admired handicraftsmanship.

His political inclinations were Tory, believing in the need for an aristocracy. He talked of the ideal government as a benevolent dictatorship. More realistically, he admitted that no such regime could be realized "except in heaven." An unabashed romantic, he said that he ought to have been born into the days of Elizabeth I, or else in Homeric Greece, much as Lovecraft wished to be an eighteenth-century English gentleman and Howard an American frontiersman.

In 1916, Eddison had privately printed a small book called *Poems, Letters, and Memories of Philip Sidney Nairn.* Following *The Worm Ouroboros,* he issued two more books. The first was a historical novel of the Viking Age, *Styrbiorn the Strong* (1926). After that came his translation of *Egil's Saga* (1930).

It is interesting to compare these two works. *Styrbiorn the Strong* is an excellent historical novel. Based on a few brief allusions in Snorri's *Heimskringla* (a history of Norway to 1176), it follows the adventures of its mighty and valiant hero and his pet musk ox in the Scandinavian kingdoms and among the Jomsvikings of the Baltic, whose headquarters were on an island off the coast of Pomerania.

Egil's Saga is one of a large body of similar writings, made in Iceland in the twelfth and thirteenth centuries. They tell the stories of eminent Icelanders who lived in the tenth and eleventh centuries. They have had many English-speaking admirers and translators; William Morris started publication of a whole saga library.

Sagas are similar to the epics of other burgeoning civilizations but are in prose, although the Icelanders had plenty of poetry and the sagas often include bits of verse. They can best be compared to modern historical novels. They supposedly tell of real people and events but are also full of fictional speeches and other details that could not have been preserved.

Nearly forty sagas have come down, in varying degrees of completeness. The biggest, such as *Egil's Saga* and *Njal's Saga,* are as long as modern novels; the latter comes to about 110,000 words in translation. They deal largely with murders, vengeance, and feuds among Icelandic landowning families. The supernatural plays little part, but the authors paid close attention to human character. The atmosphere is one of grim, somber realism, and the life portrayed is one of dreary monotony and endless petty squabbling.

While *Styrbiorn the Strong* is highly readable, a modern reader may bog down in *Egil's Saga* or in many of the other sagas. After the umpteenth episode in which an Icelandic woman nags a male kinsman or a servant into going out to ambush a member of a rival clan, in revenge for a previous killing, the reader may decide that enough is enough.

Near the end of his public service, Eddison returned to heroic fantasy with *Mistress of Mistresses, a Vision of Zimiamvia* (1935). Zimiamvia is briefly mentioned in *The Worm Ouroboros*. Preparing to climb Koshtra Pivrarcha, Lord Juss remarks: "That gap hight the Gates of Zimiamvia." When he has climbed the mountain, he tells Brandoch Daha:

> "Thou and I, first of the children of men, now behold with living eyes the fabled land of Zimiamvia. Is it true, thinkest thou, which philosophers tell us of that fortunate land: that no mortal foot may tread it, but the blessed souls do inhabit it of the dead that be departed, even they that were great upon earth and did great deeds when they were living, that scorned not earth and the delights and the glories thereof, and yet did justly and were not dastards nor yet oppressors?"

Zimiamvia is mentioned once again in *The Worm,* without details save for its "plains and winding waters and hills and uplands and enchanted woods."[3]

Mistress of Mistresses begins with an "Overture," in the form of a monologue by a younger (but still elderly) friend of Edward Lessingham, whom we met at the beginning of *The*

Worm Ouroboros. The date is about 1973—our recent past, but several decades in the author's future.

Lessingham, ninety years old but marvelously well-preserved, has just died in his castle in the Lofoten Islands, off the northern coast of Norway. (Eddison got the setting from a trip thither in 1937.) He had built up a little private kingdom there, with its own army. Determined to assert its sovereignty, the Norwegian government had just sent him an ultimatum. Lessingham was prepared forcefully to resist the introduction of modernity into his preserve. While these matters were cooking, he quietly died, seated on a bench with his latest mistress.

As the unnamed narrator muses, we learn more about Lessingham, and still more in later books of the series. He is the sword-and-sorcery hero *par excellence,* making most of the heroes of the genre look like oafs and simpletons. He is the man of the Renaissance squared. Like Lovecraft's Randolph Carter and Howard's Conan, he is (we may suppose) an idealization of his creator—the man the author would like to have been.

Six and a half feet tall, with a great black beard, Lessingham combines the qualities of Harald Hardraade, Leonardo da Vinci, and James Bond all in one. A rich, well-born English country gentleman, he is a great soldier, administrator, scholar, sportsman, painter, sculptor, writer, poet, and lover all at once. He rides to the hounds, climbs mountains, and collects art treasures. He beat the Germans in East Africa in the Kaiserian War; he overthrew Bela Kun's Communist rule in Hungary after that war; he once made himself dictator of Paraguay. He has written the definitive biography, in ten volumes, of his ancestor, the Emperor Frederick II.

Nobody has ever approached such omnicompetence in the real world, although a few, like Richard F. Burton, Theodore Roosevelt, and Lord Dunsany have done pretty well. When Eddison set himself to imagine a supermannish *alter ego,* there was nothing petty about his phantasm.

This gargantuan character has studied at Eton, Oxford, and Heidelberg. He has served in the French Foreign Legion. At twenty-five, he marries the beautiful and brilliant Lady Mary Scarnside, daughter of Lord Anmering. Lessingham's marriage is ecstatically happy; a friend tells Mary: "You and Edward are the only married people I've ever known who always seem as if you weren't married at all, but were carrying on some clandestine affair that nobody was supposed to have wind of but yourselves."[4]

After fifteen blissful years, Mary and their only child, a daughter, are killed in a train wreck. Mary had been Lessingham's favorite model for painting; now he destroys all his portraits of her but one. He burns down his stately home, with all its heirlooms and art treasures. He likewise leaves orders with his narrator-friend to burn the Norwegian castle, with its Ming vases, its rugs from Samarkand, and his last portrait of Mary. (A selfish fellow indeed, one thinks, to deprive the world of pleasant things in order to indulge his own solipsistic *hybris*.)

Recovering from his beloved wife's death, Lessingham goes back to his arts, his mistresses, and his adventuring. The reader of *Mistress of Mistresses,* however, drops this Lessingham at the end of the "Overture" and enters another world: Zimiamvia.

This place is described in *The Worm Ouroboros* as a kind of heaven or Valhalla for the souls of dead heroes from the Eddisonian Mercury. The milieu presented in *Mistress of Mistresses* is, however, quite different. Its folk are as mortal as any other, and they include a goodly quota of "dastards and oppressors."

Like Eddison's Mercury, this is a pre-gunpowder, pre-industrial world, but European Renaissance rather than Viking Age. It is like the world of Richard III and Henry VIII of England, Louis XI and François I of France, Emperor Charles V, Niccolò Machiavelli, and Cesare Borgia.

The scene is a group of lands, cut up by mountain chains and arms of the sea: Fingiswold in the North, Meszria in the South, and Rerek in between. Mezentius, king of these three lands, has recently died.

The original Mezentius was a legendary Etruscan king, supposed to have been slain by Aeneas. All the characters have names of similarly eclectic origins, somewhat as Howard later called his people "Demetrio" and "Yasmini."

The common speech of Zimiamvia, we learn, is English of a Shakespearean sort. The characters, however, drop into French, Italian, Latin, or Greek. They often quote from earthly Classical and Renaissance literature.

King Mezentius has left two legitimate children by his late Queen Rosma: a son, Styllis, who has become an arrogant youth; and a daughter, Antiope. By his mistress Amalie, Duchess of Memison, Mezentius has a bastard son, Barganax, Duke of Zayana. Mezentius' vicar in Rerek is the mighty, bull-necked, red-bearded Horius Parry. This man represents the powerful Parry family, noted for vitality, ability, brutality, and unscrupulous perfidy.

Horius Parry has a cousin and ally named Lessingham. To distinguish this Lessingham from the earthly Edward Lessingham—he of the Norwegian castle—I shall call the mundane one Lessingham[1] and the Zimiamvian one Lessingham[2].

Lessingham[2] looks much like Lessingham[1] but is more purely a soldier and politician. He has much in common with Duke Barganax, as if both partook of the qualities of Lessingham[1]. But whereas Lessingham[2] got more than his share of Lessingham[1]'s military virtues, Barganax received the larger portion of his artistic qualities. Barganax is an artist, esthete, and hedonist, albeit he can also buckle a swash or lead a charge when the occasion demands. Although on opposite sides of the conflict, he and Lessingham[2] are drawn to each other.

Barganax has a secretary and ex-tutor, Doctor Vandermast, a wizard who wears a long white beard and quotes Spinoza. In Vandermast's service are two nymphs: Campaspe, who turns herself into a water rat, and Anthea, who now and then becomes a lynx.

The story deals with the efforts of Horius Parry to enlarge his power, and of Barganax and other supporters of the late king to thwart him. Parry has King Styllis poisoned, whereupon Antiope succeeds him. Lessingham[2] loves Antiope.

Himself honorable, Lessingham[2] sticks to his cousin Parry, although he knows what a scoundrel the latter is. He says that he does this because he enjoys the danger and because he deems Parry "a dangerous horse: say I taste a pleasure in such riding."[5]

Parry insults Lessingham[2], threatens him with death, and otherwise abuses him. But not even when Lessingham[2] learns that Parry has been plotting with the vile King Derxis of Akkama does he finally break with Parry, although Derxis has murdered Lessingham[2]'s sweetheart Antiope. At last Parry has Lessingham[2], too, murdered, albeit it appears that he will be avenged by Barganax. For a man to whom such remarkable gifts are attributed, Lessingham[2] seems to have been a bit stupid in judgments of character.

It is a splendid story, quite different from *The Worm Ouroboros* but almost on a level with it. The reader, however, is liable to confusion among the many characters and the labyrinthine plots and intrigues. The tale reminds me of a remark by an Italian character in one of John Dickson Carr's detective stories: "Italian history, she's-a hot stuff. Everybody stab everybody!" There is no essential connection between this story and *The Worm Ouroboros,* save that they have different characters bearing the common name of Lessingham.

In 1937, Eddison, now fifty-four, retired from his bureaucratic labors, which during his last three years had included membership in the Council of Arts and Industry. He meant, he said, to devote the rest of his life to literature. Having built a new house at Marlborough, in Wiltshire west of London, he lived there quietly with his wife and married daughter until his death in 1945, at sixty-two. His son-in-law was killed, as a member of the Royal Air Force, in the Hitlerian War.

The first fruit of this period of leisure was another novel, *A Fish Dinner in Memison* (1941). This is a prequel to *Mistress of Mistresses* (that is, a story of which the previous tale is a sequel) with many of the same characters. Besides making clear many things obscure in *Mistress of Mistresses, A Fish Dinner* tells the story of Lessingham[1]. Interspersed with the Zimiamvian sections are passages narrating Lessingham['s] youth, his courtship of Lady Mary Scarnside, their married life, and her death.

The Zimiamvian tale, alternating with the mundane, brings in the Jovian King Mezentius; his mistress Amalie, Duchess of Memison; and their youthful son Barganax. By a lover, before she married the first of her three husbands, Queen Rosma had two children, both of whom she would have done away with had not fate preserved them to be reared by others. The elder, Beroald, is Mezentius' chancellor; the younger is the beautiful Fiorinda.

Beroald makes a political marriage for his sister. When this brother-in-law proves unsatisfactory, Beroald has him murdered and finds her another husband, as Cesare Borgia was always doing with his much-put-upon sister Lucrezia. The second husband, Lord Morville, proves too simple-minded to interest Fiorinda. Bored, she denies him intimacy, although he dotes on her. When poor Morville accuses Fiorinda—prematurely, but not without grounds for suspicion—of an affair with Barganax, the latter disarms him in a fight. The nymph Anthea, in her lynx form, then kills Morville because he had shown the bad judgment of hitting her. Fed up with the married state, Fiorinda refuses to wed Barganax but agrees to be his mistress.

The strength of the Norse influence on Eddison is shown by a passage from this book, wherein Morville first accuses Fiorinda:

"You are his strumpet." As if for the wasting of her heart's blood, Morville whipped out his dagger: then, as she rose up now and faced him, threw it down and stood, his countenance distort. There seemed to be shed suddenly about the lady a chill and a remoteness beside which a statue were companionable human flesh, and the dead marble's stillness kindly and human beside that stillness. He struck her across the mouth with his glove, saying, in that extreme, "Go your gait, then, you salt bitch."

Her face, all save the smouldering trail of that blow turned bloodless white. "This may be your death," she said.

But Morville went from the room like a man drunk, for the galling and blistering of his eyes with broken tears; and so from the house; and so to horse.[6]

In *King Olaf Trygvesson's Saga,* which forms part of Snorri Sturluson's *Heimskringla,* Olaf was a fierce and violent king, even by Viking standards. He Christianized Norway by giving any subject whom he caught the choice between baptism and instant death. In the year 998, Olaf went to visit Queen Sigrid the Haughty, whom he was courting, in Sweden:

. . . and the business seemed likely to be concluded. But when Olaf insisted that Sigrid should let herself be baptized, she answered thus:—"I must not part from the faith which I have held, and my forebears before me; and, on the other hand, I shall make no objection to your believing in the god that pleases you best." Then King Olaf was enraged, and answered in a passion, "Why should I care to have thee, an old faded woman, and a heathen bitch?" and therewith struck her in the face with his glove which he held in his hands, rose, and then they parted. Sigrid said, "This may well be thy death." The king set off to Viken, the queen to Sweden.[7]

It was, too. Sigrid married King Swend of Denmark. Two years later, she persuaded her husband and her kinsman, King Olaf of Sweden, to gang up on Olaf Trygvesson (or Trygvason), who was killed at the naval battle of Svold.

Like Lessingham[2], Mezentius is incomprehensibly drawn to Horius Parry. The king persists in trying to use the scoundrel as an ally and agent, even when he knows of Parry's plots against him.

The fish dinner of the title occupies the last quarter of the book. The diners are Mezentius, Amalie, Barganax, Fiorinda, Horius Parry, and five others. In the course of conversation, Amalie says: "If we were Gods, able to make worlds and unmake 'em as we list, what world would we have?"[8]

Among the various suggestions, Fiorinda proposes a world that works in strict accord with the laws of cause and effect, without magic or supernatural intervention. Mezentius cups his hands, and an opalescent sphere forms between them. While the diners sit for half an hour, talking and admiring the king's creation, the world he has made—ours—goes through its history of billions of years, from the Archaeozoic seas with their amebalike organisms to the present. Fiorinda suggests that she and Mezentius enter that world and lead the lives of a couple of the natives thereof.

And so it transpires: Mezentius is an incarnation of Zeus—God—and Fiorinda of his created mate, Aphrodite. Since a god can incarnate in more than one mortal body at a time, there is some Zeus in Barganax and in Lessingham[2], and of Aphrodite in Amalie and in the king's daughter Antiope. In our own world, Zeus and Aphrodite incarnate themselves in Lessingham[1] and Mary Scarnside. When dinner in Memison is over and all have had their fun, Fiorinda pricks the shimmering sphere with a hairpin, and it vanishes like a soap bubble.

When this God takes on a mortal incarnation, it is no gentle-Jesus-meek-and-mild. It is a swaggering, swashbuckling Renaissance bravo, who would as lief hew the head off an ill-wisher as swat a fly. The latent divinity of Lessingham[1] at least makes his godlike achievements more plausible than they would otherwise be, although it seems a little unfair that the rest of us mortals should have to compete with such a demigod. The Goddess, while irresistible by any male on whom she casts an amative glance, is given to caprice, mischief, and cruelty, as shown by her treatment of Morville.

Although Eddison's idea is tremendous, *A Fish Dinner,* while very interesting to the critic, is much less successful as fiction than the two previous novels. The story drowns in talk. Moreover, as if the relationships among the many characters were not hard enough to keep track of, the frequent shifts between our own world and that of Zimiamvia further confuse the reader.

Eddison's own attitude toward religion was neither a conventional, conservative form of Christianity nor an outspoken disbelief like Lovecraft's. Eddison's Quaker ancestry gave him a leaning towards moderation. His younger brother, with whom he was very close, and his mother were both Christian Scientists, but he never accepted that view. An indefinite pantheism might best describe his religious orientation.

After *A Fish Dinner in Memison,* Eddison began another Zimiamvian novel, *The Mezentian Gate.* A meticulous outliner, he had planned the whole work and had written about two fifths of it—the beginning, the end, and a few chapters in between—when he died.

Eddison evidently did not compose a novel straight through from beginning to end, but rather wrote a piece here and a piece there, like a painter filling in different parts of a picture. The incomplete novel, with "arguments" or synopses of the unwritten chapters, was privately published by Eddison's widow in England in 1958. The work was reprinted, along with the other novels described here, in Ballantine's paperback series. If Eddison had completed the novel, it would have been even longer than *The Worm Ouroboros.* Even in its present fragmentary form, it is impressive.

The story starts with a "Praeludium: Lessingham on the Raftsund." It begins with the nonagenarian Lessingham[1] in his Norwegian castle, talking with his latest mistress, another incarnation of Aphrodite. He speaks of meeting the Norwegian Air Force in the air, to "give them a keepsake to remember me by."[9] Then, as he sits in the low Arctic sun, he dies.

Back we go to the world of Zimiamvia, with its courts, plots, duels, murders, and battles. The story begins before *A Fish Dinner in Memison* and ends after it, inclosing the other novel as in a frame. The events of *A Fish Dinner,* however, are briefly summarized or alluded to obliquely, since they comprise but a small fraction of the tale.

A Prince Aktor from Akkama gets into trouble by a love affair with the neglected young wife, Stateira, of King Mardanus of Fingiswold. As a result, Aktor becomes an accomplice to the king's murder and, in remorse, kills himself. Akkama, a bleak and barbarous northern land, serves mainly as a training ground for villains.

Then we learn of the rise of Mardanus' son Mezentius and of his relations with his queen, the big masculine Rosma, who has already had husbands and children. Mezentius crushes a conspiracy headed by Horius Parry. By sheer force of personality, he compels Parry to come over to his side and help in slaughtering the other conspirators.

In the end, at a banquet, Queen Rosma tries to poison Barganax, the bastard son of her husband. In a series of switches of the poisoned cup reminiscent of those in *Hamlet,* King Mezentius drinks the poison. Foiled, the queen finishes off the draft and dies in her turn.

In its present form, *The Mezentian Gate* suggests the possibility of completion by another hand, as has been done with the unfinished works of other writers. I cannot, however, think of anybody competent for such a task. (I could certainly not do it.) Such a writer should have, not only an exuberant imagination, great technical skill, plenty of time, and a strong drive, but also an old-fashioned Eton-and-Oxford Classical British upper-class education.

Linear-minded persons like myself may wish to read the story through in chronological order of the events, instead of skipping back and forth in time as the author does. This can be approximated by reading in the following order:

1. *The Mezentian Gate,* without the "Praeludium," Books I to VI.
2. *A Fish Dinner in Memison,* Chapters I to VIII, inclusive.
3. *The Worm Ouroboros,* considered a dream of Lessingham[1].
4. The rest of *A Fish Dinner in Memison.*
5. The "Praeludium" to *The Mezentian Gate.*
6. The "Overture" to *Mistress of Mistresses.*
7. The rest of *The Mezentian Gate.*
8. *Mistress of Mistresses,* without the "Overture."

Even this scheme will not straighten things out entirely. Perhaps the reader would do as well to read a whole book at a time in any convenient order.

In judging Eddison's work, one must separate one's literary opinions from those of the author's philosophical and political ideas. Simply as literature, the tetralogy is a monument, although an egregiously imperfect one. *The Worm Ouroboros* is only tenuously connected with the rest. The other three novels are poorly integrated into a whole, and one of them is less than half finished.

Trying to make Eddison's imaginary worlds into a coherent whole merely leaves one more confused than ever. On the theme of worlds-within-worlds, one can see that the world we know is an artifact of the quasi-divine inhabitants of the world of Zimiamvia. Then the world of *The Worm Ouroboros,* being a dream of Lessingham[1] (an incarnation of Mezentius who is an incarnation of Zeus) must be an artifact of this world. But we are told that Zimiamvia is located in the world of *The Worm Ouroboros.* One need not be up on the theory of sets to realize that if A is inside B, and B inside C, C cannot be inside A. Nor is any plausible reason adduced why natives of another world should quote the Elder Edda, Keats, Sappho, and Shakespeare.

As for Eddison's outlook, there are sketches of upper-class English country life, which he evidently knew at first hand, in *A Fish Dinner*. The people express the attitudes of their time and place. Since, at the start of this century, Britain ruled not only the seas but a goodly part of the lands as well, this attitude is firmly ethnocentric. There are allusions to "that unsavoury Jew musician" with whom Lessingham[1] had a fight. Another obnoxious character is a "hulking great rascal, sort of half-nigger."

True, there are signs that the extreme British upper-class social exclusiveness is beginning to break down. Before a dinner party, Mary's father says:

" 'My dear girl, you can't have that dancer woman sit down with us.'

" 'Why not? She's very nice. Perfectly respectable. I think it would be unkind not to. Anybody else would do it.'

" 'It's monstrous, and you're old enough to know better.'

" 'Well, I've asked her, and I've asked him. You can order them both out if you want to make a scene.' "[10]

If Eddison does not share Lord Anmering's prejudice against the Spanish danseuse, he does embrace another conviction of his milieu. Like H. P. Lovecraft, he regarded the English country gentleman as the climax of human evolution, as God's chosen person.

Eddison's characters, especially Lessingham[1], are free with their view of the mass of mankind: "The vast majority of civilized mankind are, politically, a mongrel breed of sheep and monkey: the timidity, the herded idiocy, of the sheep: the cunning, the dissimulation, the ferocity, of the great ape." "Human affairs conducted on the basis of megalopolitan civilization are simply not susceptible of good government. You have two choices: tyranny and mob-rule."[11]

The way to handle the masses is that of Zimiamvia, where the strong, the "great," run things as they should be run and take no back talk:

"And yet," said Melates, "for less matter, himself hath ere this
headed or hanged, in his time, scores of common men."

"The way of the world," Barganax said. "And some will say,
the best way too: better a hundred such should die than one great
man's hand be hampered."

When Lessingham[2] is arguing a treaty with Barganax, he
reminds the Duke of "our greatness." These great men have a
short way with the ungreat who displease them:

Gabriel stood yet in doubt. "Yet, consider, my lord,—"

Lessingham gave him a sudden look. "Unless you mean to be
kicked," he said, "Begone."

And with great swiftness Gabriel went.[12]

When a lieutenant of Lessingham[2] comes to Barganax to try
to make peace between them, the Duke orders his men to pitch
the intruder off the cliff and is barely dissuaded. When a messenger tells Lessingham[2] of Antiope's murder, Lessingham[2] tries
to stab the man to death and just fails to do so. When Doctor
Vandermast warns Lessingham[2] that his recklessness will cause
his early death, Lessingham[2] nearly throttles the old man before
being talked out of it.

In short, Eddison's "great men," even the best of them, are
cruel, arrogant bullies. One may admire, in the abstract, the indomitable courage, energy, and ability of such rampant egotists.
In the concrete, however, they are like the larger carnivora, best
admired with a set of stout bars between them and the viewer.

There is some historical basis for such portrayal of the
"great" of earlier times, who serve as models for Eddison's
characters. Before the rise of bourgeois democracy, some members of ruling classes were much less careful of the feelings of
those below them in the scale than is now considered meet. But
to ask a modern reader to admire the feudal "insolence of office" is the next thing to asking him to admire heretic-burning,
the Roman arena, or cannibalism, all of which have been defended by upright, virtuous men with cogent arguments.

Eddison was not insensible of the worm's eye view:

> When lions, eagles, and she-wolves are let loose among such weak
> sheep as for the most part we be, we rightly, for sake of our
> continuance, attend rather to their claws, maws, and talons than
> stay to contemplate their magnificences. We forget, in our ne-
> cessity lest our flesh become their meat, that they too, ideally and
> *sub specie aeternitatis,* have their places . . . in the hierarchy of
> true values.

Still, we have here essentially the ancient idea of the benevolent despot: let the "strong" or "great" man have his way, and
he will make the right decisions for all of us. This theory was
most recently revived by the European Fascist movements of
the 1920s and 30s. It was even superimposed, by Lenin and
Stalin, on the nominally egalitarian and democratic Communist
movement.

This idea is mere sentimental romanticism. If, under such a
regime, people occasionally get a Marcus Aurelius or a Duke
Federigo of Urbino, they are much more likely to be saddled
with a Caracalla or a Cesare Borgia. While popular rule, for-
sooth, has often bred follies and outrages, these are petty compared to the enormities of despots. Moreover, says Eddison:

> A very unearthly character of Zimiamvia lies in the fact that
> nobody wants to change it. Nobody, that is to say, apart from a
> few weak natures who fail on their probation. . . . Gabriel Flores,
> for instance, has no ambition to be Vicar of Rerek: it satisfies his
> lust for power that he serves a master who commands his dog-
> like devotion.[13]

In other words, wouldn't it be splendid to be a member of
the ruling class (whether called counts, capitalists, or commis-
sars) in a country where the lower orders loyally served and
obeyed their betters, without thought of changing either the
system or their own status?

The nearest that this ideal has come to realization on this
earth is India, with its caste system. The history of India,

technologically stagnant and hence perennially conquered by outsiders, gives little cause for enthusiasm. If all mankind were so minded, we should probably still be cowering in caves.

One should not, of course, assume that the author believes everything he makes his characters say. Even when the author's prejudices are patent, as they are with many of the writers dealt with here, that is no reason for not enjoying their tales, provided that the stories are enjoyable: absorbing, colorful, exciting, and stimulating. And all these things, despite their faults, Eddison's four fantasy novels are.

W . B . Richmond

WILLIAM MORRIS

LORD DUNSANY

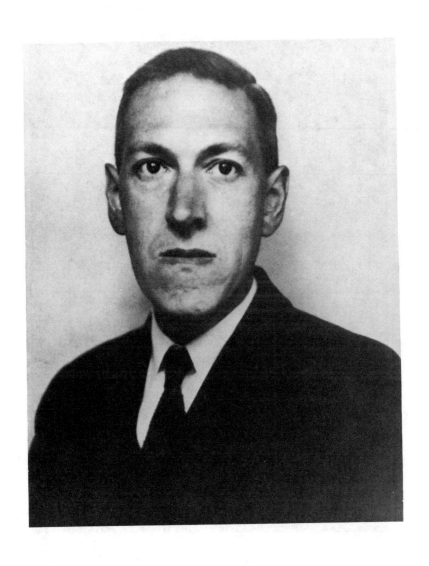

H. P. Lovecraft

E. R. EDDISON

Glenn Lord

ROBERT E. HOWARD

FLETCHER PRATT

Emil Petaja

CLARK ASHTON SMITH

Roger Hill

J. R. R. TOLKIEN

T. H. WHITE

Fritz Leiber

FRITZ LEIBER

VI

THE MISCAST BARBARIAN:
ROBERT E. HOWARD

At birth a witch laid on me monstrous spells,
  And I have trod strange highroads all my days,
  Turning my feet to gray, unholy ways.
I grope for stems of broken asphodels;
High on the rims of bare, fiend-haunted fells,
  I follow cloven tracks that lie ablaze;
  And ghosts have led me through the moonlight's haze
To talk with demons in their granite hells.[1]

HOWARD

Next to J. R. R. Tolkien, the most widely-read and influential author of heroic fantasy is Robert E. Howard (1906–36), creator of Conan. His tragic story shows one reaction between literary talent and a hostile milieu.

Howard was one of many mass-production pulp writers of the 1920s and 30s. Nevertheless, his work has shown a staying power and a capacity for inciting enthusiasm far beyond those of most of his contemporaries. This work has acquired a lasting popularity, despite the fact that it has been said of it, not unjustly, that "his barbarian heroes are overgrown juvenile delinquents; his settings are a riot of anachronisms; and his plots overwork the long arm of coincidence."[2] There must be a reason for this lasting appeal.

Robert Ervin Howard was born in the village of Peaster, Texas, near modern Weatherford. His father was Dr. Isaac

Mordecai Howard, a frontier physician. While Robert, an only child, was a boy, the family moved several times around Texas and Oklahoma. About 1919, they settled in Cross Plains, in the center of the state between Abilene and Brownwood.

The land around Cross Plains is flat, with a slight roll. In aboriginal days, it was well-wooded by an open stand of a small oak, the post oak or jack oak. Between the oaks grew a sparse cover of grass and herbs. The flora could be classed as a scrub forest of the Mediterranean type, except that the long dry season comes in winter instead of in summer. Many oaks have been cleared away for pasture or wheat, but enough still stand to give an idea of the country's former aspect.

Cross Plains stands amid this flat, limitless vastness. To the west, the level horizon is broken by a conical hill. This is the larger of the two Caddo Peaks, named for the Caddo Indians.

Today, Cross Plains harbors 1,200 people—300 fewer than when Howard lived; while Brownwood, forty-odd miles to the southeast, has grown from 14,000 to 20,000. People say that time has passed Cross Plains by. Save for some new service stations, the town has changed but little in recent decades. But Cross Plains is a pleasant-looking little town, with neat bungalows surrounded by the lawns and plantings of the typical contemporary suburban American home.

As a boy, Robert Howard was puny and bookish. To judge from his later attitudes and behavior, he must have started life, as have H. P. Lovecraft and many other writers, with a personality of the schizoid type, which I have defined and explained in the fourth chapter. When such an introverted personality is combined with a puny body and bookish tastes, the individual is a natural butt of bullies. For such an unfortunate, boy life is a jungle, with the schizoid playing the rôle of rabbit. Every day is a series of terrifying encounters with slavering monsters and Inquisitorial tortures.

This was true *a fortiori* in the small-town Texas of Howard's youth. If not the true frontier environment for which Howard nostalgically longed, it was certainly rough enough. Later, Howard was incredulous when Lovecraft assured him that public fights were almost unknown in the cities of the Northeast.

In one town, Howard could not leave his own yard for fear of being set upon by a gang. During this time, his mother read extensively to him, especially poetry. The resulting closeness between the two led both to Howard's literary career and to his eventual destruction.

As he grew up, Howard embarked upon a heroic program of weight-lifting, bag-punching, and other calisthenics. When his father asked: "Robert, what's this all about?" young Howard replied:

"Dad, when I was in school, I had to take a lot because I was alone and [had] no one to take my part. I intend to build my body until when a scoundrel crosses me up, I can with my bare hands tear him to pieces, double him up, and break his back with my hands alone."[3]

By the time he entered the Cross Plains High School, Howard was a large, powerful youth. The bullying stopped, albeit Howard did not become a bully in his turn. He remained a sport and exercise fanatic. When fully grown, he was 5 feet 11 inches tall and weighed around 200 pounds, most of it muscle. He was a boxing and football fan and himself an accomplished boxer and rider, owning a horse and attending matches of the Golden Gloves, the amateur boxing association.

Nobody bothered Howard then, but his boyhood left him with a lasting streak of cynical misanthropy.[4] Towards those who had abused him, he bore lifelong grudges and undying hatred. These bullies may have been the "enemies" of whom he spoke in later years, although he seems to have had little adult contact with them.

Howard hated school—not because of the work, which came easily, but because he disliked routine and discipline. The public schools in Cross Plains went only through the tenth grade. In 1922, therefore, his parents sent him to Brownwood for a year at Brownwood High School. He returned home for two years; then his parents sent him to Brownwood again for a year at the Howard Payne Academy, a preparatory school run in connection with Howard Payne College. He graduated from the Academy in 1927.

The following year, he took commercial, non-credit courses at the college in shorthand, typing, business arithmetic, and commercial law. Although in 1928 he expressed a scorn of college, he later wrote: "A literary college education probably would have helped me immensely. . . . I might have liked college. . . . That's neither here nor there; I didn't feel I could afford it. . . ."[5]

At Brownwood, Howard showed signs of maladjustment by sleepwalking. In fact, he once walked out the window. Fortunately his bedroom was on the ground floor, so that he was not much hurt. Thereafter he tied one toe to the foot of his bed to prevent a recurrence.

At this time, being a fast and omnivorous reader, Howard was educating himself by wide and diversified reading. Being far from any sizable library, during summers he broke into locked schoolhouses to get at the books. He carried them off on horseback in a flour sack but always returned them.

He became a faithful reader of *Adventure Magazine*. This was an aristocrat of the pulps, publishing many able writers of popular fiction. Being strapped for money, Howard made an arrangement with the newsstand to buy *Adventure* on credit, paying for each issue as the next arrived.

At fifteen, in 1921, Howard chose writing as his career. Writing, he thought, would give him more freedom and independence than any other gainful occupation. In later years, he maintained that this passion to be his own boss was a larger factor in his choice of this career than any overwhelming literary urge. He would, he said, have worked at something else if it promised equal freedom with more money.

One may, however, suspect that a man with Howard's voracious appetite for reading and his natural storytelling bent would have written, no matter what his main occupation. On the other hand, since he regarded writing as mainly a way of making a living, Howard took a hard-headed, commercial view of the craft. This contrasts with Lovecraft's gentleman-amateur, art-for-art's-sake attitude.

In 1921, Howard sent a story to *Adventure Magazine;* the story came promptly back. Throughout his career, Howard repeatedly tried to break into the highest-paying pulps, such as *Adventure, Argosy, Blue Book,* and *Short Stories.* His only success was one boxing story, "Crowd-Horror," in *Argosy All-Story Weekly* for July 20, 1929.

In these magazines, Howard was competing with such finished writers as H. Bedford-Jones, Harold Lamb, Talbot Mundy, and Arthur D. Howden Smith. While strongly influenced by these writers, Howard was not writing stories up to the standard they set. Had he lived longer and matured further, both as a writer and as a human being, while the older writers died off or left pulp writing, Howard might very well have achieved his goal.

Meanwhile, Howard wrote for the Brownwood High School magazine, *The Tattler.* He concocted several fictional characters, some of whom later became the heroes of published stories.

In 1923, *Weird Tales* was launched. In the fall of 1924, while at Brownwood, Howard sold his first commercial story: a cave-man tale called "Spear and Fang." *Weird Tales* had just come under the editorship of Farnsworth Wright, who paid Howard $16.00 for his piece.

In 1924, between his studies and miscellaneous jobs, Howard entertained thoughts of a musical career. He hired, in turn, three local musicians to teach him the violin, but this career aborted when each of his teachers either skipped town ahead of the sheriff or got shot. Unlike Lovecraft, however, Howard appreciated symphonic music on the rare occasions when he could pick it up on the radio. It is hard not to think that he might have fared better where the cultural advantages for which he wistfully yearned were more accessible.

Besides his studies, Howard held a number of jobs: clerking in a grocery store and a dry-goods shop, working in a tailor shop, soda-jerking in a drug store, secretary in a law office, stenographer, postal clerk, oil-field hand, and geological surveyor.

The drug-store job, which he held in 1926, proved the most exhausting. It required him to be on duty seven days a week until midnight. His health broke down, so that he quit and returned to Howard Payne College to study bookkeeping. He said that, after he finished the course, bookkeeping was a bigger mystery to him than it had been at the start.

He joined a coterie of eight or ten young people of literary tastes, living in or near Brownwood. The group included Harold Preece, later a professional writer, and Howard's lifelong friends Tevis Clyde Smith (with whom he later collaborated on a story) and Truett Vinson. They issued a round-robin journal, *The Junto,* to which Howard contributed. Some members published professionally, but only Preece and Howard became full-time writers. Howard also wrote for a local publication, *The Yellow Jacket,* and for the amateur journal *The All-Around,* published by his friend Smith.

Although modest about his writings, Howard took a quiet pride in being "the first to light the torch of literature in this part of the country, comprising a territory equal to that of the state of Connecticut. . . . I am, in a way, a pioneer. . . . I was the first writer of the post oak country; my work's lack of merit can not erase that fact." He accomplished this feat despite "having never seen a writer, a poet, a publisher, or a magazine editor, and having only the vaguest ideas of procedure," with "neither expert aid nor advice," and not even access to large libraries.[6]

Howard continued writing for *Weird Tales:* "The Lost Race" appeared in the issue of January 1927. During 1923–25, he also composed and sold "The Hyena," "In the Forest of Villefère," and "Wolfshead." All four were undistinguished fictions of standard *Weird Tales* type. "The Lost Race" was a tale of Celt versus Pict in ancient Britain; "The Hyena" and "Wolfshead" about African lycanthropy.

After completing his courses at Howard Payne College in 1927, Howard settled down to full-time writing. He wrote ghost, adventure, pirate, and sport stories—even the so-called "true confessions." He submitted them to many magazines, both pulp and slick, but had few sales—usually two to five a year. His earnings were, for 1926: $50.00; 1927: $37.50; 1928: $186.00; 1929: $772.50. Most of the money came from *Weird Tales*. Although this magazine paid low rates and was often late in its payments, it still proved Howard's most trustworthy source of literary income.

Such a time of groping and struggle is usual in the career of a tyronic writer. Howard's distinction is that, completely self-taught, he did so well, so soon, despite an uncongenial environment and isolation from professional contacts. From 1930 on, his earnings (except for 1933, with $962.25) were consistently over $1,000 a year. By 1935 they were over $2,000. At this time, $1,000 was a living annual wage and $2,000 a fairly affluent one.

In 1928, Howard set down on paper a fictional character whom he had long borne in mind: Solomon Kane, an English Puritan of the late sixteenth century. The story, "Red Shadows," appeared in *Weird Tales* for August 1928. Kane differs from most of Howard's heroes, who are brawny, brawling, belligerent adventurers. Kane is somber of dress, dour of manner, rigid of principles, and driven by a demonic urge to wander, to seek danger, and to right wrongs. In the Kane stories, some of which are set in Europe and some in Africa, Kane undergoes gory adventures and overcomes supernatural menaces. In these stories first appears Howard's distinctive intensity—a curious sense of total emotional commitment, which hypnotically drags the reader along willy-nilly.

In 1929, Howard began to sell to markets other than *Weird Tales,* such as *Argosy* and *Fight Stories. Weird Tales,* however, remained his most reliable market. In the decade following "Red Shadows," he appeared in about two thirds of all its issues, even though many appearances were only of poems.

Howard produced a sizable volume of poetry, nearly all of which has been published. Two of his poems appeared in *Modern American Poetry* for 1933. Like his prose, his verse is vigorous, colorful, strongly rhythmic, and technically adroit. He was modest about his talent, saying that, while he was born with the knack of "making little words rattle together," "I know nothing at all about the mechanics of poetry—I couldn't tell you whether a verse was anapestic or trochaic to save my neck. I write the stuff by ear, so to speak, and my musical ear is full of flaws."[7]

Howard's models were the major Anglo-American poets of the late nineteenth and early twentieth centuries, such as Benét, Chesterton, Dunsany, Flecker, Harte, Kipling, Masefield, Noyes, Swinburne, Tennyson, and Wilde. Howard's clanging, colorful verse, while not quite so brilliant as that of Clark Ashton Smith, is better than the rather pedestrian poetry of Dunsany or Tolkien and far superior to Lovecraft's leaden Georgian couplets.

Howard was untouched by the revolution then beginning in Anglophone poetry, which, led by Pound, Eliot, and others, resulted in the almost complete abandonment of fixed forms in favor of free verse. Where Howard used simple language and fixed forms, most contemporary poets use turgid language and no form at all. Opinions differ as to whether this is an improvement.

Since, however, poetry paid little or nothing, and Howard, however unrealistic in some phases of human relationships, had a sound sense of economic reality, he wrote very little verse after 1930.

While getting a foothold in professional writing, Howard continued to live with his parents in Cross Plains. Now and then he took off in his Chevrolet for a long drive to some historic site in Texas, or to some other noteworthy place in the Southwest (such as the Carlsbad Caverns), or to Mexico.

He continued his physical routine, walking miles every day. Lean at twenty, he became massive as he neared thirty. Despite his tremendous appetite, he tried to watch his weight; he envied men with trim figures. He drank tea but for some reason refused to touch coffee. He also accumulated a small collection of swords and bayonets.

In maturity he was a big, heavy-set man with straight black hair cut short, blue eyes under heavy black brows, and a round, slightly jowly face. Clean-shaven most of his life, he grew a mustache in his last year. He was supposed to wear eyeglasses for reading but often neglected to do so. He had a deep but soft voice, pronouncing "sword" like "sward" and rhyming "wound" (the noun) with "sound."

He usually dressed in shirt and pants, adding a sweater in cold weather, although he could appear in city-slicker clothes when the occasion demanded. He sometimes had his trouser legs cut short to clear the tops of his heavy, high-topped shoes, so that his pants would not get in his way if he got in a fight. He disliked jackets because, he said, they never fitted his bull neck and hulking shoulders, even when tailor-made. Although he hated cold, he refused to wear thick socks and heavy underwear and seldom donned an overcoat.[8] He spoke of wishing he could live in the tropics.

Howard usually went bareheaded. When he wore any headgear, it was ordinarily either a cloth cap or a cowboy sombrero. His mother once pestered him into buying an ordinary narrow-brimmed gent's felt hat, in which he had a well-known photograph taken; but he disliked that hat.

Despite his great physical strength, his health was not altogether good. He complained of rheumatism, flat feet, varicose veins, and an enlarged or "athlete's" heart. He took digitalis, which suggests that his heart had been damaged by rheumatic fever or some other cardiac ailment. He spoke of feeling prematurely old; a friendly boxing match in 1930, he complained, left him staggering with exhaustion.

Although a teetotaler for a while in youth, Howard drank—mostly beer—but did not smoke. He was known to get drunk, but not often, and he seldom or never got into fights. (One surmises that others had better sense than to cross anyone with Howard's physique.)

His letters contain many accounts of drunken brawls. My informants in Cross Plains claimed that these were imaginary and that Howard was given to the fictional elaboration of mundane events. On the other hand, the sprees are mostly said to have taken place away from Cross Plains. Possibly, in deference to his religious parents, Howard led a sober life at home but went on a tear abroad.

The same may apply to his hints of wenching. At home he displayed, until his last few years, little overt interest in women, save to complain that, at social gatherings, they passed him up for more glamorous youths. At the age of fifteen, he saw a girl who worked in a carnival, developed a violent crush on her, and for some years worshipped her image from afar. In arguments, he vigorously defended the rights and abilities of women. In 1935, he sold a story to the semi-pornographic *Spicy Adventures;* he said that he had used one of his own sexual adventures in the plot and urged H. P. Lovecraft (of all people!) to do likewise.[9]

Howard was a man of emotional extremes and of violent likes and dislikes. His hatreds, besides the bullies who had tormented him in boyhood, included such curious targets as the state of Kansas, which he had never seen, and George Bernard Shaw, whose works he had never read but whose whiskers he expressed a wish to pull out hair by hair.

Howard's personality was introverted, moody, and unconventional. He knew his own emotional instability, alluding to his fits of gloom and black moods.[10] When he felt like it, he could hold forth brilliantly on many subjects; but he might instead go into the mopes and say nothing to a friend who had come a long way to see him. Howard blamed these fits of melancholia, perhaps unfairly, on his Celtic ancestry.

He was hot-tempered, flaring up easily but quickly cooling off. Once the *Cross Plains Review* published a story that did not give Howard's mother the credit he thought she deserved. Howard marched into the newspaper office, threw a copy on the editor's desk, and told him not to send the damned paper to his house any more. The next day, Doctor Howard came in to revive the subscription.

Even Howard's friends found him an enigma. One of them told me: "He just didn't give a damn for a lot of things that other people do." This informant added: "Bob had a funny habit. He'd be walking along the street, and you'd see him suddenly start to shadow-box. He'd box for a few seconds and then go back to walking again."[11]

August Derleth wrote of Howard: ". . . he lived in a world that was at least quasi-make-believe."[12] Howard was evidently one to whom the things that he read about or imagined were more real than the people and things around him.

With so voracious a reader, it is hard to be sure that he was *not* influenced by any given predecessor. Jack London was one of Howard's favorite writers. Howard esteemed Sir Richard F. Burton's narratives of travel and adventure, although he was skeptical of Burton's truthfulness. In Howard's stories, the influence of Edgar Rice Burroughs, Robert W. Chambers, Harold Lamb, H. P. Lovecraft, Talbot Mundy, Sax Rohmer, and Arthur D. Howden Smith is plain to be seen.

An alert reader can also pick up echoes of other, older writings in Howard's stories, or in individual scenes and passages.

One of his rewritten and posthumously published stories was, in its various incarnations, titled "The Black Stranger," "Swords of the Red Brotherhood," and "The Treasure of Tranicos." I suspect that Howard got the idea of the little colony (French in one version, Zingaran in another) on a wild, distant coast from "The Lady Ursula," in Charles M. Skinner's *Myths and Legends of Our Own Land* (1896). Howard's story "The Frost Giant's Daughter" (also published as "Gods of the North") may have come either from "The Home of Thunder" in Skinner's book or from a similar incident in William Morris's *The Roots of the Mountains* (1913, p. 76)—or from both.

Other examples are the death throes of Khosatral Khel in "The Devil in Iron," where the phraseology echoes Arthur Machen's "The Great God Pan"; the incident of the poisoned prong of Zorathus' iron box, in *Conan the Conqueror* (Chapter XII), which could have come from Sax Rohmer's *The Hand of Fu-Manchu* (1917) or A. Conan Doyle's "The Adventure of the Dying Detective" (1913); and the attacks on the king in "By This Ax I Rule!" and "The Phoenix on the Sword," which closely resemble the death of Francesco Pizarro as described by William H. Prescott in *The History of the Conquest of Peru.* Where Gustave Flaubert, in *Salammbô*, described Hamilcar Barca driving his chariot "up the whole Mappalian Way," Howard, in "The God in the Bowl," has Kallian Publico driving his chariot "along the Palian Way."

Still, the man had much more than mere imitativeness. A young writer often imitates admired predecessors. Many have thus passed through a Hemingway or a Lovecraft period. If the writer is good, he assimilates these influences so that the derivations are no longer obvious. Howard, I think, was reaching this stage when he perished.

Three strong influences on Howard's fiction were, first, the romantic primitivism of London and Burroughs; second, a fascination with Celtic history and legend; and third, the racial beliefs then current. Howard's primitivism is summed up by a remark made by a character at the end of the story "Beyond the Black River": "Barbarism is the natural state of mankind. Civilization is unnatural. It is a whim of circumstance. And barbarism must always ultimately triumph."

In 1930, Howard began a voluminous six-year correspondence with H. P. Lovecraft, in the course of which Howard argued for the superiority of barbarism over civilization. They discussed the races of man, the migrations of peoples, and the rise and fall of civilizations. Sometimes their exchanges became acrimonious, with time out for one writer or the other to apologize for his vehemence.

We cannot always tell whether Lovecraft actually accused Howard of the things that Howard said he had. While we have nearly all Howard's letters to Lovecraft for the period, fewer than half of Lovecraft's letters to Howard are available.[13]

In this correspondence, Lovecraft's tone is bland, urbane and detached but much given to sweeping, dogmatic assertions on matters of which he knew but little. Howard appears as more realistic, sensible, and worldly wise. On the whole, he comes off better in these arguments than Lovecraft. But Howard also sounds defensive, prickly, and wont to take Lovecraft's grand generalizations as personal slurs, when Lovecraft probably did not so mean them.

When Howard wished that he had been born a barbarian or on the frontier of the previous century, Lovecraft (according to Howard) accused him of romanticism, sentimentality, and naïveté, and of being an "enemy to humanity." Howard retorted that Lovecraft's idealization of the eighteenth century was just as naïve and romantic. Besides, Howard said, he wished, not to be translated by time travel to a barbarian milieu, for which he admitted he was unsuited, but to have been born and reared in one, so that he would have grown up naturally in those surroundings.

Lovecraft (said Howard) accused Howard of exalting the

physical side of life over the intellectual; Howard replied that
he merely took a balanced view, sport and exercise being as
necessary to him as antiquarianism was to Lovecraft. When
Lovecraft praised Mussolini and Fascism, Howard, to whom
personal liberty was the prime political principle, denounced
Mussolini as a butcher and racketeer and Fascism as despotism,
enslavement, and a front for the financial oligarchy.

Several times, Howard told Lovecraft that he would be glad
to drop the argument and agree to disagree. But Lovecraft kept
trying to convert Howard to his own art-for-art's-sake, anti-
physical, anti-commercial estheticism. In view of his own un-
worldliness and unsuccess, Lovecraft hardly seems the man best
qualified to tell another how to run his life.

The ancient Celts fascinated Howard. Where Lovecraft was
an Anglophile, Howard was a Celtophile. Of largely Irish des-
cent, Howard made an affectation of his Celticism, sometimes
signing himself "Raibeard Eiarbhin hui Howard." One St.
Patrick's Day, he appeared in a green bow tie two feet across.
Howard was more objective toward the Celts than Lovecraft
ever was towards the Anglo-Saxons. Nevertheless, Howard harbored, throughout his life, a burning interest in Celtic history,
anthropology, and mythology.

This interest appears in Howard's fantasies of Turlogh
O'Brien, in his historical stories of Cormac Mac Art, and in
other historical and contemporary tales with heroes of Irish
names: Costigan, Dorgan, Kirowan, O'Donnell, and so on. He
wrote fantasies and historical tales laid in the British Isles, of
the struggle of Pict against Briton, of Briton against Roman,
and of Irishman against Norseman. He read Donn Byrne's Irish
novels but resented Bryne's making heroes of Ulstermen and
Anglo-Normans. He studied the eccentric phonology and or-
thography of the Irish language. He took part in the arguments
as to which of the two branches of the British Celts—the
Goidels, Gaels, or Q-Celts and the Cymry, Britons, or P-Celts—
reached the islands first.

Howard indignantly rejected Lovecraft's assertion that Americans had a duty to defend the British Empire, on the ground that his own forebears had fled from Ireland to escape British oppression. While Lovecraft fulminated against Irishmen for agitating against their "lawful sovereign," the king of England, Howard felt equally bitter about the sins of the English in Ireland ever since 1171, when the Irish chieftains submitted to Henry II.

Like Lovecraft, Howard was still under the spell of the Aryanist doctrine. This dogma identified the horse-taming Aryans, the original spreaders of the Indo-European languages, with the tall, blond, blue-eyed Nordic racial type—which seems unlikely in the light of present knowledge. Hence Howard wrote of the conquest, in Britain, of small, dark aborigines of Mediterranean type by "blond, blue-eyed giants"—the supposed Aryan Celts. According to present evidence, the conquering was probably the other way round. The Nordic aborigines were at least twice conquered by swarthy little Southerners, first by the prehistoric Beaker Folk from Spain and secondly by the Romans. Howard himself had black hair and blue eyes, a genetic combination that seems commoner in Ireland than elsewhere. Hence he was less englamorated by mere blondness than Lovecraft. Most of his heroes, in fact, are brunets.

For all his Irish sympathies, Howard was not altogether naïve about the Celts, writing of their fickleness, jealousy, and treachery. He blamed his Celtic blood for endowing him with a restless, unstable mind. In his black moods, he cursed the black Milesian blood, which filled him with nameless sorrows and instilled in him a blind, brooding rage at anything that crossed his path.

Many of Howard's views would today be called "racist." In presenting such views, Howard merely followed most popular fiction writers of the time, to whom ethnic stereotypes were stock in trade. If a racist, Howard was, by the standards of his time, a comparatively mild one. He agreed with Lovecraft's rhapsodies on the "Aryan race" and his rantings against non-Nordic immigrants. But then he noted the superior qualities of the intelligent, industrious, orderly Bohemian settlers in Texas. He admitted that every ethnos has its share of saints and scoundrels.[14]

Howard's attitudes were compounded by a conventional Southern white outlook, with sentimental sympathy for the Confederacy and a sense of outrage at the depredations of the carpetbaggers. He vented conventional Texan views of Negroes and Mexicans but noted some Negroes and Mexicans whom he admired, such as the Negro cowboy who discovered the art of bulldogging.

In defending Texas against Lovecraft's attacks, Howard told Lovecraft that Texans never persecuted any class or race; but he also noted that no Negro was allowed to pass the night in his part of the country. He insisted that Texans were really a law-abiding people, despite their terrific homicide rate, because, like many Texans, he did not consider killing an enemy in a fair fight a crime.

Howard's primitivism gave his ethnic attitudes a paradoxical twist. He might view Negroes as incorrigibly barbaric; but to him that was not altogether bad, since he thought that barbarians had virtues lacking in civilized men. Thus, in criticizing French novelists (of whom he read many in translation) he said: "Dumas has a virility lacking in other French writers—I attribute it to his negroid strain. . . ."[15] While he wrote weird stories laid in the Deep South, with gallant white men dashing about to forestall nigger uprisings, the reader also comes upon an unexpected flicker, here and there, of sympathy for the downtrodden blacks.[16] Although a few remarks about Shemites in the Conan stories suggest the hostile Christian stereotype of the Jew, Howard also made Bêlit, the Shemitish she-pirate, one of his more beguiling heroines.

Politically—racial questions aside—Howard was a vigorously anti-authoritarian liberal. In religion, he was not a Texan

Baptist like his parents but, like many writers of heroic fantasy, an agnostic who made up his own pantheon for the sake of his stories but did not take his synthetic gods seriously. He declined to take a definitely atheistic stance, as Lovecraft did, because of his respect for the opinions of his father, a believing Christian.

In 1930, Howard attended Sunday School and the Epworth League for a while, to the dismay of his iconoclastic friends of the Junto. The reason, it transpired, was that Howard had taken a shine to a girl who was active in those groups. Soon, however, he became so bored with these affairs that he dropped out, girl or no girl.[17]

During 1929–32, with the opening of wider markets for his fiction, Howard was busier than ever. He wrote several weird stories in the frame of Lovecraft's Cthulhu Mythos. He sold sport, adventure, Western, oriental, and historical stories. Most of his stories belonged to one or another of the score of series that he wrote, each series built around one character.

At the end of 1929, Howard's novel "Skull-Face" ran as a serial in *Weird Tales.* It is an obvious imitation of Sax Rohmer, with an immortal Atlantean sorcerer, Kathulos, substituted for the insidious Doctor Fu-Manchu. Howard denied that "Kathulos" was derived from Lovecraft's "Cthulhu"; he said he had made up the name himself. He started but never finished a sequel. In 1931, he also sold an article to *The Texaco Star,* the Texaco Company's house organ.

Although Howard was a versatile writer throughout his career, writing in several genres at once, his writing falls into three definite if overlapping periods. In each period, stories of one kind dominate his output. The first period, after he became an established writer, was that of boxing stories, from 1929 to 1932. The second, from 1932 to 1935, was that of fantasy. The third and last, from 1934 to 1936, was that of Westerns.

Howard's main writing, from 1929 to 1932, consisted of

stories of prizefighting. He published twenty tales about a pugilistic sailor named Steve Costigan. Over half of these were sold to *Fight Stories* and the rest to *Action Stories* and *Jack Dempsey's Fight Magazine.*

Costigan, an able-bodied seaman and prizefighter, is an invincible roughneck with fists of iron, a heart of gold, and a head of ivory. These stories are comedies, full of broad, slapstick humor, of a sort that those who know only Howard's serious stories would never expect of him. The tales deal with prizefights, usually in port cities. There are plots, skullduggery, and virtue finally triumphant. The hero is an incorrigible sucker for a hard-luck story, especially from a fair but designing female. Howard explained his preference for heroes of mighty thews and feeble minds:

"They're simpler. You get them in a jam, and no one expects you to rack your brains inventing clever ways for them to extricate themselves. They are too stupid to do anything but cut, shoot or slug themselves into the clear."[18]

The Costigan tales came so fast that they began to pile up. In 1931, Farnsworth Wright launched *Weird Tales*'s short-lived companion, *Oriental Stories* (later *Magic Carpet*). To sell some Costigan stories laid in oriental places to the new magazine, Howard changed the name of the hero, his dog, and his ship. Sailor Costigan became Sailor Dennis Dorgan. Wright bought four of these stories and published one before *Magic Carpet* folded. Six more remained in manuscript until their recent publication in a book.

These stories would never have been disinterred but for Conan's popularity in the last decade. Still, they have ingenuity, action, and broad humor. Even at his corniest and pulpiest, Howard is fun to read.

The stories also show Howard's limitations. His knowledge of seafaring, for example, was second-hand. The closest he had come to going to sea was a motorboat ride in the Gulf of Mexico. Tales of Shanghai, Singapore, and other exotic ports are obviously by one who had never been there. But Howard had neither time nor facilities profoundly to research the *ambiance* of these places.

A couple of Dorgan stories, laid in San Francisco, give a picture of "high society" by one who likewise had never been there. The Societarians flutter limp paws, stare through lorgnettes and monocles, say "my deah" and "rawthah," and swoon at the sight of blood. But then, the class of readers for whom Howard was writing had never been there, either.

After 1932, Howard's production of sport stories dropped off. Only four more in this genre were published in his lifetime.

Howard sustained his share of personal misadventures. At the end of 1933, driving with three companions in a night of pouring rain through a small town, he ran his car into a steel flagpole, set in a concrete stanchion in the middle of the main street. Howard and his passengers were all badly banged, bruised, and cut, although all recovered. Telling Clark Ashton Smith about the incident, he wrote:

> For a fellow who has always lived a quiet, peaceful, and really prosaic life, I've had my share of narrow shaves: horses running away with me and falling on me; one threw me and then jumped on me; one turned a complete somersault in mid-air and landed on her back which would have mashed me like a bed-bug if I hadn't been hurled over her head as she fell; went head-on through a bed-room window once; knife stuck into my leg behind the knee, once, a hair's breadth from that big artery that runs there; stepped right over a diamond-backed rattler in the dark, etc.[19]

Edgar Hoffmann Price, who visited Howard twice, in 1934 and 1935, described him thus:

> A complex and baffling personality one can't—couldn't—get all at once. An overgrown boy—a brooding anachronism—a scholar—a gripping, compelling writer—a naive boy scout—a man of great emotional depth, yet strangely self-conscious of many emotional phases which he unjustly claimed he could never put into writing fiction—a burly, broad faced, not unduly shrewd looking fellow

at first glance—a courtly, gracious, kindly hospitable person—a
hearty, rollicking, gusty, spacious personality loving tales and
deeds that reeked of sweat and dust and dung of horses and sheep
and camels—a blustering, boyishly extravagant-spoken boy who
made up whopping stories about the country and people and himself, not to deceive or fool you, but because he loved the sweep
of words and knew you liked to hear him hold forth—a fanciful,
sensitive, imaginative soul, hidden in that big bluff hulk. A man
of strange, whimsical, bitter and utterly illogical resentments and
hatreds and enmities and grudges. . . .[20]

There were also darker sides to Howard's character. In the
1920s, he began to toy with the idea of suicide. This is not un-
common in adolescence, but in Howard's case the idea grew
stronger instead of fading away.

In assembling Howard, the gods somehow left out the cog-
wheel that furnished love of life. When Howard's dog Patches
("Patch") died in 1930, Howard became so despondent that
his parents, fearing that he would kill himself, sent him to
Brownwood for a vacation. A notable animal-lover, Howard
once kept a pet racoon and, by feeding stray cats, gathered an
entourage of a dozen felines.

Some of his poems commended suicide and practically
shouted his intention of eventually taking that way out. In "The
Tempter," the phantom, Suicide, taps him on the shoulder and
urges him to leave the world of men, promising rest from hate
and pride. Howard went on to brood:

> I am weary of tide breasting,
> Weary of the world's behesting,
> And I lusted for the resting
> As a lover for his bride.

He voiced the wish to be quit

> Of this world of human cattle,
> All this dreary noise and prattle.[21]

As one can see from Howard's really quiet and secluded life, the din and struggle of which he complained were all within him. But they were real nevertheless. At some time in the early 1930s, he had made up his mind not to survive his aging mother. He told his friend Smith: "My father is a man and can take care of himself, but I've got to stay on as long as my mother is alive."[22] And Howard, having once made up his mind to something, was not to be dissuaded by any ordinary means.

A factor in this resolution, although perhaps a minor one, may have been a fear of old age and its infirmities. He wrote that he did not want to become old; he wished to die young, in the full tide of his health and strength.[23]

It seems obvious that the dominating factor in Howard's life was his devotion to his mother, which answers to the textbook descriptions of the Oedipus complex. We must bear in mind, however, that posthumous psychoanalysis is at best a jejune form of speculation. The results are doubtful enough when a trained psychiatrist tries to uncover the conflicts seething in the unconscious of a living person. So diagnoses of this sort, in the case of persons long dead, should not be taken too seriously.

In his late twenties, a decade after most youths do, Howard began at last to go with girls as a regular thing. While he had previously shown a normal heterosexual orientation, his actual approaches to women had been timid and tentative. For years he excused his misogyny by saying: "Aw, what woman would ever look at a big, ugly hulk like me?"[24] or quoting Kipling:

> Down to Gehenna or up to the Throne,
> He travels the fastest who travels alone.[25]

When Howard began at last to display a more active regard for young women, his mother discouraged this new interest. E. Hoffmann Price reported that, when a girl called Howard on the telephone, Mrs. Howard told the caller that he was not in, although she knew that he was.[26]

In the speculations about Howard's mother, little attention has been paid to his father. Although Price liked and admired him, Dr. Isaac Howard seems to have been a bossy, self-assertive, overbearing man—an unattractive domestic tyrant, wrapped up in his practice to the virtual exclusion of his family. Robert Howard's relations with his father seem to have been of the love-hate kind.

The two quarreled frequently and furiously, often because Robert took his father to task for neglecting his mother. The quarrels were followed by emotional reconciliations. Robert Howard had high praise for his father's medical knowledge and skill, and Doctor Howard insisted that his son "loved me with a love that was beautiful."[27] But the actual relationship seems to have been more complex than that.

Robert Howard began to display paranoid delusions of persecution. He took to carrying a pistol against "enemies," who were probably imaginary—or who at most had once bullied or otherwise offended Howard but had long forgotten all about it. He owned several pistols, his favorite being a Colt .38 automatic. When he was driving Price to Brownwood in 1934 and approached a clump of vegetation, he slowed the car and took a pistol out of the side pocket, explaining: "I have a lot of enemies; everyone has around here. Wasn't that I figured we were running into anything, but had to make sure."

The local people regarded him as a "harmless freak." He said: "These people around here think I'm crazy as hell, anyway." Now and then they asked him when he was going to quit fooling around with stories and settle down to real work, even when he was working longer hours and making more money than most Cross Plainsians. Although he knew many in Cross Plains, only Tevis Clyde Smith and Truett Vinson were close friends.

Despite this Boeotian environment, Howard stubbornly stuck to Cross Plains, saying: "I'll make the pulps, not the slicks, and I'll make them from here in Texas. I'm going to prove that a man doesn't have to live in New York to sell his stories."[28]

Ever since he had begun the Solomon Kane stories, Howard had worked on and off at heroic fantasy. In 1926, he started "The Shadow Kingdom," the first story in a new series about Kull of Atlantis. In these tales, Howard gave full vent to his primitivism.

Contrary to cultist doctrine, Howard did not assume that Atlantis was the fountainhead of all civilization. Instead, his Atlantis is backward and primitive. Kull, a Stone Age savage, goes from Atlantis to the main or Thurian continent. He becomes a soldier in the civilized kingdom of Valusia and usurps the throne, as Conan does later in Aquilonia. As King Kull, he encounters sorcerers, pre-human reptile men, and a talking cat. Some Kull tales, like two of the Solomon Kane stories, lack the supernatural element.

After he finished at Howard Payne in 1927, Howard completed "The Shadow Kingdom." From 1926 to 1930, he wrote nine Kull stories and a poem about Kull; he began three other stories but failed to finish them. At least one and possibly more of the Kull stories were sent to *Adventure* and *Argosy* but were rejected.

Eventually, the Kull stories reached *Weird Tales*. Wright bought "The Shadow Kingdom" and "The Mirrors of Tuzun Thune." He also bought "Kings of the Night," which brings King Kull and Bran Mak Morn, Howard's anti-Roman Pictish hero, together by magical time travel. The other Kull stories, Wright rejected, and they were published only long after Howard's death.

In 1932, at the beginning of his main spurt of fantasy fiction, Howard conceived his most popular character: Conan the Cimmerian. He sold seventeen Conan stories to *Weird Tales*, ranging from short stories to a book-length novel. Five more were either rejected or never submitted, and four were left unfinished.

All have since been published after editing or completion by other hands, mainly those of the present writer. One of those rejected, "The Frost Giant's Daughter," Howard rewrote as "Gods of the North." He changed the hero's name to "Amra of Akbitana" but otherwise left the story practically as it was and gave it to a non-paying fan magazine.

From 1932 to 1934, Conan stories were Howard's main preoccupation. Then he began to taper off, as Western stories took more and more of his time. His last published Conan story was the 29,500-word "Red Nails." This was completed in July 1935, although not published (as a three-part serial) until a year later. The final instalments appeared after Howard's death.

Conan first surfaced as the hero of a rewritten Kull story, "By This Ax I Rule!" Howard changed the names and introduced a supernatural element to create "The Phoenix on the Sword," published in *Weird Tales* for December 1932.

Conan was not only a development of King Kull but also an idealization of Howard himself. He is a gigantic barbarian adventurer from backward northern Cimmeria. After a lifetime of wading through rivers of gore and overcoming foes both natural and supernatural, Conan becomes king of Aquilonia. Dr. John D. Clark, in an introduction to a book edition of *Conan the Conqueror* (originally a *Weird Tales* serial, "The Hour of the Dragon") said: "Conan, the hero of all of Howard's heroes, is the armored swashbuckler, indestructible and irresistible, that we've all wanted to be at one time or another."[29]

Actually, Howard had more in common with Kull than with Conan. Kull is given to mystical broodings on the meaning of it all. Conan, on the other hand, is more the pure extrovert, much more interested in wine, women, and battle than in abstract questions. Another of Howard's fictional characters says of Conan:

> The Cimmerian might have spent years among the great cities of
> the world; he might have walked with the rulers of civilization;

he might even achieve his wild whim some day and rule as king
of a civilized nation; stranger things had happened. But he was
no less a barbarian. He was concerned only with the naked funda-
mentals of life. The warm intimacies of small, kindly things, the
sentiments and delicious trivialities that make up so much of
civilized men's lives were meaningless to him. . . . Bloodshed and
violence and savagery were the natural elements of the life Conan
knew; he could not, and would never, understand the little things
that are so dear to civilized men and women.[30]

This is a romantic primitivist's view of barbarism. Conan is
the barbarian hero to end all barbarian heroes; his later imitations seem pallid by comparison. In "A Witch Shall Be Born,"
Conan is captured and crucified. As he hangs on the cross, a
vulture flies down to peck his eyes out. Conan bites the vulture's
head off. You just can't have a hero tougher than that.

This scene may have been inspired by a similar incident in
the seventh chapter of Burroughs's *Tarzan the Untamed*. Lost
in a desert, Tarzan saves his life by luring a vulture within
reach, seizing it, and devouring it. Howard himself described
the genesis of Conan thus:

Conan simply grew up in my mind a few years ago when I was
stopping in a little border town on the lower Rio Grande. I did
not create him by any conscious process. He simply stalked full
grown out of oblivion and set me at work recording the saga of
his adventures. . . .

It may sound fantastic to link the term "realism" with Conan;
but as a matter of fact—his supernatural adventures aside—he is
the most realistic character I have ever evolved. He is simply a
combination of a number of men I have known, and I think that's
why he seemed to step full-grown into my consciousness when I
wrote the first yarn of the series. Some mechanism in my sub-con-
sciousness took the dominant characteristics of various prize-fight-
ers, gunmen, bootleggers, oil field bullies, gamblers, and honest
workmen I have come in contact with, and combining them all, produced the amalgamation I call Conan the Cimmerian.[31]

In conceiving Conan, Howard invented a whole world to go
with him. He assumed that about 12,000 years ago, after the
sinking of Atlantis but before recorded history, there was a Hyborian Age, when

> . . . shining kingdoms lay spread across the world like blue mantles
> beneath the stars—Nemedia, Ophir, Brythunia, Hyperborea, Za-
> mora with its dark-haired women and towers of spider-haunted
> mystery, Zingara with its chivalry, Koth that bordered on the
> pastoral lands of Shem, Stygia with its shadow-guarded tombs,
> Hyrkania whose riders wore steel and silk and gold. But the proud-
> est kingdom of the world was Aquilonia, reigning supreme in the
> dreaming west. Hither came Conan the Cimmerian, black-haired,
> sullen-eyed, sword in hand, a thief, a reaver, a slayer, with gigantic
> melancholies and gigantic mirth, to tread the jeweled thrones of
> the Earth under his sandaled feet.[32]

"Conan" is a common Celtic name, as in A. Conan Doyle
and several medieval dukes of Brittany. It also occurs in Geoffrey of Monmouth's largely fictional twelfth-century *History
of the Kings of Britain,* the main source of the later Arthurian
legend cycle. Most proper names in the Conan stories, like that
of Conan himself, Howard got from Classical and other history,
geography, and mythology, sometimes slightly disguising them.
Hence we read of Dion, Valeria, Thoth-Amon, Yasmina, Kush,
Asgard, and Turan.

Lovecraft criticized this procedure. In planning his Conan
stories, Howard composed an essay, "The Hyborian Age,"
which set forth the pseudo-history of Conan's world. Howard
disclaimed any intention of writing a serious theory of human
prehistory; it was avowedly fiction. In September 1935, Howard sent Lovecraft a copy of "The Hyborian Age," with a re-
quest to forward it to the fan Donald A. Wollheim for publication. Lovecraft wrote:

> Dear Wollheim:—
> Here is something which Two-Gun Bob says he wants for-
> warded to you for The Phantagraph, and which I profoundly hope

you'll be able to use. This is really great stuff—Howard has the
most magnificent sense of the drama of "History" of anyone I
know. He possesses a panoramic vision which takes in the evolution and interaction of races and nations over vast periods of time,
and gives one the same large scale excitement which (with even
greater scope) is furnished by things like Stapledon's "Last and
First Men."

The only flaw in this stuff is R.E.H.'s incurable tendency to
devise names too closely resembling actual names of ancient history—names which, for us, have a very different set of associations.
In many cases he does this designedly—on the theory that the
familiar names descend from the fabulous realms he describes—
but such a design is invalidated by the fact that we clearly know
the etymology of many of the historic terms, hence cannot accept
the pedigree he suggests. E. Hoffmann Price and I have both argued with Two-Gun on this point, but we make no headway what-
soever. The only thing to do is to accept the nomenclature as he
gives it, wink at the weak spots, and be damned thankful that we
can get such vivid artificial legendry. Howard is without question
the most vigorous and spontaneous writer now contributing to the
pulps—the nearest approach (although he wouldn't admit it
himself) to a sincere artist. He puts himself into his work as none
of the regulation hacks do.

Best wishes—

Yours most sincerely,
HPL[33]

Despite this criticism, there is much to be said for Howard's
nomenclature. Howard's made-up names are unpleasing, no
doubt as a result of Howard's linguistic naïveté. Whereas Lovecraft and Clark Ashton Smith were both fair self-taught lin-
guists, Howard's knowledge of foreign tongues was limited to
a smattering of Spanish. On the other hand, his names borrowed from ancient sources convey the glamor of antiquity
without being too hard for the modern reader, who, having
learned to read by sight-reading methods, boggles at any name
more exotic than "Smith." Most readers, moreover, are not so

erudite as to be nettled by knowledge of the true derivation of names like Thoth-Amon.

Howard envisaged the entire life of Conan, from birth to old age, and made him grow and develop as a real man does. At the start, Conan is merely a lawless, reckless, irresponsible, predatory youth with few virtues save courage, loyalty to his few friends, and a rough-and-ready chivalry toward women. In time he learns caution, prudence, duty, and responsibility, until by middle age he has matured enough to make a reasonably good king. On the contrary, many heroes of heroic fantasy seem, like the characters of Homer and of P. G. Wodehouse, to have the enviable faculty of staying the same age for half a century at a stretch.

Although self-taught, Howard achieved a sound, taut, unobtrusive prose style. He wrote in sentences of short to medium length and simple construction, as became general after the Hemingway revolution of the thirties. He could give the impression of a highly colorful scene while making only sparing use of action-slowing modifiers. Consider the opening paragraph of "The Hour of the Dragon" (*Conan the Conqueror*):

> The long tapers flickered, sending black shadows wavering across the walls, and the velvet tapestries rippled. Yet there was no wind in the chamber. Four men stood about the ebony table on which lay the green sarcophagus that gleamed like carven jade. In the upraised right hand of each man, a curious black candle burned with a weird greenish light. Outside was night and a lost wind moaning among the black trees.[34]

There the mood is set and the scene pictured with broad strokes of color, yet in straightforward, economical prose. Some contemporary writers, who try to make up for lack of an interesting story by stylistic eccentricities, could profit from a study of Howard.

An editor has little occasion to correct Howard's English. Howard very rarely made a grammatical error. True, he had some idiosyncrasies, like "surprize" and making two words of "cannot." Present-day editors might quibble about some of his punctuation, but conventions have changed since Howard's time.

Howard was a devotee of the "well-wrought tale" as opposed to the "slice-of-life" school of fiction. Stories of either kind have their place; but for pure escapist entertainment, which Howard's stories were meant to be, the well-wrought tale usually works better.

As a writer, Howard had faults as well as virtues. His faults arose mainly from haste. Like his pulp-writing colleagues, he had to turn out a large volume to make a living. He rarely wrote more than two drafts and sometimes only one. Hence his stories have many inconsistencies, anachronisms, and other examples of careless craftsmanship. Thus in Chapter XII of *Conan the Conqueror* (in its earlier editions), in the space of a few pages, Conan's helmet is variously called a morion, a basinet, and a burganet.

Howard was often inconsistent in spelling foreign words and exotic names, such as *kaffia* and *kafieh,* "Kush" and "Cush." He tended to repeat certain story elements over and over, such as the combat with a gigantic serpent or ape, the stone city built on the lines of the Pentagon, and the menace in the form of a winged ape or demon.

Many of Howard's stories are plainly derivative. Among the Conan tales, "Shadows in the Moonlight" and "The Devil in Iron" are patently inspired by Harold Lamb's Cossack stories in *Adventure;* after seeing the movie *The Cossacks,* with John Gilbert, Howard wished that he could have been one. "People of the Black Circle" is derived from Talbot Mundy's stories of India. "Beyond the Black River" traces its source to the American frontier novels of Robert W. Chambers. Outside the Conan stories, Howard wrote several tales, inspired by Arthur D. Howden Smith's Viking stories, of Norsemen in the British Isles.

Critics have blamed Howard for his fictional violence and

for his immaturity in human relationships. Conan swaggers about the Hyborian stage, bedding one willing wench after another; but he views women as mere toys. True, he at last takes a legitimate queen, but as an afterthought. Howard was evidently as uncomfortable with love as the small boy who, viewing a Western, is loudly disgusted when the hero kisses the heroine instead of his horse. Furthermore, one critic was so staggered by the splashing of gore that he said Howard's stories "project the immature fantasy of a split mind and logically pave the way to schizophrenia."[35]

What seem like excessive bloodshed and emotional immaturity, however, were normal in the pulp fiction of Howard's time. Writers did not then deem it their duty to endow their heroes with social consciousness, to sympathize with disadvantaged ethnics, or to show their devotion to peace, equality, and social justice. A story that displayed these now-esteemed qualities would not have gotten far in the pulps.

Withal, Howard was a natural storyteller, and this is the *sine qua non* of fiction-writing. With this talent, many of a writer's faults may be overlooked; without it, no other virtues make up for the lack. It is like the capacity of a boat to float; if it cannot do that, no amount of fresh paint or shiny brass does any good.

Whatever their shortcomings, Howard's writings will long be enjoyed for their zest, vigor, furious action, and headlong narrative drive; for his "purple and golden and crimson universe where anything can happen—except the tedious," spangled with "vast megalithic cities of the elder world, around whose dark towers and labyrinthine nether vaults linger[s] an aura of pre-human fear and necromancy which no other writer could duplicate."[36] One of Howard's long-standing ambitions was to visit some of these ruined cities in person.

From 1932 to 1936, most of Howard's time was taken up with the Conan stories. For months, the mighty Cimmerian obsessed him, so that he wrote:

While I don't go so far as to believe that stories are inspired by actually existent spirits or powers (though I am rather opposed to flatly denying anything) I have sometimes wondered if it were possible that unrecognized forces of the past or present—or even the future—work through the thoughts and actions of living men. This occurred to me when I was writing the first stories of the Conan series especially. I know that for months I had been absolutely barren of ideas, completely unable to work up anything sellable. Then the man Conan seemed suddenly to grow up in my mind without much labor on my part and immediately a stream of stories flowed off my pen—or rather off my typewriter—almost without effort on my part. I did not seem to be creating, but rather relating events that had occurred. Episode crowded on episode so fast that I could scarcely keep up with them. For weeks I did nothing but write of the adventures of Conan. The character took complete possession of my mind and crowded out everything else in the way of story-writing. When I deliberately tried to write something else, I couldn't do it. I do not attempt to explain this by esoteric or occult means, but the facts remain. I still write of Conan more powerfully and with more understanding than any of my other characters. But the time will probably come when I will suddenly find myself unable to write convincingly of him at all. That has happened in the past with nearly all my rather numerous characters; suddenly I would find myself out of contact with the conception, as if the man himself had been standing at my shoulder directing my efforts, and had suddenly turned and gone away, leaving me to search for another character.[37]

That, he explained, was why the Conan stories were written in a random, non-chronological order. A real adventurer, reminiscing on a wild existence, would narrate the episodes as they occurred to him rather than in the order in which they happened.

All through Howard's fantasy period, when he was writing tales of Kull and Conan, he kept pushing out into other areas of fiction. He wrote many stories of weird fantasy along conventional *Weird Tales* lines. In a couple of these, such as "The

Thing on the Roof," he used elements from Lovecraft's Cthulhu Mythos, to which he contributed the sinister volume *Nameless Cults,* by "Friedrich von Junzt."

Howard also wrote several detective stories. All have fantastic elements, like sinister oriental cults and African leopard-men. They were no great success, even though he sold them. Howard disliked the meticulous, intricate plotting called for in that genre. Moreover, never having lived in a big city, he found it hard to present the urban atmosphere convincingly.

He wrote his only interplanetary novel, *Almuric.* This was the nearest he came to science fiction proper, although he sometimes put super-scientific elements into his fantasies. *Almuric* is an obvious imitation of Burroughs. Esau Cairn, the world's strongest man, is transported by super-scientific gadgetry to a planet of a distant star. There he finds himself among brawny barbarians, fighting a race of winged beings. Howard exaggerates his hero's brawn to the point of burlesque; Esau can drive a knife into solid rock.

Howard also wrote tales of ancient, medieval, and modern adventure. Some brought in fantastic elements—magic, racial memory, monsters, lost cities, or prehistoric races—while others did not. He sold over two dozen of these tales, but others he failed to place.

Of Howard's many series of stories, built around a single character, one series has a Texan hero, Francis X. Gordon, adventuring in modern Afghanistan. Rifles crack, scimitars swish, and everybody kills everybody with gusto. These tales are derived from those that Lamb and Mundy had been publishing in *Adventure.* Gordon is an avatar of Howard's heroes Bran Mak Morn and Turlogh O'Brien: dark, of medium size but preternatural strength, speed, and agility. Another series, also laid in Afghanistan, features a doublet of Gordon called Kirby O'Donnell.

In a letter to Lovecraft, Howard scorned Broadway cowboys who wrote stories of the Wild West without having been west of Hoboken. Howard, though, wrote many stories laid in places thousands of miles from where he had ever been. He admitted his sketchy, second-hand knowledge of the Orient, confessing that his Turks, Mongols, and Afghans were merely Irishmen and Englishmen in turbans and sandals.

Still, Howard had to make a living. A writer does not live long enough to learn to write well and also to visit all the places he may wish to write about. So Howard did what others do. He read up on the places and filled the gaps with his vivid imagination.

In another series, Howard made his protagonist a modern man who is crippled. By "racial memory," James Allison recalls his incarnations as a series of heroic barbarians: Hunwulf in "The Garden of Fear," Niord in "The Valley of the Worm," and Hialmar in "Marchers of Valhalla."

Howard also sold two tales of Turlogh O'Brien, an eleventh-century Irishman, and began but failed to finish two others. Four stories of an earlier Gael, Cormac Mac Art, he failed altogether to place. Four stories of the Crusades and of the first Turkish siege of Vienna, Howard published in *Oriental Stories-Magic Carpet.*

After the demise of that magazine, however, he wrote but few tales in the straight historical vein, although he said he would like to spend his life on such fiction.[38] He had tried it often, with but meager success. The short-lived magazine of historical fiction, *Golden Fleece* (1938–39), would have been a natural for him; one of his stories was posthumously published therein.

The market for short stories of this type has always been limited, but Howard never tried a book-length historical novel, for which there was more demand. It is too bad that he was not alive in the 1950s, when the swashbuckling historical novel, for which he had a natural bent, reached its peak of popularity. Then, books by such authors as Costain, Duggan, and Renault made the best-seller lists as a matter of course.

Under the name "Sam Walser," Howard also sold several stories to *Spicy Adventures,* a magazine of the group then known as "the hots." They were supposed to be pornographic, although by present standards they were as mild as milktoast. Howard's porn consists of having his heroes and villains paw the "firm white breasts" of his heroines.

Howard early began work on Western stories, since he knew this milieu at first hand. He found the going hard. Knowing a setting too well, he said, could be a handicap.

In 1933, Howard engaged Otis A. Kline as his literary agent. At Kline's urging, he gave more attention to the Western genre. Soon his Western production all but crowded out his other work. He sold about thirty Western stories during his last three years. He said that he thought his natural bent lay in that direction.

Many of Howard's Westerns are filled with a broad frontier humor, close to burlesque, such as he had used in his Costigan and Dorgan stories: "A bullet smashed into the rock a few inches from my face and a sliver of stone taken a notch out of my ear. I don't know of nothing that makes me madder'n getting shot in the ear."[39] His humorous Western heroes are as big as Conan, even less intellectual, and genial in a homicidal way. He hoped eventually to break into the "slicks" (*Colliers,* &c.) by these stories.

Howard also wrote many non-humorous Westerns: grim, somber tales like most of his stories. To judge from those I have read, these are merely competent pulp. They are harmless amusement, with adequate dialogue and fair suspense. They are conventional shoot-'em-up yarns, wherein steely-eyed Texans, ruthless and unscrupulous but chivalrous towards women, perforate even wickeder Westerners. The view of the Wild West in these stories is superficial, as if gotten from the library instead of, as was actually the case, from personal knowledge.

In his last years, Howard hinted at writing a "Southwestern

epic." He may have had in mind something like the later "realistic" Westerns by authors like A. B. Guthrie. In his letters, he spoke of the need for something more realistic than the stereotyped shoot-'em-up stories such as he had been turning out.[40] Such an epic, however, would have needed a deeper grasp of human relationships and of the politico-economic factors in human affairs than appears in stories like his "The Vultures of Whapeton."

He might have developed this insight, for his letters show awareness of these factors. In the Western pulps of the thirties, however, such vision would have been a handicap. The stories in these magazines were the world's most conventional, cliché-filled, formula-ridden fictions, and Howard merely wrote what he knew he could sell.

In some of his last letters, Howard implied that he might quit fantasy altogether: "I'm seriously contemplating devoting all my time and efforts to Western writing, abandoning all other forms of writing entirely; the older I get the more my thoughts and interests are drawn back over the trails of the past; so much has been written, but there is so much more that should be written."[41] His true future, he said, lay in that direction.

When Howard's virtues and faults as a writer have been set forth, however, there remains that curiously hypnotic grip that his narratives have upon many readers. Apart from the headlong pace and verve and zest of Howard's storytelling, as Lovecraft put it, "the real secret is that he himself is in every one of them."[42]

The "self" that Howard wrote into his stories with such burning intensity was a very—in fact fatally—flawed human being. He suffered from abnormal devotion to his mother, paranoid delusions of persecution, and a fascination with suicide. This somber self, with its nightmarish view of a hostile, menacing universe, its irrational fears, hatreds, and grudges, and its love affair with death, comes across in his fiction. It grips the reader whether he will or no, somewhat as do Lovecraft's fictional versions of his nightmares and neuroses. Thus the very traits that help to give Howard's fiction lasting interest are those that in the end destroyed him.

In any case, Howard's stories, despite their patent faults, bid fair to be enjoyed for their action, color, and furious narrative drive for many years to come.

The years 1932–36 were busy for Howard, who—being a compulsive if spasmodic worker—no longer found time for poetry. His Western market was growing. For a while, he earned more money than any other man in Cross Plains—even more than the local banker. Of course, this was in the depths of the Great Depression, when bankers were harried, $2,500 a year was an opulent income, and Doctor Howard had to take livestock and farm produce in payment of his medical bills.

Howard's circumstances were never really easy, since word rates were low, magazines on which he counted failed, and his mother's illnesses caused him heavy expenses. Mrs. Howard had been in poor health for years and was now in rapid decline. In May 1935, *Weird Tales* owed Howard $800. Still, whatever Howard's problems, money troubles do not seem to have bulked large among them.

His circle of correspondents grew, with many letters passing between him and Clark Ashton Smith, H. P. Lovecraft, and August Derleth. He urged Lovecraft to visit him in Texas, promising a tour of the historic sights of the Lone Star State; for they had not allowed their often intense arguments to cloud their friendship. Howard was bitterly disappointed when, in the spring of 1932, Lovecraft arrived in New Orleans on one of his shoestring bus tours, at a moment when Howard (as a result of bank failures and the discontinuance of certain magazines) was broke, carless, and unable to join him. Nor could Lovecraft have stretched his travel budget to visit Cross Plains.

Howard telegraphed E. Hoffmann Price, with whom he had

been corresponding and who was then living in New Orleans, and told him where to find Lovecraft. Price was a fellow-contributor to *Weird Tales* and the only full-time, practicing professional writer whom Howard met in the flesh. (Harold Preece became a writer only after he left Texas.) Price telephoned Lovecraft and brought him to his own quarters, where Lovecraft had a memorable visit before returning to Providence. But Lovecraft and Howard never did meet.

Howard did, however, receive two visits from Price, in 1934 and 1935. Howard told Price:

"Ed, I am God damn proud to have you visit me. . . . Nobody thinks I amount to much, so I am glad to have a chance to show these sons of bitches that a successful writer will drive a thousand miles to hell and gone out of his way to see me."[43]

Howard dated a young schoolteacher, Novalyne Price, who taught public speaking in the local high school. She was thought a little eccentric, too, being a perfectionist with her pupils. The University of Texas staged an annual University Interscholastic League contest in public speaking. Miss Price coached her teams so mercilessly—usually on an abridged Shakespearean play—that they repeatedly won first prize.

In July 1935, however, Howard broke off his friendship with Miss Price by a bitter letter, in which he accused her of making fun of him, behind his back, to their mutual friend Vinson. In a subsequent letter, in May 1936, he spoke of having renewed and then broken off an old love affair, but without naming the girl. It would seem that, during his last year or two, he was not starved for female companionship, so far as he wanted to partake of it.

Mrs. Howard's health continued to sink; she had cancer. During the first half of 1936, Howard spent much of his time driving her to various hospitals. At home, he had to do most of the housework.

When Mrs. Howard took turns for the worse, Howard would

talk to his father about the condition of his literary business. Sensing that Howard was contemplating suicide, the doctor tried to argue him out of this intention. But Howard told his father that "he positively did not intend to live after his mother was gone." Early in June 1936, Howard wrote to Kline in Chicago, giving instructions for the handling of his literary estate if anything should befall him.

At this time, there was a brisk demand for Howard's fiction. Several magazines asked him for more sport, pirate, and humorous Western stories. *Argosy,* long one of his goals, requested a whole series of the last-named kind.

On the night of June 10, 1936, Doctor Howard noted that Robert seemed cheerful. Howard put his arm around his father and said: "Buck up; you are equal to it; you will go through it all right."[44]

June 11th was a fiendishly hot day. Early in the morning, Mrs. Howard was in a coma. Howard asked if she would ever regain consciousness. The nurse answered: "I'm afraid not."

Howard sat down at his battered Underwood No. 5 and typed:

> All fled—all done, so lift me on the pyre;
> The feast is over and the lamps expire.

Howard then went out, got into his car, and shot himself through the head. He died about four that afternoon without regaining consciousness, while his mother lingered until the following day.

Howard's death sent a wave of amazement, grief, and indignation through his circle of friends and admirers. Lovecraft wrote: "That such a genuine artist should perish while hundreds of insincere hacks continue to concoct spurious ghosts and vampires and space-ships and occult detectives is indeed a sorry piece of cosmic irony!"

An even greater irony was the commercial success of Howard's writings thirty-odd years after his death. If he had known that something like two million copies of his books would be sold, in over half a dozen countries. . . . But he had no way of foreseeing this, despite his speculative talk of "unrecognized forces of the future." It might not have mattered if he had.

This suicide has long been a subject of amateur psychological speculation. Suggestions include Oedipism, paranoid schizophrenia, and latent homosexuality. All are guesses. Still, when a healthy young man with versatile abilities, wide interests, a congenial occupation, excellent prospects, and a growing circle of friends and admirers kills himself over a family tragedy of a commonplace and inevitable kind, it is plain that he was not a well-balanced human being.

It has been suggested that Howard's worry over physical deterioration may have contributed to his suicide. But this cannot have been more than a small factor, since, in late letters, he wrote that he was in the best health in a long time. Nor was it a sudden onset of one of his fits of gloomy depression. He had planned the act months in advance and was cheerful—the cheerfulness of a man who has made up his mind—the night before the event.

Evidently his "fatal fixation" (as Derleth put it) on his mother was the main cause. Perhaps a good psychoanalyst might have saved him, but that is like saying that penicillin might have saved Byron. If the persuasion of his father, whose opinions he respected no matter how they squabbled at times, could not swerve him from the course he had long planned, it would have taken something drastic indeed to change his mind.

Both Howard and Lovecraft, although men of powerful intellect and many virtues, failed to come to terms with real life. Instead, they used their imaginative reveries, not as a refreshment from the round of daily living, but as a total escape from it. In fact, Howard's immersion in his world of make-believe perhaps contributed to the vividness of his fiction. Lovecraft was on the right track when he wrote:

> It is hard to describe precisely what made his stories stand out so—
> but the real secret is that *he was in every one of them,* whether
> they were ostensibly commercial or not. . . . even when he out-
> wardly made concessions to the mammon-guided editors he had an
> internal force & sincerity which broke through to the surface &
> put the imprint of his personality on everything he wrote. . . .
> He was almost alone in his ability to create real emotions of fear
> & of dread suspense. . . . No author can excel unless he takes his
> work very seriously & puts himself whole-heartedly into it—and
> Two-Gun did just that, even when he claimed and consciously
> believed that he didn't.[45]

Howard's preoccupation with and absorption in his fantasy
life, however, had a fearful price. Although Howard seemed
more realistic and practical than Lovecraft, his eventual failure
was the more complete of the two. The critic who was so appalled by Howard's fictional violence passed a harsh but not
unjust judgment on Howard's refusal to face reality:

> Howard's life is like a fable illustrating the sad consequences of
> this situation. Living in the never-never land of Conan and King
> Kull, he slaughtered enemies by the dozen. He was fearless, in-
> scrutable, desired by all women. Single-handed he toppled rulers
> from their thrones and built empires of oriental splendor. Even
> the menace of the supernatural was vanquished by the magic that
> he alone was able to control. In the real world, however, he had
> no resources. When he was faced with the loss of maternal pro-
> tection he took the way of self-destruction.[46]

There is a slight quibble here. Literally, a book is just as
"real" as a board, a boat, or a baby. Therefore, an hour spent
reading a book contains exactly as much "real life" as an hour
spent in sawing a board, sailing a boat, or nursing a baby. What
we really mean when we speak of "real life" is life containing a
representative assortment of normal human activities and interests: work and play, getting and begetting, commanding and
obeying, and so on. To concentrate on one aspect of life to the

exclusion of all the rest is to invite Lovecraft's frustration and Howard's doom.

Dr. Isaac Howard inherited Howard's estate, and the Kline agency sold several of Howard's stories after Howard's death. Counting collaborations, Howard wrote about 250 stories— more than his pen pals H. P. Lovecraft and Clark Ashton Smith together. Of these, over two dozen were published posthumously. Some had been rejected; others were bought by magazines that ceased publication before the Howard story appeared.

The agency had much trouble with the suspicious and crusty Doctor Howard, who was sure they were trying to cheat him. It is a common item in Texan folklore that all Northerners are sharpies out to hornswoggle honest Texans.

Soon after the loss of his family, Doctor Howard went to the editor of the *Cross Plains Review* and barked: "I'm going to start a Sunday School class. Round up all the men in town for Sunday night!"

Since the formidable doctor was not easily gainsaid, the editor meekly obeyed. At the meeting, Doctor Howard began:

"Now, I want every man of you, who's ever been drunk or been in a whorehouse, to stand up!"

My informant said: "Well, I stood up, and some of the others stood up; but it sure was embarrassing!"

Doctor Howard had eight years to go, during which he suffered from cataracts, diabetes, and, he said, "loneliness indescribable." He wrote: "I do not see why Robert left me. I am so lonely and desolate."[47] It is hard not to pity the cantankerous old man, even though his own acts and attitudes were probably, to some extent, to blame for the suicide.

The reader may wonder at Howard's callousness in condemning his father to such a fate. But a psychiatrist tells me that, when one has determined on suicide, one has by then become so utterly self-absorbed that nothing outside oneself really matters. At that point, Howard no longer cared about his

father, or his friends and admirers, or his career, or even his
ambition to explore the ruins of ancient cities. "All fled, all
done. . ."

Robert E. Howard had over 160 stories published in his lifetime. He left over eighty more unpublished and fragments of
still others. Many of the previously unpublished works have
appeared in recent years.

During the decade after Howard's death, his writings—
mainly of the Conan stories—were the private enthusiasm of
a few admirers with files of *Weird Tales.* In his last year,
Howard had sold British rights to *The Hour of the Dragon* and
a collection of the Breckenridge Elkins Westerns, *A Gent from
Bear Creek.* But the would-be publisher of the Conan novel
went out of business. The other publisher, Herbert Jenkins, did
not issue *A Gent from Bear Creek* until 1937, after Howard's
death.

The first serious attempt to revive Howard came in 1946,
when August Derleth's Arkham House published a collection of
Howard's fiction as *Skull-Face and Others.* Besides "Skull-Face"
itself, the volume included stories of Conan, Kull, Solomon
Kane, and Bran Mak Morn. In the 1950s, a small publisher
brought out the then known Conan stories in clothbound
volumes, and in the 1960s a major paperback house reissued
them with stories added by the present writer and his colleagues
Lin Carter and Björn Nyberg.

The success of the Conan paperbacks touched off a general
reprinting of Howard's stories, both in cloth and in paper. The
magazine *Bestsellers* has listed Howard among the eight writers
of imaginative fiction whose books have, in the last thirty years,
sold over a million copies. In the narrower field of heroic fantasy, Howard is surpassed in sales only by Tolkien—who once
told me that he rather liked the Conan stories. Howard also
begat a flourishing school of imitators.

I suspect that this revival is partly a reaction against some recent trends in fiction. Ever since the Hitlerian War, advance-guard writers have issued stories marked by certain features, carried to doubtful extremes. One is the use of experimental narrative techniques: non-sentences, stream-of-consciousness, temporal disorganization, and plotlessness. Another is extreme subjectivity, or egotistical self-indulgence on the part of the writer. Another is obsession with contemporary social and political problems. Still another is concentration on sex, especially in its more peculiar manifestations. Lastly there is the vogue of the anti-hero.

All these developments have their place, up to a point. But, since they have all come at once and have often been carried to bizarre extremes, many readers prefer, for a change, stories of stalwart heroes doing heroic deeds, with hot action in roman-tic settings, told in plain, lucid, straightforward prose, without mention of the school dropout problem or the woes of the sexual deviant or the foreign-aid situation or other contempo-rary difficulties. How far this reaction will go, no man knoweth; but while its lasts, Howard's publishers stand to benefit.

During this revival, Howard has slept beneath the large, plain gravestone in the Brownwood cemetery, where his parents also lie. A panel reads: "They were lovely and pleasant in their lives and in their death they were not divided" (2 Samuel 1:23).

According to what my sources in Cross Plains told me, the Howard family was not in fact quite so harmonious as all that. For Robert Howard himself, a fitting epitaph would have been a sentence from John D. Clark's introduction to one of the Conan books: "And above all Howard was a storyteller."

VII

PARALLEL WORLDS:
FLETCHER PRATT

*"A castle on the Pyrenean height
The necromancer keeps, the work of spell;*
*(The host relates) "of steel, so fair and bright
All nature cannot match the wondrous shell.
There many cavaliers, to prove their might,
Have gone, but none returned the tale to tell."*[1]

ARIOSTO

My friend and collaborator Fletcher Pratt (1897–1956) was
a connoisseur of heroic fantasy before that term was invented.
He read Norse sagas in the original and extravagantly admired
E. R. Eddison's *The Worm Ouroboros.* Curiously, he despised
Howard's Conan stories, next to Tolkien's *Lord of the Rings*
the most successful books in the genre, because their occasional
crudities and lapses of logic exasperated him. He had little use
for heroes who merely battered their way out of traps by means
of bulging thews, without using their brains.

Pratt also tried his own hand at such stories. Besides his
several collaborations with me, he wrote two major novels in
the genre in the late 1940s, *The Well of the Unicorn* and *The
Blue Star.*

(Murray) Fletcher Pratt, the son of an upstate New York
farmer, was born on one of the Indian reservations near Buffalo.
He claimed that this gave him the right to hunt and fish in
New York State without a license, but he had never availed
himself of the privilege.

As a youth, five feet three but wiry and muscular, Pratt un-

dertook two careers in Buffalo. One was that of librarian; the
other, that of a prizefighter in the flyweight (112-pound) class.
He fought several fights, lost a couple of teeth, and knocked
one opponent cold. When the story appeared in the Buffalo
papers, the head librarian told him that it simply would not do
to have one of their employees knocking people arsy-varsy.
Forced to choose between his careers, Pratt picked the library.

Soon afterwards, Pratt entered Hobart College at Geneva,
New York, on Lake Seneca. When the coach learned that Pratt
had been in the ring, he tapped him for an assistant in his boxing class. Word got around that this funny-looking little freshman, who was showing the boys in the gym how to do rights
over lefts, was the real thing. As a result, somewhat to his dis-
appointment, Pratt was never hazed.

At the end of Pratt's freshman year, his father fell on hard
times. Pratt had to leave college for want of money. In the
early 1920s, he worked as a reporter on the *Buffalo Courier-
Express* and on a Staten Island paper. Later, he settled in New
York City with his second wife, the artist Inga Stephens Pratt.
(His first wife had tried to make him confine his writing to
poetry.)

For several years, Pratt held a succession of fringe literary
jobs, such as editing a "mug book" (a biographical encyclo-
pedia), in which people of small importance were persuaded
to pay to have their lives and pictures published. He also
worked for one of those "writers' institutes," which promise to
turn every would-be scribbler into a Tolstoy and keep the
money coming in by fulsome flattery of the veriest bilge submitted. Later, as an established author, Pratt drew upon these
experiences in lecturing to writers' groups on literary rackets.

In the late 1920s, Pratt got a foothold as an established
writer. From 1929 to 1935 he sold a number of science-fiction
stories to *Amazing Stories, Wonder Stories,* and several other
science-fiction pulps of the time. He worked with several col-
laborators, notably Laurence Manning.

During this time, Pratt also worked for Hugo Gernsback, then publishing *Wonder Stories.* Pratt translated European science-fiction novels from the French and the German, and Gernsback ran them as serials. Like some other publishers operating on a shoestring, Gernsback had a habit of not paying his authors what he had promised, but Pratt got around him. He would translate the first installment or two of a European novel and then, when the material was already in print, say:

"I'm sorry, Mr. Gernsback, but if you don't pay me what you owe me, I don't see how I can complete this translation."

He had Gernsback over a barrel. He also took off more than a year to live in Paris on the insurance money that he collected after a fire gutted the Pratts' apartment. He studied at the Sorbonne and did research for his book on codes and ciphers, *Secret and Urgent.*

He learned Danish among other languages, spoke French with a terrible accent, and became friends with the curator of arms and armor at the Louvre. The curator let him try on the armor of King François I, who in his day had been deemed a large, stout man. The flyweight Pratt found all the armor too small except the shoulder pieces; François had tremendous shoulders from working out with sword and battle ax in the tilt yard.

Back in New York, Pratt, now a self-made scholar of respectable attainments, attacked more serious writing. One early effort was *The Red King,* about the successors of Alexander the Great and especially about Pyrrhos of Epeiros. Although written in a lively style and sparkling with interesting ideas, the book was never sold and exists today only in manuscript at the University of Syracuse. As Pratt's then agent explained, a little-known author can write about a well-known historical figure, or a well-known author can write about a little-known historical figure with some chance of success, but an unknown cannot expect to sell a book about another unknown.

Soon, however, Pratt hit his stride with books like *The*

Heroic Years, about the War of 1812; *The Cunning Mulatto,* a book of true crime stories; *Hail, Caesar!,* a biography; and *Ordeal by Fire,* a popular history of the Civil War. The last made Pratt's reputation and remained in print for decades.

The Pratt menage in New York attracted a wide circle of friends, drawn by Pratt's lavish hospitality and extraordinary sense of fun. One room of the apartment was cluttered with cages full of squeaking marmosets, which Pratt successfully raised by feeding them on vitamin tablets and squirming yellow larvae.

As a military, history, and naval buff, Pratt devised a naval war game, to which his friends were invited once a month. In odd moments between sentences, he whittled out scale models ($55' = 1'$) of the world's warships, using balsa wood, wires, and pins, until he had hundreds of these models crowding his shelves.

The game called for the players to crawl around on the floor, moving their models the distances allowed on scales marked in knots; estimating the ranges in inches of the ships on which they were firing; and writing down these estimates on pads. Then the referees chased the players off and measured the actual ranges, penalizing ships hit so many points according to the size of the shells and depriving them of a corresponding number of knots of speed, guns, and so on. When a ship had lost all its points, it was taken from the floor. There were special provisions for merchant ships, shore batteries, submarines, torpedoes, and airplanes.

For several years, the war gamers met in the Pratts' apartment. When this became too crowded, with forty or fifty players crawling around at once, the game moved to a hall on east 59th Street. After the Second World War, interest declined, perhaps because nuclear explosives made the whole thing seem too artificial. It has, however, been revived, using 1:2500 warship models made in Germany.

Pratt's many interests also included the reading of sagas

(already mentioned) and gourmet cookery. His *A Man and his Meals* was a cookbook. He taught at the Bread Loaf Writers' Conference, was a Baker Street Irregular, and served for seven years as president of the New York Authors' Club. When he declined to serve longer, the club collapsed. In 1944 he founded a stag eating, drinking, and arguing society, the Trap Door Spiders, which still meets eight or nine times a year in New York.

In 1939, my old friend and college roommate, John D. Clark, introduced me to Pratt. Being a naval hobbyist myself, I was soon an enthusiastic war gamer and a regular attendant at the Pratts' evenings, along with such colleagues as Malcolm Jameson, Laurence Manning, George O. Smith, Ted Sturgeon, and L. Ron Hubbard, long before Hubbard manifested himself as the pontiff of Scientology.

I had been free-lancing for a year and a half, having been fired as an economy measure from an editorial job on a trade journal. I was also in the midst of getting married. With the appearance of John W. Campbell's *Unknown,* Pratt conceived the idea of a series of novels, in collaboration with me, about a hero who projects himself into the parallel worlds described on this plane in myths and legends. We decided to make our hero a brash, self-conceited young psychologist named Harold Shea, who gets the vanity knocked out of him in the course of his adventures and is forced to grow up.

First we sent Harold to the world of Scandinavian myth, in "The Roaring Trumpet" (*Unknown,* May 1940). Pratt furnished most of the background for this story, since at that time my knowledge of Norse myth was limited to popular or juvenile digests and retellings. I had not yet read the original sources.

For the second episode, we transferred Harold to the world of Spenser's *Faerie Queene* in "The Mathematics of Magic" (August 1940). I was never so enthusiastic about *The Faerie*

Queene as Pratt, finding it tedious for long stretches. Years later, however, when I took to writing light verse, I composed a poem, *The Dragon-Kings,* in Spenserian nine-line stanzas. This is a very exacting verse form. Having sweated through three such stanzas, I was appalled at the feat of Edmund Spenser, whose *Faerie Queene* comprises over four thousand of the things!

The first two novellas were followed by "The Castle of Iron" (April 1941), which took Harold to the world of Ariosto's *Orlando Furioso,* of which *The Faerie Queene* was an imitation. In that year, also, Holt brought out the first two novellas as the clothbound book, *The Incomplete Enchanter,* which has been through a number of editions since. While Pratt proposed the basic themes for the first two stories, those for the later ones were worked out by discussion between us.

After the Hitlerian War, Pratt and I rewrote and expanded "The Castle of Iron" to book length, in which form it appeared in 1950. We also wrote two more novellas of the saga, placing Harold first in the world of the Finnish *Kalevala* ("The Wall of Serpents") and finally in the world of Irish myth ("The Green Magician") with Cúchulainn and Queen Maev. After magazine publication, these two stories were combined in a clothbound volume, *Wall of Serpents* (Avalon, 1960).

For obvious reasons, I cannot objectively assess the virtues and faults of these novels. I will only say that they were certainly heroic fantasy, or swordplay-and-sorcery fiction, long before these terms were invented. While Robert E. Howard is justly hailed as the main American pioneer in this genre, neither Pratt nor I, when we started the Shea stories, had ever read a Conan story or heard enough about Howard to recognize his name. By coincidence, our colleague Lester del Rey had the idea of a story laid in a parallel world of Scandinavian myth at just about the time we did. Alas for Lester! we got our manuscript in first.

Our method of collaboration was to meet in Pratt's apartment and hammer out the plot by discussion, of which I took shorthand notes. Observing the utility of Pratt's knowledge of shorthand from his journalistic days, I taught myself Gregg and have found it valuable ever since.

When I had taken home the notes, I wrote a rough draft. Pratt then wrote the final draft, which I edited. In a few cases, in our later Gavagan's Bar stories, we reversed the procedure, Pratt doing the first draft and I the second. This did not work out so well. In such collaborations, I think, it is generally better for the junior member to do the rough draft, since the senior member, as a result of experience, is likely to have more skill at polishing and condensation.

A fan magazine once asserted that, in the Harold Shea stories, de Camp furnished the imaginative element and Pratt the controlling logic. Actually, it was the other way round. Pratt had a livelier and more creative imagination than I, but I had a keener sense of critical logic. In any case, I learned much of what I think I know about the writer's craft in the course of these collaborations. Pratt's influence on me in this matter was second only to Campbell's.

In 1941, L. Ron Hubbard wrote one of his several hilarious fantasy novels for *Unknown:* "The Case of the Friendly Corpse" (August 1941). Hubbard got the basis for his story from our mutual friend John D. Clark. In the 1930s, Clark and a friend concocted a prospectus for an imaginary College of the Unholy Names. In a clever imitation of the usual deadly-dull style of such publications, they solemnly listed courses in the black arts, e.g. Advanced Thaumaturgy 112, Elementary and Advanced Transformations (Magic 56), . . . Delinquent students (e.g. those caught sleeping alone) were to be dropped —from Skelos Tower (borrowed from Howard).

Clark lent the typescript of this fabrication to Hubbard, who made it a major element in his story. The tale has some of Hubbard's funniest passages but lets the reader down badly at the end. The hero, Jules Riley, has swapped souls with an apprentice magician on another plane, who up to then has been a student at the College of the Unholy Names. Another student tells Jules (now on this other plane) that Harold Shea appeared before him, claiming to be a magician from another world. The student challenged Harold to a sporting contest: the student would turn his wand into a super-serpent, and Harold could summon up his own monster, and they would see which creature won. But ". . . the snake just grew up and then grabbed him and ate him up before I could do anything about it."

Some fans were indignant at Hubbard's so brusquely bumping off a colleague's hero. Pratt and I thought of writing a story to rescue Harold from the serpent's maw and turn the tables, but after some floundering we gave up. Another writer's *mise en scène,* we found, so severely cramps the imagination that fancy plods when it ought to soar. In the end, we ignored Hubbard and sent Harold on to other milieux.

During 1941–42, Pratt and I wrote two more fantasy novels, *The Land of Unreason* and *The Carnelian Cube,* both of which have gone through several editions. Although both were parallel-world stories, the first was only marginally heroic fantasy and the second not heroic fantasy at all.

Pearl Harbor came just as I was finishing my part of *The Carnelian Cube.* I volunteered for the Naval Reserve, was commissioned, and spent the war navigating a desk at the Philadelphia Naval Base. Heinlein, Asimov, and I did engineering on naval aircraft.

Pratt, a strong patriot and nationalist, described himself as a political conservative; although, when one discussed actual current issues with him, one found him surprisingly objective, pragmatic, and at times almost liberal. Kept out of the armed forces by age, physical limitations, and lack of a college degree, he wrote a war column for the *New York Post.* This ended when his editor forced him to guess on the outcome of the battle of the Coral Sea, and he guessed wrong. He also wrote a number of books on the war, especially the U. S. Navy's part in it.

Later, Pratt became a naval war correspondent assigned to Latin America. An old Brazilophile who spoke fluent Portuguese, Pratt visited Brazil. In tropical Bahia, he and a U.S. Navy captain were entertained by the local bigwigs. Pratt said:

"We were the only white men present—except the waiters. Moreover, our black hosts—politicians, poets, and intellectuals —were obviously men of culture and intelligence, while the waiters were equally obviously a lot of giggling dopes."

Pratt had long worn a mustache and in the early 1930s, for a while, a goatee. Now he grew a straggly full beard, graying reddish in color, and of Babylonian cut. He hated razors, and the Navy would not let him use his electric shaver on shipboard in the Caribbean. This was long before the revival of beards in the 1950s and 60s. His small size, whiskers, thick tinted glasses, and loud shirts made an ensemble not easily forgotten.

After the war, Pratt continued living in New York, while my family and I stayed in the suburbs of Philadelphia. We continued our collaboration with the two more Harold Shea novellas and the Gavagan's Bar stories. The latter were a series of barroom tall tales, comparable to (though conceived independently of) Arthur C. Clarke's tales of the White Hart. Both series may have been inspired by Lord Dunsany's stories of Jorkens. Neither Pratt nor I on one hand, nor Clarke on the other, knew of the other's enterprise until it was well under way.

In the late 1940s, Pratt wrote the two novels that (the Harold Shea stories aside) put him in the front rank of heroic fantasists, with knights and magic, castles and empires, wars and piracies.

The first was *The Well of the Unicorn,* published in 1948 by the short-lived firm of William Sloane Associates. Despite a handsome jacket and beautiful maps by Rafael Palacios, the book had three strikes against it. One: the publishers, on the dubious theory that a writer should use different names in different genres, published the book under the pseudonym of "George U. Fletcher," thus robbing it of the benefits of Pratt's considerable literary status. Two: not satisfied with Pratt's own brief introduction to the story, one of the editors wrote another introduction and printed it before Pratt's. This ran the whole idea of explanatory prefaces or "frames" into the ground.

Finally, there was the incomprehension of many reviewers, to whom at that time a "real" novel had to deal with the contemporary racial question, or the morals of adolescents, or poverty in Appalachia. Tony Boucher, reviewing the book for the much-esteemed *Fantasy and Science Fiction,* did not like the *Well* at all, although like Pratt he was an ardent admirer of *The Worm Ouroboros.* (Neither had Boucher any use for Conan.)

Not surprisingly, the book was remaindered after a year or so of poor sales. Happily, it has since reappeared in paperback.

Despite all this, *The Well of the Unicorn* is in most ways an excellent novel, well-wrought and consistently entertaining, which *aficionados* of the genre ought to know as well as they know the heroic fantasies of Dunsany, Leiber, and Tolkien.

The action takes place in Dalarna, a country resembling medieval Scandinavia. Dalarna groans under the tyranny of the Vulkings, a race-proud military caste, comparable politically to the medieval knightly orders and militarily to the Romans.

Southwest across the Blue Sea lie the main lands of the Empire, comparable to the Holy Roman one of history. The Vulkings plot to gain control of the Empire, of which they are nominal subjects. South lie the turbulent isles of the Twelve Cities, Classical Greek in their politics and Renaissance (plate-armored cavalry) in their warfare. Other powers include the pirate Earl Mikalegon to the north and the blond heathen Dzik across the sea to the west.

Taxed out of his farm by the Vulkings, young Airar Alvarson joins a plot against Vulking rule. He rises to leadership, has adventures and romances, practices magic and has it practiced on him. He makes friends and foes: the pleasantly sinister old Doctor Meliboë (Pratt's version of Merlin); the rough, passionate soldier-girl Evadne of Carrhoene (one of the Twelve Cities); and finally the Princess Argyra, one of the Emperor's daughters.

The story contains much more than derring-do. Characters argue out questions of good and evil, authority and voluntary agreement, and free will versus predestination. The central theme is the philosophy of government: how to organize men to fight effectively for freedom without losing freedom in the process? These questions are discussed with considerable subtlety, since Fletcher's sharp mind had thought much about them.

The novel is also a warning against the solution of problems by easy answers, short cuts, or gimmicks. Airar knows magic; but, whenever he gets himself out of a jam by casting a spell, he finds that in the long run he has landed himself in a worse predicament than the one he has escaped. His sorcerous friend Meliboë is an inveterate short-cutter. But, although Meliboë wishes his young protégé well, the wise old wizard's attempts to help Airar by enchantments likewise tend to go awry, until Airar is forced to exile his "second father" lest worse befall.

The novel has plenty of color, movement, conflict, and intellectual stimulation. Its main weakness lies in its central characters. Airar is a tall blond, for there was a touch of Nordicism in Pratt's *Weltanschauung*. He is upright, brave, and resourceful; rather priggish and solemn; and not really very interesting despite his many interior monologues and soul-searchings. His eventual bride, Argyra, while charming and lovely, is even less developed. As oft befalls, the best characters are minor ones, like Evadne, Meliboë, Mikalegon, and Erb the fisherman.

Moreover, in an excess of subtlety, Pratt sometimes brushed over critical events in such a brief, casual manner that the reader has to turn back the pages to try to figure out how things have come to be.

Knowing Pratt as I did, I was aware of his sources to an extent denied most readers. While writing the novel, Pratt said he was literally dreaming the episodes at night before he put them on paper. At one point, his characters got stuck on a cliff. Then his dreams wandered off the proper story line. Pratt tossed and muttered in his sleep. When this happened, his wife would whisper: "Go back to the cliff!" Then he would quiet down.

The influence of *The Worm Ouroboros* is patent in this novel, and Doctor Meliboë is the spit and image of Doctor Vandermast in Eddison's other Zimiamvian novels. Pratt, furthermore, deliberately used Dunsany's play *King Argimēnēs and the Unknown Warrior* as a springboard. He assumed that Dunsany's Argimēnēs had, some generations before the time of the *Well*, founded Pratt's Empire.

Some of Pratt's characters have names like those in William Morris's pseudo-medieval romances. In fact, the basic idea of the well may have been suggested by Morris's *The Well at the World's End.* The incident of the slaying of the Vulking deserion in Chapter XX was lifted from one of Naomi Mitchison's stories of Classical Greece, as Pratt conceded to me when I pointed it out to him. Poë's tale in Chapter XXVI is based on an actual incident that befell a well-known, red-haired science-fiction writer while he was yachting off the coast of Alaska.

At first, Pratt intended to bring the heathen Dzik on stage. He explained: "They're really Mohammedans—very nice Mohammedans, too." As things worked out, however, he found it expedient to wind up the story before the Dzik invasion.

The archaism of the language of the *Well* seems to derive largely from Morris and Eddison. Although Pratt's English is less medieval and therefore easier to read than theirs, he does not use it with quite their skill and polish, either. Some of his sentences achieve an almost Teutonic length and complexity.

Still and all, the story rates, if not at the very top of the scale, at least very close to it among tales of heroic fantasy and certainly stands far above many run-of-the-mill stories of swordplay and sorcery that have come out in the last decade as original paperbacks.

The other story, *The Blue Star,* was published by Twayne Publishers, Inc., in 1952 as the third of three novels presented in the large volume *Witches Three.* (The other two were Leiber's *Conjure Wife* and Blish's *There Shall Be No Darkness.*) The frame for this story is a Prologue, wherein three men sit of an evening, drinking and talking philosophy. They speculate about possible worlds, and that night all three dream of such a world. The dream is the story.

This time, also, Pratt has an Empire. The model, however, is the Austrian or Holy Roman Empire of the eighteenth century, say about the time of Maria Theresa. The atmosphere, with its masked balls and its noblemen attended by gangs of thugs, reminds one of Casanova's memoirs. There is not a hulking, grunting, hairy-chested barbarian in sight, and the clang of swords in combat is never heard.

Whereas gunpowder is unknown, witchcraft works, in a complicated way. The ability is hereditary, being passed from mother to daughter. But it passes at the precise moment when the daughter is deflowered; mother loses the talent as daughter gains it.

Certain witches possess a jewel in the form of a small blue pentagram—the Blue Star of the title—worn as a pendant. Each witch lends this to her lover or mate. While he wears it, he can descry people's true emotions by looking them in the eye, but only so long as he remains faithful to his witch.

Again the hero, Rodvard Bergelin, joins a conspiracy, the Sons of the New Day, against the corrupt and tottering government of the Empress. The conspirators urge him to become the lover of a potential witch, Lalette Asterhax, because they need the talent of a Blue Star wearer in their intrigues. Neither Rodvard nor Lalette is in love with the other at first. Rodvard, a clerk in a governmental genealogical office in the capital city of

Netznegon, has set his eye on a baron's daughter who visits the office. He is, however, bullied by his fellow conspirators into seducing Lalette. Lalette on her side yields to escape the attentions of the brutal Count Cleudi.

Both are trapped in various plights and forced to flee, first together and then singly. Separately they voyage to the land of Mancherei. This province is under the rule of the Amorosian sect, which harps on the theme of love-love-love. The doctrines of the sect sound like a caricature of the tenets of Christian Science. Pratt, however, can hardly have meant it so, since he was himself a Christian Scientist. How he reconciled his constant pipe and cigar-smoking and his convivial drinking with Mrs. Eddy's strictures on liquor and tobacco ("the obnoxious fumes of . . . a leaf naturally attractive to no creature except a loathsome worm"),[2] I shall never know.

Reunited by happenstance in Mancherei, Rodvard and Lalette fall afoul of the all-powerful Amorosian priesthood. They are rescued by the Sons of the New Day; for the revolution has begun.

Soon, however, the leader of the revolution, Mathurin (who had been Cleudi's valet) turns out to be a ruthless, bloodthirsty fanatic of the Robespierre-Lenin stamp. So Rodvard and Lalette must flee again.

The novel is more pretentious but less successful than *The Well of the Unicorn*. The setting is described with vivid minuteness; nearly every piece of casual conversation throws out a flash of rich detail. This is a real achievement. As in the other novel, there are searching disputes about morals, politics, religion, and everything else under the sun.

In fact, that is the trouble. The setting utterly overwhelms the chief characters. Whereas Airar Alvarson, if a bit of a stick, is at least a resolute and competent hero, Rodvard is nearer to one of those wretched anti-heroes that make so much modern fiction dismal reading.

A shy, gangling youth, well-meaning but ineffectual, with no

particular skill save that of tracing noblemen's pedigrees, Rodvard accomplishes hardly anything under his own steam. Aside
from escaping from a few tight fixes, he is the passive object of
others' actions rather than an actor in his own right. When he
does assert himself, he usually bungles. When he tries to speak,
he gets only so far as "I—" before somebody interrupts.

Lalette, with her shrewish temper, is a more positive character. But she, too, accomplishes little save, by desperate sleights
and shifts, to escape from encompassing perils, first from Cleudi
and later from the lecherous Amorosian priests. Although some
of the minor characters are vivid, most of these are singularly
repulsive middle-aged and elderly women. A Doctor Remigor-
ius plays the regular rôle of Merlin-Vandermast-Meliboë but
has a much smaller part than in other novels of the group.

Rodvard and Lalette are ever plagued by lack of money. This
was Pratt's catharsis of bitter memories of his own poverty-
stricken youth.[3]

Parenthetically, in many heroic fantasies, including these
two, there is a good deal of casual fornication, apparently without contraception of any kind. Yet none of the women ever
seems to become inopportunely pregnant.

Is *The Blue Star* worth reading? Most emphatically it is. If I
rate it below the *Well,* I should still place it well above many
contemporary works in the genre. Pratt's stories always move
right along. Something is always happening. His writing is full
of novel conceits, flashes of wit, and interesting turns of phrase.
And the setting is so lush and vivid that perhaps you will not
mind the *morbidezza* of the leading characters.

When he had finished *The Blue Star,* Pratt told his friends
that he planned a third fantasy novel. The chief character, he
said with shrewd self-judgment, would be a woman, "because
I've learned that my female characters are stronger than my
male ones." This woman, finding her modern life hard, would
wake up in the body of another woman of 1,800 years ago, on

the German frontier of the Roman Empire. There she would learn what real hardship was.

With the approach of the Civil War centennial, however, Fletcher became so busy with better-paying nonfiction that, during his last years, he gave up fiction altogether. He and I discussed possible future works of fiction, such as another Harold Shea story laid in the world of Persian myth, or a Gavagan's Bar tale about a vampire with a sweet tooth, who attacked only diabetics. But they were never written, and we shall never know how the Roman story would have turned out. I have not tried to carry on any of our series alone, because I thought that the combination of Pratt and de Camp produced a result quite different from the work of either of us alone.

About 1950, Pratt had one of his unlikely adventures. Having a lecture engagement in Boston, he reserved a compartment on the overnight train thither. He and Inga boarded the train and went to bed. Pratt was dozing off when a blue-clad arm came through the curtains and shook him, while a voice roared:

"Dis is de New York police! Come on out of dere! We know dere's two of you!"

Pratt, his hair awry and blinking without his glasses, climbed out into the aisle in his pajamas to find, not a policeman, but a Pullman conductor, six feet something and in the 200-pound class. Pratt explained that his tickets were in order and that he and Inga had been lawfully married for twenty-odd years. The conductor kept giving him lip. So Pratt, whose ancient skills had not deserted him, lefted the man behind the ear and knocked him down.

The conductor got up, departed vowing vengeance, and returned with a squad of policemen. Each told his tale. The cops looked up at the conductor, looked down at Pratt, and walked off laughing like hell.

In 1956, at 59, Pratt was immersed in books on the Civil War and had begun to hit the best-seller lists, when he suddenly fell ill of cancer of the liver and soon died. He had written over fifty books, including many science-fiction stories, books on Napoleon, biographies of Edwin M. Stanton and King Valdemar IV of Denmark, a cookbook, a book on codes and ciphers, and histories of the U.S. Navy, the War of 1812, and the Civil War. His books are still published, and the Trap Door Spiders still meet. Both, one may hope, will continue for a long time to come.

VIII

SIERRAN SHAMAN:
CLARK ASHTON SMITH

Riding on Rosinante where the cars
With dismal unremitting clangors pass,
And people move like curbless energumens
Rowelled by fiends of fury back and forth,
Behold! Quixote comes, in battered mail,
Armgaunt, with eyes of some keen haggard hawk
Far from his eyrie. Gazing right and left,
Over his face a lightning of disdain
Flashes, and limns the hollowness of cheeks
Bronzed by the suns of battle; and his hand
Tightens beneath its gauntlet on the lance
As if some foe had challenged him, or sight
Of unredresséd wrong provoked his ire. . .[1]

CLARK ASHTON SMITH

Can a poet find happiness in rural America? One poet tried
but with only meager success. This was Clark Ashton Smith
(1893–1961), in his day acclaimed as one of America's fore-
most living poets. Smith also created a sizable body of heroic
fantasy of highly distinctive quality; hence no account of the
genre is complete without him.

Yet Smith's life, outwardly uneventful, was full of contradictions and ironies. Perhaps the most brilliant single member
of the Lovecraft-*Weird Tales* circle of the 1930s, he suffered
from poverty nearly all his life. This followed naturally from

the type of work by which he supported himself; but he did not like it.

He said that he hated his home town but spent a virtual lifetime there. He deemed himself primarily a poet; yet he is mainly remembered for a body of weird short fantasies, most of them composed in one brief six-year period. His poems, once compared to those of Byron, Keats, and Swinburne, are known today to few outside of some science-fiction and fantasy fans. Few of those who nowadays make a stir in the poetic world have even heard of Clark Ashton Smith.

In the 1880s, a footloose English bachelor, Timeus Smith, wandered into north-central California, in the gold-mining country. Of respectable bourgeois family, he had spent his patrimony on travel but now settled down. In 1891, he married Mary Frances ("Fanny") Gaylord, the small, vivacious spinster daughter of a farm family of Long Valley, a few miles from Auburn. He was about 36; she, about four years older. Two years later their only child, Clark Ashton Smith, was born.

Timeus Smith was a lean man with a narrow, beak-nosed face and a small mustache. A quietly amiable but somewhat impractical person, his accent and British reserve did not make him locally popular. He moved in with his in-laws and worked as night clerk in a hotel. In 1902, he bought, under a mortgage, a tract of 44.15 acres on Indian Ridge (also called "Boulder Ridge") about a mile from Auburn. Here he dug a well and built his own house—not the "log cabin" it is sometimes called but a modest, one-story, four-room, wooden frame house sheathed in boards and shingles, with a tar-paper roof and no electricity or running water.

The tract was unpromising for farming, at which Timeus Smith made desultory efforts. A grove of California blue oak abutted the site of the house. The rest of the tract was cluttered with boulders and overgrown with scrub, green and lush in spring, brown and lifeless in the fall after the rainless Californian summer. Clark Ashton Smith described the landscape in one of his tales:

> The Ridge is a long and rambling moraine, heavily strewn in places with boulders, as its name implies, and with many out-croppings of black volcanic stone. Fruit-ranches cling to some of its slopes, but scarcely any of the top is under cultivation, and much of the soil, indeed, is too thin and stony to be arable. With its twisted pines, often as fantastic in form as the cypresses of the California coast, and its gnarled and stunted oaks, the landscape has a wild and quaint beauty, with more than a hint of the Japanesque in places. . . . Between the emerald of the buckeyes, the gray-green of the pines, the golden and dark and bluish greens of the oaks, I caught glimpses of the snow-white Sierras to the east, and the faint blue of the Coast Range to the west, beyond the pale and lilac levels of the Sacramento valley.[2]

Building the house took several years. In 1907, about the time the Smiths moved into their new house, young Smith graduated from the Auburn grammar school. He passed the examinations for the high school but decided not to attend it. Already a voracious reader, he had been writing juvenile stories —mainly oriental romances—and poems. He had, he said, decided to be a poet, and he was sure that he could educate himself better than the Auburn high school could educate him.

In this opinion he may not have been entirely wrong. The law did not then compel him to continue his formal education, nor did his parents insist upon it. The decision, however, affected Smith's later life and not in favorable ways. While his withdrawal from the normal schoolboy milieu may or may not have made him a better poet, it also, probably, contributed to his later frustrating difficulties in making a living.

Smith's method of self-education was to read an unabridged dictionary through, word for word, studying not only the definitions of the words but also their derivations from ancient languages. Having an extraordinary eidetic memory, he seems to have retained most or all of it. When he became a commercial

writer, he constantly disconcerted his readers by dropping in
rare words like "fulvous," "cerement," and "mignard." The
poem quoted at the head of this article affords examples. No
other writer, I am sure, ever called a man's head his "cephalic
appendage." The other main course in Smith's self-education
was to read the *Encyclopædia Britannica* through at least twice.

Smith passed several years of adolescence as a weedy, wiry
youth, reading, writing, doing farm chores, and sometimes hir-
ing out to other farmers. In 1909, Timeus Smith undertook
chicken farming. Clark Ashton Smith built the henhouse but
found cleaning it his most obnoxious task. To eke out the family's minute income, Fanny Smith sold magazine subscriptions
in Auburn.

The years 1910–12 brought Clark Ashton Smith a sudden
spurt of premature fame and success. Hence he can be excused
for thinking that his unconventional ideas for a poet's proper
education had been right after all.

First, he sold several stories. These were undistinguished
tales of oriental adventure but up to the professional standards
of the popular fiction of the time. Two appeared in *The Black
Cat,* published since 1895 in Boston by H. D. Umbstaetter. *The
Black Cat* was not a magazine of science fiction or fantasy but
of general popular short stories. It published tales by Ellis
Parker Butler, Octavus Roy Cohen, Jack London, Rex Stout,
and other successful entertainers of the time. It also published
an occasional imaginative story of the kind later called science
fiction or fantasy: for instance, London's "A Thousand Deaths"
(May 1899; mad scientist on a South Sea island) or Don
Mark Lemon's "The White Death" (July 1902; gigantic hypnotic Mexican tarantula).

Smith's tales were not of this kind but were simple adventures. "The Mahout" appeared in the issue of August 1911;
"The Raja and the Tiger" in that of April 1912. He sold two
similar stories to *The Overland Monthly,* published in San
Francisco.

Then, Smith's poetry began to be taken seriously. At thirteen, he had become an enthusiast for Poe's verse. At fifteen, he became likewise infatuated with that of George Sterling. Sterling (1869–1926) had moved from his native New York State to California in 1891 and had become a protégé of Ambrose Bierce—"bitter Bierce," the misanthropic writer, poet, journalist, and satirist, whose stories include several examples of imaginative fiction.

In 1913, Bierce went to Mexico to cover the civil war between Venustiano Carranza and a former bandit and cattle rustler who operated under the alias of Pancho Villa. Bierce attached himself to Villa but soon dropped out of sight forever. There are various tales of his end. One of the more plausible is that Bierce, with an exaggerated idea of his immunity as an American, walked in on Villa and denounced him to his face, calling him a mere brigand and saying that he was going over to Carranza. As Bierce left, Villa told his men: "Shoot him!" And they did.

Sterling had become the leader of the artistic colony at Carmel, on the California coast, and married Caroline Rand. A tall, handsome, athletic man, he was also an incorrigible bohemian, full of contradictions: charming and convivial, often infinitely kind and generous, but mercurial and irresponsible. He was sensible in advising others but erratic and self-indulgent in his own affairs and, like many poets, a perpetual Don Juan.

Smith now began to publish his poems in local periodicals. He was also asked to read his poems to ladies' clubs. The ladies saw a thin, shy youth not yet twenty, with a broad forehead and narrow chin, wearing a well-worn brown suit and mumbling poems of cosmic doom and degeneracy. What they could hear of Smith's verses horrified rather than edified them.

In 1911, Emily I. Hamilton, who taught English at the Auburn high school, persuaded Smith to write George Sterling to ask for criticism. Thus began a correspondence that lasted to Sterling's death.

As a letter writer, Smith was not nearly so prolific or so self-revealing as Lovecraft. Although numerous, his letters, compared to HPL's, seem rather short and dryly impersonal. With Sterling, however, Smith let down his hair. He often burst out with hatred of Auburn: "hell-hole," "sink hole of creation," "nothing but a cage, and with little gilding on the bars at that," "impested haunt of Philistines and rattlesnakes." "To most of the people here, I'm only a crazy chump who imagines he can write poetry."

Sterling showed Smith's poems to Bierce, who waxed enthusiastic. But Smith never met Bierce and always regretted the missed opportunity.

In June 1912, Smith went to Carmel for a month's visit with Sterling. It was a memorable experience, to which Smith often later alluded. But he found the pressure of many personalities, even in so relaxed an atmosphere as that of hobohemian Carmel, more painful than pleasant. When Sterling invited him back next year, he declined, saying:

"Your saying that Carmel will be livelier this summer, is no inducement to *me*. You know I don't much care about meeting people."

During the visit, Sterling introduced Smith to a translation of the poems of Baudelaire. Charles Pierre Baudelaire had been the leader of the French "Decadent" school, writing about things that the taste of the time deemed "morbid" or "unwholesome." Baudelaire lived on a small trust fund, kept a colored mistress, fought a battle with the censors, translated Poe into French, drank heavily, ate opium, tried hashish but decided against it, and died from the effects of his excesses in 1867 at 46.

Smith had hardly returned home when a retired diplomat named Boutwell Dunlap whisked him off to San Francisco to introduce him to useful people and to earn brownie points by "discovering" Smith. The latter proved shyly inarticulate with Dunlap's business-class friends but opened up with the reporters. The papers duly hailed Smith as "the boy poet" and the "poetic genius" of "the lonely Sierras," the compeer of Byron, Shelley, and Keats.

Learning that Sterling was in San Francisco, Smith tried to get in touch with him. But Sterling, in the throes of one of his love affairs, sidestepped the contact. Instead, Dunlap presented Smith to the publisher A. M. Robertson, who had brought out a volume of Sterling's verse. Smith submitted his crop of poems, and in November Robertson published them as *The Star-Treader and Other Poems.* The book got mixed reviews, some good and some abusing Smith for his "sinister" and "ghoulish" qualities.

In 1912, Ambrose Bierce wrote to a western magazine, warning that, while Smith was a very promising young poet, this premature publicity and exaggerated praise might be bad for him and lead to an equally exaggerated reaction against him. The great professional cynic's prophecy was not put to the test, for the next year Smith's health broke down. For eight years he was intermittently reduced to semi-invalidism, although it is not known what ailed him. (Lovecraft had a similar breakdown at about the same time.)

Smith complained of nervous disorders, depression, sore joints, digestive upsets, and "malarial symptoms." The local physician thought he had incipient tuberculosis. But this doubtful diagnosis was never confirmed, and Smith showed no signs of tuberculosis in later life. He declined Sterling's offer to put him into a sanitarium.

During this time, Smith continued his correspondence with Sterling. While he had not liked San Francisco on his previous visit, finding the crowds oppressive, in 1915 he went thither as Sterling's guest to the Panama-Pacific International Exposition. He entered into correspondence with Lovecraft's lifelong friend Samuel Loveman. He composed many poems and did stints of farm labor.

Smith also learned what somebody should have told him sooner: that poetry is not commercial. In twentieth-century America, in general, one simply cannot make a living at it. Therefore one must have a trade or profession or business and compose one's verse on the side. *The Star-Treader* had sold well over a thousand copies, which is good for a first volume of poems by an unknown. But Smith got only $50 in royalties from it, plus an occasional $5.00 from periodicals that published single poems.

Smith, however, had never been trained for anything but verse. In 1915, while he and his father were driving a shaft on the tract in a vain hope of striking gold, Smith wrote: "I may find myself confronted in the disagreeable necessity of earning a living. I'm really as ill-prepared for that as if I had been brought up in affluence. . . . I don't feel in the least like work, I seem unfit for anything but pleasure, and precious little of that has ever come my way."

He wrote to Sterling about his financial needs, suggesting a loan of $1,500 to $2,000 to put his father's chicken business on a sound footing. No loan was forthcoming, but in 1917 an anonymous lady admirer of Smith's verse arranged to pay him a small monthly stipend through Sterling. This continued for three and a half years. When it ended, Smith wrote resignedly: ". . . if I work for a living, I will have to give up my art. I've not the energy for both. And I hardly know what I could do— I'm 'unskilled labor' at anything except drawing and poetry. . . . Nine hours of work on week days leaves me too tired for any mental effort."

The unskilled labor into which he drifted consisted largely of woodcutting and fruit picking. He railed against Auburn: "If it weren't for my people, I'd hoof it out of this —! —! —! rotten country tomorrow. . . ." Since his parents had been around forty when he was born, they were now in their late sixties, and he did not feel that he could walk out on them.

Following a poetic tradition that was probably old in Homer's day, Smith entered upon a long series of love affairs with married women of Auburn. Rumors of his success in this department failed to enhance his popularity with their husbands. Although Smith shunned marriage, he was the one man of the Three Musketeers of *Weird Tales*—Lovecraft, Howard, and Smith—on whose normal male sexuality nobody has ever cast any doubt. In fact, he seems to have been unusually well endowed in this regard.

He published two more volumes of verse: *Odes and Sonnets* (1918) and *Ebony and Crystal* (1922), with the usual meager returns. He received kudos from Californian literary societies. In 1920, he composed a celebrated long poem in blank verse, "The Hashish Eater":

> Bow down: I am the emperor of dreams;
> I crown me with the million-coloured sun
> Of secret worlds incredible, and take
> Their trailing skies for vestment, when I soar,
> Throned on the mounting zenith, and illume
> The spaceward-flown horizons infinite . . .[3]

He assured Sterling: "Don't worry about my experimenting with hashish. Life is enough of a nightmare without drugs and I feel content to take the effects on hearsay."

As Smith's health improved through the 1920s (his late twenties and early thirties), he added mining, fruit packing, well digging, typing, and journalism to his occupations. If none of these brought him affluence, at least he showed more gumption in getting jobs than Lovecraft ever did. He had no genteel inhibitions against turning his hand to rough outdoor work of any kind. He contributed a column to *The Auburn Journal* and sometimes worked as its night editor.

In 1922, he began correspondence with H. P. Lovecraft and illustrated one of HPL's early stories in *Home Brew*. He studied French in order to translate Baudelaire and got a fair reading and writing knowledge of that tongue, in which he composed original poems. Lacking Francophone contacts, he had no way of mastering the spoken form. He dabbled in drawing and painting and sold a few pictures for $5.00 or $10.00 each.

Then Smith lost his Guru, Sterling. Unable longer to brook

his nonsupport and adulteries, Sterling's wife divorced him in 1915 and three years later killed herself. In 1926, Sterling was found dead of poison in the Bohemian Club of San Francisco. Although his death was commonly deemed suicide, attributed to failing powers and alcoholism, Smith doubted this, pointing to Sterling's lively plans for the future. He thought that Sterling had taken poison by error for a sleeping potion while confused by illness. There is no way to test this theory.

In 1929, when the Great Depression began, Smith's parents grew feebler. Timeus Smith, 74, now suffered from high blood pressure and a weak heart.

Clark Ashton Smith was now 36. He stood 5 feet, 10 and a fraction inches tall and weighed around 140 pounds, with a large chest. Although he had filled out since youth, he was still lean, but powerfully muscled from hard physical labor. He wore his brown hair somewhat long and straggly and sported a wispy mustache. His weather-worn features were not unhandsome, although heavy-lidded eyes gave him a slightly oriental look.

A fairly heavy pipe and cigarette smoker, he drank—sometimes heavily but then again restricting himself to a glass of wine—often homemade—a day. His general *persona* was politely reserved and rather taciturn, save when somebody got him to open up on one of his literary or poetic enthusiasms. He took to wearing berets, at least one of them red. Now, the beret is an admirably practical headgear, but the small-town America of that time viewed it very much askance.

Evidently, the casual labor on which Smith had relied would not suffice to keep his aged parents. Smith had long since decided that he did not wish to work regular hours, would not work indoors, hated Auburn, and could not bear to live in a city. These self-imposed tabus left him few choices. He said: "My conception of pleasure is one that the modern world would doubtless think hopelessly bucolic, idyllic and antiquated, since there is nothing I like better than to wander in the vernal woods with a beloved mistress. . . ."[4]

Through the 1920s, Smith had been reading Lovecraft's stories. During that time, Smith had written practically no prose fiction except some little imaginative vignettes in florid language, called "prose poems." He had sold several poems and one old story, "The Ninth Skeleton," to *Weird Tales.*

In 1929, one of Smith's lady friends talked him into trying his hand at prose fiction again. So he wrote "The Last Incantation," which appeared in *Weird Tales* for June 1930. It is a charming little fable, just over a thousand words long, in Smith's meticulously polished prose.

The aged Atlantean wizard Malygris commands his familiar demon to fetch him Nylissa, the sweetheart he would have wedded in youth had she not died. The demon obeys. At first, Malygris is in rapture. But then he observes that this Nylissa is not nearly so beautiful as he remembers her; in fact, she is just a very ordinary girl. Malygris dismisses the phantom and complains to the demon.

> "It was indeed Nylissa whom you summoned and saw," replied the viper. "Your necromancy was potent up to this point; but no necromantic spell could recall for you your own lost youth or the fervent and guileless heart that loved Nylissa, or the ardent eyes that beheld her then. This, my master, was the thing that you had to learn."[5]

Finding that he could make more money, even at the low rates and late payments of *Weird Tales,* than by picking plums and cherries and chopping firewood, Smith plunged wholeheartedly into his new career. During the next six years, he turned out stories at a rate of over one a month, despite the fact that he was a careful worker who revised and rewrote a lot. Of Smith's approximately 110 stories, a large majority were written during this period, although some of these were not published until the 1940s and 50s.

Over half of Smith's stories were published in *Weird Tales.* Others appeared in *Amazing Detective Tales, Amazing Stories, Astounding Stories, Fantastic Universe, Fantasy and Science Fiction, Fantasy Fiction, Fantasy Magazine, La Paree Stories, Magic Carpet, Oriental Stories, Philippine Magazine, Saturn Science Fiction and Fantasy, Scientific Detective Monthly, Stirring Science Stories, Snappy Stories, Startling Stories, Strange Tales, Tales of Wonder, Wonder Stories,* and fan magazines. Many have been reprinted in anthologies and reprint magazines. Some, like "The Holiness of Azéderac," were based upon Lovecraft's Cthulhu Mythos, to whose sinister library of pseudobiblia Smith added the baleful *Book of Eibon.*

Some stories written during this spurt were more or less conventional science fiction. Many were fantasies laid in the supposed lost continents of Hyperborea and Atlantis, in the imaginary medieval land of Malnéant, and on the magic-haunted planet Xiccarph. Others were placed on the future continent Zothique (rhymes with "seek"). This will be the last large land mass to remain above waters when the sun shall have dimmed, science shall have been forgotten, and the ancient magics shall rise again, bringing back their sinister gods and demons in more frightful guise than ever.

The stories of Klarkash-Ton (as Lovecraft called him, meaning simply "Clark Ashton") are not like anybody's else. Readers either love them or hate them but are seldom indifferent. Smith wrote in an elaborately euphuistic style, bedizened with rare words (some of which Farnsworth Wright, editing *Weird Tales,* made him take out). He had a monstrously vivid imagination. Like Lovecraft, he drew upon the nightmares that had plagued him during youthful spells of sickness. He also had a keenly ironic sense of humor and an uninhibited bent for the macabre. Nobody since Poe has so loved a well-rotted corpse.

Even one of his more conventional science-fiction stories, "The Dweller in the Gulf," is one of the most gruesome ever written. An expedition to Mars encounters a monster, which apparently subsists on interplanetary explorers' eyeballs, being equipped with special appendages for extracting them.

Most of Smith's published stories were short. He planned or began several novels but never finished any, finding the greater lengths uncongenial. Lovecraft wrote:

> Mr. Smith has for his background a universe of remote and para-lysing fright—jungles of poisonous and iridescent blossoms on the moons of Saturn, evil and grotesque temples in Atlantis, Lemuria, and forgotten elder worlds, and dank morasses of spotted death-fungi in spectral countries beyond earth's rim. . . . In sheer daemonic strangeness and fertility of conception, Mr. Smith is per-haps unexcelled by any other writer dead or living. Who else has seen such gorgeous, luxuriant, and feverishly distorted visions of infinite spheres and multiple dimensions and lived to tell the tale?[6]

Some of Smith's readers have seen what they thought was Lord Dunsany's influence in his stories. Smith himself said that while he had read Dunsany, he thought that he had been much more influenced by Poe, Bierce, and the early stories of Robert W. Chambers.

Although Smith stayed in Auburn during these years, his stories brought him a new circle of admirers—the science-fiction fans, some of whom came to see him from time to time. They found a curious menage. Fanny Smith, now in her eighties and in failing health, still ruled the family. When she sent Timeus to Auburn for supplies, she gave him a schedule, and woe betid him if he failed to adhere to the timetable. Fanny had become obsessed with the idea that, unless watched, poor old Timeus would gallop off in lustful pursuit of Auburn's damsels.

Smith's friends included Benjamin De Casseres (rhymes with "mass array") and his wife. De Casseres had contributed to *The Black Cat,* become a popular poet in the 1920s, and published a book of poems called *The Shadow-Eater*, with splendidly ghoulish black-and-white illustrations by Wallace Smith. De Casseres compared Smith's poetry to that of Poe, Baudelaire, Shelley, Rimbaud, Keats, and Blake. Other knowledgeable critics were equally enthusiastic about Smith's verse.

In 1933, Smith began corresponding with Robert E. Howard, the Texan creator of Conan. Howard, too, wrote vigorous, colorful, imaginative verse, but on a much smaller scale than Smith, who composed over 700 poems. Nor did REH take his poetry so seriously as Smith took his. For three years, Smith, Howard, and Lovecraft were the leaders of the *Weird Tales* school of fiction and close corresponding friends, although they never met. The writer of oriental fantasies, Edgar Hoffmann Price, is the only man known to have met all three in the flesh.

In 1934, the older Smiths' growing debility caused Smith's fiction to taper off. He also began to experiment with sculpture. This consisted of creepy little figurines, carved in a soft stone such as talc with a pocketknife and hardened by baking. They resemble the little uglies that tourists buy in Mexico and Central America, which are mostly modern imitations of aboriginal idols. Some of Smith's statuettes look like miniatures of the Easter Island statues. He sold many such carvings for a few dollars each.

In September 1935, Fanny Smith died. Smith spent the next two years nursing his father through his last illness. He continued his stone carving, began a few stories, and completed fewer. In December 1937, Timeus died in his turn.

His parents' deaths practically ended Smith's fictional career. The last three years had left him exhausted from single-handedly nursing two old people and running the house and tract. In a letter to the fan Robert H. Barlow, Smith had written that he had "fully and absolutely made up my mind to quit the hell-bedunged and heaven-bespitted country when my present responsibilities are over." But when the time came, he did not.

Barlow was an assiduous correspondent of Lovecraft and

other members of the HPL-*WT* circle. As a young man, he
dabbled in various arts and sciences. When Lovecraft died in
1937, Barlow acted for a while as his literary executor, precip-
itating a quarrel among some members of the Circle.

Later, Barlow went to Mexico, where he became a distinguished archaeologist. Along with Wigberto Jiménez Moreno,
he is credited with putting the chronology of the pre-Columbian
Valley of Mexico—that is, the dating of the Toltec and Aztec
cultures—on a sound basis. In 1951, he killed himself over the
threat of the exposure of his homosexuality.

In the 1930s, Barlow was in his Communist phase. He tried
to convert Smith, who would have none of it: "No matter what
system you have—capitalism, Fascism, Bolshevism—the greed
and power-lust of men will produce the same widespread injustice, the same evils and abuses. . . . I would be strictly non-
assimilable in any sort of co-operative society, and would speed-
ily end up in a concentration camp." Smith condemned authoritarian governments of any sort, recognizing their intolerance
of nonconformists like himself.

Smith even hoped to make a trip to New York, though he
still had no wish to live in a city. After his father died, he did
in fact travel a little but only to nearby places like Carmel. Having become set in his ways, he soon returned to Indian Ridge
and his mildly reclusive life.

He wrote Derleth that he was "trying to settle down to literary production again," although he found the necessary concentration "abominably hard." But somehow he never did. He
made many statuettes and composed more poems. He taught
himself Spanish as he had done with French. Fritz Leiber wrote
of a visit to Smith in 1944: "Garbed in white suit, Panama hat,
and quietly colorful batik shirt, he struck me as a cosmopolitan,
bohemian artist of the early century, very much out of place in
his rural setting."[7]

Stories, however, Smith produced only at intervals of years.
The tales actually completed after 1937 could be counted on

the fingers of two hands. *Weird Tales*'s simultaneous loss of its three outstanding writers—Lovecraft, Howard, and Smith, two by death and one by virtual withdrawal from the field—together with the dismissal of Farnsworth Wright, initiated its long decline.

Smith had the satisfaction of seeing books of his stories published by Derleth's Arkham House. The first of these, *Out of Space and Time* (1942) and *Lost Worlds* (1944) were each issued in small printings of 1,054 and 2,043 copies respectively. They sold slowly, went out of print, and became collectors' costly rarities. Derleth published five more volumes of Smith's prose and two of his verse, and at his death in 1971 had a large volume of Smith's poems in press. Many of Smith's stories have been reprinted in paperback.

Smith's last decade saw extensive changes in his life. In 1953 he suffered a coronary attack. The following year he married Carolyn Jones Dorman, who had been married before and had three children. For several years, he alternated between the house on Indian Ridge and his wife's house in Pacific Grove. He had sold most of Timeus Smith's tract. Then he quarreled with a real-estate developer who wished to buy the remaining lot and put pressure on Smith through legal and political connections to sell. In 1957, the old house burned—the Smiths said by arson; others, by accident. The Smiths sold the remaining lot and moved permanently to Pacific Grove.

To meet expenses, Smith (who now wore a small gray beard) did gardening, which he hated, for the other residents. In 1961 he suffered strokes, which greatly slowed him. In the summer of that year, I visited the West with family. My wife and I drove to Pacific Palisades to call on Smith, with whom I had corresponded.

The visit passed off pleasantly; but, between the after-effects of Smith's strokes and his wife's loquacity, Smith did not get much chance to talk. Carol Smith was a kindly, affectionate woman but also temperamental, impulsive, and excitable to an extreme degree. She would volubly recount her colorful past to anyone who would hold still long enough to hear it. After Smith's death, she married an alcoholic to reform him, soon divorced him, and then herself died of cancer.

Smith, when I saw him, was making a last attempt at a science-fiction story, of which he showed me the manuscript. Two weeks later, in August 1961, he quietly died in his sleep, aged 68. The story did not prove publishable.

The devotee of heroic fantasy is entitled to wonder; if Smith could write so many superlative stories of their kind from 1929 to 1935, why did he not resume his fiction, after his father's death, on his former scale? The answer seems to be that he regarded himself mainly as a poet who wrote prose only to pay his decrepid parents' bills.

This brings up another irony: Smith bitterly complained of being tied to hated Auburn. He implied that, but for having to care for two helpless old people, he would roam the wide world. In fact, if he had not so desperately needed money during his parents' decline, he might never have buckled down to fiction at all. So the very factor that so irked him also forced him into doing his best-remembered work.

Years before, he had written Sterling that writing prose was "a hateful task, for a poet, and wouldn't be necessary in any true civilization." He much preferred poetry and, after his parents' deaths, rock carving. The deaths of Lovecraft and Howard may also have discouraged Smith from resuming his stories, since he no longer had their voluminous correspondence to spur him on.

Smith also suffered from his own artistic versatility. He worked in poetry, prose fiction, sculpture, and picturing. Any one of these is enough to absorb all a man's energy, and to master all four at once is a practical impossibility.

In pursuing the graphic and plastic arts without formal

training, moreover, I think that Smith made a profound mistake. These arts are those wherein, as in boxing among sports, the gap yawns widest between the amateur and the professional and the self-taught man has little chance. But, living where he did and avoiding cities, Smith had no opportunity for formal training.

He realized his lack but took a stubbornly independent line: "Of course, I lack technical training, in the academic sense. But I don't care much more for the literalness of academic painting than I do for the geometrical abstractions of some of the modernists. . . . As for getting instruction, I doubt if my ideals would be understood or sympathized with by the average teacher. I'll have to work it out in my own way."[8] So his pictures remained at best talented primitives.

Lord Dunsany could likewise dabble in drawing and sculpture as well as prose and poetry. His weird drawings, in fact, are reminiscent of Smith's. But Dunsany had an inherited estate, which enabled him to do as he pleased. Smith did not.

For a last question: Whatever happened to Smith's poetry, so extravagantly praised when it appeared? One might think that it had all been buried with its author, as was said of the composer Anton Rubinstein's music.

There was nothing wrong with Smith's poetry, which is of high quality: vivid, stirring, evocative, colorful in a lush *fin-de-siècle* way, super-imaginative, and technically polished. But public taste is ever changing unpredictably; that is why there is, in one sense, no such thing as progress in the arts.

During the last half-century, American poetry, under the influence of Ezra Pound and others, has gone off in a direction quite different from the verse of Smith and Howard. Although Smith wrote some free verse, most of his poetry is in fixed forms, with rhyme and rhythm and predetermined numbers of feet per line. Nearly all contemporary American poetry is in free verse.

Now free verse, in the hands of a Whitman or an Emily Dickinson, can be very effective. But, however effective, it cannot be remembered anywhere nearly so easily as verse in fixed forms. In fact, the distinctive features of fixed-form verse—rhythm, rhyme, alliteration, fixed numbers of syllables or feet, and the rest—were invented as mnemonic devices back in primitive, preliterate days to make it easier to pass on the tribal wisdom without losing pieces of it with each transmission. Therefore, while Americans of a century hence may well remember "Half a league, half a league, half a league onward . . ." or "Lars Porsena of Clusium, by the Nine Gods he swore . . .," all the vast masses of *vers libre* now being ground out will probably be forgotten by all save writers of Ph.D. theses.

Moreover, even if free verse can sometimes be effective, most of it is not. To me at least, it looks like turgid prose, full of strained figures of speech and obscure locutions and chopped into arbitrary short lines. The main advantage of this formless "verse" is that it is easy to do. It is lazy man's poetry. Anybody, even a child or a computer, can do it. This makes it popular, since in the present climate of super-egalitarianism it is often thought that if a task cannot be done by everyone, it ought not to be done at all. To do or admire something that requires outstanding talent, arduous effort, and austere self-discipline is elitism, and that is considered a wicked thing.

Some leading poets, however, tell me that a reaction, with a return to fixed forms, is likely soon. Then Smith's verse may come into its own.

In viewing Smith's life, it is hard not to become a little impatient with the inept, unrealistic way this brilliant, erudite, decent, hypersensitive, imaginative, creative, and romantic-minded man conducted his worldly affairs. It would have been one thing if he had serenely accepted an impoverished existence on the outskirts of Auburn. But he did not; he hated Auburn and complained of his lot. At the same time, he did little to change that lot. In fact, his attitudes—his phobias against formal education, indoor work, and city life—combined with his parents' long debility to condemn him to Indian Ridge willy nilly.

But then, one ought not to expect a gifted poet to be also a model of shrewdness, prudence, practicality, efficiency, foresight, and commercial acumen. If all people were born with these qualities, the world's work might get done more briskly, but there would probably be no poetry or weird fantasies at all.

IX

MERLIN IN TWEEDS: J. R. R. TOLKIEN

Three Rings for the Elven-kings under the sky,
Seven for the Dwarf-lords in their halls of stone,
Nine for Mortal Men doomed to die,
One for the Dark Lord on his dark throne
In the Land of Mordor where the Shadows lie.
One Ring to rule them all, One Ring to find them,
One Ring to bring them all and in the darkness bind them
In the Land of Mordor where the Shadows lie.[1]

TOLKIEN

In 1954, an odd little advertisement appeared in successive issues of the *New York Times.* It showed a small drawing of a snaky flying dragon. The legend said: *The Fellowship of the Ring.* After several of these advertisements had appeared, it was disclosed that *The Fellowship of the Ring* was a new fantasy novel by an Oxford professor named J. R. R. Tolkien (pronounced TOLL-keen).

The book, published on October 21, 1954, was a sizable volume of 423 printed pages, including front matter. It contained about 220,000 words, with a large folded map of Tolkien's imaginary realms in the back. Houghton Mifflin Company of Boston had bound the book from sheets printed in England for George Allen and Unwin of London and shipped unbound to the United States.

Readers learned that this was an adult sequel to Tolkien's
The Hobbit: a child's fairy tale, published in the United Kingdom in 1937 and in the United States in 1938. *The Hobbit*
had enjoyed a gratifying success, having won the *New York
Herald Tribune*'s prize for the best children's book of the year.

Moreover, it was said, *The Fellowship of the Ring* was only
the first volume of a trilogy, to be called *The Lord of the Rings*
—or, if one prefers, *The Lord of the Rings* was a three-volume
novel, divided into six "books," of which this was the first volume and first two "books." The resulting work would come to
about two thirds of a million words.

The remaining two volumes, *The Two Towers* and *The Return of the King,* appeared during the next fifteen months. Of
the third volume, only three quarters were occupied by the story
proper. The rest consisted of appendices, in which Tolkien gave
a history and chronology of his fictitious prehistoric milieu of
Middle-Earth (something like Howard's "Hyborian Age"),
based upon a fictitious *Red Book of Westmarch* (like Howard's
Nemedian Chronicles and Lovecraft's *Necronomicon*).

The *Red Book of Westmarch* was doubtless suggested by
two real collections of medieval Welsh tales, the *Red Book of
Hergest* and the *White Book of Rhydderch.* Lady Charlotte
Guest translated these stories into English and in 1838 published them under her own title of *The Mabinogion,* by which
the collection has been known ever since. The appendices also
give genealogies of some of the characters, linguistic notes on
Tolkien's invented Elvish, Dwarvish, and other languages (including their complex rules of pronunciation), and tables of the
alphabets and calendars of some of these peoples.

The Lord of the Rings had modest American sales. For several years, the sales of each volume hovered between one and
two thousand copies a year. (The British edition did better,
selling 35,000 sets from 1954 to 1961.) Nevertheless, the
work became the focus of a cult of admirers and incited an extraordinary volume of critical comment and controversy.

Most critics lauded the story. In the *New York Times Book Review*, W. H. Auden said that Tolkien had "succeeded more completely than any previous writer in this genre in using the traditional properties of the Quest, the heroic journey, the Numinous Object." Tolkien's friend and fellow fantasist, C. S. Lewis, compared the work to that of Ariosto and spoke of its "beauties which pierce like swords or burn like cold iron. . . . good beyond hope."

Others compared the book to Spenser and Malory. Colin Wilson, when at last persuaded to read LOTR (as Tolkienians abbreviate the title) spent three days in bed, completely absorbed in Frodo's adventures.

The brilliant but opinionated Edmund Wilson, however, emphatically disagreed. Writing in *The Nation*, Wilson sarcastically titled his review: "Oo, Those Awful Orcs!" After summarizing some of the previous critical opinions, Wilson viewed the book itself as if it had crawled out from under a flat stone; he "apparently felt insulted at having to review it."[2] He said:

> The reviewer has just read the whole thing aloud to his seven-year-old daughter, who has been through *The Hobbit* countless times. . . . One is puzzled to know why the author should have supposed he was writing for adults. . . . except when he is being pedantic and also boring the adult reader, there is little in *The Lord of the Rings* over the head of a seven-year-old child. It is essentially a children's book—a children's book which has somehow gotten out of hand, since, instead of directing it at the "juvenile" market, the author has indulged himself in developing the fantasy for its own sake. . . .

Tolkien, Wilson noted, confessed that the work had developed as an outgrowth of his interest in linguistics, to provide a world for the "Elvish" language that he had invented.

> An overgrown fairy story, a philological curiosity—that is, then, what *The Lord of the Rings* really is. The pretentiousness is all on the part of Dr. Tolkien's infatuated admirers. . . .[3]

The three volumes also contained a good deal of poetry, apposite to the story and characters but little of it memorable. Most of it is set in a simple iambic tetrameter, with rhyme schemes aabb or abab, which soon becomes monotonous. In a very few places, Tolkien's imagery rises to the point of giving (at least to me) a touch of true poetic *frisson:*

> O Elbereth! Gilthoniel!
>   We still remember, we who dwell
> In this far land beneath the trees,
>   Thy starlight on the Western Seas.[4]

Auden had expressed a poor opinion of Tolkien's poetry, but Wilson chided Auden for not observing that Tolkien's prose was just as bad. "Prose and verse are on a same level of professorial amateurishness."

While Wilson conceded that the concept of a quest to get rid of the evil ring had possibilities, he did not admire Tolkien's use of the theme: "There are dreadful hovering birds—think of it, horrible birds of prey!" "The wars are never dynamic; the ordeals give no sense of strain; the fair ladies would not stir a heartbeat; the horrors would not hurt a fly." "These characters who are no characters are involved in interminable adventures the poverty of invention displayed in which is, it seems to me, almost pathetic." ". . . these bugaboos are not magnetic; they are feeble and rather blank; one does not feel that they have any real power. The Good People simply say 'Boo' to them." Wilson concludes:

> Now, how is it that these long-winded volumes of what looks to this reviewer like balderdash have elicited such tributes as those above? The answer is, I believe, that certain people . . . have a lifelong appetite for juvenile trash. They would not accept adult trash, but, when confronted with the pre-teen-age article, they revert to the mental phase which delighted in *Elsie Dinsmore* and *Little Lord Fauntleroy.* . . . You can see it in the tone they fall into when they talk about Tolkien in print: they bubble, they

squeal, they coo; they go on about Malory and Spenser—both of whom have a charm and a distinction that Tolkien has never touched.

As for me, if we must read about imaginary kingdoms, give me James Branch Cabell's Poictesme. He at least writes for grown-up people, and he does not present the drama of life as a showdown between the Good People and Goblins. . . .

One wonders: whence such wildly divergent opinions? What is the source of Wilson's animosity? He damns Tolkien's prose, which I have found, if not so superlative as some Tolkienians assert, at least a good, straightforward, serviceable, literate English (occasionally awkward, occasionally eloquent), which gets its images and ideas across with clarity and concision. This can hardly be said of the widely admired Dreiser and Faulkner. Neither is Tolkien ever incoherent—a quality which some advanced thinkers take as a sign of "sincerity."

For one thing, Wilson, like Lovecraft, was wont to divide all literature into a small group of work that he liked and therefore classed as "real literature," and a much larger class of all the rest, which he dismissed as "hackwork" or "trash."

This, however, is a subjective view of literature. The immature mind tends to divide phenomena into a few simple classes, to exaggerate their differences and distinctiveness, and to make sweeping judgments on whole classes. A more mature view realizes the infinite diversity of such phenomena and admits that classes are human artifacts, useful but not to be taken too seriously.

In the case of writing, literature comes in many kinds and genres, addressed to different readerships for different purposes. In any one class, the writing may be done well, badly, or in between. But there is no point in judging a whodunnit, a medical textbook, a child's fairy tale, and a novel exposing conditions in the alarm-clock industry by the same standards. The question in each case is: How well has each author succeeded in getting across, to the readers to whom the work is addressed, the particular information, message, or emotion he wants to convey?

To condemn a work because it appeals to children is, in effect, to jettison a great deal of adult fiction. To take *any* fiction seriously entails a degree of make-believe, since the reader knows full well that the events narrated never really happened.

Wilson was hypercritical of most fantasy. He dismissed Lovecraft's fiction as "hackwork" and found fault with Lovecraft for admiring the stories of Dunsany and Machen. It would seem that Cabell was about the only fantasy writer whom Wilson admired. Cabell was in many ways the opposite of Tolkien: a genial cynic as against Tolkien's moral earnestness; a world-weary sophisticate as against Tolkien's love of wholesome simplicity. And few dispute the exquisite perfection of Cabell's prose.

One of the many books on Tolkien makes an *ad hominem* judgment on Wilson, which may be not unfair: "Tolkien's lightness with his scholarship comes hard to Wilson, who reveres and proclaims his own self-taught erudition."[5] This doubtless refers to Wilson's published accounts of his struggles with unusual languages like Magyar.

Edmund Wilson was not quite alone in his objections to LOTR. Philip Toynbee thought it "dull, ill-written, whimsical, and childish." Mark Roberts complained that the work lacked "relevance to the human situation"; it was "contrived" and "does not issue from an understanding of reality which is not to be denied. . . ."[6]

This sounds as if Roberts disapproved of all fiction save that which, so to speak, exposed conditions in the alarm-clock industry. If being set in an imaginary world makes a story "irrelevant," the same objection applies to any fictions other than those placed in the here-and-now. A story laid in feudal times would be "irrelevant," since we no longer have the feudal system.

If Wilson, Roberts, and a few others disliked LOTR, a much larger band enthusiastically praised the work. A decade after the novel's clothbound appearance, paperbacked editions were published in the United States. These, to the delighted surprise of the publishers, became runaway best-sellers. This reprinting also incited a controversy.

When LOTR first appeared, neither Allen & Unwin in Britain nor Houghton Mifflin in the United States anticipated much demand for the books. Therefore the American edition consisted of sheets printed in the United Kingdom but bound in the United States. At the time of the importation, the "manufacturing clause" of the American copyright law withheld protection from works in English, printed outside the United States and imported into it, unless certain formalities were complied with. In addition, the publisher would have to begin publication of an American edition within a certain time.

This law, which discriminates against works printed abroad in English, has been kept in force for many years by the efforts of the printing unions' lobby. It was partly nullified by the Universal Copyright Convention, signed at Geneva in 1952; but this only became effective on September 16, 1955, too late to help the first two volumes of LOTR. (The third may have been protected.)

In the middle 1960s, two paperback publishers brought out editions of LOTR: Ballantine Books, which published under a normal royalty contract, and Ace Books, which published without any contract, assuming that LOTR was in public domain in the United States. Tolkien wrote in his introduction to the first Ballantine volume:

> . . . it was the product of long labour, and like a simple-minded Hobbit I feel that it is, while I am still alive, my property in justice unaffected by copyright laws. It seems to me a grave discourtesy, to say no more, to issue my book without even a polite note in-

forming me of the project: dealings one might expect of Saruman in his decay rather than from the defenders of the West. However it may be, this paperback edition and no other has been published with my consent and co-operation. Those who approve of courtesy (at least) to living authors will purchase it and no other.[7]

The paperbacked editions of the work had enormous success, especially among science-fiction fans and college students, to whose youthful minds its rather simplistic view of good and evil appealed. Sales ran into the millions. Science-fiction fans and authors, stricken with sympathy for Professor Tolkien, vociferously sided with him against Ace Books, threatening Ace with boycotts. At last, Ace Books reached an agreement with Tolkien, paid him royalties on the copies already sold, and withdrew from further publication of LOTR.

John Ronald Reuel Tolkien (1892–1973; "Ronald" to his friends) was born in Bloemfontein, South Africa, the son of a bank manager from Birmingham, England. Since young Tolkien's health was delicate, his mother took him, aged three, and his brother back to England. While they were gone, the older Tolkien died. Tolkien's mother stayed in Birmingham, taught school, and died in 1910.

Meanwhile Tolkien went through King Edward's School, a Catholic institution in Birmingham; his parents had been converts. One of Tolkien's guardians was the Rev. Francis X. Morgan. Father Morgan strongly influenced him, so that he remained a devout and practicing Catholic.

Tolkien went to Oxford on a scholarship, graduated with honors from Exeter College in 1915, entered the Lancashire Fusiliers, married Edith Bratt, and served through the Kaiserian War. He was severely wounded and recovered, got his M.A. from Oxford in 1919, and settled into his lifelong rôle as a teacher. He never did take his Ph.D. and therefore was properly addressed as "Professor," not "Doctor."

Tolkien remembered his childhood with ambiguous feelings. He once said: "But no, it was not an unhappy childhood. It was full of tragedies but it didn't tot up to any unhappy childhood." Another time, however, he recalled his school days as "really a sad and troublous time."[8]

After getting his M.A., Tolkien's first job was as an assistant on the *Oxford English Dictionary*. Then he got a readership in English at the University of Leeds and settled into a comfortable academic career. In 1924 he was advanced to professor; in 1925 he moved to Pembroke College at Oxford, as Professor of Anglo-Saxon. There he remained for twenty years, until he moved to Merton College of Oxford University. He proved an excellent teacher.

Tolkien specialized in Old and Middle English and became prodigiously learned in all the Northern languages, literatures, and mythologies. His publications during this time included *A Middle-English Vocabulary* (1922), a critical text (with E. V. Gordon) of the anonymous fourteenth-century poem *Sir Gawain and the Green Knight* (1925), "Chaucer as a Philologist" (1934), and *"Beowulf:* The Monsters and the Critics" (1936).

Tolkien and his wife had four children, three boys and a girl. About 1933, Tolkien formed the habit of telling his children fairy tales about an imaginary milieu that he had invented, which he called Middle-Earth. It was placed—as far as it was connected with our present world at all—in a vaguely prehistoric time, perhaps before the last advance of the Pleistocene ice. Its beings and nomenclature were largely derived from Norse mythology.

About 1936, Tolkien conceived the idea of making a book out of these tales. He was correcting examination papers at Pembroke—the most tedious of all professorial tasks. He said later:

"I came across a blank page someone had turned in—a boon

to all exam markers. I turned it over and wrote on the back: 'In a hole in the ground there lives a Hobbit.' I'd never heard the word before."[9]

The resulting novel, *The Hobbit, or There and Back Again,* appeared in 1937, with drawings and end-paper maps by Tolkien. It had, as noted, a gratifying success. The story begins:

> In a hole in the ground there lived a hobbit. Not a nasty, dirty, wet hole, with the ends of worms and an oozy smell, nor yet a dry, bare, sandy hole with nothing in it to sit down on or to eat: it was a hobbit-hole, and that means comfort.

The prose has a juvenile flavor, as if Tolkien were talking to his own children and improvising as he went along. This tone is maintained throughout. Tolkien often addresses the reader in the second person: "And what would you do, if an uninvited dwarf came and hung his things up in your hall without a word of explanation?"[10] He also uses onomatopoeia: *"ding-dong"* and so forth.

This may put off some adult readers, who consider it "talking down" or "writing down." Even Tolkien's own children told him, when he asked them after finishing the story, that they did not like it, so he dropped it in later writings. The right tone for a children's book is a debatable question. Not all adult literature is suitable for children; likewise, not all children's books can be enjoyed by adults—none at all, apparently, by Edmund Wilson.

A few works can be read with pleasure by both, although the young reader may miss many allusions and meanings that he will grasp and enjoy when he rereads the same work as an adult. *The Hobbit* comes close to this universal appeal, but it might have come closer if it had more sternly avoided this Disneyesque chattiness. On the other hand, while reading *The Hobbit* is not absolutely necessary for an appreciation of LOTR, it helps.

Hobbits, we learn, are a humanoid species about four feet

tall, plump and round-faced, with large, hairy bare feet. They live in a bucolic land called the Shire, modeled on the English countryside. Tolkien points up the contrast between this landscape and that of smoky Birmingham, where he passed most of his childhood. Like Morris, Lovecraft, and C. S. Lewis, Tolkien was an unabashed rurophile. As the Durants once said: "Word peddlers tend to idealize the countryside, if they are exempt from its harassments, boredom, insects, and toil."[11]

Modern rurophiles, like Tolkien and Lovecraft, who condemn the Industrial Revolution and all its works, are in an anomalous position. Since 1800, when the Industrial Revolution was just getting under full steam, the world's population has quadrupled. Some of this increase can be credited to putting additional lands, like the American West, into cultivation; but most of it resulted from the Industrial Revolution.

To abolish modern machinery, therefore, would mean that the world could support only a fraction of its present population. The rurophiles do not say what to do with the rest. Let them starve? Shoot them? The stand of a Catholic like Tolkien is especially illogical, because of his Church's adamant opposition to any practical, humane method of stopping the population explosion. All this, however, is off the track from heroic fantasy.

Some Hobbits live in cave or tunnel-houses excavated out of their fertile soil. They love eating, parties, and genealogy; like Lovecraft, they are sexually tepid. Nobody has to work hard there.

In fact, Tolkien's Hobbit heroes, Bilbo and Frodo Baggins, never work at all when home but live comfortably on their incomes. Along with the other blights of the higher civilizations, economics has never come to Hobbit-land. In a juvenile fairy tale, this is perhaps just as well, although it may bother some socially-conscious adult readers.

Some, in fact, have taken Tolkien to task for complacently accepting class distinctions like those of Edwardian England.

This is silly, because class distinctions have existed in all human societies above the most primitive hunter-gatherers. Doing away with the ruling class has merely resulted in putting another ruling class, called by another name, in its place.

Bilbo's placid, unadventurous life continues for decades, until one day he receives a visitor:

> All that the unsuspecting Bilbo saw that morning was a little old man with a tall pointed blue hat, a long grey cloak, a silver scarf over which his long white beard hung down below his waist, and immense black boots.[12]

The newcomer is Gandalf, once well known to the Hobbits for his displays of fireworks and his tales of wild adventures, but whom Bilbo has almost forgotten. Next day, Gandalf is back with thirteen Dwarves, similar to the gnomes of other fantasies: Dwalin, Balin, Kili, Fili, Dori, Nori, Ori, Oin, Gloin, Bifur, Bofur, Bombur, and an important Dwarf chieftain, Thorin Oakenshield.

These names are straight out of Norse mythology. The great thirteenth-century Icelandic historian and mythographer, Snorri Sturluson, lists over sixty Dwarves, including those mentioned by Tolkien, in a catalogue in his *Prose Edda.* A similar list occurs, with variations, in the earlier *Poetic Edda,* doubtfully attributed to another Icelander, Sæmund the Wise. Gandalf is one of the dwarves in these lists. The name is also a perfectly good Old Norse one; a King Gandalf Alfgeirson of Ranrike was slain in the late ninth century by Harald Fairhair, when the latter was conquering and uniting all of Norway.[13]

Gandalf and the Dwarves enlist Bilbo, against the latter's better judgment, in a quest to recover the Dwarves' treasure from the dragon Smaug. This monster, whose greatest pleasure (like Fáfnir's) is to sleep on a heap of gold and gems, drove the Dwarves' forebears out of their caverns in the Lonely Mountain and took their hoard for himself.

Off they go, only to be captured by a gang of trolls. The Cockney-speaking trolls, named Bert, Tom, and William, prepare to eat their captives. The victims are rescued by Gandalf, who by ventriloquism gets the trolls to quarreling until the sun comes up and turns them to stone. (In the *Poetic Edda,* it is Dwarves who are petrified by sunlight.)

At Rivendell, at the foot of the Misty Mountains, they are entertained by Elrond, a half-elf. In the mountains, Bilbo and the Dwarves, who do not act like very competent adventurers, are captured by goblins. Again Gandalf rescues them. In the flight underground, Bilbo loses his companions and, groping in the dark, finds a ring.

Bilbo next meets an ex-Hobbit, Gollum, who lives underground. Gollum subsists on fish and, when he can sneak up and strangle them, on goblins. He tries the same on Bilbo, who holds him off with a riddle game. Bilbo discovers that the ring he has found was recently lost by Gollum and, when put on, makes one invisible. By its aid, he escapes from Gollum and the goblins.

The reunited party encounters wolves, eagles, and a friendly were-bear. Giant spiders waylay them in sinister Mirkwood. This name, too, comes from Norse myth; in the Icelandic *Lokasenna,* Loki declaims:

> The daughter of Gymir   with gold didst thou buy
>   And sold thy sword to boot;
> But when Muspell's sons   through Myrkwood ride,
>   Thou shalt weaponless wait, poor wretch.[14]

The adventurers are imprisoned by Elves—not butterfly-sized Little Folk, but man-sized, suspicious, immortal, and magically potent. In pre-Christian European mythology, the elves, fairies, fays, Sidhe, sprites, and so forth (the terms are more or less synonymous) were generally thought of as man-sized. The idea of such supernaturals as Little Folk seems to have arisen in Elizabethan times, with Spenser:

> And forth he cald out of deepe darknes dredd
> Legions of Sprights, the which like litle flyes
> Fluttring about his ever-damnéd hedd,

> Awaite whereto their service he applyes,
> To aide his friendes, or fray his enimies.

and Shakespeare likewise:

> Where the bee sucks, there suck I:
> In a cowslip's bell I lie;
> There I couch when owls do cry.
> On the bat's back I do fly. . . .[15]

Escaping to the lake town of Esgaroth, on Long Lake, they get help from the human dwellers there for their assault on Smaug. Bilbo burgles the dragon's lair and steals a gewgaw. Suspecting the lake towners, Smaug destroys the town but is slain by the captain of their archers.

A quarrel arises among the surviving townsfolk and the avaricious Dwarves over Smaug's treasure. Before they come to blows, they are attacked by hordes of wolves and goblins.

In the end, Bilbo is happily back in his hole. In later editions of *The Hobbit,* Tolkien made changes to eliminate inconsistencies with LOTR.

At Oxford, Tolkien became a member of one of those persistent discussion groups that spring up wherever enough articulate intellectuals are gathered to keep the coterie going. There have been many such groups, like Lovecraft's Kalem Club and Howard's Junto, with varying degrees of organization and formality. The set at Oxford was called the Inklings. In the middle 1930s, an undergraduate formed a literary society of that name, in which he enlisted Tolkien and another professor, Clive ("Jack") Staples Lewis (1898–1963).

This club soon expired, but Lewis and Tolkien continued to meet and gathered a group of friends who met informally, still using the name of Inklings. They assembled on Thursday evenings, usually in Lewis's rooms but sometimes in a pub like The Eagle and Child. Old-fashioned English pubs had a semiprivate room for such gatherings. On Tuesday mornings, less formal meetings were held at The Eagle and Child.

As far as the group had a leader, this was Lewis. The son of a Belfast solicitor of Welsh origin, Lewis went to Oxford, left to serve in the Kaiserian War as an officer, was wounded by shell fragments, returned to complete his education, and graduated with honors. He taught at Oxford from 1924 to 1954. Then, believing with some reason that he had not been given due recognition, he switched to Cambridge. He was described as "a big man with a large red face and shabby clothes" and "a loud, booming voice," and as kindly and impulsive.

Lewis's personal life was a bit unusual. In 1918, while convalescing from his wound, he formed an attachment to a widow twenty-six years his senior, Mrs. Janet Askins Moore, with a young daughter. They lived together off and on for over thirty years, until Mrs. Moore died in 1951 at seventy-nine. The exact nature of their relationship is not known. Lewis, who in later years wrote in enthusiastic praise of Christian chastity, refused to say or write anything about his association with Mrs. Moore.

After Mrs. Moore died, the bachelor Lewis met an American poetess, Helen Joy Davidman Gresham. The daughter of non-observant Jews, Mrs. Gresham had married a gentile writer, William Lindsay Gresham. They had two sons and became active Communists. Mrs. Gresham contributed to *The New Masses;* Gresham paraphrased the opening sentence of Marx's *Communist Manifesto* in a novel, *Nightmare Alley* (1946), about the adventures of a carnival grifter. Despite ideological differences, Gresham was a member of Fletcher Pratt's large circle of friends.

Then the Greshams were converted to Christianity, fell out, and separated. Gresham got a divorce and remarried. Later he came down with terminal cancer and killed himself.

Joy Gresham put her boys in school in England. In 1957, when she was forty-two and he nearly sixty, she married Lewis. She was already suffering from cancer. The disease remitted, and they had two good years together. Lewis and his friends described this time as ecstatically happy. Then Joy's condition worsened, and she died in 1960. Lewis followed her on November 22, 1963—the day of the deaths of John F. Kennedy and Aldous Huxley.

An atheist in his youth, Lewis in his thirties investigated theology and converted himself back to Anglican Christianity of a notably orthodox, Fundamentalist sort, complete with devils. He became convinced of its truth, he said, while on his way to the zoo one day. On his own account, however, his conversion seems to have been an emotional compulsion rather than a logical necessity. Zeal for his faith formed a major element in his novels, of which he wrote a dozen besides his many scholarly and theological works. He became a leading Christian apologist.

Most of Lewis's fictions may be classed as theological fantasies. Seven formed the juvenile fairy tales of the Narnia series. In these, a group of children find themselves in the parallel world of Narnia, with witches, talking animals, and similar wonders. The dominant figure is a super-lion, Aslan (presumably from the Turkish *arslan,* "lion"). Aslan, it turns out, is another incarnation of Christ. Although these stories have enjoyed considerable popularity, I cannot say that I care for them. Like Tolkien, I find them didactically "too explicit."

Lewis also wrote three adult science-fiction novels, the Perelandra or Ransom series. Strictly speaking, they are, like many of Lovecraft's stories, on the borderline between science fiction and fantasy.

In the first of the trilogy, *Out of the Silent Planet* (1943), the evil scientist Weston sends the protagonist Ransom to Mars. There Ransom finds a beautiful world, where all life coöperates under the guidance of the planetary ruling spirit or Eldil. Weston follows and begins shooting the natives until this spirit stops him. Ransom learns that things are not so harmonious on earth because our planet's Eldil has become "bent"— that is, wicked or psychotic. This is Christianity with touches of Gnosticism and Neo-Platonism—both of which, to be sure, influenced early Christianity.

In *Perelandra, World of the New Temptation* (1944), Ransom goes to Venus, a planet of vegetable islands floating in a worldwide ocean. Ransom meets the Venerian Eve, a beautiful green girl. Satan (the Terran Eldil), having taken possession of Weston's body, turns up and tempts the green girl by suggesting that she wear clothes.

The last of the trilogy, *That Hideous Strength* (1946), takes place on earth. A gang of evil scientists is gaining control of Britain by means of a National Institute of Co-ordinated Experiments, or N.I.C.E. Ransom leads a group opposing the N.I.C.E. The cast also includes Merlin the enchanter, the severed but living head of an evil scientist, and Horace Jules, the figurehead director of the N.I.C.E. Jules, a pudgy little man who speaks Cockney and pontificates on things he knows nothing about, is a venomous caricature of H. G. Wells, although Lewis unconvincingly denied this.

Lewis, in his way, was an able and erudite novelist. The first two Ransom novels, however, sag under the author's didacticism. His Mars and Venus, which have never known the Fall, are such pretty, perfect worlds as to be insipid. Lewis also uses symbolic names for his characters, "Weston" standing for "Western" (modern industrial) culture. This is what writers of the seventeenth and eighteenth centuries did, with their Squire Allworthys and Lady Sneerwells.

Lewis's villains are scientists, to whom he attributes such outré intentions as exterminating all unnecessary plant and animal species and all backward races of man. Science-fiction writers, says Lewis, are "obsessed with the idea . . . that humanity, having sufficiently corrupted the planet where it arose, must at all costs contrive to seed itself over a larger area. . . ." His books may be classed as anti-science fiction, of the kind written by Aldous Huxley and Ray Bradbury. Although enormously erudite, Lewis seems to have known little about science; in school and college he had been unable to master simple algebra.

Still, whether one agrees with its premises, *That Hideous Strength* is an extraordinarily good, gripping piece of story-telling.

Another Inkling was Charles Williams (1886–1945), an editor for the Oxford University Press. Williams had been compelled by poverty to drop out of Oxford. His wife refused to live in a small town and remained in London, whither Williams went on weekends to visit her and their son.

Williams wrote seven novels: erudite, subtle, moralistic, weighty, and slow-moving theological fantasies. *Shadows of Ecstasy* (1933) follows the spirit of a recently-dead girl and a world-conquering sorcerer. In *Many Dimensions* (1931), the Stone of Solomon gets loose in modern London. In *The Place of the Lion* (1931), amateur theurgy causes the things of this world to merge back into their Platonic archetypes. Williams also wrote the nonfiction *Witchcraft* (1941), an excellent introduction to and history of this subject.

Lewis was a close friend both of Williams and of Tolkien, though the latter two themselves were not intimate. A remark attributed to Tolkien implies dislike of Williams; Lewis, he said, had been "taken in" by Williams, as he had by Mrs. Moore and Mrs. Gresham. In denying that Williams had influenced his writing, he also said: "I didn't even know him very well." For that matter, Lewis, while he acknowledged that he and Williams had influenced each other, asserted: "No one ever influenced Tolkien—you might as well try to influence a bandersnatch." He once told Tolkien: "Confound you, nobody can influence you anyhow. I have tried but it's no good."

Although critics have professed to detect the influence of various precursors, such as Coleridge, Morris, MacDonald, Yeats, and Chesterton in Tolkien's fiction, Tolkien himself denied any influences on him save the North European legends and Rider Haggard's *She*. Of MacDonald he said: "I now find that I can't stand George MacDonald's books at any price at all."[16]

In 1938, Tolkien was invited to give the annual Andrew Lang lecture at the University of St. Andrews in Scotland. Lang (1844–1912) was an eminent Scottish writer, historian, journalist, mythographer, and poet. One of his monuments is a series of collections of fairy stories, gathered (with much help from his wife) from all over the world. These twelve volumes began with *The Blue Fairy Book* of 1889 and went on with the *Red,* the *Green,* and so on through the spectrum. (I had a copy of *The Red Fairy Book* as a child. It scared the daylights out of me, with its wicked stepmothers made to dance in red-hot iron shoes until they fell dead and its severed heads bouncing all over the place.)

Tolkien called his lecture, "On Fairy-Stories." Later he expanded and published it. He began by explaining that he did not necessarily mean a story about the Little Folk.

A fairy story, in Tolkien's sense, meant a story about Faërie, Elfland, the land of enchantment and imagination, filled with unearthly joys and sorrows and beauties and perils.

> In that realm a man may, perhaps, count himself fortunate to have wandered, but its very richness and strangeness tie the tongue of a traveller who would report them. And while he is there it is dangerous for him to ask too many questions, lest the gates should be shut and the keys be lost.

Not all children, any more than all adults, enjoy such fiction. The main distinction of Faërie from the everyday world, says Tolkien, is that it contains magic that works. The writer must take his magic seriously and neither laugh at it nor explain it away. Hence dream narratives (like Lewis Carroll's *Alice* books), beast fables (like those of Peter Rabbit), and travelers' tall tales (like those of Captain Gulliver) do not qualify.

Tolkien discussed what he considered the purposes of a fairy story. These are three: Recovery, Escape, and Consolation.

Recovery, he said, was the regaining of a clear view of the

things of this world, which he called the Primary World, by living for a while in an imaginary Secondary World. One might liken it to stirring up one's sense of wonder so that one can view commonplace things with it. "We should look at green again, and be startled anew (but not blinded) by blue and yellow and red. . . . We need, in any case, to clean our windows; so that the things seen clearly may be freed from the drab blur of triteness or familiarity—from possessiveness." In an oft-quoted sentence, he concludes: "By the forging of Gram cold iron was revealed; by the making of Pegasus horses were ennobled; in the Trees of the Sun and Moon root and stock, flower and fruit are manifested in glory."[17]

Next is Escape. People have a deep desire to do many things that they cannot do in the Primary World: to plumb the depths of time and space; to converse with nonhuman intelligences; and to live forever. Fairy stories provide these, at least while the reader is immersed in them. In his own childhood, Tolkien said:

> I desired dragons with profound desire. Of course, I in my timid body did not wish to have them in the neighbourhood, intruding into my relatively safe world, in which it was, for instance, possible to read stories in peace of mind, free from fear. But the world that contained even the imagination of Fáfnir was richer and more beautiful, at whatever the cost of peril.[18]

As for those who condemned imaginative fiction as "escapist" (like Roberts, who complained of LOTR's lack of "relevance"), that, said Tolkien was the point: "Why should a man be scorned if, finding himself in prison, he tries to get out and go home? Or if, when he cannot do so, he thinks and talks about other topics than jailers and prison-walls?" To Tolkien and like-minded persons, life in the Industrial Age had some of the qualities of life in prison.

And then there was Consolation: the Happy Ending. We all know that, in real life, everybody dies. Tolkien calls the happy ending a "eucatastrophe." In Greek, *katastrophê* meant literally "an overturn" and figuratively the end of a play, when its plot was resolved. A "eucatastrophe" would be a "good outcome" or "happy ending."

Tolkien viewed a fictional eucatastrophe as an echo of the story of the Resurrection in the Gospels. "But this story is supreme; and it is true."[19] This was a rare occasion on which Tolkien explicitly showed his Christianity.

He discussed the problems of composing a fairy story that should, while the reader was immersed in it, seem real to him. The writer is a "subcreator," creating a Secondary World, real to the reader while he reads. To make such a world convincing, the writer must take great care to have it self-consistent and logically thought out. In this sense, to make such a world is harder than to spin a yarn about everyday events in the here-and-now, where the ordinary laws of cause and effect are known and agreed upon.

At the Thursday night meetings of the Inklings, members lit pipes and addressed themselves to their tea. Then C. S. Lewis would ask: "Well, has nobody got anything to read us?"[20]

Out would come manuscripts. Members were candid to the point of brutality in their criticisms.

In 1938, after finishing *The Hobbit,* Tolkien began reading selections from what the members called "his new *Hobbit.*" It was *The Fellowship of the Ring.* When he gave his lecture at St. Andrews, said Tolkien: "At about that time we had reached Bree, and I had no more notion than they had of what had become of Gandalf or who Strider was; and I had begun to despair of surviving to find out."[21]

The other members found that it did no good to give Tolkien the sort of criticism they were used to. Either he ignored it altogether or got discouraged, discarded the piece he had read, and started over.

Tolkien worked on his gargantuan novel off and on through

the Hitlerian War and the bleak period of shortages afterwards, when Britons had to learn to breakfast on baked beans. When he finally turned the work in to the publishers, he said, it was like having "a great tumor" removed.

The Fellowship of the Ring starts with a Prologue, in which Tolkien describes Hobbits and their Shire and summarizes the story of *The Hobbit.* Then the tale proper begins:

> When Mr. Bilbo Baggins of Bag End announced that he would shortly be celebrating his eleventy-first birthday with a party of special magnificence, there was much talk and excitement in Hobbiton.
>
> Bilbo was very rich and very peculiar, and had been the wonder of the Shire for sixty years, ever since his remarkable disappearance and unexpected return. The riches he had brought back from his travels had now become a local legend, and it was popularly believed, whatever the old folk might say, that the Hill at Bag End was full of tunnels stuffed with treasure. And if that was not enough for fame, there was also his prolonged vigour to marvel at. . . . At ninety he was much the same as at fifty. . . . At ninety-nine they began to call him *well*-preserved; but *unchanged* would have been nearer the mark.[22]

Thus leisurely the story opens. Some readers may be put off by the kiddie-book tone, but if they perservere through the first chapter of fifty pages, the juvenility clears away. Tolkien's Secondary World is envisaged in great and plausible detail.

The story line parallels that of *The Hobbit,* although on a vaster scale. This time, the Quest is not to get something but to get rid of something.

Bilbo takes the occasion of his party to disappear, by means of Gollum's ring, in front of his guests. He means to go away to wild, mountainous country and finish his book on the adventures narrated in *The Hobbit.* He has promised Gandalf to leave the ring to Frodo, a younger cousin whom he had made his heir. ("Frodo" comes from the Old Norse names "Froði" and "Froða," related to the adjective *froðe,* "wise." Tolkien explains in an appendix that he had changed the final vowel to *o* to make the name sound more masculine to English-speaking readers.)[23]

Years later, Gandalf comes to see Frodo. Like Bilbo, Frodo has shown a remarkable resistance to aging. Gandalf explains that this is an effect of the ring, which is the One Ring made by Sauron, the Dark Lord, briefly referred to in *The Hobbit* as the Necromancer. ("Sauron" comes from the Greek *sauros,* "lizard.") This being, an incarnation of evil, was killed once, centuries before, in a war involving Elves and men; but he has not stayed dead.

The One Ring is one of twenty magical rings, distributed among men, Elves, and Dwarves. Possession of the One Ring will enable Sauron to enslave the Earth. Like the Heart of Ahriman in Howard's *Conan the Conqueror,* the One Ring has a mind of its own. It has a knack of getting itself found by people who could be tempted into taking it back to Sauron.

Early readers of *The Lord of the Rings* could not help seeing parallels with their own recent history, with the Ring playing the rôle of the Bomb. Tolkien emphatically denied any such intention. He had, he said, no use whatever for allegory and did not mean his story to be interpreted as such.

Still, it is hard not to think of Sauron as a fictional prototype of Adolf Hitler, the most Satanic figure of modern history. Moreover, despite his disclaimer, Tolkien did write two short stories, "Leaf by Niggle" (1947) and "Smith of Wootton Major" (1967), which are as plainly allegorical as anything could be.

Gandalf tells Frodo that the world's only hope is to cast the One Ring into the Cracks of Doom in the volcano Orodruin, in Sauron's land of Mordor. That is the only fire hot enough to melt it.

After more delay, Frodo sets off with Sam Gamgee, a local gardener who acts as Frodo's squire, and two younger cousins. They head for Rivendell, where Bilbo lives in retirement. On the way, they are menaced by the Black Riders, servants of Sauron. They are saved from graveyard spooks called barrow wights by Tom Bombadil, a kind of timeless nature spirit, whose irrepressible jolliness becomes a bit tiresome.

At Bree, they fall in with a weather-beaten Ranger, locally called Strider. This man turns out to be Aragorn, heir to the throne of the southern kingdom of Gondor. After more perils, they attend a council of Hobbits, Elves, and men at Rivendell, to plan a campaign against Sauron.

After much discussion and recapitulation of the history of Middle-Earth, a party of nine sets out to destroy the One Ring. These are Gandalf and Aragorn; an Elf, Legolas; Gimli, a Dwarf; Boromir, a lord of Gondor; and Sam, Frodo, and Frodo's two young cousins. (Gimli or Gimlé is a place mentioned in the Eddas.) Elves and Dwarves normally dislike each other, but the growth of friendship between Legolas and Gimli is one theme of the story.

Then come tremendous adventures. In the underground realm of Moria, built by Dwarves before they were driven out, the Fellowship are attacked by goblins. In this story, goblins are called by the Elvish name of "Orcs" (from Latin *orcus,* "Hades," "death," "Pluto," cognate with "ogre"). Perhaps Tolkien had decided that "goblin" had too light and humorous a connotation. Wolves are now called "wargs" (Anglo-Saxon *wearg,* "criminal").

While Tolkien can build up excellent suspense and sense of danger, his orcs, when they appear, are too easily slaughtered to be fictionally effective menaces.

In conflict with a kind of demon called a Balrog, Gandalf falls into an abyss. The Balrog, mostly made of flame and smoke, seems to be original with Tolkien, unless by some remote chance it is derived from the Boyg (Norwegian *Böig*). This is an invisible monster, with whom Peer Gynt grapples in Act II, Scene 7 of Ibsen's play and in the Norse folk tales on which the play is based.

The rest find refuge in Lothlōrien, ruled by an Elven king and queen. When they leave, divisions arise. The party splits up. Boromir, overcome by greed, tries to rob Frodo of the ring. Frodo escapes, invisible. He and Sam flee towards Mordor, while the rest head for Gondor, threatened by Sauron's forces.

In *The Two Towers,* Boromir, repenting his evil deed, is slain by Orcs while defending the two younger Hobbits. These are captured by Orcs, escape, encounter a race of treelike beings called Ents, and are finally reunited with Aragorn, Legolas, and Gimli. The latter have taken part in a great battle. This battle was fought against the Orckish hordes by an army of heroic barbarians, the Rohirrim, who have Anglo-Saxon names but otherwise resemble the ancient Goths.

Gandalf, resurrected, rejoins them. It transpires that he is one of a group of good wizards, the five Istari, sent from higher quarters to guide Middle-Earth through its perils. The head of that Council was the wizard Saruman. But Saruman has become corrupted by greed and has formed an uneasy alliance with Sauron. Saruman holds sway from his own tower of Orthanc (Anglo-Saxon for "gadget") and is training his own army of Orcs. Gandalf has now taken his place. Asked about Gandalf's resurrection, Tolkien said: "Gandalf is an angel."[24]

So, presumably, are the other wizards of the Council. So, too, are the remote superhuman beings called the Valar, who live in Valinor, the Blessed Realm or Undying Lands in the forbidden West. ("Valar" sounds suspiciously like the Old Norse *Valir,* "Frenchmen.")

The introduction of a land of immortality creates the same awkward complication in the story that it does in Morris's *Glittering Plain.* I think I have figured out why this element in some fantasies, as in those of Lloyd Alexander and L. Frank Baum, has always made me uneasy when I came across it. To a rationalistic reader, any problem can be solved, given enough time, by the application of intelligence. An Undying Land, which gives an intelligence infinite time in which to work, would enable that being to solve all problems, including such intractable ones as war and peace, the production and distribution of wealth, and the relations between the sexes. This being the case, what task could take precedence over attaining immortality? Or given the existence of an Undying Land, why have not all problems been solved?

The white wizard, of which Gandalf is an example, has long posed a puzzle for literary but pious Christians. The Churches long insisted that there was no such thing as white magic. Holy men might achieve miracles, with divine help; but all magic was performed with the help of devils and was therefore wicked.

Still, there is an obvious place in fantasy for the good magician, and medieval romancers toyed with giving Merlin that rôle. Shakespeare finally broke the tabu with his Prospero; although, to placate critics, he has his wizard give up his magic at the end. (Prospero may be viewed as a combination of Merlin and Dr. John Dee, the scholarly Elizabethan astrologer and occultist.) Since then the white wizard, long beard and all, has been a fixture in heroic fantasy. Gandalf's angelhood is Tolkien's way of getting around the contradiction in orthodox Christian doctrine.

While the Rohirrim and the Ents are overthrowing Saruman, Frodo and Sam struggle towards Mordor. They have many narrow escapes; the Black Riders, now mounted on pterosaurs (Mesozoic flying reptiles) shadow them. Their closest shave occurs when Frodo is paralyzed by the bite of Shelob, a giant spider who lairs on the borders of Mordor, and is seized by the Orcs.

The Return of the King tells of the final efforts of Sam and Frodo to reach Orodruin. They have been joined by Gollum, with whom they are on terms of unstable truce. At the same time, Aragorn's forces reach Gondor and take part in tremendous battles against the hosts of Mordor. These battles keep Sauron's attention fixed on Gondor, so that he fails to notice the approach of Frodo to Orodruin.

In the volcano, Frodo prepares to throw away the Ring; but its lure is too powerful. Instead, he puts it on, crying: "I do not choose now to do what I came to do. I will not do this deed. The Ring is mine!"[25]

Gollum attacks Frodo, bites off Frodo's ring finger, and takes the Ring. As he capers in triumph, he falls over the edge into the lava. Sauron, having invested so much of his own power in the Ring, disintegrates, and his hosts disperse. The war is over.

Aragorn takes the throne of Gondor. He is now called Elessar, otherwise Dúnadan; several characters have a confusing multiplicity of names. Aragorn also weds his part-Elf longtime fiancée, Arwen. Frodo and the other Hobbits return to the Shire, which they find corrupted—that is to say, industrialized—by the fugitive Saruman.

That situation is soon put to rights. But Frodo has sustained a wound that can be healed only in the Elves' Grey Havens, in the West. The Elves set out on their final migration thither. Since Arwen has given up her place on the ship, Frodo is allowed to take it, and he passes beyond the ken of men.

This is but a sketch of this tremendous work. A vast amount of the history of Middle-Earth is brought into the story in driblets and is summarized in the appendices.

For example, there is the story of Númenor—Tolkien's Atlantis—sunk beneath the ocean, long before the time of LOTR, because its people, seeking immortality, tried to take the forbidden Undying Lands by storm. To an unbeliever who enjoys life, this seems an altogether reasonable desire; but theology finds abstruse reasons for condemning it.

Two of the realms of Middle-Earth were founded by survivors from Númenor. These are Arnor in the North, extinct in the time of LOTR, and Gondor in the South. (Arnor Thordson is a Norse skald in Snorri's *Heimskringla,* while Gondor is a province of Ethiopia.)

At least a dozen books about Tolkien and LOTR have been published, as well as a multitude of articles. These explore every aspect of the work: literary, philosophical, religious, moral, and linguistic.

For example, Tolkien took pains with his invented languages, which furnished the core around which the novel grew. Elvish is a musical tongue, in which the consonants called "sonorants" (*l, m, n, ng,* and *r*) predominate. For instance, one stanza of the previously quoted Elvish song, in the original, is:

> A! Elbereth Gilthoniel!
> silivren penna míriel
> o menel aglar elenath,
> Gilthoniel, A! Elbereth![26]

The harsh Orckish, on the other hand, is full of velar consonants: *k, g,* and their related fricatives or "gutturals," such as occur in some oriental languages.

In the appendices, Tolkien rides his philological hobby hard. We learn that the Rohirrim do not "really" speak Anglo-Saxon; Tolkien has just Saxonified their names to make them more familiar. Sam's name was not "really" Samwise but Banazîr, nicknamed "Ban," and Tolkien has Anglicized it. All of which seems a bit much.

LOTR is virtually as sexless as Lovecraft's writings. There are few women, no mothers, and not so much as a hint of mankind's ancient sport of fornication. Three of the main characters marry at the end, but in the most proper, decorous way.

In an adventure story, this is not necessarily a fault. Women's Lib to the contrary notwithstanding, it is a fact that men have, throughout history, lived on the average more active, adventurous lives than women, and that for a few simple, obvious reasons. It is only logical that adventure fiction should reflect this fact. The theme of manly comradeship in perilous adventure, without sexual implications, is an age-old and respectable one, whatever umbrage some contemporary critics may take at it.

In any case, saving the world from Sauron would keep anyone too busy to develop the arts of Don Juan de Tenorio.
As my colleague Marion Zimmer Bradley has said: ". . . heroes
of adventure fantasy are rarely comfortable figures among the
ladies; and I don't know which pleases me the less: the treat-
'em-rough tactics of Conan or Aragorn's embarrassed courtli-
ness."[27] This is unfair to Conan, who has a rough sense of
chivalry towards women and never maltreats them; but it expresses the right idea.

Several themes recur often in the story. Among these are the
impermanence of men and their works; the value of heroism,
resolute struggle, responsibility, and renunciation; the evils of
possessiveness; and the permanence of evil. Sauron or his equiv-
alent, no matter how often scotched, always bobs up again.

Critics have noted that Tolkien has skillfully combined
Christian optimism with Northern pessimism. Norse myth
looked forward, not to any Millennium or Second Coming, but
to the eventual destruction of the earth and the principal gods
in a final cosmic battle with the forces of evil. Others describe
Tolkien's attitude as "Christian romanticism."[28]

Tolkien, unlike Lewis, keeps his religious orientation so well
hidden that I had read the trilogy thrice and had met Tolkien
without even suspecting his Catholicism. I first learned about it
by reading Lewis. When an interviewer cornered Tolkien on
this question, he finally replied: "I am a Christian and of course
what I write will be from that essential viewpoint."[29]

I met Tolkien in February 1967, on my way back from
India. Tolkien and I had corresponded. I had sent him a copy
of my little anthology, *Swords and Sorcery;* he said he found it
interesting but did not much like the stories in it. In particular,
referring to "Distressing Tale of Thangobrind the Jeweller,"
he spoke of "Dunsany's worst style," especially at the end,
where Dunsany, for the sake of a joke, pricked his own illusion. When I said I should be in England, he invited me out.

I found Tolkien very cordial and friendly. He said: "You

look just the way I pictured you. What do they call you? 'Sprague'?"

So we were "Sprague" and "Ronald" thenceforth. This rather surprised me, since Tolkien had a reputation for crustiness, and I always thought that the British were not so free with given names as Americans. Perhaps the fact that I was not trying to exploit him by pumping him for some project of my own had something to do with it. On a later occasion, he had tart words for one interviewer, who had, said Tolkien, "talked for hours about himself" and then gone off to write a notably superficial book on LOTR.

Tolkien was not altogether happy in his situation. His wife, whom I met, was badly crippled by arthritis, so that Tolkien had to do the housework. They were, however, proud of having just become great-grandparents. When Tolkien had become professor emeritus, Oxford had moved him out of the house he had occupied into a much smaller one, so that he had to convert the garage into a library.

We sat in the garage for a couple of hours, smoking pipes, drinking beer, and talking about a variety of things. Practically anything in English literature, from *Beowulf* down, Tolkien had read and could talk intelligently about. He indicated that he "rather liked" Howard's Conan stories.

I asked him two specific questions about LOTR. One was, why were the landscapes of Middle-Earth so devoid of large animal life? In the days before the population explosion and the perfection of the gun, practically all the earth's land surface, except for the most extremely dry, cold, or mountainous parts, swarmed with such megafauna.

This was true *a fortiori* back in the Pleistocene, before the wave of extinction at the end of that period. This Great Death, for example, eliminated mammoths, mastodons, ground sloths, camels, horses, tapirs, and giant species of peccary and beaver from North America, together with the lions, saber-toothed cats, and giant wolves that preyed upon them.

Tolkien and I agreed that this faunal poverty of Middle-

Earth reflected Tolkien's memories of the English countryside in his boyhood. Save for two species of deer, large wild animals have been extinct in Britain for centuries.

The other question, which others have also brought up, was: Why did the Middle-Earthians have no formal religion, as all historical peoples have had, with temples, priests, rituals, and a hierarchy of gods?

I was not sure that I understood Tolkien's reply. He said something to the effect that in those days (he assumed) good and evil had not become so mixed up as they were later.

I left it at that. When I learned of Tolkien's Catholicism, however, much became clear. Some of the most effective writers of prehistoric or other-world fantasy, like Dunsany, Lovecraft, Howard, and Leiber, have been unbelievers. Such skeptics could freely invent all the gods they pleased and give those gods whatever qualities their stories required.

A devout Christian or other monotheist, however, has a problem. He cannot make his people good Christians, Muslims, or Jews back in the Pleistocene or in a parallel world. If they worship "pagan" gods, he must make it plain that these gods are either demons in disguise or nonexistent, even though such a story could often make good use of a nice if fallible little godlet.

Tolkien sidestepped the issue by keeping his references to religion few and subdued. There are occasional allusions to Eru, or the One—that is, God. This God, however, seems an otiose deity, like that of the eighteenth-century Deists, who once wound up the universe but leaves its day-to-day running to subordinates.

The Valar and the Council of wizards are implicitly angels. They are supposed to guide and protect mankind, although they do a most incompetent job of it. The Elves sing to El-bereth, wife of Manwe and queen of the Valar, in terms that suggest a kind of prefiguration of the Virgin Mary. (And married angels?) Sauron was not originally evil. He was probably, like Saruman, an angel gone wrong. He is not Satan; Gandalf explains that Sauron is merely the tool or emissary of another evil power.

Another theme, which Tolkien touches in a gingerly way, is that of free will versus predestination or Fate. Bilbo and Frodo are repeatedly told that the things they do and suffer are part of a cosmic plan. At the end of *The Hobbit,* Gandalf tells Bilbo: "You don't really suppose, do you, that all your adventures and escapes were managed by mere luck, just for your sole benefit? You are a very fine person, Mr. Baggins, and I am very fond of you; but you are only quite a little fellow in a wide world after all!"

Early in LOTR, Frodo tells Gandalf that he ought to have killed the sniveling, treacherous, murderous Gollum. Gandalf replies:

> "Deserves it! I daresay he does. Many live that deserve death. And some that die deserve life. Can you give it to them? Then do not be too eager to deal out death in judgement. For even the very wise cannot see all ends. I have not much hope that Gollum can be cured before he dies, but there is a chance of it. And he is bound up with the fate of the Ring. My heart tells me that he has some part to play yet, for good or ill, before the end; and when that comes, the pity of Bilbo may rule the fate of many—yours not the least."[30]

Sure enough, in the final scene in Orodruin, Gollum unwittingly saves Frodo from the loss of his own resolution to discard the Ring and also destroys it and himself. When free will fails to make the cosmic plan work, Fate steps in to help.

This is convenient but not very convincing. The author assumes that good and evil are absolute values, not subjective or relative, and that there is a moral order in the universe. In other words, Fate is on the side of good. But, if theologically respectable, this idea is fictionally awkward. If the reader grasps it, then the feeling that God will save the characters is bound to take the edge off the suspense. In fact, Tolkien works the long arm of coincidence to the point of bursitis.

So, one might say, God must be working behind the scenes to make things come out right and provide these convenient happenstances. But that brings up a basic paradox, on which monotheistic theologians have broken their teeth for centuries. If God is all-good, all-wise, and all-powerful, how can evil exist? Or, if God runs things, why does he do such a sloppy job of it?

Theologians have propounded various answers. The standard Christian answer, for instance, is that God has given man free will, so that man can earn his salvation. But this is a mere quibble. If God is indeed all-wise, he knows exactly what any of his creatures will do in advance. If a man he has created does wrong, God is just as responsible as a mechanic, who knowingly assembles a faulty machine, is responsible for that machine's breakdown in use.

The Gnostic and Yezidi answer is that God delegates the running of the world to a subordinate, a Satan or an Eldil, whose incompetence or wickedness causes the trouble. But this is just as much a quibble. Having made this subordinate, God also knows just what that retainer will do and what the results will be. The Mazdaists or Parsees say that Satan is an independent power, opposed to and more or less equal to God.

Or the theologian may try to turn off questions by saying: "It is a mystery," "It is not meant for us to know." This is merely excusing ignorance by making a virtue of it and at the same time trying to shut off awkward questions.

Polytheists never had that trouble. They assumed that the gods were glorified human beings, with human lusts, vices, and follies. When things went awry, they could always say: "What can you expect, with a gang of idiotic gods like ours?"

When, however, the monotheistic faiths began competing for converts, they found that people would buy the biggest and shiniest God they could offer, regardless of logic. In the same way, a man may buy the biggest and shiniest automobile he can afford, even if it will not fit into his garage. The most market-

able God proved to be an omnipotent, omniscient, and omni-
benevolent God. Converts were not deterred by the state of the
world, which implied that it could not possibly be run by a
God having all those qualities at once. One or two, perhaps,
but not all three.

A fairy story, however, is not really adapted to settling such
philosophical questions. I bring them up only because Tolkien
did, although he wisely did not try to solve them. In Faërie, as
Tolkien says, "it is dangerous to ask too many questions."

Another aspect of LOTR is Tolkien's use of traditional
versus original concepts. Edmund Wilson complained of the
author's "poverty of invention." By this, I suppose Wilson
meant that Tolkien stuck close to traditional themes and elements from existing myth and folklore.

Indeed, Tolkien does bring in a multitude of traditional
elements: the Quest (compare the Argosy); the magical ring
of invisibility (Gyges' ring); the ring that bears a curse (And-
vari's ring); the hero's incurable wound (Philoktetes, Am-
fortas); the wicked, gold-hoarding dragon (Fáfnir);[31] the
reforging of the hero's broken sword (Sigurð's Gram); the
return of the True King (Odysseus); the hero's humorous,
commonsensical lower-class retainer (Sancho Panza, Dunsany's
Morāno, and Wodehouse's Jeeves).

Traditional, too is Tolkien's making the swarthy southern
Haradrim and the nomadic Easterlings villains, sent by Sauron
against Gondor. Europe has a long tradition of invasions from
the East and the South, by Persians, Cathaginians, Huns, Arabs,
Mongols, and Turks, to whom the attackers of Gondor roughly
correspond. An Asian or an African could, of course, present
an equal bill of complaints against Europeans for invading and
conquering his continent.

When Tolkien introduced original concepts, his results, in
his critics' view, were mixed. Most approved of his Hobbits
and Ents but were less impressed by Tom Bombadil, Shelob,
and the Balrog.

An advantage of using traditional materials in their traditional rôles is that these things already have images and associations in the readers' minds. One need not describe a dragon in much detail, because nearly all readers have a mental picture of a dragon. The traditional materials also invoke strong feelings in the readers, because they stir up childhood memories, impressions, and emotions. (This may be less true than formerly, because the traditional tales, the stories of Odysseus and Sigurð and Arthur, tend to be crowded out of children's usual reading by the enormous spate of new and more "relevant" juvenile writings by contemporary authors.)

On the other hand, too close an adherence to traditional precedents may make the work hackneyed. This applies not only to the concepts but also to the way in which they are used. Traditionally, wolves, reptiles, and spiders are all feared. Therefore they are easily made into symbols of evil, and thus Tolkien uses them. But a well-informed modern reader knows that all these animals have useful places in nature; that wolves, in their private lives, display many qualities admired among human beings; that most reptiles are not only harmless but also useful; and that spiders are effective foes of the more pestiferous insects. As somebody said in a Disney nature movie, there are no heroes or villains in nature.

A fantasist who wants to take advantage of modern knowledge may reverse the traditional rôles and put a dragon or a ghost on the hero's side instead of against him. In a minor fairy story, *Farmer Giles of Ham* (1949), Tolkien did just that. After the king's gallant knights have failed to cope with the ravages of the dragon Chrysophylax, Farmer Giles subdues and domesticates the beast.

This suggests why Edmund Wilson admired Cabell but castigated Tolkien. Tolkien, with a few variations, sticks close to traditional materials, rôles, and themes.

Cabell, a man of thoroughly "modern" outlook, treats these materials in original, sophisticated ways. He stands them on their heads, burlesques them, and makes them ridiculous. In

Cabell, the heroes of legend all have feet of clay, prominently displayed. The heroines are no better than they should be. And the Creator of the Universe turns out "not particularly intelligent . . . omnipotent . . . . well-meaning, but . . . . rather slow of apprehension." This realization "went far toward explaining a host of matters which had long puzzled Jurgen."[32]

Edmund Wilson evidently admired this approach but was bored by the older, more traditional one. A story that took the traditional materials seriously and upheld the moral values of the old epics and romances, he dismissed as "juvenile trash." Wilson—forward-looking, experimental, a tabu-breaker, a one-time admirer of Lenin—was not one who could become again as a little child, if only to enjoy a traditional fantasy. The loss was his.

So the writer of heroic fantasy has a choice. He can use traditional materials in traditional ways. This has the advantage of evoking already familiar images and childhood emotions in his readers. Or he can use these materials in modern, unconventional ways, using modern knowledge that did not exist in ancient and medieval times, when the traditional epics took form. This method gives the writer more scope for humor and originality, although he risks making his story trivial, because he cannot tap his readers' buried childhood memories and the emotions that go with them. Or he can use new materials, but in that case he may find himself writing science fiction instead of fantasy.

Each course has its advantages. Tolkien chose the first method and did a bang-up job of it; others find the other approaches more congenial.

Soon after my visit to Tolkien, he moved to Devonshire and holed up, hoping to be left alone so that he could finish a long-planned prequel to LOTR. This work, *The Silmarillion,* is said to have been finished. But the perfectionistic Tolkien kept working it over to assure its consistency with what he had already published about Middle-Earth.

He persuaded his publisher to screen his correspondence, since he had long been snowed under by letters from admirers. He disliked the Tolkien cult, with its clubs, its amateur publications, its meticulous analyses of LOTR and of the author's motives and psychology. At least, he wished they would let him alone to get his work done.

In 1971, his wife died. At the beginning of 1972, he turned eighty and was named a Commander of the Order of the British Empire. In 1973, he quietly died. The editing of *The Silmarillion* passed to his second son, Christopher Tolkien—another Oxonian professor and by all accounts as meticulous a perfectionist as his sire.

In any large work, like LOTR, one can find flaws on rereading. There are plenty in the Conan saga and in the works of Morris and Eddison. But one need not, while reading a heroic fantasy, worry about a few inconsistencies or philosophical contradictions. In this genre, few have equaled and none has surpassed LOTR in vividness, grandeur, and sheer readability. And that is accomplishment enough for any one man.

X

THE ARCHITECT OF CAMELOT:
T. H. WHITE

O brother, had you known our mighty hall,
Which Merlin built for Arthur long ago!
For all the sacred mount of Camelot,
And all the dim rich city, roof by roof,
Tower after tower, spire beyond spire,
By grove, and garden-lawn, and rushing brook,
Climbs to the mighty hall that Merlin built.[1]

TENNYSON

According to the sixth-century Breton priest Gildas, when in the previous century the Saxons invaded post-Roman Britain, the Britons

> . . . took arms under the conduct of Ambrosius Aurelianus, a modest man, who of all the Roman nation was then in the confusion of this troubled period by chance left alive. . . .
>
> After this, sometimes our countrymen, sometimes the enemy, won the field, to the end that our Lord might in this land try after his accustomed manner these his Israelites, whether they loved him or not, until the year of the siege of Badon Hill, when took place also the last almost, though not the least slaughter of our cruel foes. . . .[2]

About the year 800, Nennius wrote a *History of the Britons,* drawing on Gildas and introducing mythical elements. After a garbled expansion of Gildas's account of Ambrosius, Nennius adds: "Then it was that the magnanimous Arthur, with all the kings and military force of Britain, fought against the Saxons. And though there were many more noble than himself, yet he was twelve times chosen their commander, and was as often conqueror." Nennius lists twelve battles, of which: "The twelfth was a most severe contest, when Arthur penetrated to the hill of Badon. In this engagement, 940 fell by his hand alone. . . ."[3]

This is the oldest known mention of Arthur, about 300 years after Arthur is supposed to have died. These passages from Gildas and Nennius are almost the sole historical basis for the Arthurian legend cycle, which became medieval England's *Iliad.*

Three hundred and fifty years later, a Welsh monk, Geoffrey of Monmouth, took as sources Nennius and others, such as the churchly historian Bæda or Bede, the *Welsh Annals,* and the *Anglo-Saxon Chronicle.* Using Virgil's *Aeneid* as his model, Geoffrey constructed a largely fictional *History of the Kings of Britain.* This work enlarged the rôle of Arthur still further; in fact, nearly all the latter half of the book is devoted to the Pendragon family of Ambrosius, Uther, and Arthur. The book ends when, soon after Arthur's death, the Britons are finally driven back into Wales and Cornwall by the Saxons.

Then the romancers took over, adding magic, miracles, monsters, quests, love affairs, and other elements of medieval romance. If Arthur existed, he would never have known himself.

They are still at it. Between 1857 and 1885, Tennyson, in his *Idylls of the King,* made Arthur into a proper Victorian gentleman, about as much like a real Dark Age monarch as the Rev. Billy Graham resembles Attila the Hun. In 1889, Mark Twain burlesqued chivalric romance and damned the Middle Ages with *A Connecticut Yankee in King Arthur's Court.*

In the last half-century, many novels have appeared on the Arthurian theme. They range from the realistic (Duggan, Sutcliffe, Treece), which try to reconstruct actual conditions in post-Roman Britain, to those (Stewart, Erskine, White) that more or less accept the assumptions of Arthurian romancers.

Among modern Arthurian novels, at the romantic end of the spectrum stands the great tetralogy, *The Once and Future King,* by T. H. White. Published at intervals from 1939 to 1958, the combined work can (like Tolkien's *Lord of the Rings*) be considered either a single long novel in several parts or as separate novels forming a chain of sequels. Of the modern Arthurian tales, White's tetralogy is currently the best-known to Americans as a result of becoming a successful musical comedy, *Camelot,* and subsequently a motion picture. John F. Kennedy's administration was sometimes compared to White's Camelot.

White's tetralogy is mainly based upon the *Morte d'Arthur* of Sir Thomas Malory. By the time Malory got to work on the story, the original theme of the struggle of the Britons against the invading Saxons had disappeared, which is a little like a life of George Washington that does not mention the American Revolution.

Malory even made Arthur an Englishman (that is, an Anglo-Saxon) instead of a leader of the Anglo-Saxons' mortal foes, the Celtic Britons. The romancers filled post-Roman Britain with knights, 600 years before knighthood became a regular institution, clattering around in Renaissance plate armor 800 years before such armor was invented.

Sir Thomas himself does not seem to have been quite a parfit gentle knight, since he spent much of his life in jail for assaulting and robbing his neighbors and raping their wives. In the 1460s, while doing time for one of these offenses, he lightened the tedium of prison by combining several French versions of the Arthurian story and translating the resulting conflation into English. In 1485, fourteen years after Sir Thomas's death, Caxton published the work.

White took Malory as his basis. Since, however, the milieu

that Malory described never existed, the White novels can best be viewed as laid, not in this world, but in an imaginary parallel one. White hints that this is what he has in mind. His characters allude to the real kings of England and other historical characters as legendary or mythical, and White assures us that his Arthur "was not a distressed Briton hopping about in a suit of woad in the fifth century."

White's scenery, customs, and costumes are, like Malory's, essentially those of the fourteenth and fifteenth centuries: the time of the Hundred Years' War, Joan of Arc, and the Wars of the Roses in real history. Edward III of England (1327–77, the victor of Crécy) has been suggested as the model for White's Arthur. The Norman Conquest is mentioned, Arthur being termed of Norman lineage. To enjoy these stories, the reader had better forget whatever he knows about medieval English history.

Of Terence Hanbury White (1906–64) it has been said, as of H. P. Lovecraft and Robert Howard, that he was "far more remarkable than anything he wrote."[4] Like Lovecraft, "Tim" White was a bundle of contradictions, which complicated his life. He was a sexual deviant; an intermittent alcoholic; a highly cultivated man who often displayed dreadful manners; a sensitive, sympathetic, tender-hearted man who tended to shout down the slightest disagreement; a celebrant of courage who passed the Hitlerian War safely in Ireland. In fits of childish rage, he sometimes quarreled with his best friends. He was afraid of many things, such as flying, but forced himself to do them. According to his biographer, "White, who was modest about his creative powers, was conceited about his intellect— which was second-rate."[5]

White had an effective way of coping with his problems. In *The Sword in the Stone,* Merlyn tells young Arthur:

> "The best thing for being sad . . . is to learn something. That is the only thing that never fails. You may grow old and trembling

in your anatomies, you may lie awake at night listening to the disorder in your veins, you may miss your only love, you may see the world about you devastated by evil lunatics, or know your honour trampled in the sewers of baser minds. There is only one thing for it then—to learn."[6]

Often sad, White took his own advice. He passionately pursued versatility, boasting:

> . . . I can shoot with a bow and arrow, so when the next atomic bomb is dropped poor old White will be hopping about in a suit of skins shooting caribou or something with a bow and arrow. . . . I won a prize for flying aeroplanes about thirty years ago. I can plough with horses. I used to ride show jumpers; I have taught myself to be a falconer. One of the odder things I have done is to learn to go down in diving suits—the old brass hat diving suit. I have had to learn to sail. I swim fairly well. I was a good shot until I took to spectacles—clay pigeons and geese and things of that sort. Fishing. I was a very good fisherman. I used to drive fast cars—God knows why. I had to be good at games. . . . I had to teach myself not to be clumsy. Compensating for my sense of inferiority, my sense of danger, my sense of disaster, I had to learn to paint even, and not only to paint—oils, art, and all that sort of thing—but to build and mix concrete and to be a carpenter and to saw and screw and put in a nail without bending it. . . . I had to get first-class honours with distinction at the University. I had to be a scholar. I had to learn medieval Latin shorthand so as to translate bestiaries.[7]

Not everyone agreed that White was a master of all those skills. His longtime friend David Garnett, eminent author and critic, said that their friendship was based on a mutual misunderstanding. Garnett had an exaggerated idea of White's prowess at fishing and other sports, while White had an equally inflated notion of Garnett's scholarship and authorship. Garnett said: "I can testify that he was a rough and ready fisherman, an indifferent shot and up until 1946 a ludicrously incompetent carpenter."[8]

Still, the man's gusto, energy, and drive for omnicompetence cannot fail to arouse admiration.

Like some other writers in this series, White had a bad start. His father was a police official in India; his mother, the daughter of another Anglo-Indian official. Constance White was another monster-mother: beautiful, vain, cold, demanding, jealous, and utterly selfish and self-absorbed. Hating sex, she refused it to her husband after young White's birth. The husband took to drink and became abusive. The boy saw them struggling for a pistol above his crib, each shouting that he was going to kill the other or himself or the child.

The mutually hating couple were eventually divorced. Years later, White got even with his mother by putting her into his Arthurian novels as Queen Morgause of Orkney, mother of Gawaine, Agravaine, Gaheris, Gareth, and—by Arthur, illegitimately—Mordred.

White went through English "public" (=private) schools, surviving a sadistic headmaster, and on to Cambridge. There he did well, living penuriously and tutoring to eke out his costs.

Falling ill in his third year, White took a year off for a sojourn in Italy, where he became fluent in Italian. He also fell in with homosexuals and became a practicing homosexual. As I think most psychiatrists would agree, his family background was of just the sort to predispose him to this abnormality.

He was not happy about his peculiarity, fervently wishing he were normal. He wrote: "I want to get married too, and escape from all this piddling homosexuality and fear and unreality."

A few years after he graduated from Cambridge (with distinction, in 1929) he had himself psychoanalyzed to cure the deviation. The treatments seem to have been only partly successful. In later years, White carried his love for his dogs to extravagant extremes and was badly broken up when, one by one, they died. In 1946, in Yorkshire, he became engaged to a local girl about half his age. She gave him the air, and again he was heartbroken. According to the exuberantly normal Garnett, White late in life explained:

> . . . that he was a sadist. I am so little attracted by this perversion
> that I had never used my imagination to realize the unhappiness
> which inevitably attends it. Tim explained that the sadist cannot be
> happy unless he has proved the love felt for him by acts of cruelty,
> which naturally are misinterpreted by normal human beings. It had
> been Tim's fate to destroy every passionate love he had inspired.
> He had found himself always in the dilemma of either being sincere and cruel, or false and unnatural. Whichever line he followed,
> he revolted the object of his love and disgusted himself.[9]

Altogether, a complicated man. For six years after leaving Cambridge, White earned his bread by teaching in preparatory schools. He is said to have been an excellent teacher. He was tall, big, and strikingly handsome, with prominent blue eyes. He wore an intermittent beard in a clean-shaven era, when such an ornament was a virtual monopoly of the artist class.

He rode in fox hunts and wrote some contemporary novels, which had very modest but still encouraging sales. Not at all mechanically inclined, he drove an old black Bentley. Once, driving at night with a few whiskeys aboard, he drove it through the wall of a house and into the bedroom, to the understandable dismay of the occupants. He professed the Communist sympathies then fashionable among young intellectuals, although his real political orientation was towards a medievalistic, agrarian Socialism of William Morris's kind.

In 1936, White quit teaching for full-time writing. His total output was twenty-four books (both fiction and nonfiction), thirteen short stories, minor publications, and unpublished or unfinished works. For several years he suffered the typical financial ups and downs of the free-lance writer, with a few ups and many downs. In 1938, he was living on credit when the success of *The Sword in the Stone,* a Book of the Month and the subject of a Disney animated cartoon feature, gave him a financial cushion.

In 1939, White settled in Ireland. There he stayed through

the Second World War, writing, practicing falconry, and often drinking heavily. Visiting the Dunsanys at Dunsany Castle, he thought Lord Dunsany "a decent, amusing, interesting, selfish, vain, enlightened fellow," but "not a patch on his wife, who remarked in a tone of acute nostalgia, à propos of a Daimler which they had once owned: 'Ah, that was a splendid car. It was simply riddled with bullets.' "[10]

White wrestled with his conscience about the war. A pacifistic patriot, he was over age for conscription, while weakness of eyesight and a brush with tuberculosis disqualified him for active service. He made desultory efforts to get a war job, for instance as a ferry pilot in the RAF Volunteer Reserve. But nothing came of these efforts, and White ended the war in Ireland.

Of the Arthurian novels, the second volume, *The Witch in the Wood,* came out in 1939 and the third, *The Ill-Made Knight,* in 1940. The fourth section, *The Candle in the Wind,* was never published as a separate volume. Instead, White went back, revised the first three volumes, and added the fourth story as the final book of a single big four-deck volume, *The Once and Future King.* (1958). In this omnibus volume, he changed the title of *The Witch in the Wood* to *The Queen of Air and Darkness.* White planned and wrote a fifth story, *The Book of Merlyn.* But his inspiration seems to have failed; the work turned out badly and has never been published.

In the long interval between the first three novels and the omnibus volume, White was busy with other projects. One was a fable, *The Elephant and the Kangaroo,* which transplanted the myth of Noah and the Flood to an Irish locale. White poked mild fun at the Irish, especially his landlord and landlady (thinly disguised), and at the Catholic Church. His former hosts were deeply offended when they found out.

More successful was an imaginative novel, *Mistress Masham's Repose* (1946), which became an American Book of the Month. This is an adventure-comedy on the borders of fantasy and science fiction. A ten-year-old orphaned heiress, Maria, is brought up in a crumbling mansion by a wicked governess and a wicked vicar, who plot to rob her of her inheritance. Maria discovers, on the overgrown estate, a colony of six-inch Lilliputians. These were kidnapped from their native Lilliput in Captain Gulliver's time and brought as freaks to England, where they escaped and set up a secret settlement. Although the tale drags a bit in places, it is on the whole excellent of its kind.

The Sword in the Stone tells of Arthur's boyhood, from the time when Merlyn is hired as his tutor to the day when Arthur pulls out the sword and is thus proved the rightful king. Arthur, called "the Wart," is living at Sir Ector's castle, his older companion being Ector's son Kay. White makes Kay a natural leader and Arthur a natural follower. (In Mary Stewart's recent Arthurian novel, *The Hollow Hills,* it is just the opposite: Arthur being the natural leader and Kay the follower.)

Merlyn explains that he is a time traveler who has come back from the future to rear Arthur. The aged, all-knowing, all-wise white wizard is pretty much a fixture in stories of this kind, as we have seen. Their common prototype is the Merlin of Geoffrey and Malory, who may in his turn have a prototype in the Nestor of the *Iliad.*

As White's Merlin explains to the Wart, living backwards is confusing. This assumption, however, lets White indulge in what Fritz Leiber has called "controlled anachronism"; that is, dropping allusions to psychoanalysis and other modern things for laughs. Since the story is laid in an imaginary "secondary world" anyway, the question of straining the reader's credulity does not arise. At the same time, the reader of White learns a tremendous lot about real medieval usages and techniques.

Mark Twain did the same in *A Connecticut Yankee,* furnishing his hero's partisans with bicycles and revolvers. When *A Connecticut Yankee* was first made into a movie with Will Rogers, the bicycles had evolved into motorcycles. The second time around, the motorcycles became compact cars. Trust Hollywood.

White also models his supporting characters on human types from later periods. Sir Ector is a bluff, huntin' Victorian squire, while Morgan le Fay is a Vogue model. (Blame me not for using a masculine article with a feminine name; that is Malory's French.) Sir Palomides, the Saracen knight of the later volumes, is a Bengali babu, modeled on Kipling's Hurree Chunder Mookerjee. Robin Hood, usually placed about 1200, appears.

To widen Arthur's consciousness, Merlyn turns him into nonhuman creatures, such as a fish and a hawk. The story is great fun. At times it becomes hilarious, as in the joust:

> Slowly and majestically, the ponderous horses lumbered into a walk. The spears, which had been pointing in the air, bowed down to a horizontal line and pointed at each other. King Pellinore and Sir Grummore could be seen to be thumping their horses' sides with their heels for all they were worth, and in a few minutes the splendid animals had shambled into an earth-shaking imitation of a trot. Clank, rumble, thumpity-thump, and now the two knights were flapping their elbows and legs in unison, showing a good deal of daylight at their seats. There was a change in tempo, and Sir Grummore's horse could be definitely seen to be cantering. In another minute King Pellinore's was doing so too. It was a terrible spectacle. . . .
>
> With a blood-curdling thumping of iron hoofs the mighty equestrians came together. Their spears wavered for a moment within a few inches of each other's helms—each had chosen the difficult point-stroke—and then they were galloping off in opposite directions. Sir Grummore drove his spear deep into the beech tree where they were sitting, and stopped dead. King Pellinore, who had been run away with, vanished altogether behind his back. . . .
>
> "Hi, Pellinore, hi!" shouted Sir Grummore. "Come back, my dear fellah, I'm over here."[11]

The Witch in the Wood (=The Queen of Air and Darkness) is only half as long as *The Sword in the Stone*. While it covers

Arthur's young manhood, most of the story tells of Queen Morgause of Orkney and her brood. It ends with her seduction of Arthur. It also recounts King Pellinore's pursuit of the Questing Beast and his romance with the daughter of the Queen of Flanders.

Chapters alternate, in John Carter-Dejah Thoris fashion, between Arthur's court and Orkney. Although the novel does not come up to its predecessor, it has good scenes. For instance, when Queen Morgause's sons are talking with the bibulous Irish priest, Saint Toirdealbhach, one mentions a story of interest to Howard fans:

> "Or the one," said Gawaine, "about the great Conan who was enchanted to a chair. He was stuck on it, whatever, and they could not get him off. So they pulled it from him by force, and then there was a necessity on them to graft a piece of skin on his bottom —but it was sheepskin, and from thenceforth the stockings worn by the Fianna were made from the wool which grew on Conan!"[12]

Some blame the decline in quality on White's obsession with his mother, who appears as Morgause:

> The Queen picked up the cat. She was trying a well-known piseog to amuse herself, or at any rate to pass the time while the men were away at the war. It was a method of becoming invisible. She was not a serious witch like her sister Morgan le Fay—for her head was too empty to take any great art seriously, even if it were the black one. She was doing it because the little magics ran in her blood—as they did with all the women of her race.
>
> In the boiling water, the cat gave some horrible convulsions and a dreadful cry. . . .

The Ill-Made Knight, about the same length as *The Sword in the Stone,* concerns Lancelot and the triangle with Arthur and Guenever. (This is Malory's and White's spelling, but the name has many other forms, including Jennifer and Vanora.) White treats the story sympathetically; he is thought to have put a good deal of himself into Lancelot. The ill-made knight, being physically ugly, feels that he must excel in other achievements to make up. White shrewdly philosophizes:

> There is a thing called knowledge of the world, which people do not have until they are middle-aged. It is something which cannot be taught to younger people, because it is not logical and does not obey laws which are constant. It has no rules.[13]

Finally, the short *Candle in the Wind* tells of the revenge of the Orkney brothers, led by Mordred, on Arthur and his court. At the end, the aging Arthur, the night before the final battle of Camlan, calls in a page named Tom and tells him his story. We are given to understand that this Tom grows up to be Malory.

There is much of White's philosophizing, some of it appealing; but, as his biographer said, his intellect was second-rate. Although his father was half Irish and his mother more than half Scottish, he gave the back of his hand to the Celts:

> They were the race, now represented by the Irish Republican Army rather than by the Scots Nationalists, who had always murdered landlords and blamed them for being murdered—the race which could make a national hero of a man like Lynchahaun, because he bit off a woman's nose and she a Gall [=stranger]—the race which had been expelled by the volcano of history into the far quarters of the globe, where, with a venomous sense of grievance and inferiority, they could nowadays proclaim their ancient megalomania.[14]

There are reasons why the Celtic peoples, boasting such impetuous, warlike valor, nevertheless succumbed to the Romans in Gaul, the Saxons in England, and the Normans in Ireland. But those reasons would take us into anthropology and sociology, which were not White's métier. White also presented the most idealized Middle Ages ever: "It was the age of fullness, the age of wading into everything up to the neck," with plenty

to eat, fine craftsmanship in castle and cathedral, priestly sa-
vants, scientists like Pope Silvester II, and all the other orna-
ments of refined civilization.

White was not just being naïve. This imagined Middle
Ages, he says, is that which followed Arthur's pacifications.
White knew the darker side of the age, portrayed in the des-
cription of conditions before Arthur:

> . . . then you would have met the mendicants by the roadside, mu-
> tilated men who carried their right hands in their left. . . . In the
> baron's castle, in the early days, you would have found the poor
> men being disembowelled—and their living bowels burned before
> them—men being slit open to see if they had swallowed their
> gold, men gagged with notched iron bits, men hanging upside
> down with their heads in smoke, others in snake pits or with
> leather tourniquets round their heads, or crammed into stone-filled
> boxes which would break their bones. . . . Legendary kings like
> John had been accustomed to hang twenty-eight hostages before
> dinner . . . or, like Louis, had decapitated their enemies on scaf-
> folds under the blood of which the children of the enemy had been
> forced to stand. . . . There had been roasting heretics on one hand
> —forty-five Templars had been burned in one day—and the heads
> of captives being thrown into besieged castles from catapults on
> the other.[15]

Mark Twain, in his bitterly anti-medieval *Connecticut
Yankee,* would have agreed with this picture of the Middle
Ages. Twain condoned the Terror of the French Revolution on
the ground that it was only a fair revenge by the lower orders
on the aristocracy for all the oppressions inflicted by the latter.
This is ridiculous, since the several thousand who lost their
heads in 1794 had had nothing to do with oppressing medieval
peasants. Ancient wrongs can never be righted, because both
perpetrators and victims are long since dead, and nothing one
does to or for their descendants affects them.

If one hunts, one can find examples a-plenty of both White's
imagined Arthurian and his pre-Arthurian conditions in the
real Middle Ages. Good and evil—or what most of us consider

to be such—were inextricably mixed, as they are in all known human societies.

At the end, White, in the person of Arthur, thinks about war and peace—not originally or profoundly, but with a certain common sense:

> He remembered . . . where all those puffins, razorbills, guillemots and kittiwakes had lived together peacefully, preserving their own kinds of civilization without war—because they claimed no boundaries. He saw the problem before him as plain as a map. The fantastic thing about war was that it was fought about nothing—literally nothing. Frontiers were imaginary lines. There was no visible line between Scotland and England, although Flodden and Bannockburn had been fought about it.[16]

An ethologist specializing in the territorial instinct might not agree on the pacifism of puffins and so on; a historian might take exception to the assertion that wars are fought about "nothing." For example, the American Civil War was fought mainly about slavery, which is hardly "nothing." Still, White had a point.

In preparing his tetralogy for one-volume publication, White revised the first three novels—*The Sword in the Stone* the most drastically. No man to leave well enough alone, his changes were more for the worse than for the better.

In *The Sword in the Stone,* the Wart and Kay go hunting. When they kill a rabbit, the Wart shoots an arrow straight up to celebrate. A crow seizes the arrow and flies off with it. Kay says: "It was a witch." Searching for the arrow, they come upon a cottage with a brass plate:

> MADAME MIM, B.A. (Dom-Daniel)
>
> PIANOFORTE
>
> NEEDLEWORK
>
> NECROMANCY
>
> No Hawkers, circulars
> or Income Tax.
> Beware of the Dragon.

Madame Mim, "a strikingly beautiful woman of about thirty, with coal-black hair," lures the boys in, imprisons them, and prepares to eat them, merrily singing:

> Two spoons of sherry
> Three oz. of yeast,
> Half a pound of unicorn,
> And God bless the feast.
> Shake them in a collander,
> Bang them to a chop,
> Simmer slightly, snip up nicely,
> Jump, skip, hop.

Merlyn rescues the boys and fights a duel with Madame Mim, with Hecate as referee. The duel consists of each duellist's turning himself into something, each trying to top the other's transformation in order to destroy the other. If one becomes a mouse, the other turns into a cat, and the first into a dog, and so on. When Merlyn becomes an elephant, Madame Mim assumes the form of an aullay, "as much bigger than an elephant as an elephant is larger than a sheep. It was a sort of horse with an elephant's trunk."[17] (It sounds like a *Baluchitherium*.) Merlyn then turns himself into a swarm of deadly bacteria, wherefrom the aullay dies, and good riddance.

Whether because he deemed the episode too juvenile, or because he did not think he should have two evil enchantresses in one story, White cut out the whole episode after Kay's remark: "It was a witch." That leaves the crow's theft of the arrow unexplained.

Later, the boys go with Robin Hood and his band to rescue some captives of Morgan le Fay. Morgan's castle "had neon-lights around the front door, which said in large letters: "THE QUEEN OF AIR AND DARKNESS, NOW SHOWING." If the Wart and Kay eat anything in the castle, they will become prisoners, too. The interior is a gourmand's dream:

> The fourth floor . . . was all shining with white and silver, and
> the floor was of ivory. At the other end of the room was a huge

chromium bar, covered with twinkling crystal taps, out of which
there poured incessant streams of whipped cream, fruit juice, boil-
ing chocolate, and ice. Every possible kind of ice-cream sundae was
conveyed along the top of this bar, together with plates of cream
buns, éclairs, and pâtisseries belges. Behind the bar, twenty charming negro minstrels were singing soulfully:

> Way down inside the large intestine,
> Far, far away,
> That's where the ice cream cones are resting,
> That's where the éclairs stay.

Queen Morgan is

> . . . a very beautiful lady, wearing beach pajamas and smoked
> glasses, and she was smoking a cigarette in a long green jade
> holder as she lay full length on a white leather sofa. All round
> the walls and on the grand piano there were photographs, signed
> "Darling Morgy from Oberon," "Best Wishes, Pendragon R. I.,"
> . . . or "Love from all at Windsor Castle."[18]

The rescue is duly accomplished. In the revision, however,
White substituted a much less delightfully imaginative version.
The castle is made entirely of food, and Morgan is "a
fat, dowdy, middle-aged woman with black hair and a slight
moustache."

White made further changes in Chapters 13, 18, and 19. In
the original, Merlyn changes the Wart to a snake; in the revision, to an ant. The motto of the anthill is: EVERYTHING
NOT FORBIDDEN IS COMPULSORY. While competently
done, the ant episode seems dated, since it is an obvious takeoff
on the Nazi government. This regime, naturally, was in the
minds of millions when White wrote; but now it has been done
to death.

Later, in the first version, the Wart visits Athene with Archi-
medes, Merlyn's pet owl. He is captured by and rescued from
the giant Galapas. White cut out these episodes and substituted
a sojourn by the Wart in the form of a wild goose. The goose
episode is one of White's best and should not be missed; but

neither should the parts deleted to make room for it.

Perhaps the best way to read the tetralogy is first to read the original version of *The Sword in the Stone.* Interrupt it at the end of Chapter 18 to read Chapters 19 and 20 of the revision. Then go on with the rest of the older version; then read the rest of *The Once and Future King.*

After the war, White returned to England, where Garnett lent him a cottage he owned in Yorkshire. Here White led a solitary life except for his abortive engagement and occasional visits from friends. With the friends, however, he sometimes went into fits of ungovernable rage. He blamed these outbursts on having fallen downstairs on his head in Ireland while drunk.

The success of *Mistress Masham's Repose* made White prosperous, and *Camelot* made him rich. To avoid the murderous British income tax, he moved to the Channel Islands and bought a house on Alderney. There he had a brief but hot heterosexual love affair. He abandoned *The Book of Merlyn* as hopeless. He did volunteer work for the deaf and the blind. He sailed, wrestled with his alcoholism, finished revision on *The Once and Future King,* and tried but failed to write a novel about Tristram.

In 1957, White published a book on which he had been working off and on for sixteen years. This was a science-fiction novel, *The Master*, about a sesquicentenarian mad scientist in a lair on Rockall. This is a small, cliff-bound island, which protrudes from the stormy Atlantic 300 miles west of Scotland. A duke, his rich American brother-in-law, and the duke's two children land on the island, supposing it to be uninhabited. The children are non-identical twins, a boy and a girl of twelve.

The mad scientist's henchmen seize the children. Supposing them drowned, the grieving Duke sails away on his brother-in-law's yacht. The scientist has developed a "vibrator," by which he can afflict or destroy life on earth within any desired radius.

By this means he proposes to force mankind to submit to his benevolent dictatorship.

This is an old, well-worn plot, freshened by White's eloquent writing. The plot is, however, too slight to sustain a story of over 50,000 words. To pad it out, White becomes excessively long-winded, with minute descriptions of things and endless conversations. Admirers of White will find the story interesting and moderately entertaining. Other adult readers may be put off by the kiddie-book tone (like that of *The Hobbit*), while children may find it too slow and wordy.

In his last years, White's wandering libido settled on a boy. For four years he struggled with this obsession, not wishing to pervert the lad but unable to tear himself loose: "a small boy —whom I don't need sexually, whose personality I disapprove of intellectually, but to whom I am committed emotionally, against my will. The whole of my brain tells me the situation is impossible, while the whole of my heart hangs on." Then the child's father, taking alarm, removed his son from White's orbit.

Now fat and full-bearded, White was called "an extremist"; "always good fun"; "kind and generous"; "a warm and considerate host"; "overbearing"; "domineering"; one who "never admitted himself wrong"; and sometimes "a drunken bore," who dominated the conversation, roaring out the same jokes and stories time and again.[19] He hired a raffish Neapolitan family as feudal retainers.

In 1963, White went to the United States for a lecture tour. The tour was successful; but, on the way back by ship in 1964, he suddenly died of heart failure.

White was, much of the time, an unhappy man, and he sometimes made those around him unhappy, too. But the pleasure that he has given multitudes through his books makes up for it.

XI

CONAN'S COMPEERS

The ghost kings are marching down the ages' dusty maze;
The unseen feet are tramping through the moonlight's pallid haze,
Down the hollow clanging stairways of a million yesterdays.[1]

HOWARD

During the great period of *Weird Tales* for heroic fantasy—
roughly, 1929–36—one regular writer for that magazine made
contributions comparable to those of Robert E. Howard and
Clark Ashton Smith. This was C. L. Moore, with her six tales
of Jirel of Joiry.

Catherine Lucile Moore was born in 1911 in Indianapolis,
the daughter of a designer and maker of machine tools. Her
girlhood was plagued by ill health, which often interrupted her
schooling.

Her storytelling bent appeared early. She told Sam Moskowitz: "As soon as I could talk, I began telling long, obscure
tales to everyone I could corner. When I learned to write, I
wrote them and have been at it ever since.

"I was reared on a diet of Greek mythology, Oz books, and
Edgar Rice Burroughs, so you see I never had a chance. Nothing used to daunt my infant ambition. I wrote about cowboys
and kings, Robin Hoods and Lancelots and Tarzans thinly disguised under other names."

One adolescent series concerned a princely hero, Dalmar
j'Penrya, beloved by all women. "This went on for years and
years, until one rainy afternoon in 1931 when I succumbed to

a lifelong temptation and bought a magazine called *Amazing Stories,* whose cover portrayed six-armed men in a battle to the death. From that moment on I was a convert. A whole new field of literature opened out before my admiring gaze, and the urge to imitate it was irresistible."[2]

Meanwhile Miss Moore had grown into a strikingly beautiful brunette, slender and a little above average height. She entered Indiana University but, after a year and a half, was compelled by the Great Depression to quit and work as secretary in a bank, while writing on the side. After one or two abortive efforts, she succeeded with "Shambleau" in *Weird Tales* for November 1933.

"Shambleau" introduced Miss Moore's protagonist Northwest Smith, a dour interplanetary adventurer with "colorless eyes" and a fast hand with a heat gun. Smith rescues a girl from a pursuing mob in a raffish frontier town on Mars. Taking her to his quarters, he learns the hard way that she is not what she seems. She is in fact a gorgonlike organism of hypnotic powers, from whom Smith is rescued in the nick of time by his Venerian partner Yarol.

The story showed such narrative skill, professional finish, and sensuous emotional power that it drew wide praise. H. P. Lovecraft wrote to the magazine:

> *Shambleau* is great stuff. It begins *magnificently,* on just the right note of terror, and with black intimations of the unknown. The subtle evil of the Entity, as suggested by the unexplained horror of the people, is extremely powerful—and the description of the Thing itself when unmasked is no letdown. It has real atmosphere and tension—rare things amidst the pulp traditions of brisk, cheerful, staccato prose and lifeless stock characters and images. The one major fault is the conventional interplanetary setting.[3]

Lovecraft had long taken a toplofty attitude towards "conventional interplanetary" stories (which he had relished as a youth) and stories focused on action rather than on mood and atmosphere. To him, stories of mood and atmosphere—espe-

cially an atmosphere of horror—were the only ones worthy of
being called "art." One difficulty in writing a good horror story
is the fact that different people are horrified by such different
things. Robert Howard hated snakes and so used them to stir
horror in his readers; but, to a wild-life lover, a snake is merely
an interesting organism.

In later years, Lovecraft took a somewhat broader view. One
of his last writings, in fact, was a collaboration on "In the
Walls of Eryx," a story of men in the jungles of Venus.

Miss Moore signed her stories "C. L. Moore," and not for
some months did her admirers learn that the writer was a
woman. Moskowitz called her the most important female writer
of imaginative fiction since Mary Godwin Shelley, author of
Frankenstein.

Four more stories of Northwest Smith soon followed. The
first, "Werewoman," was rejected by Wright and later published in a fan magazine. The others appeared in *Weird Tales*
through 1934. Then, besides continuing the Northwest Smith
series with several more stories, she launched the series that
places her firmly in the heroic-fantasy genre: the tales of Jirel
of Joiry.

The first of the six Jirel stories, "Black God's Kiss," appeared
in *Weird Tales* for October 1934 and the others during the
next five years. Jirel is a medieval warrior girl, tall, powerful,
red-haired, and passionate. Jirel resembles Red Anne in the
quasi-medieval novels of Leslie Barringer, but this likeness is
happenstance. Miss Moore had never heard of Barringer's
novels when she wrote the Jirel stories.

Although the tales are plainly laid in medieval Europe,
there are few clues to their precise time and place. Names of
characters are a mixture of English and French. A plausible
guess would place the stories in the west of France, in lands
that the English and French fought over during the Hundred
Years' War, and that the time is about the fourteenth century,

when this war was being fought in fiction by Conan Doyle's Sir Nigel and in real life by Bertrand du Guesclin and Joan of Arc.

In "Black God's Kiss," Jirel is conquered and humiliated by a neighboring lord, Guillaume. Imprisoned in her own castle, she stuns a sentry and gets loose. Down in the dungeons, she takes a down-sloping passage that she has explored once before.

At the bottom, she enters a trans-dimensional world. It is night time. Herds of blind horses gallop through the starlight; little lights, like mini-meteors, fall out of the sky. Jirel learns that, for the ghastliest revenge on Guillaume, she must kiss a black, one-eyed statue in a temple and then kiss Guillaume. She approaches the image:

> Gradually the universal focusing of lines began to exert its influence upon her. She took a hesitant step forward without realizing the motion. But that step was all the dominant urge within her needed. With her one motion forward the compulsion closed down upon her with whirlwind impetuosity. Helplessly she felt herself advancing, helplessly with one small, sane portion of her mind she realized the madness that was gripping her, the blind, irresistible urge to do what every visible line in the temple's construction was made to compel. With stars swirling around her she advanced across the floor and laid her hands upon the rounded shoulders of the image—the sword, forgotten, making a sort of accolade against its hunched neck—and lifted her red head and laid her mouth blindly against the pursed lips of the image.[4]

In the other stories, too, clangorous battle alternates with visits to trans-dimensional worlds and planes. In one of the Jirel stories, "Quest of the Starstone," Miss Moore collaborated with her husband, Henry Kuttner. In this tale, they brought Jirel and Northwest Smith together by time travel. Although the story duly appeared in *Weird Tales* (November 1937), the authors became dissatisfied with it and refused to allow its reprinting.

Always attractive, Miss Moore became engaged to a local

young man, who was an enthusiastic hunter. Early in 1936, while Miss Moore and her mother were traveling in Florida, Miss Moore's fiancé perished when a gun he was cleaning went off.

About that time, Miss Moore became a correspondent of a fellow pulp writer, Henry Kuttner. They met in 1938 and in 1940 were married. Thereafter most of their writing was done in collaboration. They left *Weird Tales* for the better-paying science-fiction magazines; Miss Moore had no stories in *Weird Tales* after 1939 and Kuttner only a few. Miss Moore declined urgings to write more stories in the vein of Northwest Smith and Jirel of Joiry, saying that both she and the public taste had changed.

In the 1950s, both the Kuttners enrolled in college and obtained their bachelor's degrees. Kuttner died in 1958. After that, Miss Moore's work was largely confined to motion-picture script writing. She also taught, obtained her MA, and finally married a businessman, Thomas Reggie. Fans of heroic fantasy, holding bad Moore to be still better than many writers' best, regret that they have been unable to lure her into writing more tales in their favored genre.

Leslie Barringer (1895–1968), just alluded to, was like Eddison, a British civil servant. At other times he was an editor for Thomas Nelson & Sons and for Amalgamated Press. Besides several historical novels laid in medieval England, he wrote three novels on the borderline of heroic fantasy: *Gerfalcon* (1927), *Joris of the Rock* (1928), and *Shy Leopardess* (1948).

These stories are laid in a medieval kingdom called Neustria. There was once a real Neustria; the name was applied to the northwestern corner of Merovingian France. But this name vanished from the maps in the ninth century.

The author, however, makes it plain that his tales take place in the late fourteenth or early fifteenth century. Characters look back to the Crusades and forward to the fall of Constantinople to the Turks. Cannon are mentioned but do not appear on stage.

Barringer's "Neustria" is thus a fictional doublet of the real medieval France, and his provinces of Nordanay and Honoy are doublets of Normandy and Brittany. Germany is called "Franconia," while England and Italy appear under their real names.

I suppose that Barringer wanted to tell medieval tales, but with his own cast of kings and nobles, whom he could not put through such paces as he wished without tripping over the history of the real medieval world. Here is the advantage of using a wholly fictitious world for a story of heroic fantasy. Although Barringer wrought skillfully, the juxtaposition of real and imaginary geography may make the reader uncomfortable.

Barringer's main hero is Raoul, Baron of Marckmont: a small young man with poetic and musical talents, a strong sword arm, and pure morals. We see Raoul as a boy in a monastery school, then as a ward for his uncle, Count Armand of Ger. Raoul gets into a scrape, is flogged, and runs away. He rescues the witch Sabelle from an attacking peasant and so gets the local coven on his side. Sabelle gives him refuge (much as Zelata does Conan) and a password to the other witches.

After further adventures, Raoul becomes a page to Red Anne, mistress of the "butcher Count" Lorin of Campscapel and mistress, in another sense, of a witch coven. When Count Lorin captures another count by treachery and is gloating over his mutilated victim, Raoul kills Lorin and escapes from the castle.

Following more adventures, Raoul reclaims his barony and succeeds his uncle as count of Ger. He leads his men-at-arms against a raid of Vikinglike "Easterlings" and cleans out the robbers' hold at Campscapel. He is besieged in a church tower by Joris of the Rock, a brigand, and finds his true love.

Joris of the Rock is a prequel-sequel to *Gerfalcon,* since it deals with the same locale and characters, begins earlier, and ends later. It enfolds the other story somewhat as Eddison's uncompleted *The Mezentian Gate* embraces *A Fish Dinner in Memison.* The main characters are the bandit Joris, his sweetheart Red Anne, and his son Juhel by a girl he once raped. The siege of Raoul in his tower by Joris is told again, this time from the side of the attackers instead of the defenders.

Then King René dies. His illegitimate son Conrad revolts, trying to seize the throne. In the end, Conrad, Joris, and Anne are all dead.

Shy Leopardess begins about ten years later. The main characters are Yolande, the 14-year-old daughter of the duke of Baraine, and two pages, Lioncel and Diomede. Yolande's castle is captured by a gang of outlaws in the pay of her villainous uncle. While the pages escape and go adventuring with an old-fashioned knight-errant, Yolande is forcibly wed to her uncle's sadistic son Balthasar.

With the help of her kinsman, Raoul of Ger, she exposes a plot by Balthasar against King Thorismund and destroys Balthasar himself. Both squires have become her lovers, and the reader wonders which will get her. Barringer solves this question, in a brusque and rather far-fetched way, in the course of a battle.

Despite the witches and their covens, the stories are only borderline heroic fantasy, because the supernatural element is but slight. There are one prophetic trance and one ghost, both in *Joris of the Rock.*

Of the three, I like *Gerfalcon* best. Raoul, if a bit of a Galahad, is still an intelligent, lively, and likable hero. *Joris* suffers from sprawling over a longer period, numerous shifts in point of view, and the massive unattractiveness of its protagonists Joris and Juhel. *Shy Leopardess* starts well, drags in the middle, and rates somewhere between its predecessors. On the whole, these novels are well worth reading.

When Robert Howard killed himself in 1936, he left a gap in American fantastic fiction. Nobody was writing anything much like his stories of Conan and Kull, although Clark Ashton Smith and C. L. Moore, in their separate and highly individual ways, were contributing greatly to heroic fantasy. The novels of Eddison and Barringer were little known in the United States, and Tolkien had not yet begun *The Lord of the Rings.*

Nictzin Dyalhis,[5] a minor pulp writer who contributed eight stories to *Weird Tales,* published one, "The Sapphire Goddess," in the issue of February 1934. This is a mildly entertaining if slightly amateurish tale of a man who projects himself into another dimension and finds himself a king, locked in struggles with dwarfs and wizards and seeking his ensorcelled mate. Dyalhis did not pursue the genre further.

Several writers undertook to fill the hole left by Howard. First was Clifford Ball, with three stories in *Weird Tales:* "Duar the Accursed" (May 1937), "The Thief of Forthe" (July 1937), and "The Goddess Awakes" (February 1938).

In "Duar the Accursed," the imitation of Burroughs and Howard is painfully evident. Duar, the barbarian adventurer, has black hair, blue eyes, and the "nerves of a jungle animal." He runs about in loin cloth and sandals. An ex-king who has lost his memory, he has a female guardian spirit who appears to get him out of tight fixes. She tries to explain that he is a member of the Elder Race and a priest of the High God. Duar just shakes his head in a dull sort of way, muttering an unlikely "Faith!"

With the help of his sprite, Duar destroys the Rose of Gaon, a great red jewel in the Tower of Ygoth. This jewel is really the heart of a demon. Thus Duar wins Nione, queen of Ygoth.

Ball had some portentous ideas but did not know what to do with them. Instead of clearing up the mysteries about Duar— for instance, why he was "accursed"—he dropped Duar with an audible thud and laid the next story in the neighboring kingdom of Forthe.[6]

Here, Karlk the magician persuades Rald, Forthe's leading

thief, to steal the necklace of the Ebon Dynasty from King Krall and his sister Thrine. Rald, who also favors breechclout and sandals as his working garb, discovers that Karlk is not what he seems. . . .

The story is an improvement over the first of the triolet. In "The Goddess Awakes," Ball sticks to Rald. This hero is now a mercenary soldier. This occupation fascinates many authors of adventure stories, although from all I can gather it is likely to be extremely dull in real life.

This time, Rald is captured by a race of warrior women and put in an arena to be eaten by the cat goddess. The Etrusco-Roman institution of the arena, although almost unique among the peoples of this earthly plane, has been a favorite plot element with writers of imaginative fiction ever since the Warhoons tossed John Carter into one in *A Princess of Mars*. Speaking of which, "Duar the Accursed" mentions the "great white apes of Barsoom." In the following tales, Ball caught himself and changed Barsoom to Sorjoon.

With "The Goddess Awakes," the series sputtered out. The next contender for Howard's mantle was Henry Kuttner (1914–58), one of the most prolific and versatile imaginative writers of his time. Born in Los Angeles, Kuttner worked as a youth for a literary agency and began writing professionally in the 1930s. His first success was a celebrated Lovecraftian horror story, "The Graveyard Rats," in *Weird Tales* for March 1936. He followed it with a number of stories of pure horror for this and other magazines.

Kuttner was a small, slight, swarthy man with a small mustache and a quiet, shy, gentle, almost timid manner. His friends found in him a marked vein of deadpan humor, which he used in many stories. For some years, he was one of the two science-fiction writers most noted for fictional humor—although both were, in private life, persons of rather serious mien.

When he became established as a writer, Kuttner lived alternately in or near New York, which he detested, and in California. He collaborated with C. L. Moore on a story of Northwest Smith, and in 1940 they were married. They became science fiction's leading married writing team, collaborating on most of their fiction regardless of whose by-line or pseudonym the story appeared under.

Although physically frail, Kuttner was a hard worker. When absorbed in a major piece of writing, he let almost nothing divert him from the job. His writing, however, had two characteristics, which kept him from the highest rank among his colleagues. One was his addiction to pseudonyms, of which he used at least sixteen. Readers were surprised when, in the 1940s, they learned that several of their favorite writers were really Henry Kuttner.

Another quirk was a tendency to imitate whatever other writer had recently achieved fame. Hence Kuttner wrote stories in the style of Lovecraft, Howard, Merritt, Weinbaum, van Vogt, and others. That a tyro should copy admired predecessors is natural. A mature writer, however, assimilates these influences, so that his writing no longer betrays imitation. Kuttner never reached this stage. This fact, together with his lavish use of pen names, suggests a deeply-rooted lack of self-confidence.

Kuttner's contribution to heroic fantasy consists mainly of four stories in *Weird Tales:* "Thunder in the Dawn" (May and June 1938), "Spawn of Dagon" (July 1938), "Beyond the Phoenix" (October 1938), and "Dragon Moon" (January 1941). The hero is Elak, a "lithe adventurer" in lost Atlantis. Elak has a comrade, Lycon, whose only interest in life is getting drunk. Since Lycon is neither able, clever, nor very funny, it is hard to see what good he is, save to play the conventional Sancho to Elak's Quixote.

Elak is the elder brother of King Orander of Cyrena, the northernmost kingdom of Atlantis. With Mider the Druid, Elak goes home from the city of Poseidonia to save Cyrena from the warlock Elf and the Viking leader Guthrum.

In "Spawn of Dagon," the pair are brawling and robbing in the city of San-Mu when they become involved with a gang of Lovecraftian fish-men. "Beyond the Phoenix" takes them on a trans-dimensional journey to save the western Atlantean kingdom of Sarhaddon. The last story puts them back in Cyrena, where Orander has been murdered by magic.

These stories have their weaknesses. The character of Elak is hardly developed; he lacks the personality of a Conan or a Northwest Smith, let alone an Aragorn. Like Howard, Kuttner uses historical names for his prehistoric people and places, but he does it with even less care and discrimination.

Still, these stories have power and vividness. In fact, the supernatural episodes are developed on such a cosmic scale, with supernatural entities taking possession of the characters, that the human actors are dwarfed. While not the best of Kuttner, the tales are still well above the *Weird Tales* average.

Kuttner also sold two stories in the genre to *Strange Stories*, a short-lived competitor of *Weird Tales*. The stories were "Cursed Be the City" (April 1939) and "The Citadel of Darkness" (August 1939). Prince Raynor of the prehistoric Gobi Empire is captured when King Cyaxares seizes the capital, Sardopolis, by magic. Cyaxares is controlled by the demon Necho. Raynor escapes with the help of a Nubian friend, Eblik, and seeks magical revenge.

In the second story, Raynor, Eblik, and the girl Delphia are involved with an astrological magician, Ghiar. This is the only use of astrology in the genre that I know of.

The stories are literate and readable, even when obviously derivative. But Kuttner did not carry the series further, nor did he write any more stories of heroic fantasy. Soon the paper shortage got the magazine, and the army got Hank.

Kuttner served in the medical corps but was released before the end of the Hitlerian War on a medical discharge. He had suffered from heart trouble among other things. He went to

college in California, 1950–54, got his BA, and was working
on his master's thesis when a coronary attack carried him off.

The launch in 1939 of *Astounding*'s fantasy companion,
Unknown,[7] gave an opening to authors of swordplay-and-
sorcery fiction. This chance was seized by Norvell W. Page,
author of two novels: "Flame Winds" (June 1939) and "Sons
of the Bear-God" (November 1939). Page based his series on
the legend of Prester John. He ingeniously derived the name,
not from the Greek *presbyteros,* "elder," but from *prêstêr,*
"hurricane."

In the first story, Prester John, a.k.a. Wan Tengri and Am-
lairic the Scythian, is a gigantic adventurer, ex-gladiator, and
nominal Christian, born of mixed ancestry in first-century Alex-
andria. He comes to the city of Turgohl in Central Asia, ruled
by evil magicians. John kills a few people, picks up as comrade
a small, apish thief, Bourtai, is captured and fights in the arena,
overcomes the wizards, but is tricked out of the rule of the city
by a woman and forced to flee.

In the second tale, John and Bourtai come to the city of
Byoko, ruled by evil magicians. John kills a few people, is captured and fights in the arena, overcomes the wizards, but is
tricked out of the rule of the city by a woman and forced to
flee. One can see why the series did not become a trilogy.

Page's characters are certainly eloquent. Nobody grunts "Me
Tarzan, you Jane." John is a vivid curser. In fact, the characters are often too garrulous for the good of the story, which
stands still while they shout picturesque billingsgate for a page
at a time. If essentially a red-bearded Conan, John is a livelier
and more humorous hero than his grim, sullen prototype.
There are plenty of color, action, and imagination.

The stories, however, drag for long stretches, and one tires
of the windy bombast. John's prowess is enlarged to the point
of burlesque. He fights a hundred foes at once, single-handed,

and slays them all. He strangles a tiger with a chain and breaks the back of a huge bear in a wrestling match.

Page also invited difficulties in laying the stories in a known historical setting. As Leiber found in "Adept's Gambit," it is harder to make the reader believe in such a setting plus sorcery than it is in a wholly imaginary world.

Page evidently tried to pick a time and place whose known history is blank. He did not succeed. In real life, the stories would have taken place in the midst of a powerful Hunnish empire, which could hardly have been overlooked. Page tried to bridge the difficulty of combining magic with the known historical world by hints that the magic is only hypnotism or precocious science, but the effect is lame.

In the autumn of 1934, Fritz Leiber (rhymes with "fiber") opened a letter from his friend Harry O. Fischer, writing from Lexington, Kentucky. Leiber was then a young actor. He was traveling with the Shakespearean repertory company of his father, a noted Shakespearean actor also named Fritz Leiber. The letter was one of a series that the younger Leiber and Fischer had been exchanging, in which they tried out imaginative ideas in fragments and vignettes. Fischer wrote:

> For all do fear the one known as the Gray Mouser. He walks with swagger 'mongst the bravos, though he's but the stature of a child. His costume is all of gray, from gauntlets to boots and spurs of steel. His flat, swart face is shadowed by a peaked cap of mouse-skin and his garments are of silk, strangely soft and coarse of weave. His weapons: one called Cat's Claw, for it kills in the dark unerringly, and his longer sword, curved up, he terms the Scalpel, for it lets the heart's blood as neatly as a surgeon. And this one was well feared, for he was sly as a wolverine, and while a great cheat and hard to engage in a fair quarrel, yet he did not fear to die and preferred great odds to single combat. And his style of fencing was peculiar, intermixed with strange side-steps and glides and always an attack wavering and elusive, and the sudden end at the upward flash of Scalpel from the very air it seemed. And many

who claimed enmity to this one were found strangely strangled, as by their own hands. So the Gray Mouser was feared and only drunken bravos dared a quarrel and they dissuaded quickly by wiser companions.

Until one night, the market night, the huxters all acry and horns blaring wares and smoky, stinking torches flared yellow-red in the foggy air—for the walled city of the Tuatha De Danann called Lankhmar was built on the edge of the Great Salt Marsh—there strode into the group of lounging bravos a pair of monstrous men. The one who laughed the merrier was full seven feet in height. His light chestnut hair was bound in a ringlet of pure gold, engraved with runes. His eyes, wide-set, were proud and of fearless mien. His wrist between gauntlet and mail was white as milk and thick as a hero's ankle. His features were clean cut and his mouth smiled as he fingered the ponderous hilt of a huge longsword with long and nimble fingers. But ne'er the less. . . .

Anyhow, they met, and the saga of how the Gray Mouser and Fafhrd of the Blue Eyes came to the innermost vaults of the City of the Forbidden God and there met death in the moment of victory in no common fashion, was begun.[8]

From this fragment grew one of the most popular heroic-fantasy series. Fritz Leiber, the author, looks like a more mature Fafhrd (rhymes with "proffered"). Over six feet four, he has large, handsome features and stiff gray hair, once blond.

Leiber was born in Chicago in 1910, the son of Fritz and Virginia (Bronson) Leiber. The elder Leiber was of German parentage; both he and his wife were Shakespearean actors. When Fritz Junior was an infant, he was taken along on the company's tours. When he reached school age, he was parked with relatives in Illinois while his parents continued their tours.

Leiber graduated from the University of Chicago in psychology in 1932. While an undergraduate, he had studied various sciences, learned chess and fencing, met Fischer, and begun a voluminous lifelong correspondence with him. During the summer of 1932, he entered the Episcopal Church. He enrolled in the General Theological Seminary in New York and was assigned, as minister and lay reader, to two small churches in

New Jersey. By the end of the 1932–33 school year, however, he decided that he had no priestly vocation and withdrew.

In 1934–35, Leiber went on the road with his parents, playing minor characters. Because of the Great Depression, the tour was an economic failure; but the senior Leiber moved to Hollywood. There for the next fifteen years, until his death in 1949, he made a good living playing character parts in the movies.

After some months in Hollywood, the young Leiber returned to Chicago, attempted commercial writing, and married Jonquil Stevens, an English girl. The pair made an unusual appearance, since Jonquil was under five feet. They had one son, now a professor of philosophy. They went to Hollywood, where Leiber played a couple of bit parts in movies, became a pen pal of H. P. Lovecraft, and hobnobbed with the bibulous John Barrymore.

Leiber continued his oscillation between Chicago and the Coast: an editorial job in Chicago in 1937; teaching speech and dramatics in California; a war-production job in California as aircraft inspector for Douglas; then Chicago again as an editor on *Science Digest* until 1956. After that, he dwelt in California as a free-lance writer. Since the death of his wife in 1969, he has lived in San Francisco.

Leiber began selling stories regularly about 1938. When *Unknown* was launched the next year, Leiber became a regular contributor. During the last forty years, he has published around two hundred stories, in all lengths, as well as a number of popular-science articles. Most of the stories are science fiction. The next largest group is horror-fantasy. There are a few detective stories, a few juveniles, and the two dozen heroic fantasies of Fafhrd and the Gray Mouser.

The Fafhrd-Mouser series had a tangled beginning. Building on the vignette in Fischer's letter, Leiber began the novelette "Adept's Gambit" in 1935, while living in Beverly Hills, and finished it early the next year. He sent it to Lovecraft and got good advice. He and Fischer each began a full-length Fafhrd-

Mouser novel, but neither was completed for many years. Leiber's was "The Tale of the Grain Ships."

"Adept's Gambit" begins in Tyre under the Seleucid kings— that is, in the Hellenistic Era, between Alexander and Augustus. Leiber had started but abandoned a Fafhrd-Mouser tale in Imperial Rome.

In "Adept's Gambit," the two adventurers are much as Fischer had described them, save that Fafhrd has become more Scandinavian and less Celtic. They are "dallying in a wine shop" when they make the shocking discovery that any girl whom Fafhrd kisses is temporarily turned into a pig. To free Fafhrd from this curse, they seek out Fafhrd's supernatural guardian, Ningauble of the Seven Eyes. All we see of Ningauble is a hunched, black-cloaked figure. From the neck of his garment rise, betimes, seven eyes on stalks, like those of a snail but glowing green.

In other stories, it transpires that the Mouser, too, has such a guardian, Sheelba of the Eyeless Face. The two guardians are bitter rivals but sometimes get together to help out their protégés.

Ningauble tells them that, to nullify the spell, they must get certain things: "The shroud of Ahriman, from the secret shrine near Persepolis . . . . powdered mummy from the Demon Pharaoh, who reigned for three horrid and unhistoried midnights after the death of Ikhnaton . . . . the cup from which Socrates drank the hemlock, fourthly a sprig from the original Tree of Life, and lastly . . . the woman who will come when she is ready."[9] They must take these things to the Lost City of Ahriman, somewhere east of Armenia. . . .

Leiber submitted "Adept's Gambit" to *Weird Tales*. Farnsworth Wright rejected it, although some critics consider it the best Fafhrd-Mouser story. Several book publishers, also, turned it down. Leiber rewrote it from time to time, but it did not see publication until 1947. Arkham House then brought out a collection of Leiber's fiction, *Night's Black Agents*, including

"Adept's Gambit" and one short Fafhrd-Mouser story, "The Sunken Land."

During the next few years, the substance of a series of Fafhrd-Mouser stories took shape in Leiber's mind. When *Unknown* appeared, Leiber "took the silver bit in my teeth, devised a somewhat choppier, more action-packed style of narrative than Harry and I had used in our letters, set up for myself the rule that my heroes should be not Conans or Troses but earthy characters with earthy weaknesses, winning in the end mostly by luck from villains and supernatural forces more powerful than themselves, and turned out the novelet 'Two Sought Adventure,' which appeared in the August [1939] issue of *Unknown. . . .*"[10]

The story tells of a quest for treasure in the house of Urgaan of Angarngi. This house turns out to be dangerously capable of defending itself. When the tale was reprinted in 1957 in a clothbound collection, *Two Sought Adventure* was chosen as the title of the book. The short story was renamed "The Jewels in the Forest," under which title it has been reprinted since.

During *Unknown*'s short life, Leiber sold it four more Fafhrd-Mouser stories. He also tried some on *Weird Tales,* but Dorothy McIlwraith rejected them. Since she also turned down Lovecraft's "The Dream-Quest of Unknown Kadath," one can see why the magazine did not flourish better under her editorship.

During the next two decades, Leiber sold only three more Fafhrd-Mouser stories to magazines. Beginning with "Two Sought Adventure," he abandoned this world as the scene of his tales. Instead, he placed his rogue-heroes on a world called Newhon (an anagram of "no when"), in a parallel universe. Their actions center in Lankhmar, the City of the Black Toga, mentioned in Fischer's original letter.

The discontinuity between Newhon and the world we know is awkward. Leiber papered over the gap by hints that, while his heroes lived mainly on Newhon, their supernatural guardians could send them to other universes. He also dropped a reference to "Lankhmar" into later printings of "Adept's Gambit." Still, excellent a tale though "Adept's Gambit" is, I think I might have enjoyed it even more if it had been laid on Newhon like the rest.

With the revival of fantasy in the 1950s, Leiber found his Fafhrd-Mouser stories popular again and turned out a number. He completed "The Tale of the Grain Ships." First he made a novelette, "Scylla's Daughter," of it. Then he expanded it into a book-length novel, *The Swords of Lankhmar.*

He also took the 10,000 words that Fischer had written for his unfinished Fafhrd-Mouser novel and added 24,000 more, to make the novella "The Lords of Quarmall." Fischer had meanwhile gone into the making of corrugated-paper cartons and given up his literary ambitions.

Leiber also wrote shorter pieces. He began to set the stories in chronological order, with tales about the youth of his heroes to begin the series. Before, they had been timeless and unchanging, like the characters of Homer and Wodehouse.

These witty, ironic, light-hearted, action-packed tales are, I should say, as enjoyable as any stories in the genre being written today. I hope that they will keep coming for many years to come.

What is the attraction of heroic fantasy? Specifically, what is the lure of the typical hero of such fiction? He is usually a mighty barbarian, or at least an uninhibited adventurer, operating on

> ... the good old rule ... the simple plan,
> That they should take, who have the power,
> And they should keep who can.[11]

First, let us consider what is "natural" man—that is, what all men have in common under the modifications imposed by culture and custom. The philosopher Henri Bergson once wrote: "Man was designed for very small societies. That primitive societies were such is generally admitted, but it must be added that the primitive human soul continues to exist, concealed under habits without which civilizations could not have been created. . . ."[12]

Being the world's most adaptable species, mankind adjusts itself to a civilized life very different from that which it led for at least a couple of million years. But this adaptation entails effort and nervous strain. There is always a buried tendency to revert to a more primitive pattern, like a piece of silicone putty, which, however distorted, begins slowly to resume its original shape as soon as the pressure is taken off.

In this primitive pattern, one feels sentiments like loyalty and altruism only towards a small circle of kith and kin, corresponding to the clan of the barbarian and the hunting band of the food-gathering savage. The rest of mankind is viewed as fair game.

In the first chapter, I said that, while real barbarians normally tend to be very conventional, conservative, tabu-ridden folk, under rare circumstances they may lose their inhibitions. I mentioned the chaos that ensues when such people get control of once civilized lands. Such states of affairs are remotely reflected in the legends of the Trojan War, of Sigurð-Siegfried, and of the Red Branch of Ulster, from all of which our present-day heroic fantasies descend. The British historian Chadwick described these fictional milieux thus:

> The qualities exhibited by these societies, virtues and defects alike, are clearly those of adolescence. . . . The characteristic feature . . . is emancipation—social, political, and religious—from the bonds of tribal law. . . . For a true analogy we must turn to the case of a youth who has outgrown both the ideas and the control of his parents.[13]

Hence such fictional heroes, like their real-life prototypes, are permitted to indulge a more or less universal human tendency: a tendency to revert to the small-group attitudes of primitive life.

Now, we all carry memories of our emotions as we were at every age we have passed through, from childhood on. This includes ourselves at the time of adolescent emancipation. It is notorious that we then tend to quarrel with our families and to try out deeds of daring and self-assertion to see what we can get away with.

So it is no coincidence that many heroes of heroic fantasy behave like juvenile delinquents. Even long after we have left adolescence, we keep a hankering for that time when, for once, we enjoyed a sense of liberation from rules and restrictions.

That feeling, of course, was mostly illusion. We soon discovered that the world around us—the laws of nature, our fellow men, and our own limitations—would impose upon us as strict a set of rules as anything our parents applied. But the memory of the emotion still lingers.

So it is not surprising that multitudes enjoy, if only vicariously, the uninhibited life of the conqueror, especially the barbarian conqueror of the Sigurð-Siegfried type. Therefore Conan and his fictional colleagues will probably continue popular for many years to come.

NOTES

Chapter I (pages 3–30)

1. Alfred, Lord Tennyson, "The Bugle Song" from *The Princess,* Part IV.
2. Rudyard Kipling, *The Jungle Books* (New York: Dell Publishing Co., 1964), p. 327.
3. According to E. Hoffmann Price (*Amra,* II, Sept. 1966, p. 20), Burroughs got the name "Barsoom" (Martian for the planet Mars) from the Armenian rug dealer Barsoom Badigian, a friend both of Burroughs and of Price.
4. Edgar Rice Burroughs, *Tarzan the Untamed* (New York: Ballantine Books, 1963), pp. 13, 72.
5. Michael P. Orth, "The Vaults of Opar," *ERB-dom,* No. 83 (Sept. 1975), p. 16; No. 84 (Nov. 1975), pp. 8, 48.
6. Robert E. Howard, *Conan the Conqueror* (New York: Lancer Books, 1967), p. 92.

Chapter II (pages 31–47)

1. William Morris, *The Earthly Paradise,* Prologue 11.17–20.
2. Brian Ash, *Faces of the Future* (New York: Taplinger Publishing Co., 1975), p. 100.
3. Philip Henderson, *William Morris: His Life, Work, and Friends* (New York: McGraw-Hill, 1967), p. 28.
4. Margaret R. Grennan, *William Morris, Medievalist and Revolutionary* (New York: King's Crown Press, 1945), p. 105.
5. William Morris, *The Roots of the Mountains* (London: Longmans, Green and Co., 1913), p. 76.
6. William Morris, *The Wood Beyond the World* (New York: Ballantine Books, 1969), pp. 2f.
7. William Morris, *The Water of the Wondrous Isles* (New York: Ballantine Books, 1971), p. 1.
8. "Fax" (Anglo-Saxon *feax*) is an old English word for "hair" or "mane."

Chapter III (pages 48–63)

1. Lord Dunsany, "The Probable Adventure of the Three Literary Men"; Hazel Littlefield, *Lord Dunsany: King of Dreams* (New York: Exposition Press, 1959), p. 74.
2. Oliver St. John Gogarty, "Lord Dunsany," *Atlantic Monthly,* CXCV (Mar. 1955), p. 72.
3. Lin Carter, ed., *New Worlds for Old* (New York: Ballantine Books, 1971), p. 125.
4. Mark Amory, *Biography of Lord Dunsany* (London: Collins, 1972), p. 278; *Twentieth Century Authors, First Supplement* (New York: H. W. Wilson Co., 1955), p. 291.
5. For this mission, see William L. Shirer, *The Rise and Fall of the Third Reich,* Chap. XV.
6. Amory, pp. 33f, 180.
7. Lord Dunsany, *While the Sirens Slept* (London: Hutchinson & Co., 1944), p. 62.
8. Amory, p. 231.
9. Lord Dunsany, *Patches of Sunlight* (New York: Reynal & Hitchcock, 1938), p. 213.
10. *Ibid.,* p. 280.
11. *Twentieth Century Authors* (New York: H. W. Wilson Co., 1942), p. 407.
12. Letter from Lady Dunsany, 18 Oct. 1963.
13. Lord Dunsany, *The Sirens Wake* (London: Jarrolds, 1945), p. 127.
14. H. P. Lovecraft, "Supernatural Horror in Literature," in *The Outsider and Others* (Sauk City, Wisconsin: Arkham House, 1939), p. 549.
15. From "The Hoard of the Gibbelins" and "Chu-bu and Sheemish."
16. See, e.g., "The Last Wolf," in *Mirage Water* (London: Putnam, 1938), p. 56.
17. *While the Sirens Slept,* p. 93.
18. From "The Hoard of the Gibbelins."

Chapter IV (pages 64–113)

1. H. P. Lovecraft, "Supernatural Horror in Literature," in *The Outsider and Others,* p. 509.
2. Steve Eisner, "H.P.L.—Imagination's Envoy to Literature," *Fresco,* VIII (Spring 1958), p. 3; address by Samuel Loveman to the Eastern Science Fiction Assn., Newark, N.J., 2 Mar. 1952.
3. Lovecraft to J. F. Morton, 1 Mar. 1923.

4. Lovecraft to M. W. Moe, 18 May 1922; 30 July 1927; to F. B. Long, 21 Aug. 1926; to D. Wandrei, 10 Feb. 1927.

5. In 1948, the psychiatrist and former *Weird Tales* writer, Dr. David H. Keller, wrote an article (reprinted in *Fresco, num. cit.,* pp. 12–29) arguing that Lovecraft suffered from hereditary syphilis, presumably inherited from his father. Other physicians have denied this, saying that the idea was based on obsolete medical theories, and that Lovecraft showed no known syphilitic symptoms.

6. Lovecraft to B. A. Dwyer, 3 Mar 1927.

7. Lovecraft to R. Kleiner, 27 Aug. 1917; 23 May 1917; 22 June 1917.

8. W. Paul Cook, *In Memoriam: Howard Phillips Lovecraft* (North Montpelier, Vermont: Driftwind Press, 1941), p. 9.

9. Lovecraft to A. W. Derleth, Dec. 1927; Sonia H. Davis, "Howard Phillips Lovecraft as his Wife Remembers Him," *Books at Brown,* XI (Feb. 1949), p. 9.

10. Lovecraft to E. H. Price, 13 Jan. 1935.

11. Vincent Starrett, *Books and Bipeds* (New York: Argus Books, 1947), p. 120; Lovecraft to R. Kleiner, 13 May 1921.

12. Lovecraft to F. B. Long, 26 Jan. 1921.

13. Lovecraft to R. H. Barlow, 10 Apr. 1934.

14. Donald Wandrei, "The Dweller in Darkness: Lovecraft, 1927," in *Marginalia,* by H. P. Lovecraft (Sauk City, Wisconsin: Arkham House, 1944), pp. 368, 364.

15. Lovecraft to R. H. Barlow, 10 Apr. 1934.

16. Lovecraft to A. W. Derleth, 9 Sept. 1931.

17. Bertrand Russell, *The Impact of Science on Society* (New York: Simon & Schuster, 1953), p. 108.

18. H. P. Lovecraft, "The Crime of the Century," *The Conservative,* I (Apr. 1915), pp. 2f.

19. Lovecraft to R. Kleiner, 25 Nov. 1915.

20. Lovecraft to F. B. Long, 21 Aug. 1926.

21. Lovecraft to R. Kleiner, 8 Nov. 1917.

22. Cook, *op. cit.,* p. 13; Lovecraft to R. Kleiner, 23 Apr. 1921; Samuel Loveman, "Lovecraft as a Conversationalist," *Fresco, num. cit.,* p. 36.

23. Lovecraft to R. Kleiner, 11 June 1920; to A. T. Renshaw, 10 Dec. 1921; to E. Toldridge, 26 Feb. 1932.

24. Frank Belknap Long, *Howard Phillips Lovecraft: Dreamer on the Nightside* (Sauk City, Wisconsin: Arkham House, 1975), p. 110; Lovecraft to L. P. Clark, 8 Aug. 1925; *The Outsider and Others,* p. 6.

25. T. O. Mabbott, "Lovecraft as a Student of Poe," *Fresco, num. cit.,* pp. 38f.
26. Arthur S. Koki, *H. P. Lovecraft: An Introduction to his Life and Writings* (unpublished master's thesis, Columbia University, 1962), p. 208; Lovecraft to R. F. Searight, 31 Aug. 1933.
27. Lovecraft to J. V. Shea, 13 Oct. 1932; to E. H. Price, 31 Aug. 1934; 2 Feb. 1935.
28. Lovecraft to M. W. Moe, 18 May 1922; Davis, *op. cit.,* p. 7.
29. Lovecraft to B. A. Dwyer, 26 Mar. 1927; to F. B. Long, 21 Mar. 1924.
30. Davis, *op. cit.,* p. 7.
31. Lovecraft to L. P. Clark, 1 Aug. 1924; H. P. Lovecraft, *Selected Letters I* (Sauk City, Wisconsin: Arkham House, 1965), p. xxvii.
32. Davis, *op. cit.,* p. 10; Lovecraft to F. B. Long, 21 Mar. 1924; 21 Aug. 1926; to L. P. Clark, 13 Aug. 1925; to D. Wandrei, 10 Feb. 1927.
33. Lovecraft to J. V. Shea, 29 May 1933; 30 July 1933; 14 Aug. 1933; 23 Aug. 1933; to F. B. Long, 21 Aug. 1926; to H. V. Sully, 15 July 1934.
34. Lovecraft to J. V. Shea, 8 Nov. 1933.
35. Davis, *op. cit.,* p. 11.
36. *Ibid.,* p. 12.
37. *Ibid., loc. cit.*
38. Lovecraft's letters indicate that he meant the name to be pronounced something like "tlhülhü," the *lh* being a voiceless *l* like the Welsh *ll.*
39. H. P. Lovecraft, "The Dream-Quest of Unknown Kadath," in *Beyond the Wall of Sleep* (Sauk City, Wisconsin: Arkham House, 1943), p. 77.
40. M. W. Wellman, pers. comm., c. 1937; Lovecraft to J. V. Shea, 14 Aug. 1931.
41. Fritz Leiber, "The Works of H. P. Lovecraft," *The Acolyte,* II (Fall 1944), pp. 3ff; Lovecraft to J. V. Shea, 21 Aug. 1931.
42. Lovecraft to J. V. Shea, 21 Aug. 1931; to E. H. Price, 15 Aug. 1934; to H. V. Sully, 15 Aug. 1935.
43. Lovecraft to R. Bloch, 7 Feb. 1937; to A. Galpin, 17 Jan. 1936; to R. H. Barlow, 5 Sept. 1935.
44. Lovecraft to E. H. Price, 15 Aug. 1934; to H. V. Sully, 15 Aug. 1935; to R. H. Barlow, 1 Feb. 1934; to J. V. Shea, 5 Dec. 1935.
45. Lovecraft to R. H. Barlow, 27 Jan. 1937; H. K. Brobst, pers. comm., 11 Feb. 1971.
46. Lovecraft to J. V. Shea, 9 Dec. 1931; to E. H. Price, 15 Aug. 1934.

Chapter V (pages 114–134)

1. *Njal's Saga,* trans. by Magnus Magnusson and Hermann Pálsson (Baltimore: Penguin Books, 1960), p. 349.
2. E. R. Eddison, *The Worm Ouroboros* (New York: E. P. Dutton & Co., 1952), p. xv; (New York: Ballantine Books, 1967), p. 1.
3. Jean Eddison (Mrs. W. J.) Latham, pers. comm.; Eddison, *op. cit.* (1952), pp. 176, 182, 358; (1967), pp. 212, 219f, 420.
4. E. R. Eddison, *A Fish Dinner in Memison* (New York: Ballantine Books, 1968), p. 209.
5. E. R. Eddison, *Mistress of Mistresses* (New York: Ballantine Books, 1967), p. 359.
6. *A Fish Dinner in Memison,* pp. 158f.
7. Snorri Sturluson, *The Olaf Sagas,* trans. by Samuel Laing and Jacqueline Simpson (New York: E. P. Dutton & Co., 1964), p. 58.
8. *A Fish Dinner in Memison,* p. 247.
9. E. R. Eddison, *The Mezentian Gate* (Plaistow, England: Curwen Press, 1958), p. xix; (New York: Ballantine Books, 1969), pp. xxif.
10. *A Fish Dinner in Memison,* pp. 4, 206, 39.
11. *Ibid.,* pp. 211, 284.
12. *Ibid.,* p. 75; *Mistress of Mistresses,* pp. 174, 177.
13. *The Mezentian Gate* (1969), pp. xiif.

Chapter VI (pages 135–177)

1. Robert E. Howard, "The Singer in the Mist," in *Always Comes Evening* (Sauk City, Wisconsin: Arkham House, 1957), p. 7.
2. L. Sprague de Camp, *Science-Fiction Handbook* (New York: Hermitage House, 1953), p. 80.
3. I. M. Howard to E. H. Price, 21 June 1944; E. Hoffmann Price, "A Memory of R. E. Howard," in *Skull-Face and Others,* by Robert E. Howard (Sauk City, Wisconsin: Arkham House, 1946), p. xxv.
4. R. E. Howard to H. Preece, c. 1928.
5. R. E. Howard to H. Preece, 20 Oct. 1928; to H. P. Lovecraft, Feb. 1933.
6. R. E. Howard to W. B. Talman, c. Jan. 1931; to H. P. Lovecraft, June 1933.
7. R. E. Howard to H. P. Lovecraft, July 1931; to H. P. Lovecraft, Feb. 1933.
8. Some letters (e.g. to H. P. Lovecraft, c. Oct. 1934) imply that Howard never wore any underwear at all, but this seems to be an exaggeration.

9. R. E. Howard to H. P. Lovecraft, 5 Dec. 1935.

10. R. E. Howard to H. Preece, 5 Sept. 1928; to H. P. Lovecraft, early Feb. 1933.

11. Interview with Jack Scott in Cross Plains, 1 Apr. 1965.

12. A. W. Derleth to Glenn Lord, 25 Sept. 1961.

13. Apparently, Doctor Howard unintentionally destroyed the originals of these letters when he moved away from Cross Plains, so that they exist only in the form of transcripts made under the direction of Derleth and Wandrei when they borrowed the letters.

14. H. P. Lovecraft, "The Crime of the Century," *The Conservative*, I (Apr. 1915), p. 3; H. P. Lovecraft to F. B. Long, 13 May 1923; R. E. Howard to H. P. Lovecraft, winter 1931; late Feb. 1931; early June 1931; to H. Preece, c. 1930.

15. R. E. Howard to H. P. Lovecraft, early Feb. 1933.

16. R. E. Howard to H. P. Lovecraft, early Feb. 1933; the stories "Black Canaan" and "The Dead Remember."

17. Harold Preece, "Women and Robert Ervin Howard," *Fantasy Crossroads*, I (May 1975), pp. 20ff.

18. E. Hoffmann Price, *op. cit.*, p. xxii.

19. R. E. Howard to C. A. Smith, Feb. 1934.

20. E. H. Price to H. P. Lovecraft, 25 June 1936.

21. "The Tempter," in *Always Comes Evening*, p. 80.

22. Tevis Clyde Smith, "Report on a Writing Man," *The Howard Collector*, No. 4 (Summer 1963), p. 7.

23. R. E. Howard to A. W. Derleth, 9 May 1936.

24. Harold Preece, pers. comm.

25. Rudyard Kipling, "The Winners," Stanza 1.

26. E. H. Price to *The Acolyte* (1945), in *The Howard Collector*, No. 5 (Summer, 1964), p. 34.

27. I. M. Howard to H. P. Lovecraft, 29 June 1936.

28. E. Hoffmann Price, *op. cit.*, pp. xix–xxii; T. C. Smith, *op. cit.*, pp. 9f; *Pecan Valley Days* (Brownwood, Texas: privately printed, 1956), p. 44.

29. Robert E. Howard, *Conan the Conqueror* (New York: Gnome Press, 1950), p. 12; *Conan the Freebooter* (New York: Lancer Books, 1968), p. 12.

30. "Beyond the Black River," *Weird Tales*, XXV (June 1935); *Conan the Warrior* (New York: Lancer Books, 1967), p. 200.

31. A. E. Perry, "A Biographical Sketch of Robert E. Howard," *The Howard Collector*, No. 5 (Summer 1964), p. 5; R. E. Howard to C. A. Smith, 23 July 1935.

32. "The Phoenix on the Sword," *Weird Tales*, XX (Dec. 1932), p. 769; *Conan* (New York: Lancer Books, 1967), p. 34.

33. H. P. Lovecraft to D. A. Wollheim, 7 Oct. 1935. *The Phantagraph* was Wollheim's fan magazine.

34. *Weird Tales*, XXVI (Dec. 1935), p. 658; *Conan the Conqueror* (1950), p. 15; (1967), pp. 13f.

35. H. R. Hays, review of *Skull-Face and Others*, in *New York Times Book Review*, 29 Sept. 1946, p. 34.

36. H. P. Lovecraft, "Robert Ervin Howard: A Memoriam," in *Skull-Face and Others*, p. xiii.

37. R. E. Howard to C. A. Smith, 14 Dec. 1933.

38. R. E. Howard to H. P. Lovecraft, Sept. 1933.

39. Robert E. Howard, "Guns of the Mountains," in *A Gent from Bear Creek* (West Kingston, Rhode Island: Donald M. Grant, 1965), p. 72.

40. R. E. Howard to H. P. Lovecraft, c. Jan. 1932.

41. R. E. Howard to A. W. Derleth, 28 Nov. 1935.

42. H. P. Lovecraft, *op. cit.*, p. xv.

43. E. Hoffmann Price, "Robert Ervin Howard," *The Howard Collector*, No. 1 (Summer 1961), p. 9.

44. I. M. Howard to H. P. Lovecraft, 29 June 1936.

45. *The Cross Plains Review*, 19 June 1936, quoted in *Amra*, II, 2 (1959), p. 10; H. P. Lovecraft to E. H. Price, 20 July 1936. The second line of the couplet typed by Howard before his death is paraphrased from a poem by Ernest Christopher Dowson (1867–1900), a minor Victorian poet who died young of tuberculosis and alcoholism.

46. H. R. Hays, *loc. cit.* My own speculation as to Howard's death (purely amateur, but based on reading and observation in my work as a science writer) is that, eventually, most cases of suicide and mental breakdown will be traced to the interaction between environmental circumstances and congenital, hereditary biochemical (e.g. glandular) abnormalities.

47. A. W. Derleth, pers. comm.; I. M. Howard to E. H. Price, 21 June 1944; to Frank Torbett, 22 June 1936.

Chapter VII (pages 178–194)

1. Lodovico Ariosto, *Orlando Furioso*, Canto IV, st. vii.

2. Mary Baker Eddy, *Science and Health with Key to the Scriptures* (Boston: Trustees Under Will of Mary Baker G. Eddy, 1934), p. 407.

3. John D. Clark, pers. comm.; Doctor Clark married Pratt's widow, Inga Stephens Pratt.

Chapter VIII (pages 195–214)

1. Clark Ashton Smith, "Don Quixote on Market Street," in *The Dark Chateau* (Sauk City, Wisconsin: Arkham House, 1951), p. 25.
2. Clark Ashton Smith, "The Ninth Skeleton," in *Genius Loci* (Sauk City, Wisconsin: Arkham House, 1948), pp. 26f.
3. Lin Carter, ed., *New Worlds for Old*, p. 279.
4. C. A. Smith to Samuel Loveman, 14 Apr. 1929.
5. Clark Ashton Smith, "The Last Incantation," in *Lost Worlds* (Sauk City, Wisconsin: Arkham House, 1944), p. 90.
6. H. P. Lovecraft, "Supernatural Horror in Literature," in *The Outsider and Others*, p. 538.
7. C. A. Smith to R. H. Barlow, 16 May 1936; Fritz Leiber, review of *Zothique*, by Clark Ashton Smith, in *Fantastic Stories*, XX (Feb. 1971), p. 107.
8. C. A. Smith to G. Sterling, 28 Sept. 1926.

Chapter IX (pages 215–251)

1. J. R. R. Tolkien, *The Fellowship of the Ring* (Boston: Houghton Mifflin, 1954), p. 5; (New York: Ballantine Books, 1965), p. vii.
2. Lin Carter, *Tolkien: A Look Behind "The Lord of the Rings"* (New York: Ballantine Books, 1969), pp. 4f; Robert J. Reilly, "Tolkien and the Fairy Story," in *Tolkien and the Critics*, ed. by Neil D. Isaacs and Rose A. Zimbardo (Notre Dame. Indiana: University of Notre Dame Press, 1968), p. 133.
3. Edmund Wilson, "Oo, Those Awful Orcs!" *Nation*, CLXXXII (14 Apr. 1956), pp. 312ff.
4. *The Fellowship of the Ring* (Houghton Mifflin), p. 89; (Ballantine), p. 117.
5. William Ready, *Understanding Tolkien and The Lord of the Rings* (New York: Paperback Library, 1969), p. 81.
6. Isaacs and Zimbardo, pp. 37, 134.
7. *The Fellowship of the Ring* (Ballantine), pp. xiif.
8. Ready, p. 10; J. R. R. Tolkien, *Tree and Leaf* (Boston: Houghton Mifflin, 1965), p. 42.
9. "Hobbits' Master Quietly Turns 80," *San Francisco Chronicle*, 4 Jan. 1972, p. 6.

10. J. R. R. Tolkien, *The Hobbit* (Boston: Houghton Mifflin, 1937), pp. 11, 17.

11. Will and Ariel Durant, *The Age of Voltaire* (New York: Simon & Schuster, 1965), p. 45.

12. *The Hobbit,* p. 14.

13. Snorri Sturluson, *The Prose Edda,* trans. by Jean I. Young (Berkeley: University of California Press, 1954), pp. 41f; *Heimskringla,* III, i, ii; *Völuspá,* st. 10–15. "Gandalf" (spelled "Ganndálf" in the *Prose Edda*) means "mighty Elf."

14. *The Poetic Edda,* trans. by Henry Adams Bellows (Princeton: Princeton University Press, 1936), p. 165. See also pp. 306, 476, 483. In the original, the name is "Myrkviþ." "þ" is the Anglo-Saxon, Icelandic, and Old Norse letter representing the sound of *th* in "thing."

15. Edmund Spenser, *The Faerie Queene,* I, Canto I, st. xxxviii; William Shakespeare, *The Tempest,* Act V, sc. 1, 11.88–91.

16. Roger Lancelyn Green and Walter Hooper, *C. S. Lewis: A Biography* (New York: Harcourt, Brace, Jovanovich, 1974), pp. 140, 164, 184; C. S. Lewis, *Surprised by Joy* (New York: Harcourt, Brace and Company, 1955), p. 237; Edmund Fuller, *et al., Myth, Allegory, and Gospel* (Minneapolis: Bethany Fellowship, 1974), p. 91; Carter, pp. 18ff.

17. *Tree and Leaf,* pp. 3, 57ff.

18. *Ibid.,* p. 41.

19. *Ibid.,* pp. 60, 72.

20. C. S. Lewis, *Letters of C. S. Lewis, apud* Glen GoodKnight, "The Social History of the Inklings," *Tolkien Journal,* No. 12 (Winter 1970), p. 7.

21. *Tree and Leaf,* p. vii.

22. *The Fellowship of the Ring* (Houghton Mifflin), p. 29; (Ballantine), p. 43.

23. The Anglo-Saxon letter "ð" represents the sound of *th* in "this."

24. Edmund Fuller, "The Lord of the Hobbits," in Isaacs and Zimbardo, p. 35.

25. *The Return of the King* (Houghton Mifflin), p. 223; (Ballantine), p. 274.

26. *Ibid.* (Houghton Mifflin), p. 308; (Ballantine), p. 381.

27. Marion Zimmer Bradley, *Men, Halflings, and Hero Worship* (Baltimore: T-K Graphics, 1973), p. 9.

28. Robert J. Reilly, in Isaacs and Zimbardo, pp. 83, 130.

29. Fuller, *et al.,* p. 141.

30. *The Hobbit,* p. 315; *The Fellowship of the Ring* (Houghton Mifflin), p. 69; (Ballantine), p. 93.
31. Plato, *The Republic,* II, 359; *The Prose Edda,* pp. 111–15.
32. James Branch Cabell, *Jurgen* (New York: Robert M. McBride & Company, 1919), p. 332.

Chapter X (pages 252–269)

1. Alfred, Lord Tennyson, "The Holy Grail."
2. Gildas, 25f.
3. Nennius, 56 (50 in J. A. Giles, *Six Old English Chronicles,* 1848).
4. T. H. White, *The Once and Future King* (New York: G. P. Putnam's Sons, 1958), p. 564; Sylvia Townsend Warner, *T. H. White* (New York: Viking Press, 1967), p. 46.
5. Warner, p. 183.
6. White (1958), pp. 185f; T. H. White, *The Sword in the Stone* (New York: G. P. Putnam's Sons, 1939), p. 278. The wording differs slightly in the 1939 and 1958 versions.
7. Warner, p. 23.
8. David Garnett, ed., *The White/Garnett Letters* (New York: Viking Press, 1968), p. 7. This volume contains (p. 308) an interesting sidelight on another curious character, T. E. Lawrence ("of Arabia"), also reputed to have been a homosexual. White wrote, "But T. E. Lawrence wasn't a homosexual. I know that for a fact as I have read a correspondence which I could not publish between him & a friend who was a homosexual. . . . He was a masochist, in the strict sense of the word."
9. Garnett, pp. 11, 8.
10. Warner, p. 141; Garnett, p. 70.
11. Fritz Leiber, "Controlled Anachronism," in *The Conan Swordbook,* ed. by L. Sprague de Camp and George H. Scithers (Baltimore: Mirage Press, 1969), pp. 132–147; White (1958), pp. 61f.
12. White (1958), p. 245.
13. *Ibid.,* pp. 221, 394.
14. *Ibid.,* p. 548.
15. *Ibid.,* pp. 563, 559f.
16. *Ibid.,* p. 676.
17. White (1939), pp. 66ff, 82.
18. *Ibid.,* pp. 160ff.
19. Warner, pp. 288, 304ff, 317.

Chapter XI (pages 270–289)

1. Robert E. Howard, "The Ghost Kings," in *Always Comes Evening,* p. 31.
2. Sam Moskowitz, *Seekers of Tomorrow* (Cleveland: World Publishing Company, 1966), pp. 305f.
3. *Weird Tales,* XXIII (Jan. 1934), p. 132.
4. C. L. Moore, "Black God's Kiss," in *Warlocks and Warriors,* ed. by L. Sprague de Camp (New York: G. P. Putnam's Sons, 1970), p. 191; (New York: Berkley, 1970), pp. 190f. The original title in *Weird Tales* was "The Black God's Kiss," but the article was dropped in the several reprintings.
5. Dyalhis's father was a Welshman (hence the surname) fascinated by the Aztecs (hence the given name).
6. Ball gives no indication of which way he meant his characters' names to be pronounced.
7. Technically, the title of the magazine was *Street & Smith's Unknown.* In 1941, when it went to larger size, Campbell changed the title to *Street & Smith's Unknown Worlds,* because magazine sellers looked blank when asked for an unknown magazine.
8. Fritz Leiber, *Night's Black Agents* (Sauk City, Wisconsin: Arkham House, 1947), pp. ixf; L. Sprague de Camp and George H. Scithers, eds., *The Conan Grimoire* (Baltimore: Mirage Press, 1972), pp. 105f. The Tuatha Dé Danann, one of the legendary groups of invaders of Ireland (now considered euhemerized Celtic deities), do not appear in Leiber's Fafhrd-Mouser stories.
9. *Night's Black Agents,* pp. 171f; Fritz Leiber, *Swords in the Mist* (New York: Ace Books, 1968), pp. 120f.
10. *The Conan Grimoire,* p. 121. The reference to "Troses" is to the novels by Talbot Mundy about Tros of Samothrace, a Greek of the time of Caesar and Cleopatra.
11. William Wordsworth, "Rob Roy's Grave."
12. Henri Bergson, *Les Deux Sources de la Morale et de la Religion* (Paris: F. Alcan, 1932), p. 24, *apud* Toynbee, *A Study of History.*
13. H. Munro Chadwick, *The Heroic Age* (Cambridge: Cambridge University Press, 1912), pp. 442ff.

INDEX

ACKNOWLEDGMENT

Quotations from the letters of Robert E. Howard are by permission of Glenn Lord, agent for the Howard heirs.

Five thousand copies of this book have been printed and bound by The Lakeside Press, R. R. Donnelley & Sons Company, from Linotype Garamond composed by Fox Valley Typesetting, Menasha, Wisconsin, by Web Offset on 50# Nekoosa Vellum. The binding cloth is Holliston Black Novelex.